The Will and the Wisp

JAMES D. ARMSTRONG

WITH

SHARON KIZZIAH-HOLMES

To David & Sherry (Dooze)
I love you, cuz!
Y'all enjoy!
Sharon

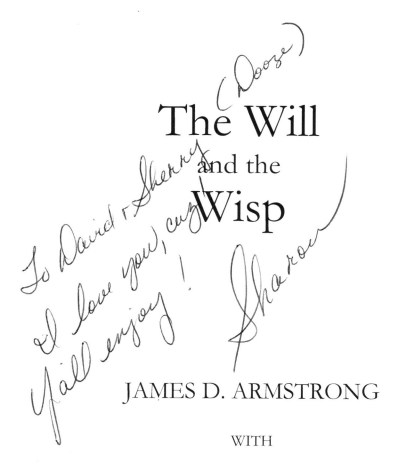

This is the first episode in the serial release of the full length novel, The Will and the Wisp. This is a work of fiction based on the true story of the Armstrong family.

Paperback-Press
Springfield, Missouri
an imprint A & S Publishing, A & S Holmes, Inc.

ISBN: 0692301356
ISBN-13: 978-0-692-30135-7

ACKNOWLEDGMENTS

Thank you to Mr. James Hussy for allowing us to use his beautiful artwork, HIDAWAY, for the cover of The Will and the Wisp.

Thank you to our spouses for allowing us countless hours in front of our computers, writing, re-writing, checking emails or maybe even talking on the phone. Without your support, Dennis and Susan, we may not have completed this project.

CONTENTS

PROLOGUE

Fall 1761

"Man overboard! Another man overboard!"

Little Jean Trebeaux barely heard the Captain's voice. The huge French ship Victor was losing its battle with the raging sea. Howling wind, pounding rain and the roar of thunder filled the air.

Johnny, as his grandfather called him, held on to his granddad, Tom Red Blair, with all of his might. The big ship tossed violently in the pitch black night. His heart thumped against his chest like never before.

Without warning the storm hit. It was like nothing he'd ever witnessed in all of his ten years. Not even the plague, that had taken his parents' life a few months earlier, scared him as much. He was glad his grandfather was left to take him in.

"Wind is moving the ship too fast, Captain! It's impossible to man the wheel!" The crewman held on to anything tied down as he staggered across the deck of the rocking vessel.

A huge gust of wind sent a deafening sound of wood cracking somewhere behind them. A booming thud shook the big ship when something hit the deck.

"The main sail mast has gone down! It was the last one standing, Captain!"

"There is nothing we can do but wait it out! Stay still, I don't want to lose any more men!"

Through sudden bursts of intense lightning, Johnny saw the devastation on the ship's deck. Crewmembers screamed in pain, some bleeding, and some dead, but most held on to anything that would keep them from going over the side.

"Land on the port side, Captain!" The crewmember pointed. "Where do you think we are?!"

"It must be Cat Island!"

Tom Red Blair stood as best he could. "Johnny, there's a secure tarp over there! I want you to get under it! I'm going to see if I can help some of the injured crew members!"

Was this a nightmare? Would he ever wake up? He feared he would never see his grandfather again. "No, Granddad, don't leave me!" It hurt his throat to yell above the noise.

"It'll be okay, son! I'll return! You'll be safe under there!

He followed orders and crept under the temporary cover. It seemed a bit quieter now. Though the wind still howled, it wasn't blowing directly in his ears. He peeked out from under the tarp to see the older man walk unsteadily away.

He missed his parents, but he loved his grandfather very much and liked living with him. He peered out again. This time, there was no sign of his granddad. He hoped the man would come back soon.

****

The sun began to rise and Tom Red Blair couldn't believe what he saw. "Good God help us." The ship's devastation, along with the loss of life, was immense. He listened as the able bodied crewmembers reported to the Captain.

Wind continued to push the ship forward at a frightening speed. He had seen many ocean perils, but never this kind of weather. However, he knew all too well that this was the deadly Gulf and anything could change in an instant. It was extremely dangerous when wind and down-pouring rain stained a person's vision, making disorientation grow.

He gazed out across the water. They were definitely not close to Cat Island as the Captain had thought. He took in his surroundings and realized the wind had pushed them so fast they had already crossed Lake Borgne, gone through the St. Louis

Bay and had entered the flooded swamp. He had to tell the Captain they were in danger.

A huge bump on the port side knocked him off his feet. “Trees. Trees! We’re in the trees!” He tried to stand, but with each hit of the giant cypress, the ship listed from side to side. Victor stopped abruptly and pitched him against the railing. It took all of his strength to keep from going into the rough waters.

Almost as sudden as the wind and rain started, they stopped. He finally got his footing and made his way back to the main deck. Thick fog slipped over the ship like a blanket. He saw the outline of the giant trees. Damn it all! They were on top of the Mississippi swamp.

“Captain!” A crewman yelled. “The lower decks are flooding!”

“All that are able help the ones who are not to starboard! The ship is heavy with what we captured from the pirates.”

The Victor creaked, rocked and tilted to port side at a forty degree angle. She settled onto the swamp bottom under the deep murky water. The loud groan from below said the cargo had shifted from its casing and it drove through the ship's hull. Not knowing exactly what the French had gotten from the pirates, he knew for sure it was a heavy load.

He began to help get the injured to the higher starboard side. All was quieting and Johnny hadn’t stirred. He hoped the boy was sleeping. It would be good for the youngster to rest.

When his grandson snuck onboard, the boy had no idea Victor was heading for the French and Indian war. The French army hired Tom because of his knowledge of the Gulf waters and he vowed this would be the last time he would sail. After his daughter and her French husband’s death, he was left to care for Johnny and soon the two of them would head back to his beloved England.

There was no reason to stay in France now. Not when his daughter and her beautiful French mother, who died with pain in her chest a few years back, were both in heaven. He only had Johnny left, and he would take care of the boy until the day he died.

He didn’t know the boy had stowed away until they were too far out to go back. So far the child had been safe, however with this new development, he couldn't predict how long he could keep him that way. Looking to the sky, he said a silent prayer, but something was wrong.

A bright, eerie glow flew from the swamp. "What the hell?" Then another came and another. "Arrows? Fire Arrows!"

He stood as hundreds of fire arrows hit the deck. Men fell all around him. Crewmen reached for their guns, but the powder was wet and they were useless. Tom grabbed a French sword and ran back to where Johnny was. The tarp was wet and surely wouldn't burn.

Crawling beneath the cover beside his grandson, he prayed the Indians wouldn't board the ship. Maybe if he hid for a while, they would stop their attack and retreat.

Finally, it became silent but he stayed still. He waited for a few minutes before looking out from under his cover. The Indians had indeed retreated and the deck was clear.

"Johnny, you stay here. I'm going to assess the damage then I'll come back after you."

"Yes, sir."

Tom rolled onto the deck and got to his feet. So many had been killed, including the Captain. It looked to him like about twenty-five men survived. Most were injured, but a few were still healthy. Nothing burned. That was the only reason to be thankful for the storm.

A few days had passed since they ran aground, and no more signs of the Indians. The first seaman had taken control of the crew. Tom approached the man. Something had to be done.

"Sir, infection is spreading like fire through the wounded."

"Yes, and our supplies are dwindling from spoilage. In a couple of days, the water will subside even more. At that time I plan to take some of the stronger men and try to get to shore."

"We only have one fit lifeboat. Are your plans to leave the rest of us here?"

"Of course not Mr. Blair. I intend to build a shelter then return for all others."

Tom knew the first seaman was a strong man and very capable of doing the job. He only hoped the man was telling the truth. "I'm satisfied with that." He had no choice.

In the following days, the first seaman and a few men left on their quest. They had taken a large, heavy box with them. Some of the cargo they had gotten from the pirates he supposed. But why? It was none of his business; all he was worried about was the safety of Johnny.

He expected the men to return within two days, but they never came back. Over the next week his health deteriorated. Something, maybe the water, was affecting all aboard except the boy. It had been at least twenty five days since they landed. There were few crew members left. If he died, what would become of his grandson?

The Victor creaked and cracked as the waves sometimes rocked the ship. Johnny knew something was terribly wrong with his grandfather. The older man was talking out of his head and sweat rolled from his brow.

Later that night, Johnny heard a commotion on the bow. He ran to see what it was. Two crew members had jumped into the water. "What happened?" he asked. "What are they doing?"

A crewmember pushed him back. "It's your grandfather. He became disoriented and fell overboard."

Johnny ran to the railing of the ship. He could barely see in the dark of night. "Granddad! Granddad!"

One crewman popped out of the water. "It's too late. He's gone."

"No! Granddad!" He tried to jump into the water, but someone's hands surrounded his waist and pulled him back.

"You can't do that, kid. You're grandpa's dead. Just like the rest of us will be soon if we don't get off this hell ship."

Wrenching out of the man's grip, Johnny couldn't stop the tears that stained his cheeks. He ran to the tarp that had been his only shelter since this ordeal started. First his parents, now his grandfather. What was he going to do? Darkness overtook him as he cried himself to sleep.

Pounding and shouting drew Johnny from his slumber. He threw back the covering and stood. "What are you doing?"

"We're building a raft. We're getting the hell off here."

He watched as six of the seven remaining men manned the vessel they'd built from barrels. They set off to find…anything.

"We'll be back."

He turned and walked away, but before long, he heard the men screaming. He ran back to the railing to see what had happened. The Indians were back.

"They'll be after us next, kid."

Johnny hated to see the cover of darkness come as night fell. Would the Indians come to kill them? He hid under his tarp and prayed.

When the morning sun lit the sky, Johnny realized he was still alive. The Indians hadn't come after all. He stepped out to relieve himself over the side of the ship. His breath caught in his throat and his heart fell to his stomach. The last crewman lay on the deck, dead from an arrow in the head.

Surely his legs were going to buckle beneath him as he backed away. He couldn't stop trembling. What was going to happen to him now? He fell to his knees. Pray, that's what he'd do, pray.

He bowed his head, then held his breath and slowly turned to see what had made a noise behind him. The most fearsome sight he could have ever imagined glared down at him. Unable to move, he soiled himself with urine when the man pulled a large knife from its sheath..

Chapter One

THE WARNING OF THE WISP

Summer 1846

The night was full of strange and eerie sounds. Not the noises that usually inhabit night, like crickets and frogs, but voices, loud yet not argumentative. In some way, uneasy. They came from the main room of the house.

"When Bud gets back inside, he's gonna have to get down here."

"Dis is heavy. I don't know how weez gonna carry it."

Carl rubbed his eyes, turned over in his bed and fought to go back to sleep. The sun had set hours earlier. The sweltering hot day was over, but the night wasn't much cooler.

No matter how hard he tried, he couldn't block out the voices.

"Be careful, Neil. I swear, nobody can know about this."

"Yes, Mr. O.C."

Carl threw back the sheet, thankful for the blessed wind that whistled through the open window. It relieved, in some way, the dreaded night mosquitoes that were terrible in lower Mississippi this time of year.

"We'll manage. We have to. Let's not talk so loud."

Sitting up on the side of the bed, Carl fixed his eyes on the window and the bright moon that had risen over the ancient cypress forest outside. The woods hanging over the swollen waters of the swamp were scary enough in the daytime, but at night they terrified him.

Well, he was only nine years old. What did he expect? He'd probably get over it when he was ten. At least he wanted to believe that.

He moved off the bed and stepped onto the swelled, almost wet wood floor. It creaked under his summer callused feet and he pulled in a deep breath to calm his pounding heart. He wasn't supposed to be out of bed, but his curiosity got the best of him. What was going on in there?

On tiptoe, he made his way across the lean-to bedroom he shared with his two older brothers, Charles, who was twelve, and Joe, fourteen. They were fast asleep in their homemade beds. He, on the other hand, was wide awake. He remembered his pa's warning, "curiosity killed the cat", but he had to find out what was going on.

The lump in his throat went down hard when he turned the knob on the old door. Maybe if he just opened it a little, no one would know he was watching. If he got caught, his pa, who everyone called O.C., would give him a whipping.

The floor was hard under his knees, but he got as comfortable as he could, then peeked through the sliver of an opening. What were his Uncle Bud and the hired hand, Neil, doing there at that time of night? Putting in the new stove? Why would they be doing that now?

His pa and uncle were tenant farmers, and O.C. bought a large smut black coal stove with the cash he'd made from the summer crops. The money wasn't much after he paid the landlord, Mr. Plummer, his part for rent and such. However, the family needed a new heating stove so O.C. got it, but why would they put it in now? In the middle of summer instead of fall, and in the dark?

Shadows from the coal oil lanterns flickered on the walls. He thought sure his heart was going to jump out of his chest when he heard a loud thud. His pa didn't sound any too pleased.

"Easy, Neil, we don't want to wake those boys."

"Sorry, Mr. O.C., but all dis is makin' me nervous as hell.

"Everything's gonna be okay." O.C. wiped his forehead. "Hurry up, Bud, we've only got four hours 'til daylight, Dammit.

You're the tallest, so you're gonna have to get down here and pass this to us."

Carl strained to see what his Uncle Bud dragged across the floor. Why, it wasn't the new stove at all. It was a big ol' black pot like his ma washed their clothes in. What the hell? How come they had one of them pots?

He cracked the door a bit more. Bud left the pot and climbed down through a dark spot in the floor. When did that hole get there? He'd never seen it before. Had they killed somebody or something? He wasn't sure he wanted to know, but couldn't stop himself from watching.

Man, that hole was pretty deep. His uncle Bud stood tall, and he could only see the man's shoulders above the floor as he passed a flour sack to Neil.

Whatever was in that sack sure wasn't flour, it was too heavy. Neil looked like he was going to bust a gut when he lifted it from Bud's hands.

One sack after another came through the opening. He watched until his eyelids got too heavy, then he stretched out on the floor to rest for a minute.

* * *

The aroma of frying bacon was one of Carl's favorite smells. He lay there enjoying the fragrant odor and the sound of his ma whistling and singing while she made breakfast. Footsteps got closer to the door and the sound of his ma's voice made him open his eyes.

"Carl, get yourself up off that floor, boy. Your breakfast is gettin' colder by the minute and the coals are goin' out, too. What are you doin' down there anyway? Someone put rocks in your bed?"

She was kidding him, but he remembered the activities of the night before and knew he couldn't tell her what happened. With a shrug of his shoulders he said, "I don't know. Maybe I was walkin' in my sleep."

"Well, you get dressed now, your brothers have been up and working for hours." She turned and headed back toward the kitchen.

"Yes, ma'am." He grabbed his overalls from the foot of his bed. It was going to be hot, so he decided not to wear a shirt, and shoes made his feet sweat.

He gave the overalls a good shake, just in case a scorpion had crawled in during the night. The denim was cool when he stepped into the legs, then he slipped the straps over his shoulders. This would probably be the only cool thing he felt all day.

He clumped out of the bedroom to the kitchen and sat down at one of the six chairs placed around the old wooden table. "Where's Pa?"

His mother set his plate in front of him. "He's still asleep. He worked all night on that darned floor over there." She nodded toward the living room and a patch of wooden planks.

His gaze went to where the floor boards had been put back in place. That was where the hole had been the night before. "Ma, what was wrong with the floor?" Homemade biscuits dripping with crystal white syrup and butter were his favorite part of breakfast. He took a bite and wondered if his ma knew about what his pa and them were doing in the hole.

"The new stove was too heavy for that floor. Your pa said he needed to add some support under the house to hold it. He wanted to get it done before time to put the stove in so when it gets here, he can just bring it inside."

She turned her attention to the biscuits she was making. "But, this is a swamp house. It's built off the ground. For the life of me, I don't know why they had to cut a hole in the floor. Looks like they could've just crawled under to shore it up."

"Not enough room under there to dig holes and stuff, Ma. 'Sides, there's too many spiders."

She furrowed her brow and pointed to his food. "Hey, don't you worry about it anyway. You finish that breakfast and get to work. I catch heck enough around here about you never doin' anything. So hurry up, young man, before I take a switch to you."

The threat fell on him feather light, softened by the love in his ma's eyes. But, not wanting to push his luck, he finished the last bite on his plate, hopped off the chair, ran out the door and jumped off the porch. The screen smacked shut behind him.

It was going to be a great day! He didn't know why he was in such a good mood. Maybe he needed to sleep on the floor all the time.

He glanced at Joe and Charles in the field working away. Skipping and hopping, he grabbed his chopping hoe from the side of the shed and raced down one of the long rows to join his brothers.

Charles stopped working, leaned on the handle of his hoe and grinned. "What happened little brother? Boogers keep you awake all night?"

"Yeah," Joe said, "we had to step over ya to get out this mornin'."

Trying to ignore his brothers' teasing and laughter, he started to chop weeds.

"You'd better work harder durin' the day so you can sleep at night instead of lyin' around on the floor," Joe chided then winked at Charles. "You know, Charles, it's that time of the year. I bet that ol' Wisp is back. It's not good for little boys to roam around alone in the night when the Wisp is lurkin' about."

"Yep, and I've heard that little white boys is his favorite food."

Why did they have so much fun scaring him? "The Wisp didn't keep me awake! Pa did, puttin' in the new floor."

Charles went back to his work. "Oh, sure. Just get busy now, squirt."

The sun was at its height and the kidding had stopped long ago. He was hot and tired and wished he could sit down, but he didn't dare. His pa might show up any time and he sure didn't want to get caught sitting on his butt. Joe's voice brought him back from his thought.

"Hey, look yonder." Joe pointed to the south.

Charles smiled. "I'll be damned; it's Little Boy Horse and Johnny One Horn."

Carl saw the two big Indians in the distance and wondered where Grey Wolf was. Grey Wolf was a chief of some sort and had hidden his little band of renegades deep in the vastness of the swamp. Horse and Johnny were part of Grey Wolf's people.

Nobody knew how long Grey Wolf and his natives had lived in the swamp, but he was old, even older than O.C. "Hey,

Joe, how old do you think Grey Wolf is?"

"I don't know. Seventy or so, I guess"

"Wow, that's old. Is he scared of the Wisp, too."

"Yeah, and he's not the only one. None of the Indians like the Wisp. They all think it's collecting souls. You know that."

"Yeah, but I bet Little Boy Horse ain't scared. Why, he's big as a tree."

Joe glanced at the two men coming up the lane. "He can throw a knife, too. Pa throws one good, but he says no one's better with a knife than Horse. Pa said he figured Horse could slip up and steal the hoot right from an owl. I'm sure Grey Wolf's proud to have Boy Horse as a son."

Charles wiped his brow. "Is Johnny One Horn Grey Wolf's boy, too, Joe?"

"Naw. Some say he's part French and that his real name is Jean La Beau or somethin' like that, but nobody really knows for sure. He's some older than Horse. I've heard tell he's a medicine man and can cure almost any ailment with his secret potions."

Charles laughed. "Maybe he can cure little brother of his night jitters so he can get some sleep. Johnny says sometimes the wisp is a warning that evil lurks."

"Shut up, Charles," Carl said.

Johnny One Horn and Little Boy Horse looked like giants to Carl. He had to force his mouth shut as he gawked at them. Somehow he didn't remember them being that big.

Joe stuck out his hand. "Horse, Johnny, good to see ya."

Horse stepped forward to accept the shake. "Yes, long time."

Carl went back to work but listened carefully to the conversation between his brother and the giants. He was surprised how good they spoke English. Broken, but good enough to understand. Nobody knew where Johnny had learned the language, but nobody cared either, except he was the one that taught Horse.

Joe rested against the hoe handle. "Grey Wolf didn't bring any furs this spring. He okay?"

"Yes, he is good. Has many furs to bring this fall. Will be trading with your father. Wolf want sweet potatoes, corn and onions."

"I'll tell Pa. He'll have 'em ready."

"Wonder where ol' Neil is this mornin'? He's always here by now. He'll be sorry he missed you, Boy Horse." Charles said.

Carl shook his head. "He's probably still asleep like Pa. I told y'all they worked on the floor all night."

"You didn't say nothin' 'bout Neil."

"Well, he did, and so did Uncle Bud. So there."

Boy Horse stepped forward. "I like get Neil riled up. He funny when scared. He think I mean."

Carl knew Horse was right. He would tease the colored man something awful. Never cracking a smile, Horse would stare at Neil, usually while cleaning his fingernails with one of the two razor-sharp Arkansas Toothpicks he carried. He'd scare that poor old man half to death, then walk off laughing to himself.

Looking up at Horse, Carl stopped working. "Hey, Mr. Horse, do you remember the time you rubbed the top of ol' Neil's curly black hair? He was so afraid it was all Pa could do to keep him from unloadin' his old ten-gauge double barreled shotgun on you."

"I remember. We never see man that dark skinned. So, when I stare at him he get scared. His woman try calm him, but he not listen."

"Yeah, he still thinks you might want his curly hair hangin' from your belt."

Joe gave him a stern look. "Carl, shut up!"

He was probably in big trouble, but that had just come out. He hadn't meant to say it. To his relief, Boy Horse and Johnny both busted out laughing and it wasn't long before they took their leave.

As he worked, Carl thought about Neil Carter and his wife Minnie. They had been part of his life since he was born. His pa and Neil were like brothers, except one was colored and one was white.

He loved to go places with Neil and Minnie. Why, last time he went to Gulfport with them, eyebrows raised all over the place, especially when he called them Grandpa and Grandma. They didn't care. They just laughed at the looks and went on about their business.

Hours went by and finally the air began to cool. Not much,

but enough that Carl noticed it was getting late. The blood red sun hung low on the horizon and shimmered through the heat waves that rose from the ground.

Joe stood straight and stretched his back. “Let’s go home, boys.”

“Yeah,” Charles replied. “I’m starvin’.”

Hard clods of sun-baked dirt dug into Carl’s feet as he walked down the long row toward the house. Even the soft dirt was hot and he jumped from one clump of grass to another. He was glad the day was over. “I can almost taste Ma’s fried chicken from here.”

“That’s the smartest thing you’ve said all day, squirt.” Joe playfully patted the younger boy’s head.

The closer to the small dwelling he got, the more Carl anticipated the family’s evening meal. He had no doubt his ma was the best cook in the world, and Minnie wasn’t far behind.

Today had been a hard one. His pa couldn’t afford to buy gloves to protect their hands, so he had raised some pretty good blisters.

“Joe, why does Ma make us soak our hands in coal oil when we get these sores.”

“To keep down infection.”

“Well, I don’t like the smell. It stinks.”

Charles poked Carl in the chest. “Stop whinin’, sissy.”

“I ain’t no sissy.”

“It stinks! It stinks! Sissy,” Charles mocked then took off running.

Sometimes his brother made him so mad. “Dammit, Charles, I said I ain’t no sissy.” His legs were shorter than his sibling’s, but he was going to try like hell to catch him, and when he did he’d beat the tar out of him!

CHAPTER TWO

Carl pushed his chair back from the table and patted his stomach. "Ma, that was the best chicken I ever had."

"Sure was, Ma." Joe picked up his plate, took it to the wash bucket and pumped water on it. "Oh, Pa, Johnny One Horn and Little Boy Horse stopped by today. Said Grey Wolf has furs for you."

"Okay."

Carl got up and added his plate to the stack in the bucket. He realized his pa had barely heard what Joe said. What was he thinking about?

Joe looked out the open kitchen window. "It's a pretty night out there."

"Yeah," Charles added. "There's a nice breeze, too. No mosquitoes." He placed his plate on top of Joe's. "I'll get my banjo and, Pa, you can get your guitar. We'll sit on the porch and pick a little."

Carl liked it when the family played music in the evening. It was relaxing after a long day of hard work. When there was no wind blowing, the mosquitoes were so bad they had to stay inside and that wasn't nearly as much fun.

O.C. cleared his throat. "Not tonight. Y'all worked hard today. I want you to soak your hands then get in bed early. You've got another hard day in front of you tomorrow."

Unable to believe his ears, Carl saw disappointment on his brothers' faces. He glanced at his ma. Her shrug said she didn't understand either, but one thing you didn't do was argue with

O.C.

By nine o'clock, he and his brothers were in their room getting ready for bed.

Joe unbuttoned his ragged cotton shirt. "Wonder why Pa made us come to bed on one of the few nights we could sit outside without being 'et up by those damn mosquitoes?"

"Hell, Joe, he doesn't have to have a reason." Charles climbed under his sheet and picked up a book. "You know that."

"I guess so, but sometimes it gets me riled."

Carl grabbed his sheet, threw it around his shoulders and went to the open window. He sat on the cool floor and stared out at the night sky.

Joe got into bed. "Don't stay up all night, Carl. You hear?"

He nodded but his attention was on the moon that glowed ever so bright. It was almost like daytime above the trees, but below in the forest it was dark as could be. It wasn't long before he heard his brothers' steady breathing. He hoped he didn't get pooped out that easy when he got that old.

Settling down, he leaned against the wall and enjoyed the cool breeze from the open window. After a while he looked to the north toward the cypress thicket close to the swamp. The hair on back of his neck stood straight out and he shivered. His flesh bumped up all over his body.

He stared for a minute without thinking then looked away and blinked. A tight fist of fear gripped his belly, but he forced himself to breathe. He turned his head once again toward the thicket and squinted, then his eyes focused.

Yes, there it was! A tiny, unnatural light glistened in the distance. The light grew and grew. It glowed as bright as the full moon itself as it crept across the swamp changing shapes from time to time.

The strange phenomenon had happened every summer that he could remember, but he never knew when it would come about, and he sure didn't know why. Silent, it snuck through the giant trees. His heart was going to pound its way free, he just knew it. He swallowed hard. No doubt about it, the Wisp was back.

The Indians believed the evil Wisp searched for the lost souls of warriors killed in night battle. It collected them in its never-ending quest fueled by a ravenous hunger. Invisible until it captured a soul, the Wisp then glowed with a blinding radiance created by the burning of the soul's life force.

He pulled the sheet more tightly around his neck, and watched the strange glow become larger as it joined its own reflection in the murky swamp water. Damn he hated that thing, but he watched it until it devoured all the souls, then made its ghostly disappearance just as it had arrived.

The night grew still. No wind. The mosquitoes moved in through the holes in the old screen like sharks in a feeding frenzy, buzzing and eager for a blood feast. Not wanting to cover himself in kerosene so they wouldn't bite him, he closed the window.

He went to bed, glad he wasn't covered with the sickening smell of the lantern fuel. It was unbearable and sometimes the misery of the stench kept him up all night.

This was the worst summer for the pesky rascals and he wished the wind would return so he could open the window again. The heat was stifling as he tossed and turned, trying to get comfortable. He was exhausted, and finally sleep overtook him.

****

What the hell? Carl was wrenched from a fitful sleep by a flash of light and the rumble of thunder like cannons in the night. Then he heard it, the wind, the blessed wind.

He jumped out of bed and opened the window. Joe did the same on the other side of the room.

"Thunder wake y'all up, too?"

"Yep."

A cross current of air whistled through the small space, cooling and freshening the smell of stale air. Inhaling deeply, Carl welcomed the aroma of rain. Man, oh man, sweet rain.

Charles flung open the backdoor that opened out on the swamp side of the house. "Come on. Let's take a bath."

It didn't take much coaxing. He and Joe charged out the door into the downpour of warm, clean rainwater, a prayer answered.

"My mosquito bites don't itch so bad now," Joe blurted. "I

think we must be in Heaven."

Carl and his brothers romped and played for he knew at least half an hour. It had been a long time since he'd felt this good, and he was disappointed when the water slowed and it was time to go back inside.

Grabbing his sheet, he plopped down in front of the opened window to watch the dwindling storm. Sitting at the window looking out was one of his favorite things. Except, of course, when the ole Wisp was around.

Joe and Charles lay on their beds and were soon asleep. Cool and refreshed, Carl, awed as always by the force of Mother Nature, started to turn away from the window when his eyes were drawn to a light coming from the swamp. The Wisp? Not again.

He pulled the sheet up over his shoulders then up over his head and hoped he didn't have to wake his brothers. "I pray you evil Wisp go away!" Why not? His prayers had worked with the wind.

His heart pounded as he slowly brought the sheet down below his eyes, and peered toward the place he'd last seen the Wisp.

The light was still there, but it looked different. Maybe it wasn't the evil Wisp after all. The rain had all but stopped; now he could see much better. It wasn't one light either, it was three and they flickered in the distance like candles in the wind.

He watched for what seemed like an hour. Sometimes the lights would move from side to side then stay in one place for a while. His muscles tensed when he realized the lights were getting closer. Closer and closer they came. He heard low voices carried on the night air. Who, or what, was it?

Running across the room he thought his legs would shake right out from under him. "Charles, wake up. Someone's comin'!"

"Oh, go to sleep, Carl, you're dreamin' and I've had enough excitement for one night." The older boy turned to face the wall.

Carl turned to Joe who was already awake. "Joe, someone's comin'!"

"Calm down, Squirt." Joe replied quietly. "I'll take a look."

Joe moved over to the window with Carl right behind him.

Nothing was going to tear him away from his older sibling. Not tonight.

Joe scratched his head. "Sounds like Pa and Bud talkin'. Wonder what they're doin' out there this late and in this kind of weather. They have the wagon and mule team, too."

When Carl saw Joe put on his pants, he grabbed his overalls and slid into them. "Where are you goin', Joe?"

"To try to see what's goin' on. You stay here."

"Nuh uh, I'm comin', too. I ain't gonna be left in here by myself."

"You're not by yourself, Charles is here."

"He's asleep!"

Joe headed for the door. "Alright, but keep quiet. If we get caught, it'll be our hides."

The clouds were breaking up and Carl welcomed the beams of moonlight that shone through. The tumbling billows of clouds cast huge shadows that flitted slow and strangely across the ground.

In the broken moonlight, the lantern torches flashed through the partially open door of the old barn. He followed Joe as quiet as possible to the side of the building and peered through a large crack in the warped wood.

Inside, water dripped off his father, Uncle Bud and Neil. They were soaked to the bone. Hopefully they wouldn't catch their death. He watched as the three men dried as best they could using some hay and old tow sacks.

O.C. began unharnessing the two mules from the wagon when he turned to Neil Carter. "Well, Neil, one thing about it, nobody'll ever find any trace of where we buried it.

Neil sat on a bale of hay. "I'z plumb wore out, Mr. O.C., but if you ever said anythin' right, you said it dis time."

Bud moved around slowly and rubbed his chest. "I'm still not feelin' so good. If y'all can finish up, I'm gonna get dry and get some rest. It's been one hell of a night."

Watching his Uncle Bud walk wearily down the path to the small shotgun house where he lived, Carl was worried about the older man. He just didn't look right. His color was funny. Maybe he really was sick.

As soon as Bud disappeared into the dark, Joe grabbed Carl

by the arm and nodded toward the house. He got the hint and followed Joe as he slipped away.

Back in the warmth of their room, Carl climbed into his bed but was unable to sleep. "Joe," he whispered, "You awake?"

"Yeah,"

"Why do you think they was out in the storm buryin' somethin' in the cypress thicket?"

"Don't know, but more important, what was it they buried?"

Chapter Three

The next morning brought a peculiar silence to the breakfast table. O.C. sat deep in thought through most of the meal. Carl couldn't meet his father's gaze. He and Joe knew a secret; they just didn't know what it was. He wondered if they'd ever find out.

The day's work ahead of them, he was glad he'd soaked his hands in coal oil the evening before. They weren't nearly as sore today. It was too wet from last night's rain to work in the field so he wouldn't have to use a hoe, but they would be able to pull weeds with their hands.

When he and his brothers left the house for the field, he dared to look in the direction of the woods where his pa had been the night before. Would Joe go to look for what they buried? He sure wasn't going. The Wisp was out there.

****

Fall 1847

Before Carl knew it, the crops were in. The fall rain came more often, the whole world was soggy and the water level in the swamp rose daily. The family needed money, and thankfully Grey Wolf had gotten there for his autumn fur trade with O.C.

Always in awe of the old Indian, Carl could hardly keep from staring at him. He guessed that Joe and Charles were more used to the man, so they didn't seem interested in the trade.

O.C. greeted Grey Wolf with a smile. "My friend, it's good to see you." He looked at the furs on the pack animal's backs. "You had a good year."

"Many furs for you to trade."

Walking toward one of the horses, O.C. asked, "What all you got here?"

Grey Wolf was proud and held his back straight. "Muskrat, beaver, mink."

O.C. studied the goods and Carl remembered what his father had told him. Grey Wolf and his clan survived well in the swamp. Fishing and hunting came natural to them. The Indians knew the swamp like he knew his own back yard.

They brought their booty to O.C. to take to Gulfport because Indians weren't allowed in town. Especially not Grey Wolf and his little band of renegades. They feared they would be shot on sight or hanged at the town's convenience if they even tried to enter.

O.C. rubbed his hand across one of the hides. "You timed this just right, Wolf. Neil and I are goin' into town tomorrow. You can camp out in the barn and we'll bring your supplies back to you."

"You get pots, fishing line, traps and spices from town?"

"Sure, and I've got your sweet potatoes, corn and onions already."

Grey Wolf smiled. "You good man, O.C. Armstrong."

"You and your men make yourself comfortable. I'll have the wife fix us some supper."

Carl was amazed at how tall and strong this old Indian man still was. He looked grand standing there. With a brief nod, Grey Wolf led his small group and their animals toward the barn.

****

"Neil, let's get the wagon hitched up and get goin'."

"Yes, Mr. O.C."

O.C.'s voice rang loud and clear. The sun peeked over the horizon, and a slight chill drifted on the air. Fall was nipping at the heels of summer and Carl was glad for that. "Pa, can I go?"

"Not today. Bud's goin' with us. He hasn't been feelin' too

good so he's gonna to see the doc. There ain't no room."

His Uncle Bud had been looking kind of ashy colored ever since they'd put the hole in the floor and buried…whatever it was in the swamp.

They must have buried something bad because no one had ever brought it up again. Even he and Joe had never talked about it. He guessed things like that were better left alone, but it didn't stop him from thinking about it from time to time. "Hope the doctor can find out what's wrong."

O.C. opened the barn door. "Me, too. Now quit jawin' and let's get these furs loaded up." He glanced at the sky. "I want to get out of here before the rain starts."

Carl peered upward. Didn't look like rain to him but that didn't mean anything, recently rain came most every day. His pa said if it didn't stop they might not have a good crop next season. Too much rain could make it too muddy and they couldn't afford a bad year.

"You going to stand there, Carl, or you going to help?"

He turned to see which Indian was talking to him. To his surprise, it was Johnny One Horn. "Johnny, when did you get here?"

"In night. You sleeping like papoose after suckle."

"I'm ten now, Horse, goin' on eleven. I ain't no baby no more."

"Sleep like one." Boy Horse laughed.

The tall man was worse than his brothers when it came to teasing him. However, it didn't bother him as bad. Maybe it was because there wasn't a chance in hell he could beat Boy Horse up. At least he liked to think there would come a day when he could put a hurtin' on Charles or Joe.

Carl waved to his pa, Neil and Uncle Bud as the horses led the wagon down the dirt road and out of sight. They'd be gone until well after dark.

He got his chores done, then headed for the barn. Maybe Johnny One Horn would tell him a story. He figured Johnny was probably the world's best storyteller.

Luck was on his side. Horn was in the barn by himself. Gray Wolf and the others had gone somewhere for the time being and that suited him just fine. That way, he could have

Horn all to himself.

The older man studied the barn walls. Carl quietly walked up beside him and tried to see what he was looking at so intently. There it was. Funny, he'd never noticed the writing on the boards before.

"What's that say, Johnny?"

"I do not know."

"Where'd it come from?"

Johnny reached up and ran his fingers over the faded letters. "A Ship."

"A Ship? What kind of ship? You mean like one that goes in the water?"

The Indian turned and took a seat on a pile of loose hay. "Sit, I tell you about it, but you tell no one."

Carl sat beside Johnny eager to hear what he had to say. "Cross my heart." He made an imaginary X on his chest with his finger.

"Many years ago in 1759 or '60, there was a war. White men call it French and Indian War, but the fighting was between French and British."

"Why would they call it that if the Indians wasn't even fightin'? That's pretty dumb."

"The swamp was flooded during war. There was a bad storm and one French ship, The Victor, lost its way in the swirling wind and sailed too far into bay St. Louis. The Captain did not know he sailed over swamp and Cyprus forest. It was big, strong ship but when the bottom hit trees, the ship broke open. The Victor sank right there."

"Where?"

"Just a ways behind this barn is where it was found. Resting in the trees."

"Who found it?"

"The same band of Indians that Grey Wolf is now Chief of. My People"

"Was Grey Wolf Chief then?"

"He was not born. Long time ago."

"What did the Indians do when they found The Victor?" Carl saw a sadness fill Johnny's eyes.

"Some men already drowned in deep water. Some escaped,

but died in the swamp trying to get out. My people killed some of the Frenchmen. There was a small one with the French. A Boy. My people took him and let him live."

"Why was a boy on the ship?"

"I do not know that."

"What did the Indians do with the boy?"

"They took him to their camp and raised him like one of their own. He grew and married a beautiful Indian woman and taught her his language, but while she was with child he went hunting and was killed by a bear. He never got to see his son."

"Wow, that's a sad story. Wonder where his son is now?"

"The Frenchman's son was my father. I am the Frenchman's grandson."

Carl had to force his jaws shut. "You, One Horn? You're his grandson?"

With a distant look in his eye, Johnny nodded. It was true what Joe had said. Johnny One Horn was part French. He couldn't stop staring at the older man. He guessed he'd always noticed his skin wasn't as dark as the others, but never really wondered about it.

He swallowed hard and hoped he wouldn't make Johnny mad with his next question. "D-do you have a French name, too?"

"My mother gave me two names. One French, and one Indian, like my father's name, but I only wanted to be called One Horn."

"Can I ask what your father's name was, Horn?"

"Jean La Beau Running Horse. That is it."

Damn, Joe was right about that, too. Maybe Joe was smarter than Carl gave him credit for. "So that's why they call you Johnny."

"You are right my young friend. You are smart."

"Yeah, I know."

One Horn laughed and lay back on the straw. "The Indians took all they could use off the ship then left it. When the swamp went down, Plummer's father claimed this land. He made this barn with the wood from the ship. These are very hard boards. Will withstand lots of bad weather. Half of the house is built from ship boards, as well." He paused and glanced at the walls.

"When I was a boy I watched the old man build this place from the ground up. He tore the great ship apart one board at a time and used everything from it he could. He almost had it finished when he died."

"He died?"

"Bit by a cottonmouth. The old man's wife and son, moved to town. The son grew up, his mother died, then he married. Now he's dead, too, and his wife owns this."

"That's kind of confusing, Horn."

"Don't worry about it, it doesn't matter. What matters is that O.C. came along and became Plummer's tenant farmer. Then soon, you were born, Carl."

"That's the best thing of all, Horn. Me." Carl liked to make Johnny laugh. The man was so jolly when he did. However, he had one last question. "Horn, why is it you speak English so good? I mean, it's not perfect, but better than most Indians. You and Horse both."

"I listen well and learn. My grandmother taught the language to my father then he taught me. You, too, are a good listener. That is why I like to share my stories."

"Sure 'nough." This story was a special one. One Carl wouldn't forget for the rest of his life. He lay back on the straw beside Johnny One horn. Dust danced on the sunbeams that streamed through the boards that held such history.

Shortly the sky proved O.C. right. A shadow covered the barn and rain began to fall.

Chapter Four

Winter 1848

"Carl, Carl, get up, quick!"

He opened his eyes and shivered under his quilt. The chill in the room went all the way to his bones. "What's wrong, Charles?"

"It's snowin'."

"What?"

"Snowin', get your lazy butt up and look out the window."

Carl joined his big brothers at the window. He'd never seen snow before. Matter of fact, he didn't know if Joe or Charles had either. It just didn't snow much in southern Mississippi.

White flakes like goose down floated from the gray sky. He wasn't going to miss the opportunity to stand in it and feel it on his face. "I'm goin' outside." He started for the door when Joe stopped him.

"You'd better get some clothes and shoes on, or you'll freeze to death."

Was he stupid or something? He was about to run out in nothing but his long johns. Man would that have been a shock. After he dressed, he stepped out into the night. Joe and Charles weren't far behind.

The white flakes didn't stick to the ground and melted as soon as they hit his skin. He'd never experienced anything like it in his life. He wondered if his mother had ever seen snow before.

"Did y'all tell Ma?"

"No, we didn't wake her up. She and Pa were at Uncle Bud's house 'til late. He's real bad sick. Pa says he probably won't make it through winter."

Bud was one of Carl's favorite people. He hated to see the old man suffer the way he had over the last few months. With pains in his chest and such. The doctor said it was a bad heart. If he wasn't going to get better, maybe dying was the best thing that could happen to him. He'd been working this old farm for years and was probably pretty tired.

The flakes were fewer now, and the ground was wet from the snow melt. It didn't take much to soak it since all the rain. The swamp had risen by a few feet and water crept into the field.

Joe opened the door leading into their room. "Come on, boys, let's go in before we catch our death."

Carl was reluctant, but the snow had all but stopped now, so he had no reason not to go back into the stale smelling room. However, his bed was still warm when he got in it, and he welcomed the return of peaceful sleep.

****

Spring 1849

"Amen."

O.C. closed the Bible and Carl watched his father wipe a tear from his cheek. It was the only time in his life he'd seen his pa cry.

Joe and Charles shoveled dirt onto the wooden coffin. Bud was gone. He glanced over at his Aunt. She was sobbing and it made him sad for her. She'd be alone now, except for them. She said she was thinking of moving back to Vicksburg where her family was. He'd miss her, but it would probably be best if she did, she might be happier there.

He felt sorry for his ma, too. After all, her brother Bud was her only living kin besides him, Charles, Joe and his pa of course. Now them and O.C. was all she had left.

O.C. approached his wife. "Martha, you gonna be okay?

She wiped her nose with a handkerchief. "I think so.

"You want to walk Estelle home?"

"Yes. O.C., and I think I should stay with her a few nights. Until she gets used to the fact Bud's gone. I guess I have to get used to it, too."

"Do what you have to, hon."

Carl knew his ma would be home to fix meals, but he'd never spent a night in the house without her there. What was he worried about anyhow? He was going on twelve years old now and didn't need his ma by his side every minute.

Charles dried the last of the dishes and Carl put them away. When his pa entered the kitchen, the man had a worried look on his face.

"Joe, come in here."

"What is it, Pa?" Joe asked.

"All three of y'all sit down. I got somethin' I want to say."

They hadn't gathered up at the table like this for a family talk in a long time. Carl wondered why O.C. was doing it now, without his ma here.

"It's time to plant the crop. The swamp water's so high, we ain't gonna have nearly the land to plant on this year. It's gonna be a rough year. If things don't get better soon, we may have to move."

Carl didn't want to move, this was his home. The only one he'd ever known. "Move, Pa?"

"I'm not sayin' we have to right now, I'm talkin' down the road."

Joe sat back in his chair. "What does Ma say?"

"I ain't talked to her about it, and don't y'all either. I don't want her to know how bad things are and start her worryin' more than she does already. This is just between us men. Hear me?"

"Yes, sir," Carl said at the same time his brothers did.

"The garden behind the house will keep us eatin', long as the water don't get too high. We're gonna have to work extra hard this year to make the best crop possible. I'm countin' on y'all. Now that Bud's gone, you boys are my partners."

Charles leaned forward. "What about Neil?"

"Y'all know Minnie's been sickly. With Bud dyin', she's worried she's gonna go, too, and she don't want to die out here in the swamp. She and Neil have thought about movin' to Missouri for some time so she can be closer to a doctor."

Carl's world was falling apart around him. Damned rain. "Why Missouri? There's doctors close around here."

"I don't know, Carl. That's not for me to question. It's what Minnie wants and Neil's gonna give it to her, I guess."

"When do you think they'll be leavin', Pa?" Joe asked.

"I'd say pretty quick. They're gatherin' their belongin's already."

Tears welled in Carl's eyes. Bud was gone, his aunt was moving to Illinois, and now Neil and Minnie, too. He blinked and fought to keep the salty drops from falling. He didn't want his brothers to make fun of him for crying, but he was worried about what his family was going to do?

O.C sat back in his chair. "We still have the livestock and the furs Grey Wolf brings in the fall will help us get supplies to last through the winter. Your ma will do some cannin' with things from the garden, but that's a ways down the road, too. Right now, we need to pray it stops rainin' every day and the water goes down."

It was scary thinking about all the changes that could be ahead of them, but Carl had confidence that O.C. would be able to keep the family together.

"Well, that's it, boys, it's you and me now." O.C. offered Joe a handshake. "Partners?"

Joe accepted. "Partners."

Then Charles received the shake. "Partners."

Carl felt something swell in his chest when his pa offered him his hand. Somehow it made him feel more grown up. Older in a way, and proud.

"Partners, Carl?"

He placed his hand firmly in his father's then lifted the corners of his mouth. Surely his smile went from ear to ear. "Partners, Pa."

****

Loading the last wooden box into the wagon meant Neil and Minnie would be on their way soon. O.C was right about their move to Missouri, but Carl didn't have to like it.

Minnie had steadily gone downhill in the last couple of months since they'd buried Bud. Carl didn't want her to die, so he was sort of reconciled to their going someplace where she could find the right doctor to help her.

He ran to ole black Neil, threw his arms around the old man's chest and hugged him tight. He loved him and Minnie like family. Hell, they were family. "I wish you didn't have to go." He couldn't stop the tears this time.

Neil gently wrapped him in an embrace. "Now, you knows wez got to. Never fugit we loves ya, boy."

Minnie stepped forward and joined in the hug. "We sho does, Carl. Maybe if wez all pray hard enough, we be seein' each other again by-n-by."

He couldn't stop sobbing and vowed to pray harder than he ever had. He backed away, wiped his eyes and nose with the sleeve of his shirt. "I love y'all so much."

He turned and ran sobbing back toward the barn. He jerked the door open, plunged into the blessed dimness of the barn and fell on a pile of hay. What the hell did he care if Charles and Joe laughed at him? His heart was breaking, he was going to miss his good friends, and it was okay to cry about it!

****

Early Spring 1850

It was Sunday and Carl sat in the barn and gazed at the strange boards of the walls. This was a day of rest, but lately there'd been a lot of time to rest. He stuck one end of a piece of hay in his mouth and allowed his mind to wander.

The harvest the past fall had been little more than nothing. The family struggled from day to day just to get by.

The rain. The ever-present rain. The swamp was at an almost all-time high. He had never seen the water such a short distance from the back of the barn. Why, it couldn't be more than twenty feet away.

Over the winter, their meager supplies were all but used up and some of livestock had to be sold. Now the remaining farm animals were their biggest food source and he wasn't sure how long it would be before they were gone, too. Of course, they could hunt for squirrel, rabbit and such, and the garden spot would start to produce soon so that would get them through for a while.

And his poor ma hadn't been the same since her brother died. She still worked hard every day, but there was a faraway look in her eyes and he worried about her.

It had been almost a year since Neil and Minnie moved away. He'd gotten a letter from them that said Minnie was doing better. He was glad for that.

He inhaled a deep breath and spit the hay straw out. Getting older was supposed to be easy. At least that's what he thought. Now that he was thirteen, things seemed to be getting harder.

"Carl, you in there?"

He jumped to his feet. "Yes sir, Pa."

"Find your brothers and y'all come in the house."

"Yes, sir." As usual, water began to drizzle from the sky. He'd better hurry and find the other boys before it started to pour. He didn't have to go far; they were both walking up the soggy road toward the house.

He fell into step with them as they trudged through the Mississippi mud. "Y'all, Pa wants us."

"For what?" Charles asked.

"Hell, I don't know."

"Hey, you'd better stop that cussin'. Ma hears ya and you'll be feelin' a rawhide strap across your behind."

"I'm too old to get a whuppin', Joe."

"I'm eighteen and I bet she could still give me a good one if I was askin' for it."

"Maybe so." His ma wasn't physically as strong as she used to be, but Joe was right, there was no doubt that she could still swing a strap if it was called for. 'For your own good', as she would say.

O.C. stood on the porch. The rain fell heavier as they approached the house. There was a strange look on his pa's face. A look Carl didn't like.

"Y'all come on in. I've got somethin' to talk to ya about."

Martha stepped out the door. "You boys take those muddy

boots off first, you hear?"

Carl left his boots outside and shook off as much rain as he could before following the others inside.

O.C. went to the table and pulled out a chair. "Come on and sit down. We may as well get this over with."

Carl, his brothers and his mother took their usual seats at the table. An uncomfortable silence filled the room. In a voice void of emotion O.C. cleared his throat and began to speak. Carl didn't think he wanted to hear what the man had to say.

"This may sound bad, but it's got to be said. We've got to sell more of the livestock. That will leave only enough to slaughter and eat on for a few more months. There's still some canned goods from last year and the garden will get us by for this year but–. "

Martha met her husband's gaze. "We've always got by somehow or another. We've got to do what we've got to do."

"I know that, hon. That's why I've got to leave the farm and go look for work."

Eyes wide, Martha gasped. "Leave? What are you talking about, O.C. You can't just leave us here."

"We've gotta get out of this hellhole. I'll find work and send money to y'all. Hell, we'll starve to death this winter if I don't do somethin'."

Carl was scared. More afraid then he'd ever been, even of the Wisp. He wanted to cry but he was too old for that.

Martha peered down at her hands. Tears flowed freely from her eyes. "You promise you'll send for us?"

O.C. took her hand. "I promise. Soon as I can."

"We'll make it 'til winter, then we'll come wherever you are."

Nodding his head, O.C. stood. "I'll be leavin' to Gulfport come mornin'."

Chapter Five

LEAVING THE FARM

It was late, but O.C. couldn't sleep. He'd never been away from his family for more than a day or two. Now, he couldn't predict how long he would be gone.

He stood on the porch of the house where they'd lived for most of his sons' lives. The smell of the wet ground invaded his nostrils. It was time to tell his secret. Someone had to know before he left.

Inhaling a deep, labored breath then slowly releasing it, he turned and entered the house where his family slept. He opened the door to the small lean-to bedroom and studied the three young men sleeping in the beds. He loved each one of them, but hadn't told them so. He'd never been one to show his emotions and figured now wasn't the time to start.

He crossed the small area and placed his hand on his oldest son's shoulder. "Joe, wake up."

Joe slowly opened his eyes. "What is it, Pa?"

"Get dressed and meet me in the barn."

"Yes, sir."

O.C. left the house, went into the barn, lit a lantern and waited. He realized how proud of Joe he was as he watched him walk through the barn doorway. What a tall, good looking man he'd grown into. He was sure Joe could keep the secret and do what needed to be done.

"Let's sit up here." O.C. was perched on the back of the wagon. Joe swung effortlessly up beside him.

"I'll be sorry to see you go, Pa."

"It's somethin' I gotta do and I'm gonna leave before the other boys wake up. You know, being the oldest, the care of the family'll fall on you now. Your ma won't take my leavin' well and will need lots of extra care."

"I know."

"But," How was he going to say this? "I've been keepin' somethin' from y'all for the last few years. Somethin' important you need to know before I get on my way."

Joe's brow furrowed. "What's that?"

It was best just to get it out, he knew that, but still it wasn't easy. O.C. swallowed hard. "You can't tell this, son. Not until it's time, anyway."

"Okay."

"Remember when we got the new heatin' stove four years ago?"

"Yes, sir."

"Well, me, Neil and Bud, Lord rest his soul, were trying to make the floor strong enough to hold it up. So we cut a hole and went under the house. When we was diggin' to make room for the support poles, our shovels hit somethin'. It was an old wooden box. We cleared out around it thinkin' maybe we'd found a dead body. The box was about six feet square, too big for a coffin."

"It was hard wood. The hardest I ever seen." O.C. glanced around the barn. "Now that I think about it, it was made from boards just like these walls." He wondered why he didn't realize that before. "Anyway, we pried it open and lo and behold it was full of some kind of gold coins."

"Gold?"

"Yep."

"How'd it get there?"

O.C. shook his head. "Hell if I know. Don't suppose anyone else knows either."

"Where is it now?"

"I'm gettin' to that. Just let me talk. Most of the coins were bigger than fifty dollar gold pieces." He remembered the strange looking money. "I don't know what in hell they were. All I know is they was made of pure gold."

O.C. glanced at Joe who sat with his jaw dropped. He smiled at the look on the young man's face and continued, "Joe, it took two whole nights to move the stuff. Like to have worked all of us to death.

"We fought them damned mosquitoes, a hell of a rain storm, everything you can imagine. Neil was afraid the Wisp was gonna get us, Bud was gettin' sick about then, and we all knew we had to be quiet about it.

"You boys was smaller then, and we didn't want none of you to find out for sure. You might have slipped and told somebody."

"Pa–."

"Wait, let me finish. Two wagon loads of black washin' pots full we hauled down to the cypress thicket. We dug a hole while you boys was workin' in the field. The hole was pretty big. 'Bout six foot deep and eight foot square.

"We had hauled a load of rocks from the knoll above the house. In the night we put those wash pots in the hole and filled them with the bags of coins then covered the coins with candle wax. After that we packed the rock on top then filled the rest with dirt. We put some of the rocks on top and tried to make it look as natural as possible."

Joe shifted on the back of the wagon. "Carl saw y'all, Pa."

His breath caught in his throat and he looked into Joes eyes. "What are you talkin' about?"

Joe met his gaze. "The night y'all buried the gold. We went out and took a bath in the rain. When we came back in, Carl sat by the window watchin' the storm. When the rain slowed, he saw the lanterns in the thicket. He thought it was the Wisp. Then he realized it was somebody comin' toward the house. He got scared and woke me up."

"Why didn't y'all ever tell me?"

Joe glanced down at the floor. "We figured we'd get a whuppin' if you found out. After y'all got back in the barn, we came outside to see what you were doin'. We didn't see anything, so after Uncle Bud left, we went back inside."

O.C. shook his head and laughter made its way to the

surface. "I should have known I could trust you boys to keep quiet. If you could hold that inside, you can keep a secret from anyone." He was glad to see a smile on Joe's face, and happy the mood had lightened.

Running his fingers through his hair, Joe asked, "Why'd you move it, Pa? We could've been rich, moved out of this godforsaken place and lived like people should. I don't understand."

"One day we will be rich, Joe, but at that time, we had to move fast. See, after his ma died, young Mr. Plummer was gonna sell this place out from under us. I never told y'all, but I was afraid the new owner might make us leave. When we found the gold, we decided we had to move fast. At the time we thought we did what was best. As it proved, we should have thought it out better."

"How come Plummer didn't sell?"

"He was killed before he could get it sold, and his Mrs. decided not to sell. After all that passed, I tried to go get some of the coins, but by then it was under water. I figured the swamp would go down like it always did, but it just got worse. None of us was strong enough anymore to swim down and try to get to it. Now it's under even more water."

"How do you know where it is out there in the swamp?"

"It's by two tall Cypress trees that are almost grown together. One was struck by lightning and the top's blown out. The other one your Uncle Bud marked by choppin' the bark off about three feet above the ground on the side that faces the house. Course, you can't see that now cause it's under water."

"Can you still tell where they are?"

"You can, but you have to look hard. A few feet of the tops of the trees still show above the water. The two we buried it under are among them.

"You have to look for the one that's burned, the one hit by lightning. It's the tallest of the two of them."

"Pa, I bet it would be next to impossible to get the gold out now."

He nodded. "That's why I have to go somewhere for work." He wanted to take in one last good look at his oldest son. He jumped off the back of the wagon and turned to face the young man. “If somethin’ happens, Joe, that I don’t’ get back, you know where the gold is. You can tell the other boys when it’s time. Hear me, Joe? When it’s time.”

“Yes, sir, when it’s time.”

He studied Joe’s face. “You’re a good boy, son. I know you’re a man now, but you’ll always be my boy.”

Joe stepped to the ground and hugged O.C. “I love you, too, Pa.”

Tears welled in O.C.’s eyes and he backed away. He didn’t want emotion to change his mind about leaving. “I’m gonna be goin’ in about an hour. I’d like to spend a little time with your mother. Tell Charles and Carl about the gold only if I don’t come back. Like I said, you’ll know when it’s time. You’ll know.” He turned and walked toward the house.

This had been a good farm for many years. He loved and hated it, but it had fed his family through the years of hard work. If only Grey Wolf was still well enough and could bring furs to trade, he might be able to stay. Maybe he could talk to one of the other Indians and they would bring them. No, he had to get that kind of thinking out of his head. The decision was made. Besides, furs weren’t as plentiful either, now that the swamp was up.

He entered the small dwelling. The kerosene odor was only slight as the mosquitoes weren’t bad enough yet to have to rub it on. The door of the bedroom he’d shared with Martha for the last twenty some years squeaked open, and he stepped inside.

****

Joe lay in his bed. There was no way he could sleep knowing his father was leaving and he might not see him for a long while. Hell, after being told the story of the buried treasure, he might not ever sleep again. Knowing about it gnawed at his gut. Why, why had they buried it all?

He couldn’t think about that now. He had other worries at hand. His ma… he hoped she would handle O.C.’s leaving better than he expected her to.

It seemed only a short time until he heard the front door of the house shut. His father was gone. He heard his ma crying quietly, but he didn't go to her for he was sure she didn't want anyone to know.

In a few minutes the clip clop of the horses' hooves against the ground faded into the distance. His heart leaped to his throat and he wanted to run after his father and beg him not to go.

He was more scared than he had ever been. The responsibility of taking care of the family was now on his shoulders. He drew a deep breath and tried to swallow the lump in his throat. There was no choice; he'd just have to do it.

Joe felt something tug on the covers of his bed. He opened his eyes and saw it was daylight. He must have slept after all. Another tug. He turned to meet the watery eyes of his youngest brother. "What is it, Carl?"

"Is Pa gone?"

"Yeah, he's gone. Don't worry, everything's gonna be all right. The next couple of months are gonna pass in no time a'tall."

Carl wiped a tear from his cheek. "It just don't seem right. I'm afraid I'll never see him again.

"Oh, stop it. He'll be back. You'll see." Joe sat up on the side of the bed wishing he were as confident as he sounded. "Hey, I tell you what. Since the crops are all rained out, how bout we build that raft you've always wanted? We can use it to fish the swamp. We need the fish anyway." Carl didn't suspect the motive behind the offer, and Joe was delighted to see a sparkle return to the boy's eyes.

"Really, Joe?"

"Sure." He stood. "I'll get some fresh eggs out of the henhouse and fix somethin' to eat. We won't bother Ma right now. I'm guessin' she's pretty tired. You get that lazy brother of yours up and let's get started!"

Joe built a fire in the wood stove, and cooked a hearty breakfast of eggs and warmed over cornbread left from the night before. He sat at the table with his brothers. "Seems strange without Pa here."

Charles chomped on his breakfast. "It don't seem like he's gone yet. It's just like he's still in bed sleeping with Ma."

Carl took a bite of egg. "Yeah, that's the way I'm gonna think about it, too. Like he's still asleep or just took some furs to town."

Joe thought it was time to change the subject. "Hey, let's talk about that raft. I think once we get the stuff together this mornin', we can have it done by sundown."

"Wow, then we can go fishing first thing tomorrow." Carl put his plate in the wash bucket.

Following his brothers outside, Joe made a plan in his head. He pointed to the north. "Carl, you go that way and gather logs, old boards, whatever you think we can use on the raft. Charles, you go south and do the same thing. I'll go east. Let's not get too far away from the house. If you need help carryin' somethin' whistle. I'll come help you."

He watched his siblings go in their appointed directions. Hopefully this raft would really float and he could check out the swamp and find the burned-out tree.

The day passed swiftly and finding the material to build the makeshift boat was harder then Joe thought it would be. There was a look of disappointment in Carl's eyes.

"Damn, Joe, we didn't even get started puttin' the thing together today."

"Just because Pa ain't around, don't mean you can start cussin' all the time."

"But I thought we'd be able to go fishin' in the mornin'."

"We're gonna build this right or we ain't gonna do it at all. Be patient, little brother." It was easy for him to tell Carl that, but his heart pounded in anticipation of what they'd find. His biggest question was, how would they get to the bottom of the swamp to retrieve the treasure?

Chapter Six

Joe hadn't realized it would take almost a week to get the materials together to build the raft, but finally it was time to begin.

He invited Martha to come outside, sit on the porch and watch them at their task. Her moods were better now and she even smiled from time to time. Surprised she called him aside; he followed her to the far end of the porch.

"What are you going to do with that thing, son?"

"We're gonna catch some catfish in the swamp."

"You sure you're not going treasure hunting?"

He'd wondered if she knew about the gold. Now he was sure she did. "It's for fishin', Ma. Pa said I'd know when it was time for that other." The look on her face relaxed.

"Good. That water's deep and I don't want you boys diving off that thing into that murky stuff. It's full of cottonmouths, and leeches, too. No telling what's in there."

"Don't worry."

She patted him on the back. "Okay. Y'all get after it. I wouldn't mind havin' a mess of catfish."

The rocking chair creaked when she sat back down. Joe was pleased to see the smile on her face when he, Carl and Charles started working in earnest to finish the raft.

It was an all day job, but they finished and Joe was proud of what they'd done. He put his arm around Carl's shoulders. "Now that, little brother, is how a raft should be built."

"It's perfect, ain't it, Joe?"

"Pretty close."

Martha came out of the house and wiped her hands on her apron. "My, my, you boys did a fine job." She stepped off the porch. "Fine indeed."

Charles straightened his back. "Thanks, Ma."

Turning toward the house Martha waved for her sons to come inside. "I've got supper ready. Y'all have worked hard all day and we're having something special. In the morning you can go and get me some fish."

****

Joe brought Seemo, one of the two mules they had left, out of the barn. "Let's hook her up to the raft and drag it to the edge of the water."

Carl wrapped the rope around one side of the handmade craft and Charles did the same on the other. Joe hooked the rope to the old wagon hitch he'd already put on the mule. He couldn't wait to get the raft into the water and make way to the money tree. He only hoped it would be as easy to find as O.C. had said it would.

"Carl, go get the cane fishin' poles out of the barn and the worms we dug. Charles, you grab the oars we made last night and the push poles and let's get." He did some last minute adjustments on the mules harness and noticed his mother come out of the house.

"You boys be careful, now."

"Yes, ma'am, we will. We'll get some good fishin' in today."

"Don't try nothin' stupid, Joe."

He smiled, walked to the porch and put his arm around her shoulder. "Don't fret. Everything's gonna be all right. I swear."

She grinned and nodded her head.

"Mornin', Ma." Carl came from the barn, and put the homemade poles, the bucket of dirt and worms on the raft.

"Mornin'."

Charles laid the oars down. "How you feelin' this mornin', Ma?"

"Pretty good, but I'll feel better when you bring back some fish for supper."

Joe walked to the mule and grabbed the reins. "We'd better get or we ain't gonna get no fishin' in before the rain starts." He began to walk glad they were finally on their way.

Leading the mule to the edge of the swamp, Joe struggled in the thick mud that sucked at his feet and made walking almost impossible. "Damn soggy ground. Once we get this thing in the water, we'll leave it. It'll be too hard to pull it down here every time we want to go fishin'."

"Okay," Carl said as he helped push the raft into the mucky water.

Charles tied the mule to a tree and Joe grabbed a push pole. "Get on, boys. We're goin' fishin'."

Using the long poles they moved the raft through the shallow water fairly easy. It was quiet on the water. Peaceful. Joe was lost in thought when Charles' voice got his attention.

"My push pole ain't touchin' ground no more. We'd better start rowin'. How far out are we goin', anyway?"

Studying the waters around them Joe's heart threatened to stop. That was it. The lightning blasted cypress his pa talked about. He sat down and picked up an oar. "That old burned-out tree over there looks like a good spot." Trying to stay calm so his brothers wouldn't suspect anything, he began to whistle.

Thoughts of what his pa told him raced through his mind as they drew closer to the ancient money tree. It was just as O.C. said. The top was all but gone, jagged remnants of broken branches reflected in the dark water. As they approached, he saw the scorch marks made from the lightning strike.

"Charles, tie that rope to one of the bigger branches. Tie it tight. I don't want it to come loose if the wind comes up or a storm catches us out here. Carl, grab them worms, let's catch some fish." The smile on Carl's face warmed Joe's heart.

"Sure thing."

Joe had put extra-long line on his pole. He wanted to check the depth of the water. From the looks of it, it was probably about twenty feet. A little higher than O.C. had thought. It was amazing to him that their house hadn't flooded yet. It and the barn were built on a small hill, just high enough to keep the water from reaching it yet. Even through their hardships, they had some things to be thankful for.

One of the things he could be thankful for rested about twenty feet below the raft. He gazed into the cloudy water that was the only thing between him and the gold that could make his family rich.

Charles sat for a long while with his line in the water. "It was just a few years ago, Joe, that we played in this thicket. Hard to believe it's under water now. We probably played under this very tree."

Carl shook his head. "Not me! I don't like this creepy old tree. This is where the Wisp lives at night."

Laughing, Charles asked, "What makes you think that? Sometimes your imagination runs away with you, squirt."

"I'm not kidding. Every time I've seen that awful thing, it starts right here by this creepy tree." Carl shivered. "I don't like this place. Besides, we ain't catchin' anything."

"He's right, Joe. Maybe the fish are up closer to the bank."

Now that Joe knew the depth of the water and exactly where the tree was, they could leave. "Well, alright, we'll head on back."

About the time they got close to shore, Carl caught the first fish. Joe was happy for the younger boy. After all, it was Carl that had always wanted to fish from a raft. "Hey, that's a nice one, Carl."

Carl stood proud and took the flopping fish off the end of his line. "Probably the biggest one we'll catch all day. Don't you think?"

The enthusiasm in Carl's voice did little to stop Joe from thinking about the gold. He stared at the money tree in the middle of the water. "Probably so, little brother, probably so."

****

Summer 1850

O.C. peered out over the vast expanse of a basin of the Texas plains. In the distance was another mountain range he'd have to cross.

It had been four months since he'd left Mississippi and headed west. He'd found odd jobs here and there in Louisiana and East Texas, but only made enough to keep himself and his horse fed. Was it a mistake? Had he chosen the wrong thing to do?

He missed his family something awful, but he couldn't turn back now. He couldn't get to the gold he'd buried, but there was gold in California and that's where he was headed. It was a long way, but he'd make it. He had to.

Ginger hues of the setting sun rippled behind the spiky peaks of the distant mountains. It was hot in this state, but it was a dry heat. Not like the heavy heat of Mississippi. That oppressive heat and those nasty, blood-thirsty mosquitoes were two things he didn't miss.

Darkness fell and the wind began to blow. O.C. didn't think he could keep his sore butt in the saddle one more minute. Then a flicker in the distance caught his eye. What was it? A fire? A campfire. He caught a second wind and headed toward the bright spot hoping to find a friendly face.

As he neared the flames, he reined in his enthusiasm. He had to be careful. There was no telling who he would find at the camp. He stopped a good ways away and watched from a distance the men around the fire eating.

The wind blew and a lone tumbleweed drifted across the space between him and the men. One of the men whirled and looked in the direction of the wind-blown weed, his hand rested on the butt of his holstered revolver.

Were they a posse out looking for someone? It wouldn't fill his empty stomach to stay there guessing. He figured he'd make himself known, but decided to stay on his horse just in case he had to make a run for it.

Cautiously he approached. "Howdy!" The men all stood and looked toward him. Two drew their guns. "Howdy, y'all." He entered the circle of light made by the fire. "My name's O.C. Saw you and wondered if I could share your campfire for the night." The tallest man looked into the expanse around them.

"You alone?"

"Yep."

"Where'd you come from?"

"Mississippi. On my way to the California lookin' for gold." He didn't know how to take the laughter of the other men as they once again took their seats. The tall man walked toward him and offered a handshake.

"O.C., you say?"

"Yep."

"Come on down and have a bite. You look like you could use it. Don Boggs is the name."

O.C. dismounted, made sure his knife was tucked in his boot, then tied his horse. "Thank ya, Don."

After taking a tin plate from Boggs, O.C. filled it with beans and sat next to the man. "What are y'all doin' out here?"

Don rolled some tobacco in a paper and lit it. "We're following a cattle herd to Arizona. We work for the guy that owns them."

"So you're on a cattle drive?" A couple of men snickered and elbowed each other. He wondered what that was all about.

"Not exactly, we do, well, we kind of clean up. We collect the hides from the dead cattle. Each hide we get gives us a fifty cent bonus and we get a salary of fifteen dollars for a month's work."

"Fifteen dollars! Hell, I haven't seen that much money in I don't know when." O.C. took another bite of beans. "I'd love to be able to send money like that back to Mississippi to my family."

"You good with a gun?" Don looked him straight in the eye.

"Fair, but I can hit a bee on a tree with a knife."

Don nodded. "How fast do you want to get to California?"

O.C. knew Don had something up his sleeve. "Why?"

"Well, we lost a man last week. He was, shall we say, put in his place by the big man. So, we're looking for a hand. You interested?"

There was something in Don Boggs' eyes that bothered O.C., but how could he pass it up? "Fifteen dollars for a month and fifty cents a hide?"

"Yep. It ain't easy work, but it pays regular."

Visions of being able to send money to his family flashed through his mind's eye. Getting them out of the swamp was worth almost anything. "I'm in." He shook Don's hand. The rest of the men offered their howdys, and welcomes. They looked pretty rough and didn't smell none too good, but a man couldn't judge another by his smell. He smiled to himself, hell he probably smelled the same way.

However, none of that mattered. The important thing was that he would be able to send Martha and the boys some money soon. He curled up in his blanket and pillowed his head on his saddle. He had a job.

Chapter Seven

Fall 1852

The morning sun streamed through the window of the living area in the Armstrong house. Joe went into the kitchen where his brothers sat at the table. "What are y'all doin'?"

Carl met Joe's gaze. "Listenin' to Ma cry."

"It's been two and a half years, Joe. I can't believe Pa would just walk off and leave us like this." Charles went to the stove and filled his cup. "This is the last of the coffee, we've barely survived these last couple of years and he's off gallivantin' around. What are we gonna do?"

Joe heard the frustration in his brother's voice. He had his own questions about O.C. not returning, but… "Y'all know somethin's bound to be wrong or Pa would have been back by now. Hell, he may be dead for all we know, so don't talk bad about him, you hear me?!"

Charles took his seat once again. "Okay, but what are we gonna do about Ma? She don't eat, she cries all the time and she hardly ever talks anymore."

He'd watched his mother's health dwindle away over the last few months. At twenty years old, Joe shouldn't miss the strength his pa had always provided for the family. Today, more then ever, he missed him because he had to make a very important decision. "I'm worried about Ma, too. I've been thinkin' about it, and I believe it would be best to take her to

Vicksburg to Aunt Estelle's. I've written Estie a couple of letters, but haven't heard back."

"How did you send letters to Vicksburg?"

"Through some passersby." He shook his head. "I don't even know if she got them, but I'm hopin' she did."

"How you gonna get Ma to agree to travel that far?" Charles asked.

Carl choked back his tears. "I don't think she's even able to make the trip."

"If she stays here, she's sure to die. Now, we'll have to fix up the old wagon. Make it as comfortable for her as possible and I think we ought to get started on it today." Joe spoke with a conviction that concealed the fear that gnawed at his insides.

He had written the letters to Estelle out of desperation, trying to find a solution to his ma's fading health. "Let's don't say anything to her about it until we're ready to leave. It won't take us long to get her packed with what she'll need to take along."

By the end of the day the wagon began to shape up. Joe was pleased that Carl and Charles had given it all they had in spite of the heartbreak they felt at the thought of their ma leaving.

After everyone had gone to bed, he sat alone on the porch well into the quiet night. One of those times where a man put pure thought into what he was doing. He felt sure the right thing was to get his mother out of the hellhole they were in. Footsteps behind him pulled him from thought.

"Joe, what are you doing sittin' here in the dark? This is just like somethin' your pa would do," she said. "I declare, you get more like him every day," she continued with a smile.

"Ma, why are you up? You shouldn't be. You need your rest." He stood and got the rickety old chair from the other end of the porch. "Here, sit down."

"Thank you, son."

Now was as good a time as any to get his plan off his chest. "I want to talk to you about somethin', Ma. You're not gonna like it too much at first, but hear me out."

He sat on the damp wood beside her chair. "I'm takin' you to Vicksburg in a few days." He held his hand up to stop her protest. "It's not that far, and we can make it in a couple of weeks. Ma, you've got to get away from this godforsaken place. Just look at yourself. Why, you're nothing but skin and bone. You've lost at least thirty pounds in the last few months."

"I know I'm weak, but I'll get better, and there's no way I can go off and leave you boys. You're all I got now. I can't go."

He heard her quiet sob and saw her frail shoulders tremble under the thin faded dress. "Please don't cry. It hurts me to think about not seeing you every day. But not like this, Ma. Think about us, what would we do without you? Here, you worry yourself to death, those damned mosquitoes have sucked your blood all summer and now it's goin' on winter. I can't see you living like this much longer."

"I can't just leave my home. I've spent most of my married life here, good times or bad. The family's always managed to survive somehow."

"Things are different now than they've ever been, Ma. You know that." Joe wiped his eyes on his shirtsleeve grateful for the darkness.

Martha stood. "What will your pa think when he comes home and finds we're not here."

Joe looked down at the old wooden planks of the porch. How could she think O.C. would return? "It's been almost three years. He ain't comin' back. Now, I'll hear no more about it. Me and the boys have already started workin' on the wagon."

He watched his mother put her hands to her face, and in silence, walk into the house, the screen door slapped softly shut behind her. That was the first time he'd ever talked to her like that, but it was for her own good. He wanted to follow her, hold her and tell her everything was alright but she'd try to talk him down again. This time it might work. He was better off to keep his distance.

O.C said he'd know when it was time. He sure hoped the man was right. As Joe walked into the house and toward his room, he saw the soft flicker of the kerosene lantern from under his mother's door. She wouldn't sleep this night. He knew what he must do.

The rest of the week was spent getting the wagon roadworthy. Joe was proud of the work he and his brothers had done.

Carl had the idea to take the feathers out of one of the old mattresses and make a new one. Charles had helped him using some of the quilts his ma had made. They sewed them together, stuffed them, and as far as Joe was concerned the new mattress was as good as any he'd ever seen.

They repaired the old canvas cover, put it in place then made the wagon bed as close to a real bed as possible. Charles built some long wooden boxes and hung them on the sides of the wagon where food and fresh water could be stored.

Joe stood back and inspected what they'd all put together as his brothers watched. He was pleased at what he saw. "Charles, I like these boxes you built. Looks like Ma's gonna ride like a queen in a fancy carriage on that bed y'all fixed. And Carl, looks like you got us stocked up on food real good."

"Thanks. I put six dozen eggs, enough salt pork and beans to last at least a month and the last sack of potatoes."

"That should be plenty for sure then I'll hunt for meat." Joe ruffled Carl's hair. The boy was growing up but even at fourteen years old, he was still Joe's little brother.

Charles stepped up and opened one of the wooden cubicles. "Here's the oil for the lamp, and the matches."

"I know how hard matches are to come by these days and I appreciate all you did to round those up." Joe patted Charles on the Back. "You did a good job, boys. This will make Ma's trip a lot easier."

It would be their last night together for a while and Joe had been thinking all day about what he would say to his brothers. He guessed when the time came, he'd think of something. "Carl, why don't you go help Ma with supper while me and Charles finish up here." He knew in his heart his youngest brother would have to cook the meal by himself. Their ma wasn't able to be much help these days.

"Okay."

Carl walked away and Joe was sure he'd made the right decision that Carl and Charles should stay behind. It would be crowded enough with just him and his ma traveling in the small wagon. And besides, maybe his ma would feel like someone had stayed behind to look after things and this might be a temporary move for her. Even though, he knew different.

Martha had gone downhill even more in the last week. It was almost as if when she found out she had to leave her home, she gave up. But Joe told himself she'd die for sure if she stayed here. At least she had a chance in Vicksburg.

He gazed at the swamp. What had happened to his pa? If he could only get to that gold, everything would be okay. Well, maybe not okay, but better anyway.

Carl's voice rang from the distance. "Come and get it."

He took a deep breath, turned and followed Charles into the small dwelling they called home. The gold would have to wait.

After he washed up he took his seat at the table. His ma looked weak sitting in her chair. "Ma, you okay?"

She nodded. "We'll talk later. Y'all eat now before your supper gets cold."

Carl took the last of the fried chicken out of the skillet, put it on a plate and carried it to the table. "I picked out the toughest old rooster of the lot for you two outlaws." He set the plate on the table. "Yes sir, one that'll give you muscles in your jaws as strong as a mule's behind."

He placed a bucket of bread in front of them. "Got biscuits hard as the knot holes in the barn and 'taters wrapped in the original dirt they growed in. But, thanks to my great cookin' magic, you'll like it just fine."

Charles glanced at Joe and shook his head. "Well, if that's the old rooster I think it is, it'll take a lot of magic to get the tough out."

Joe grinned. "Yeah, maybe Johnny One Horn's been teachin' him some of that hocus-pocus he knows." He glanced at his ma. It was nice to see a grin on her face.

Taking the plate of meat from Charles, he met the younger man's gaze. "You know what to do 'round here."

"Yep."

"I'll be back as soon as I get Ma delivered safe and sound."

Charles took a bite of biscuit. "I know."

"You've got some canned goods and you can take care of yourself. So can Carl." He winked at the younger boy. Carl smiled but Joe saw a tear glisten in his eye.

"Don't worry about us, Joe, we'll be fine. You just take care of Ma." Carl reached over and put his hand on Martha's. "You've gotta get well before Pa gets home, Ma, else he'll give us all a whuppin' for not takin' good care of ya."

They finished the meal in silence. Joe didn't feel like making conversation. Now he knew how his pa felt on those nights he wanted everyone to go to bed early. He sat back in his chair and pushed his plate away from him. "That was pretty good, little brother."

Carl stood and picked up his plate. "You ain't tellin' me nothin'."

Martha, who talked very little these days, rose unsteadily from her chair and walked slowly holding to anything she could to help keep her on her feet. Joe wondered if he was doing the right thing. Did she even have the strength to survive the trip to Vicksburg?

"Joe, I'd like to talk to you alone, son." Martha rested beside her son's chair and held on to its wooden back.

"Yes, ma'am." He glanced at his brothers and nodded his head toward the door leading to the front room.

The two boys left the room then he pulled out the chair next to him. "Sit down here, Ma."

She took the seat and for a moment fought to catch her breath. "Even that short walk wore me out." She met his gaze. "I don't think I'm up to making the trip, Joe. I'm too sick."

"But, Ma–."

"No, you listen to me now. I'm afraid for you boys and for myself. Honey, I think your pa must be dead. He'd not stay away from us. He'd at least send a letter or something if he was alive." She dabbed her eyes with a cloth from her apron pocket. "I miss him so. 'Cept for the last couple of years, we've been together all our lives. It seems so empty here without him, but I can't bring myself to leave.

She looked at the silver band on the third finger of her left hand. "I hope and pray every day that he'll come back, but he would have been here by now if he was alive and well."

Joe didn't know what to say. His heart ached for the lonely old woman sitting beside him. Looking at her weakened state, he realized just how much she had gone down in the last few days. He agreed with her, the trip to Vicksburg was off. No need to argue. "Pa's probably working on a job up north. Or maybe he found gold out west." He leaned forward in his chair. "That's it, Ma. I bet he's built up a fortune and is on his way home right now. You'll see."

A smile lifted the corners of her mouth. "You're a lot like your father, always trying to find a silver lining, and that's one thing you can surely be proud of."

"Are you sure you can't make the trip, Ma? We won't stay long. As soon as you get better we'll head home." He knew what the answer would be but he wanted to give her the option.

"I'm just too sick." She stood on wobbling legs.

Joe got up and took her in his arms. "Okay. Okay, we'll try to stick it out a while longer. But, if Pa don't show up soon, we're all gonna leave this damned place."

He helped his mother to her bedroom and made her as comfortable as he could. "Tomorrow we'll bring that new bed the boys made in here for you to sleep on. It's a good-un."

"Whatever you say, son."

Before he pulled the door closed he whispered, "Good night, Ma. I love you."

"Good night. Maybe I'll feel better tomorrow."

Closing his eyes, he fought back tears. "You will. I'm sure of it." He quietly shut the door behind him.

CHAPTER EIGHT

He walked out on the porch and joined his brothers. "She ain't goin'."

Carl looked up at Joe. "What?"

"Ma don't wanna go to Vicksburg. Says she's too sick."

Charles spit off the porch into the grass. "Is she?"

Joe sat on the top step and slumped against a post. "Yeah, she's not good. Not good at all." He fixed his eyes on the swamp. The moon shone like the sun over the rippling water. Small waves lightly washed the shoreline. The wind was crisp and cool, almost spellbinding as it moaned like the voices of lost spirits through the ancient trees.

He noticed his brothers stared, like he did, without saying a word. They were lost in a world where it seemed they were all alone.

Only minutes passed before Charles stood. "I'm going to call it a day."

"Me, too." Carl followed. "You comin', Joe?"

"No, I'm gonna sit here a while. Y'all go ahead, I'll be in directly."

Long after his brothers went to bed, Joe still sat in the same spot. Night sounds slinked throughout the darkness and the lantern in his ma's room flickered through the window.

All he wanted was to get out of this place. So far away he couldn't remember what it even looked like. What was gold when you couldn't get to it? And this place, what was this place without his pa? The man was dead, he just knew it. He also recognized the fact the swamp water was never going down.

His mind turned to strange tales he'd heard about faraway places west. Places waiting for someone to claim it. So exciting it sounded like a dream. He remembered how his pa's eyes would sparkle when he talked about those same mystical places.

Joe rose from the porch and slowly, dreamlike headed for the barn. One of his favorite things to do was cuddle up in the soft hay in the loft. It gave him a sense of independence and was more comfortable than his own bed. Early spring and fall were the only times he could really enjoy it because the air wasn't thickened with mosquitoes.

Entering the barn, he glanced at the feed box that held his pa's jugs of homemade whiskey. He walked over, grabbed one then made his way up the ladder. Jug in tow, he plopped down on the hay covered floor of the loft, drawing the attention of the two mules below.

The old critters were used to the scene since O.C. didn't drink in public, around Martha or the boys. He'd always come to the barn and drink by himself or with Bud or Neil. He realized now as he pulled the cork, he was a lot like his father.

He lifted the heavy brown crock container to his lips and took a long swig. After he coughed and sputtered he finally caught his breath. "Damn, Seemo, that stuff burns like hell!"

He leaned back and remembered how some years ago he'd named one of the mules Seemo. He smiled at the memory of Neil Carter. The old man's voice rang clear as a bell in his mind.

"Dat mule spooks so damned easy, he mus be able to see mo' den t'otha crittas."

From that moment on, Joe called the mule Seemo and everyone else did the same. He took another gulp of the vile liquid and thought how Shadrack, the other mule, had gotten his name. Poor thing had caught his tail on fire by knocking over a kerosene lantern. Of course, Carl, the all-knowing, had named him Shadrack after the Israelite who'd survived Nebuchadnezzar's firey furnace.

Lifting the jug to his lips, he noticed it didn't seem as heavy as it had before, and he was beginning to feel its claim. Exactly what he wanted.

"Shadrack, are you ready to get out of here?" Silence. "I thought so. Seemo, I can see you're ready to go. You just won't talk to anybody like you did when Pa was here."

His taste buds were numb as he guzzled another mouthful of whiskey. It wasn't long before he fell over sideways into the soft straw. The room began to spin. "Whooo weee, Seemo, I'm good and drunk now!" Conversation with the mules seemed as normal to him as any he'd ever had with a human.

"If I ever get outta this swamp, I'm goin' west. Far… far… wesss…." His mind faded into darkness.

****

ARIZONA DESERT

O. C. sat head in hand. If he even ever got the chance, how would he explain to his family why he hadn't returned? He was deeply ashamed. So ashamed he might not send them a letter of explanation, even if he could!

Loving them had nothing to do with not going back to the swamp. He loved them with all his heart. And Martha, how he longed to hold her in his arms. Her health hadn't been good when he left. He wondered how she was doing and if the boys got her out of there yet.

It had been almost three years and he still dreamed about her every night. The crops, the boys. He could only imagine how grown up they were now. Carl was going on fifteen years and from the way he was growing when he'd left, the boy was probably taller than Joe by now.

He left them in a heck of a spot. Not much food, the crops all but gone because of all the unyielding rain, only a few farm animals. He pulled stale air from the small room into his lungs and lay back on his bunk. Hell, he almost felt guilty because he had a warm place to stay and ate three meals a day, such as they were. The work was hard, and he took a lot of grief, but he supposed it was better than being dead.

If only the rain hadn't come, ruined the crops and caused the damned ole swamp to flood, he and his family would still be together with nothing to worry about. Joe could have been married by now with young-uns of his own. Come to think of it, Joe was older than he was when he married Martha. For all he knew, his oldest may be married now. Anything can happen in the amount of time since he'd left.

Was his family looking for him? Did they think he was dead? Or left them high and dry for bigger and better things? If only he knew what was going on in Mississippi, but he was stuck in Arizona with no way out.

****

A lone whippoorwill whistled its lonely song from in the distance. Joe lay unmoving in the hay. The familiar sounds of the swamp had a way of capturing him. He opened one eye lid. Sure enough, the early morning light was starting to show, the brightness magnified by the pounding in his head.

The slam of the barn door hitting hard against the wall jolted him upright. "What the hell!"

"Joe, get up!"

His heart pounded in response to the panic in Charles' voice. "What's the matter?"

Charles stepped on the bottom rung of the ladder. "Somethin's terrible wrong, Joe. Ma won't move or talk."

Joe's foot hit the top of the ladder before he even knew he'd stood up. In a flash he was on the barn floor running. He almost tore the barn door off its hinges in his frantic rush toward the house. Charles yelled from behind.

"I tried to wake her up, but she won't open her eyes," Charles cried.

His younger brother's voice was hoarse with fear. Joe was inside the house and in his ma's room in a matter of seconds that felt like minutes.

Fearing what was behind it, he pulled back the curtain that surrounded his mother's bed. Her face was peaceful and pale... very pale. His heart thumped hard in his chest and he swallowed to force back the bile that had rose in his throat. He bent over and picked up her frail little hand. Cold. So cold and lifeless.

His deepest fears realized, he fell to his knees beside the bed, his mind completely blank. What was he supposed to do?

Damn O.C. for abandoning them!

Joe knew he should be a strong man by now, but he'd never had to face anything like this. He rose to his feet and gazed at his mother's serene features.

Her hair was soft to the touch and she looked like she was asleep. Death had erased the marks of pain and loneliness.

He took a clean sheet from the old wooden dresser drawer and spread it, very gently, over her. "Forever rest, Ma," he whispered then slowly pulled the sheet up and covered her face. "Forever rest."

When he opened the front door, Charles, with his hand on his forehead, leaned against one of the four by fours that supported the porch. Joe reached out for his younger brother and embraced him. Charles sobbed on his shoulder uncontrollably. It was all Joe could do to keep from totally breaking down. Silent tears streamed down his face. He couldn't stop them even if he wanted to. "We're really alone now, brother, just the three of us."

He held the younger man for a short while and gave him time to catch his breath before releasing his hold. "You gonna be okay?"

Charles wiped his eyes with the back of his hand. "What are we gonna do? How are we gonna tell little Carl? He loved Ma so. I don't think he's strong enough to handle it."

Joe turned away and rubbed his swollen eyes with his fists. "I'll wake him up and tell him"

"Should you wait 'til he gets up on his own? You know how he is when you wake him up before he's ready."

"No, I'm gonna do it now. Waitin' won't make things any easier." He walked the few steps through the house and opened the door to their room. Slowly, he closed it and went back to where Charles was still standing. "He ain't in there. You got any idea where he might be?"

"Ain't there? No, I don't know where he'd be at this time of mornin'?"

"I got a feelin' he already knows 'bout Ma. Probably heard us talkin' or somethin'."

"We know where most of his hidin' places are, Joe. Why don't we split up and check 'em out. We'll find him sooner or later."

Joe started to walk away and glanced over his shoulder at Charles as he headed out to look for Carl. His brother was becoming a man fast. Well, after all, he was eighteen years old now and the past three years had sure been enough to make a boy into a man. Joe faced forward once again. Where the hell was Carl?

He looked everywhere he knew to look, but it did no good. Carl was nowhere to be found. Deciding to go back to see if Charles might have already found their younger brother, Joe made his way through the woods. When he reached the house, one look at Charles' face said it all. No Carl.

"Damn, Joe, we've got a hell of a lot to worry about without this. We need to do somethin', even if it's wrong."

"You're right. When Carl gets his self together, he'll come back. But if he don't show up in a few hours, we'll get Boy Horse and One Horn to help us look for him. Somethin' tells me he's okay."

"I hope so."

"We'd better find a place and start digging a grave."

"Jesus Christ, Joe, we found our ma dead a few hours ago. Now we have to dig a hole in this godforsaken place and put her in it to spend the rest eternity. It just don't seem right."

"I know, but we gotta do it. If there was another way, we'd do that, but there ain't. Let's get it done today, get it over with and go on. It's the only thing to do."

Charles sat hard on the top step and stared into thin air then nodded. "Any ideas where? Is there someplace we can dig down more than two feet without hitting water?"

Joe took a seat on the step beside him. "I thought maybe that knoll behind the house."

A frown creased Charles' brow. "That's an old Indian burial ground. You sure you want to put her there?"

Forcing a smile, Joe said, "Well, she's half Indian. I don't think she'd mind. Besides, that's the only place I know that's high enough, like you said, where we won't hit water."

He stood and walked toward the barn. "Come on, Charles. We only got one shovel, I'll get it, you get the pickaxe and we'll get started."

CHAPTER NINE

QUEST FOR GOLD

Charles leaned against the pickaxe. "We've been diggin' for four hours. We ain't never gonna get it right."

Wiping sweat from his forehead Joe stood at the edge of the grave. "It's good enough." He glanced around the hillside then raised his gaze to the swamp. "Ya know, when Pa left here I thought we would soon be out of this hellhole?" It was time to tell the secret.

"Charles, there's somethin' I need to let ya in on." He turned and began to walk down the knoll, his brother by his side. "Pa, Neil and Uncle Bud buried some gold by some old dead trees in the swamp."

"Gold? Real gold?"

"Yep. I never told y'all 'cause Ma was afraid you and Carl'd try to get to it and drown or get snake bit."

Charles stopped in his tracks. "Where the hell did they get it?"

The story took up the rest of the walk back to the house. Joe explained it as well as he could remember and thought he got it right.

"You mean we went all this time just barely gettin' by and we have gold? Damn you, Joe, for not tellin'! Me and you could have figured a way to get that gold and we could have all got outta this place!"

His brother's anger was to be expected, but he couldn't let it go on. “It was a promise I made to Pa, then to Ma. I had to keep it. Besides, you know we can’t swim good enough to dive into the swamp and get to the bottom.”

Looking at the ground Charles said, “Ah, I guess you’re right, but you not telling me about it just put a burr under my saddle, that’s all.”

“After this is over, we’ll see if we can figure some way to get it.” He glanced up to see Carl sitting on the porch. “There he is.”

“I bet the little guy’s dyin’ inside. No tellin’ where he’s been. I feel sick, Joe. This whole thing is sick!”

“You hold yourself together for Carl’s sake. I’m dependin’ on ya.”

“I’m tryin’, but I’m not tough like you.”

“Tough my ass. I’m fightin’ with every breath I take, and what’s worse, tonight we have to build Ma’s coffin. It’s time we got hold of ourselves.”

At the well, Joe washed the dirt and mud off. “Your hands are bleedin’ from that rough ole pickaxe handle, Charles. You’ll have to soak ‘em in kerosene this evenin’.”

“Damn. I didn’t even feel the blisters ‘til I seen ‘em. It’s hard to feel anything right now.”

“Just look at it this way, you won’t have to help with the coffin.”

He started for the house. Carl stared toward the ground. The boy looked up for just a second then back down. How was the little guy going to act? He didn’t know, but one thing was for sure, he was damned worn out.

Approaching his youngest brother Joe asked, “How ya’ doin’?”

Carl kicked at the dirt under his feet. “I was up this mornin’ when Ma died. I heard a noise in her room and when I went in and asked her if she was okay, she didn’t answer. She just laid there all still and white. When she didn’t say anything, I knew.” He sniffed and continued, “I laid by the bed for a while then went out, got on the raft and drifted into the swamp. I just wanted to be by myself.”

The youngest of them was more grown up than Joe would have ever thought. “She’s not hurtin’ anymore.”

Carl grabbed a handful of rocks then stood. "No, she's not hurtin'."

Joe heard the thickness in Carl's voice of unshed tears. He knew when the boy was troubled he'd skip rocks across the mucky swamp water. Sometimes for hours. As he watched Carl walk away a strain came in his throat that wouldn't go away. He turned toward the barn; he had a chore to do and hoped he could find enough boards to complete the job.

The morning sky was clouded over, the air heavy with humidity. Joe shook Charles' shoulder. "Wake up. Looks like rain and we've gotta move."

Sprinkles of water created small dark spots in the dirt. Joe walked in silence and watched Charles open the barn door. The gloomy day mirrored his mood as he looked at the crude box that would be his ma's last resting bed. "Come on, Charles, let's get it to the house."

Charles picked up one end. "It's heavier than I thought it'd be."

"Let's just get it to the house." The walk was short. "Put it here on the porch and let's go get Ma."

"You gonna wake Carl up?"

"No, he don't need to help us put her in the ground. He said his goodbyes last night and I told him he could pick the quilt to bury her in."

He followed Charles into the bedroom where their mother lay dead. Carl had chosen the Double Wedding Ring quilt. "Get some blankets to wrap her in, Charles."

Charles moved the quilt Carl had put next to their mother's body. "Ma made this with her own two hands. Who'd of thought she'd be buried with it?" He lay the quilt aside, turned and took two soft blankets from the chest of drawers, opened them and laid them neatly atop each other on the bed next to Martha's body.

Joe's breath caught in his throat when he helped pick her up and move her onto the covers that would incase her for eternity. "She ain't no heavier than a sack o'feathers."

They carried her through the house then he and Charles laid the body in the coffin. Charles stroked her hair and Joe bent to kiss her on the forehead, then tucked the Double Wedding Ring quilt lovingly around her. Tears ran down his cheek as he noticed the water coming from the sky. "Oh, God, Charles, help me get the lid on. It's startin' to rain."

They placed the wooden top on and Joe nailed it as good and fast as he could. "Come on, let's go."

"Maybe we should wait 'til tomorrow, Joe. It's gonna be muddy up on the knoll."

"No, Charles, we have to get on with it, you know in this country it could rain for a week. Then what would we do?"

His brother nodded and picked up his end of the casket. Joe did the same and led the way to the knoll. The rain was coming down, light, but enough to make the hill slick. "We gotta hurry or we ain't gonna make it to the top." His foot slipped and he fell to his knees. "Damn." The impact of his fall brought Charles down, too.

"Don't try to stand up, Charles. Let's just stay on our knees and you pull, I'll push."

"Okay, I'll try."

The clouds opened up and the light rain became a downpour. Thunder crashed and huge drops pounded around him. The noise was all but deafening. With everything he had inside, he heaved at the coffin. It was for damn sure it wasn't his sweet mother that made it so heavy.

He fought to catch his breath. He was used to hard work, but this was above and beyond anything he'd ever tried to do. Maybe they should have waited.

Closing his eyes, he pushed with his entire body. Suddenly, he felt something, opening his eyes he saw Carl dropped to his knees beside him. Soaked to the bone, hair dripping wet around his face, the young man's strength was evident.

Joe had tried to keep his composure until now, but he couldn't help breaking down at the sight of determination on Carl's face. They were almost to the top and he had to keep going. Carl didn't say a word, but let out a few little groans as he put his full weight behind the coffin.

Charles reached the top. "Just a little further and we've got it!"

Trying to keep the box as flat as possible when it slid over the crest of the hill, Joe stood and helped Carl to his feet, and with his brothers waited to catch his breath. When he felt they were all breathing close to normal again, Joe said, "Charles, get the ropes. We're gonna have too much water in the grave if we don't get this done pretty quick."

The ropes lay on the ground and Joe helped slide the coffin on top of them. Without a word, he took the ends on one side while his brothers took the ends on the other side. They dragged the coffin to the edge of the open grave, then lifted it and slowly lowered it into the ground.

Joe picked up the shovel. "Let's get this dirt in while some of it's still dry." He shoveled as fast as he could while Charles used a hoe and Carl his bare hands.

They hadn't worked very long when, as if the good Lord decided they had been through enough hell, the rain let up. It took them quite a while to finish, and Joe was glad it was over. As soon as they had pushed the last of the dirt onto the mound above the grave, the sky opened up again.

Looking at his water and mud covered brothers, Joe knew he looked the same. "Let's each say a silent prayer for Ma then get back to the house. We'll hold a better service for her when the rain stops."

Joe lost his footing on the way down the muddy mound. Blinded by tears and rain, he slipped and slid. His brothers moved silently through the downpour behind him. This would be a day none of them would forget.

Lightning flashed and the crashing cannons of thunder shook the old house as they tumbled onto the porch. Joe unbuttoned his shirt. "Let's get these clothes off and wash up in the rain before we go inside, boys." What they usually did in the summer for fun, this time he knew was sad for all of them. He wondered if he'd ever get clean again.

The croaking of thousands of frogs and countless swamp sounds filtered through the walls. Joe turned over in his bed. Damn, his back was sore. His muscles were stiff clear down to the bone.

Thunder rumbled in the distance, but the rain had finally stopped. It was cooler in the room and the old house creaked and popped with every shift in the temperature and humidity.

Joe figured it was about four in the morning but couldn't be sure. Thoughts of his mother filled his mind and he drifted in and out of sleep. Suddenly he sat up in bed, jerked to full consciousness by the sound of voices in the distance? At this time of morning? Who the hell could it be?

He got up, pulled on his pants and walked to the front door. When he opened it, the voices were much clearer and a fire flickered close to the edge of the swamp.

The shot gun they used for hunting stood in the corner of the front room. He grabbed it, went slowly to the edge of the porch then stepped off. Mud oozed deeper between his bare toes with every step. The gun rested on his hip pointed toward the intruders. The knot in his stomach relaxed as soon as the faces of the trespassers came into view. He smiled and stepped into the circle of light from the campfire.

"Joe, that you?" A voice rang out from across the pile of burning logs.

"Yeah, it's me," he answered, grinning. He knew they were aware of who he was. Those two were never oblivious of their surroundings.

Johnny One Horn stood. "Don't shoot. We are too tired to duck."

Little Boy Horse offered a handshake. "Hello, friend."

Joe firmly grasped the red man's callused hand. "It's been a hell of a long time. Where've you been?"

One Horn took his seat again. "Things are not too good. Grey Wolf is dead. The tribe separated. Some went south. We come here to see you."

"What happened to Grey Wolf?"

"He went hunting, got killed by a big cat of some sort. Very rare in the swamp. He wanted to die a brave, not an old man. It was a good death." He warmed his hands by the fire. "O.C. Armstrong home?"

"No, he never came back, and yesterday we buried Ma." He turned and looked at the hill behind the house. "She probably died of a broken heart thinkin' Pa was dead, too."

Johnny One Horn followed his gaze to the knoll. "You bury her there?"

Joe faced his friend. "It might not have been right, but it was the best place. We meant no disrespect to your people"

"No, it is good. Martha Armstrong had Indian blood. The spirits of our people will protect her soul."

Johnny One Horn spoke gently and placed a comforting hand on Joe's shoulder. Joe drew in a breath, a sense of relief washed over him. "I needed to hear that, Johnny. You just don't know how bad." A shiver went through him and he wasn't sure if it was the cool dampness, or the spirits giving him their approval. "It's gettin' colder. Let's go inside."

****

The sun peaked over the horizon and the stove had taken the early morning chill from the house. The coffee Horse and Johnny brought went down hot and smooth when Joe took a sip. "Damn, that's good. We haven't had coffee in over a week. Where'd y'all get it?"

He joined the two big Indians at the table. They looked like giants sitting on the small chairs. If Joe didn't know their gentle nature, he would be terrified.

Johnny took a swig from a tin cup. "Traded furs for it." He looked at Joe. "What you going to do now?"

"We're gettin' outta here as fast as we can. Goin' as far as we can, probably headin' out west, maybe north west. If Pa's still alive, maybe we can find him." He sat thoughtfully. "But there's something we gotta do first."

An idea flashed through his mind. Why hadn't he thought of these two before? They were prefect for the job. With their help, he knew they could pull it off. "Johnny, how good can you swim?"

Johnny's brow furrowed. "Swim? In water?"

"He swims like a beaver," Horse said. "I am a good swimmer, too."

Horse's words ignited a spark of hope Joe had held in his heart over the years. "Good. I've got somethin' to talk to y'all about." How was he going to put this? He might as well just say it straight out.

"Pa told me he found gold under the house and buried it in

the swamp. Me and my brothers know where it is and we're gonna try to get it. Maybe y'all could help."

Johnny shook his head. "Gold is bad, Joe. Makes brother fight brother. Makes people do things that are not right." He sat straighter in the chair. "I already know about this gold. Grey Wolf told me of story his father told him of how it got here.

The gold you look for came from my grandfather's great wooden boat. The one this house and barn was built from. It carries much sadness and is now the property of the wisp. Not meant for man to have."

"No disrespect, John, but this has become a white man's country and in this land today, if you have gold, you can do anything." He couldn't read the look on Johnny's face. Was it curious or concerned?

"Where did O.C. Armstrong get it?"

"From under this old house."

"Under this house? No one knew where the French men buried it. When Old Plummer built this place, I am sure he didn't know he built over it." Johnny remarked.

Joe got up to pour himself some more coffee. "Look, if you help us, part of the gold will be yours. You could go west with us. There's nothing for you here. Hell, we could all be rich. We could own thousands of horses, herds of cattle… anything you could ever want."

The way the two men looked at each other told Joe he might be getting somewhere. No words were exchanged, but he knew they were communicating with each other silently, an Indian's ability that had always fascinated him.

Several minutes passed and he was eager to know their answer. "Well?" He walked to the doorway.

John met Joe's gaze. "We will help you, but we are not sure we are ready to leave our home to go west. We will talk after we see the gold."

Boy Horse crossed his arms. "The Wisp and its spirits protect the gold. Maybe that is why O.C. did not come back."

Joe had never thought of that, but he couldn't let it stop him now. He was determined to get out of the swamp. "Let's talk about how we're gonna do this, then y'all can get some rest and I'll start gettin' things ready."

Chapter Ten

With Johnny and Horse asleep on the porch, Joe walked through the early morning mist to the barn to ready for the effort to retrieve the gold. His brothers were still sleeping and he welcomed this time alone. How many nights had he laid awake thinking of ways to get this job done? Now, with Johnny and Horse's help, they were going to finally give it a try.

Against the side of the old barn leaned a broken plow. He struggled to roll it to the edge of the swamp, then labored to lift it onto the makeshift raft. He realized he'd have to wait for his friends to help him get the raft into deeper water. Then they'd find out if it would float with the extra weight.

Inside the barn door, he reached up on the wall and grabbed a fifty-foot rope. That would be more than long enough to reach the bottom of the swamp. Leaving the barn, he crossed the yard to the well, and studied the two wooden water buckets. They would do fine for lifting the gold.

He gathered everything he could think of that could help them, the shovel, the hoe, the pickaxe, even stuff from the kitchen that might be used as digging tools.

He began to arrange things on the raft so there would be plenty of room for all of them to sit. Would the raft be able to float with all that gear and three men?

"So you're goin' gold huntin' one day after we put Ma in that muddy hole?"

Joe turned toward his brother. "Damn, Charles, you scared

the hell outta me." He saw through the sarcasm in Charles' voice and knew he was speaking from the depth of his grief. No matter, there was no time to explain. "I thought you and Carl might make Ma a grave marker today. I know you're sad, we all are, but I also know you do the best job of it."

Charles kicked the side of the raft. "Dammit, Joe, I don't even know if I can do that. I never thought markin' Ma's grave would be something I'd have to do."

"I know how you feel, Charles. Hell, she was my mother, too, but we have to go on livin'. She would have wanted it that way. We can't just sit around here and wait for something' to happen. We've done that for three years. It's time to make something' happen. Can't you see that?" He put his hand on his brother's shoulder.

Charles raised his eyes and looked at Joe. "Maybe."

After a moment, Joe turned back to his work again. "Whatever we decide, we'll stick together. At least if we can get some of that gold up, we'll have some hope."

"I guess that's more than most folks have," Charles said. "Hope's something' we ain't seen much of around here for a long time."

"And we've got help, Charles. Johnny and Boy Horse are here, and they've agreed to do some divin' and diggin'." He was glad to see his brother warming to the idea.

Charles glanced toward the house. "Yeah, I seen them two big bears spread out all over the porch. They must of traveled most all night to be sleepin' in the daytime."

Joe could tell by his brother's tone of voice he'd settled down some inside. He watched him turn and walk back toward the house. His words were faint, but Joe understood.

"Me and Carl'll start on the marker as soon as I can pull him outta bed and we get some breakfast. Is that coffee I smell?"

Charles voice faded as the distance lengthened between them. Some time passed before Joe finished up. He saw Carl step out onto the porch and figured he'd fixed something to eat.

"Hey, Joe!"

He smiled when Johnny and Horse jumped when the boy yelled. "What?"

"Come eat!"

"I ain't hungry just yet." Food was the last thing on his mind. Things were almost ready to go, and by the time the others finished eating, he'd be prepared to deal with the swamp.

"Good God, Johnny, leeches? I hate leeches!" Carl rubbed his arms and shivered as if it were cold.

Johnny One Horn smiled. "Many white mouth snakes, little man. Very dangerous in the water of the swamp."

"You can bet your bottom dollar I ain't goin' in there." Carl declared.

"We did not ask you to." Little Boy Horse grinned and patted the top of Carl's head. "You are getting taller."

"Course I am. I'm goin' on fifteen."

"Good cook, too. Like a squaw."

"Kiss my foot, Horse! See if you get supper tonight."

Joe watched Carl huff back to the house. "One of these days he'll be big as you, Horse, and he's gonna try to whup your butt."

A chuckle escaped the big man. "He is growing up. Will be good man someday, but never big enough to whip Horse."

Joe joined in their laughter. It was good to have lifted spirits after the events of the day before, but they had a task ahead. "We'd better get going."

"Yes, the fog has not moved in yet, but it will come soon and we will not be able to see." Johnny tied a tow rope to the canoe he and Horse brought. They would use it for passage to and from the bank.

Joe anxiously stepped onto the raft while Horse and Johnny shoved it into the water. It was actually going to float. He breathed a sigh of relief. His attempt to balance the weight had paid off.

He stood steady, while the two men stepped effortlessly on. Traces of fog meandered on the surface of the water. Using the long pole he pushed further into the swamp. Visibility was good; the water was at a dead calm.

When the water got too deep for the pole to work, Joe pulled it up. Horse and Johnny began to row; Joe stood at the back to steer. He enjoyed the quiet peacefulness as they made their way toward the money tree. The water was mirror-like and his reflection stared back at him like a ghost beckoning from beyond.

Countless swamp creatures sang their soft morning songs and every once in a while the splash of a gar or fish would cause a ripple. The peaceful day, full of promise was a comforting contrast to the powerful rain and raging emotions of yesterday. The pain of the past began to relax its hold on Joe's heart. Fall was at its best. Too cool for mosquitoes and blessed relief from the oppressive summer heat.

He snapped back from his reverie when the top of the old cypress came into view. He pointed toward the blown out treetop. "That's it right over there." Still rowing steadily neither turned to look. He was proud that they trusted him. They stopped and he kept the raft steady while his friends tied it to the tree.

Horse gazed down into the water. "Leeches. Many leeches."

When Joe had pulled the pushing pole up earlier, at least six of the disgusting beasts slid from the wood. "We brought coal oil to help keep them off." He placed the bucket of kerosene in front of them.

Horse rubbed a dab on his arm, then smelled it. His brow furrowed as he wrinkled his nose. "You sure this work?"

Joe shrugged. "It works with mosquitoes."

Johnny One Horn laughed. "I thought you were not afraid of anything. The mighty Horse, afraid of a small leech. Maybe your mother should have named you Mouse instead."

Horse glared at Johnny playfully. "Do not talk so brave, One Horn. Nobody asked how you got your name."

The lightheartedness lasted only a short while. Joe was ready to get down to business. "Let's tie the rope to the plow and ease it into the water. Then we'll get the coal oil on."

They eased the anchor over the back of the raft and played out the rope until it touched the muddy bottom. Securely tied and with the plow as an anchor to hold them, Joe was confident they wouldn't drift far from that spot.

"We can pull ourselves to the bottom by using the rope tied to the plow," Joe said. "When I get down there, I'll feel around to see if anything tells where the gold might be. We better get started."

The first to strip naked, Joe smeared himself with coal oil.

The last three years had seemed like a lifetime, but now they were ready to do what he'd been waiting for. He cut a piece of rope, tied it to his waist, then tied the shovel and hoe heads to it.

He saw Johnny sprinkle something out of a small leather pouch over the top of the water. "What's that?"

"It's good medicine. The gold holds many evil spirits. This will help us."

Joe slipped over the side. A shiver ran the length of his body when the water surrounded him. Was it the cool water or the thought of spirits deep in the depths below? He didn't know, but he was glad for Johnny's good medicine. He held to the edge of the raft while Johnny said an Indian prayer. It somehow calmed his rapidly beating heart.

Without a word, he took the deepest breath he could and slipped below the surface. It didn't take as long as he'd thought to reach the bottom. There was no visibility in the dark water, so there was no way to see where his uncle had chopped the bark from the tree. This must be what a blind man felt like, he thought as he grasped about over the muddy bottom of the swamp.

He pushed away at the slimy, sticky sludge. His lungs were tight with the air trying to force itself out, but he kept on. He knew only a minute or so had passed. Were they in the right place? When he was about to start for the surface, he touched something sharp with his hand. Eagerly he felt them, again and again. Rocks!

He untied the rope from his waist leaving the shovel and hoe in place. Now he knew his lungs would burst if he didn't get to the top. He pushed hard off the bottom with his feet and in seconds burst through the surface to catch his breath. "Wooo-eee, boys! We're for sure in the right place!"

With the help of Horse, he climbed onto the raft. "You can't see anything down there, but the mud's easy to move. I felt the rocks Pa covered the gold with. It ain't gonna be easy, but we can do it."

Boy Horse was busy looking Joe over. "Leeches! Two of them. Looks like coal water does not work!"

"There'd probably be more if I didn't have it on. We'll have to put more on every time we go down."

The Indian shook his head in disgust. "I do not want leeches on privates." He pointed to his groin. "I will put leathers back on!"

Johnny stood. "Sounds like a good idea."

It was hard for Joe to hold his tongue and his laughter. These men were bigger than anyone he'd ever seen and they didn't want to go in naked. However, he hadn't thought of one of the creatures attaching itself there. Well, he'd done it once, he could do it again.

He splashed himself with oil and went back over the side of the raft. After he drew a deep breath, he went into the depths again. Several dives later, he'd gotten most of the thin layer of rock away from the area, but now he was too tired to dive safely. Horse and Johnny pulled him onto the raft as he tried to catch his breath. "I got some of the rock moved. I think we can start diggin'"

Horse stood and put on a double dose of coal oil. "I will go now."

"The shovel and hoe are directly at the bottom of the rope. The sludge and mud keep slidin' back in so you'll have to feel around for 'em."

Joe was amazed at how long Little Boy Horse could stay down and how many times he dove. Finally, he decided he needed to rest and it was Johnny's turn. One Horn left the raft and Joe checked Horse for leeches. "Only one."

"Hmmmph."

When Johnny surfaced, Joe didn't like the look on his face.

Climbing onto the raft, Johnny said, "I feel many angry spirits down there. This place holds much pain and sorrow. Many men died over this gold. Maybe us, too, if we are not careful." Johnny sat as Horse searched for leeches on his skin.

"Then you think the gold is really there?"

"Yes, Joe, it is there. So are the screams of the dead. I will pray to the Mighty Spirit of water, wind to protect us from the evil ones."

By late afternoon they each had made several dives. The hole in the murky depth was gradually getting bigger. Inch by inch, Joe was getting closer to grasping his dream. In his mind, he saw his father telling him he would know when it was time. He hoped it was now. For everybody's sake.

Chapter Eleven

Joe opened his eyes and stretched. Every muscle and bone in his body was sore. Four days of diving and digging in the swamp was taking its toll, yet he felt himself getting stronger.

He sat on the side of the bed and leaned his head from side to side to work the stiffness out of his neck. Sunup to sundown he and his friends had worked hard in the water. When would they find what they were looking for? If something didn't happen soon he could easily– no, he couldn't give up. Besides, Horse and Johnny wouldn't let him. After all, this was all his idea.

Charles entered the room. "Come get ya somethin' to eat. The canoe's packed and ready to go."

"I'm comin'." Horse and Johnny's canoe had come in handy. Being able to leave the raft in place saved a lot of time and work.

Charles and Carl had made the headstone. Joe was surprised at how much work they'd put into it. From cutting out a large slab from one of the giant cypress trees to carving in the letters, they'd given it their best and he was impressed. All they needed to do now was to take the marker to the gravesite and erect it.

Carl cooked breakfast and supper for them every day. Food was getting so sparse he'd have to kill a duck or a rabbit or maybe a squirrel, but somehow he managed. The hens were being saved for their eggs. In midday they'd eat Indian bread or jerky that Horse and Johnny brought. Everything would run out soon and he didn't know what they'd do if the gold wasn't found by then.

Horse and Johnny paddled their way through the swamp. Joe sat in the bottom of the canoe so it would stay stable. Once they reached the raft, he was the first to get out.

Thankful they had plenty of coal oil Joe undressed and applied a thick layer to his skin. Horse was the first to go into the water. After a few minutes, he came up for a quick breath, and without a word, went back down. This time he stayed under so long, Joe began to worry. He looked at Horn. "You think he's okay?"

Johnny nodded and about that time Horse's head broke the surface.

"I found something. I am not sure what." He put the thing on the raft.

Joe's heart raced and his hand trembled as he picked it up. He stuck it in the water and washed the mud away. It felt hard, yet soft. What could it be? As soon as he saw it clean, he knew. "Wax. It's a big ole piece of wax!" If his heart beat any faster, it would surly come out of his chest. "Pa melted candle wax over the top of the pots to cover the gold. My God, y'all, we're damn close. Damn, close!"

He couldn't stop himself he had to go down. Without thinking, he dove in with Horse still in the water. When he reached the bottom, he scoured the entire hole. Where was it? Where was the gold?

Slowly letting out the air he was holding, he made his way back up. He shook the water from his hair and pushed it out of his face. "Nothing! Not a damn thing. Where'd you find it?"

"You move too fast. It's not in the big hole. It is the side of hole."

Horse pointed toward the house. West. Joe went back down. He'd find it this time, he just knew it. He dug at the mud, went up for a breath, then right back down. He worked until he thought his lungs would burst. He broke the surface and caught his breath. "I know it's there, dammit." After only three dives, he was exhausted and accepting help, pulled himself out of the water. "I know it is."

Horse oiled himself. "I know where to go." He jumped into

the water with a splash and disappeared.

Joe waited for the man to return. When he did, he threw another chunk of wax on the deck and plunged in again. “This piece is bigger than the other one, Johnny. The gold’s underneath it!” His breath caught in his throat and he thought he would puke with excitement.

Good Christ! Horse stayed under longer than Joe could ever imagine anyone could. He glanced at Johnny who gazed into the distance. “Are you worried?”

“Yes. Looks like storm clouds in the south.”

“I’m talkin’ about the bear at the bottom of the swamp, John. Jesus!”

One Horn smiled and looked at Joe. “I worry when you don’t come up for a long time. But Horse is like a fish and can stay longer than this when grabbing catfish.”

Soon Joe began to panic. Horse had been under for at least five minutes. Something was wrong. He stood. “I’m going down after him.” Before he could jump in, one large hand broke through the calm water.

Horse threw a hand full of mud onto the deck. Joe thought it was more wax, but as the slush began to slide to the deck, he saw a slight shimmer. Everything in his belly was caught in his throat as he watched Horse pour a handful of water on the pile. Gold. Pure gold.

“You did it, Horse.” He fell to his knees, snatched up one of the coins and washed it off. His heart swelled and tears spilled onto his cheeks as he held his dreams in one hand. His voice escaped just above a whisper, “You did it.”

Damn, he was acting like a kid in front of his friends. A man wasn’t supposed to cry over something like this. He wiped his face, picked up the four coins and turned toward Boy Horse. “How many did you find?”

“Many.”

Joe picked up one of the water buckets he’d brought. “Think you can put ‘em in here.” When Horse nodded, Joe tied the buckets to a rope and filled them with water so they wouldn’t float up as Horse pulled them down. Horse made another dive.

Joe thought the big man had stayed down a long time before; this time seemed ten times as long. One thing he knew for sure was he couldn't have done this without the two big lovable Indians who had become his friends over the years. His best friends.

"Hey, Johnny." He gazed at the coin he held. "I ain't never seen a coin this big. Have you?"

"Nope. And I have never seen gold."

Now that he thought about it, neither had he. "Charles and Carl will be impressed." He laughed at the thought of their amazement.

Johnny studied the dark sky in the far distance. "Definitely a storm brewing. It is getting closer."

The surface of the water broke and Horse gasped for air. Between breaths he said, "Horn, pull the rope."

With a few mighty heaves, the buckets rose to the top. Joe reached to gather them onto the raft, but to his surprise, he couldn't lift them. "Hell, that's heavier than rocks," he said as Johnny reached over his shoulder to help.

After Boy Horse made a few more dives, Johnny took over then it was Joe's turn. He loaded the buckets with gold time after time, while Horse and Johnny waited. Dusk was approaching when Joe made his last trip of the day.

The storm looked like a bad one. It was getting closer and he wanted to get to the house before it hit. Exhausted, Joe put his clothes on. The gold coins lay in a pile on the deck of the raft. The weight of the gold, and the three men, would be too much for the canoe. "Let's put some of the gold into the canoe. I'll wait here while y'all take it to shore."

Johnny helped place the coins into the smaller craft. "Yes, be careful. Gold is very heavy. We do not want to damage the canoe. It is delicate."

They put their plan into action. Charles was sitting at the shoreline when the two Indians approached. He stared at the bonanza of coins. "Gold."

"That is right, but there is more to bring." Johnny looked at the sky. "We must hurry before the storm gets here."

Charles stood. "What do you need me to do?"

Johnny helped Horse unload the coins. "Have Carl hook up one of the mules to the wagon. Bring some potato sacks back with you and we will fill them up, put them in the wagon and let the mule pull it to the house."

Charles turned and ran to the house shouting Carl's name.

After the two men made a couple more trips with the riches, it was time for Joe to leave the raft. Little Boy Horse was alone in the canoe. Joe handed the last of the remaining treasure pieces to his friend, then checked everything to make sure it would be ready for the next day's treasure hunting.

Wind whistled through the treetops, small waves grew bigger and slapped the side of the raft. It was hard for him to step into the canoe gently, but he managed. "Let's get outta here, Horse."

When they reached the shore, Joe saw that everything was already loaded onto the wagon. The only thing left was the last of the coins. The rain was still light, but the wind made the droplets sting when they hit his skin.

Horse followed Joe out of the canoe. "We'd better put the canoe in the barn, too. We don't want to lose it."

He glanced at Carl and Charles while they helped load the last of the coins and he helped Horse heave the canoe onto the wagon. Tired as he was, he couldn't help but laugh at the looks on his brother's faces as they studied the load of coins. "Well, Charles, what do you think?"

Charles lifted a coin. "Damn."

"Is that all you can say, brother? We're rich. Rich I tell ya!"

****

Lying in bed that night, Joe could barely keep his eyes open. Thunder rolled and rain pounded the roof of the house. He glanced over at Horse and Johnny who were in his brothers' beds. They had already succumbed to sleep even with the storm raging outside the thin walls of the lean-to bedroom.

He'd left Carl and Charles sitting in the floor of the front room counting the gold pieces for the second time. Their down beds, a collection of old quilts, blankets and pillows lay beside them. Their Ma's bedroom was empty, but it was still Ma's room and no one wanted to sleep in there. The floor would have to do for the two younger boys.

The first count of the gold was eight hundred coins. It was a fortune. Too bad his ma and pa couldn't be there now. Thinking about the events of the last few days, Joe finally drifted off to sleep.

Charles stacked the gold pieces by tens. A crack of thunder made him jump. "This is the worst storm we've had in a while."

"I've never heard thunder roar like this for so long," Carl said.

Charles furrowed his brow and listened. "You're right, it is roarin'." He stood, went to the front door and opened it. Big waves plummeted the shoreline next to the barn. Lightning flashed causing an almost daylight brightness, and thunder shook the house.

The wind got stronger as Carl joined his brother at the open door. He pointed toward the sky. "Look!"

A funnel cloud lurked in the distance. The noise was getting louder. "Run, go get Joe and the Indians!"

Joe opened his eyes. The same commotion must have wakened his friends. Carl rushed into the room.

"Tornado!"

Johnny jumped up. "We need to get out of the house!"

Joe had never heard such a loud rumbling. He followed the others out of the house and jumped off the porch. The wind was stronger than he'd ever felt. It was almost strong enough to blow any man off his feet. Broken limbs and branches flew suspended in the air. "Go to the mound behind the house!"

Carl slipped on the wet earth and Boy Horse grabbed him before he hit the ground. Joe brought up the rear as they struggled to reach the downhill side of the mound, hoping to find shelter from the howling wind. He saw a branch hurling among the debris and before he knew it, the thing stuck into Charles' shoulder.

He couldn't tell how serious it was, but the look on Charles' face told him it hurt like hell. Grabbing his brother, he helped steady the younger man's gait so they could make it to their destination.

Just as he helped Charles to sit and hunkered down with the rest, he glanced up at the sky. The funnel was directly overhead and the top part of the barn had been sucked into its giant jaws. Straw, ropes and tools hurled through the air. He covered his head with one hand, held Charles with the other and prayed the animals would survive.

What only lasted minutes, seemed like hours, but as fast as it came, it left. However, Joe continued to hear the rumble to the north for many minutes to follow. The unrelenting rain poured as he glanced at the others. He then realized that they held to each other in life threatening terror. As if they could have stopped the devil from plucking them away if it had wanted to.

Joe stood and looked over the mound. The roaring was all but gone now. "I think it's safe."

Charles couldn't stand on his own, but with the help of Horse and Johnny, he made it to his feet. The moans and cries that escaped him were ones of sheer pain. Joe didn't know how serious the injury was, but was glad for Johnny One Horn to be there to help with the medicine.

To Joe's astonishment, the house hadn't been damaged in the storm. How could that be when the barn lost its roof only a short distance away? Strange things happened in the swamp land.

Inside, Carl instructed, "Y'all put Charles in Ma's room. I cleaned it all up."

Too weak to protest, Charles lay on the bed and moaned. With one quick jerk One Horn pulled the branch from his shoulder. Joe thought he would lose his stomach at the sight of the wound and the sound of his brother's scream of agony.

Johnny studied the injury. "It is not too bad." He gathered a pouch from his waistband. "This will help."

The substance he smeared on the injury was oily and like nothing Joe had ever seen. Charles began to relax as if the potion numbed the pain. The knot in his stomach began to release as his brother finally lay quiet.

Boy Horse pulled a ceremonial pipe out of his gear. "Here, we will all smoke the pipe of dreams." He lit a match and puffed until smoke billowed.

Joe took the pipe. He'd never smoked anything before but he knew it would be an insult if he didn't try. Putting his lips around the mouthpiece, he drew a breath. The smoke was harsh and seared his lungs, but he held it until spasms of coughing forced him to let it out.

Horse smiled. "This make you sleep good."

It was true, before Carl and Charles took their puffs, a peaceful feeling came over Joe and his eyelids began to get heavy. All of his muscles relaxed and he caught himself grinning foolishly about nothing in particular.

Johnny One Horn took the pipe from Charles and began to laugh. "Horse, you snake. That is strong medicine. Not for young boys."

Horse replied defensively, "It will be good. These sparrows have been through much."

Joe's head began to spin. He had to lie down before he fell down. Passing through the front room, he noticed Carl already asleep on his pallet. Funny, he hadn't even known Carl left the bedroom.

As soon as his head hit the pillow, he was asleep. Or was he? He wasn't sure, but he did know the drug he'd smoked was strong. Yes, he was asleep and in some kind of dream state. Dreams, versus reality. He allowed himself to drift from one dream to another.

He couldn't understand how past events seemed as clear as if they'd happened only minutes ago. What was this? What he was seeing now hadn't happened before. Was it the future? Could it be real?

Drifting deeper and deeper into sleep. . .

He walked slowly down the lengthy corridor. Where was this place? What was it?

Chains rattled in the distance, voices moaned with pain. Rancid odors filled the air. He tried to calm his pounding heart. Why was he here? Then in the distance he saw a figure.

He stopped in his tracks and squinted into the darkness. "Pa?" A mixture of sweat and blood ran from the man's forehead. "Pa? Can you hear me? Can ya see me?"

"Wait for me, Joe. Wait for me," the apparition begged.

The ghostly voice faded along with the figure and face of his father. "Pa?"

Suddenly his mind raced into another place. Another dream. A land like none he'd ever seen before lay before him. A land full of great peaks that reached toward the sky and deep canyons of enchantment.

In the distance, silhouetted by the sun, a lone rider led his horse over the canyon floor. Closer and closer it came until Joe could see clearly it was an Indian.

A Great Chief like those he'd seen in pictures years earlier in Gulfport. Then he noticed that behind the man were warriors, thousands of warriors that faithfully followed in the wake of the Great Chief's splendor.

For only moments Joe gazed into eyes filled with immeasurable wisdom. The four winds gently waved the feathers in the magnificent war bonnet proudly displayed atop the Chief's head. The man turned, pointed toward the setting sun and motioned for Joe to follow.

A wave of peace came over him. He didn't know where he was going, but he would do as instructed. When he started toward the Chief the great man shot him a reassuring smile, then like a puff of smoke, he floated away. A breathtaking scene was the only thing that remained. Then came serene, quiet darkness.

Chapter Twelve

The sun had just begun to rise when Joe awoke. The small room gradually filled with early morning light. His dreams from the night before resurfaced in his mind. What had that all been about? What did it mean? He didn't know, but there was time to think about all of that later, it was time to get back to work retrieving the gold.

Fully awake now, he stood and went into the living area. Anticipation of what the day might bring excited him. Little Boy Horse was sitting on the porch in his usual cross legged Indian fashion, staring at the sunrise.

Horse turned to face Joe. "Old tree marking the gold is gone. Raft, too."

Joe couldn't believe his ears. He hurried through the doorway, jumped off the porch, and ran to the swamps edge, which was considerably closer to the house than it had been the day before.

The wind had calmed, but waves still slapped against the shore. "The storm. The damned storm! It broke the tree!" He didn't know why he was shouting. No one was there to hear him.

He searched the swamp with his eyes, and spotted the raft. It had to be a hundred yards or more away from its original location. He had to get it. That was all there was to it. He ran to the barn, grabbed the canoe, flipped it right side up and dragged it toward the shore. A warm hand on his arm stopped him. He turned to see Little Boy Horse.

Horse shook his head. "Waves too big. Will capsize canoe. Do not go."

Gazing once again at the rough water, Joe realized it was a lost cause. He tried to suppress his anger as he dropped the canoe and walked to the barn. If he couldn't get more gold, he would get on to his next step.

It wasn't going to be easy to build a false bottom in the wagon, but he was going to give it a hell of a try. It had to be a place so concealed that if someone looked right at it, it wouldn't be seen.

Boy Horse entered the barn. "Storm make mules run away. They are not hurt, just scared. I will go find them."

Funny, he hadn't noticed the mules were gone. Now, as he looked around at what was left of the old barn, he realized the storm had played havoc with the stuff inside its walls. Most everything was out of place. After the roof had blown off he hoped he could find the tools to build the false floor in the bottom of the wagon.

Carl, Charles and Johnny One Horn sat at the wooden table in the kitchen. Carl finished up his breakfast and said, "I wonder if anyone's ever seen as much gold as we found. You know we're all rich, John?"

Johnny smiled. "Carl, you better watch what the evil of white man happiness can do. Do not mess with what you do not understand."

"What's there to understand about gold?"

"Many men will die for what we found."

Charles cleared his throat. "Why do you think that? We can use the money for the good of us, and others. We don't have to do mean things with it."

Shaking his head, Johnny replied, "Gold has many evils. It is not what you do that matters. If you give your gold to a poor man, he becomes rich. Then someone kills him for his gold. The wicked person becomes rich and uses the money for bad things. The evil grows.

"Take my word for it, sparrows, men will suffer over the great sin we uncovered in the swamp. After the big wind yesterday, I am sure I am right."

"Well, it's over and done now. I guess we'll just have to live with it and do the best we can." Charles grinned, pushed his chair under the table and walked out of the room. "I'm gonna go help Joe."

Joe glanced up as Charles then Carl and Johnny entered the barn. "One thing about it, we don't have to worry about havin' enough light to work by."

Carl looked up at the sky. "That's for sure."

Joe started to hammer once again. "With the raft gone, our treasure huntin' days are over, for now anyway. The way I got it figured is we can come back someday and try to get more. There's a hell of a lot down there."

He didn't want to stop working. The wagon was their ticket out of there. "If we finish the wagon today, we can leave tomorrow."

"That's great with me." Charles picked up a board and began helping his brother.

Little Boy Horse entered the barn with the mules in tow and a chicken under one arm. He gave a toothy grin and stuck out his chest in a mocking fashion. "Me great hunter," he said, holding the chicken up as it were a prize animal. "Me bring supper."

Joe chuckled as his brothers made fun of Horse when he handed the hen to Carl. At that time he decided there was nothing he could do about the past, so he would look to the future and make the best of it. If not for himself, he'd do it for his brothers, who were quickly growing into men.

Johnny and Horse walked out of the barn. Joe hadn't asked them if they were going to join him and the boys on their journey out of the swamp. When they made up their minds, they'd tell him.

The two big men's faces looked different when they walked back through the doorway. He knew their decision had been made.

"Joe," said Johnny, "as you say, we have nothing here anymore. We will go with you and help you find O.C. Armstrong. When we find him, we can come back here if we want to."

Joe's fright of the unknown disappeared in that moment and was replaced by an overwhelming sense of relief. He couldn't help but hug his friends, who were now like family.

Charles and Carl hugged them as well. Joe gave instructions while everyone pitched in on the wagon. He thought of the faraway places and the great adventures that lay in their future. Were they truly going to look for his father, or were they going to follow a different dream?

Everyone got a good night's sleep before heading out; Joe was the first to rise. Everything was packed and ready to go. He only had one last task before they left this wretched place.

He went to the barn to look at the work they'd done. He was convinced nobody, but nobody, would ever suspect the shimmering fortune that lay between the double wagon floors.

A sound behind him drew his attention. It was Boy Horse. Without speaking, Joe walked over beside the large grave marker his brothers had finished, and picked up a small cross he'd made the night before. Carved in the wood of the cross were the letters WIT.

He and horse would be the only ones to know about this. Joe picked up a saddle bag. "Horse, I need to bury this next to Ma. If Pa ever comes back, he will know what these letters mean and see that I've left him some of the gold."

The big man looked at the cross then took hold of the large wooded grave marker. "What does it mean?"

"When it's time." Joe knew Horse wouldn't understand the importance, but he remembered his pa's words and was assured, O.C. would recognize he'd been left some treasure.

Horse rolled the headstone from the barn up the steep burial mound, Joe followed with the cross, saddle bag the shovel and pickaxe. It would be a relief to get this done, over with and be gone.

They dug a long narrow trench, set Martha's marker in and tamped the dirt down hard around it. Once they got it in place, Joe tried to push it over, but it didn't budge an inch. "Looks like we got it pretty steady. It'll take a pretty hard hit to knock it down."

Horse nodded then began to dig a hole for the saddle bag. Joe started one for the cross. He hoped this wasn't a tribute to his pa's death, but one to their reuniting. However, he doubted O.C.

was still alive. If he was, he'd have returned by now, but in some way, this gesture gave Joe hope. A person couldn't live without hope.

Once the task was finished, Joe started down the hill. "I'm gonna wake the others. It's time."

With everyone up and around, Joe made sure his brothers loaded just enough personal things to get them to the nearest town. They'd buy new stuff when they got there.

"Charles, Carl, y'all ready to say your goodbyes to Ma?"

Carl started toward the door. "I reckin."

The others followed the youngest boy up to the grave, Joe brought up the rear, wondering what they'd say about the cross, then he heard Charles.

"Where'd that cross come from?"

"That's somethin' I had to do. Just for me, Charles." When his brother seemed to accept it was personal, the boy didn't pursue the subject. Joe was proud of him for that and after a few moments of silence he asked, "Carl, you want to say anything?"

The boy sniffed. "I've got a lot to say, but I've said it all before."

It seemed to Joe they were all just waiting for someone to say the right thing, as they stood for several long minutes in hushed silence atop the knoll. He couldn't bring himself to open his mouth for fear he'd break down and bawl.

Finally, he glanced at Carl who, with tears streaming down his face, cupped his hands and put them to his mouth. The lonesome sound of a whippoorwill's call escaped through his fingers. Seconds afterward from somewhere in the sadness of the swamp, a solitary whippoorwill answered.

Johnny and Horse looked at each other as if they had just heard from the dead. The two of them turned and walked to the base of the mound leaving Joe with Carl and Charles. Joe looked at his brothers. "You two did a good job on the marker. Ma would have been proud. Let's say goodbye now and go."

Moments later his brothers left him alone at the gravesite. He stared at the grave marker. The dates were there, but the words engraved on it were perfect.

Our Mother, Martha Armstrong, rest in everlasting peace. We love you.

He went down the hill and directly into the barn where he gathered the last gallon of kerosene. He splashed the coal oil into the hay in the corner.

His heart was heavy. He'd spent his whole life on this farm and it brought nothing but heartache in the end. He hated this place and would be damned if he'd leave his ma and pa's stuff for someone else to pillage.

After lighting a match, he threw it into the coal oil soaked hay, then went to the house. Surprised nobody said anything to him about his actions; he spread the remaining liquid on the floor of the dwelling and torched it, too.

Outside his brothers and friends waited, without a sound, in the wagon. He got in the driver's seat, picked up the reins and coaxed the mules to start down the rutted road.

Within seconds the house and barn were fully engulfed in flames. A short distance away, Joe stopped the wagon and along with the others watched the building and barn turn to ashes.

He'd dreamed of leaving, but now that the time was here, there was sadness about going. Even with the gold, he longed for the happy life they'd had when he was younger. His mother and father, their love and discipline, even if they were poor, made them a happy family.

He turned and headed down the road. The wagon squeaked, creaked and groaned under the weight. Just enough gold coins to get them about anywhere they wanted to go were all he kept out.

Carl's voice seemed distant over the noise of the wagon, but it penetrated Joe's daydream.

"Joe, how do we know where we're goin'?"

"We don't, but we're gonna take any road that leads west. Even if it's just a trail."

Charles said, "If we go west, we'll run into the Mississippi River sooner or later. What are we gonna do then?"

"When we get there, we'll have part of the trip behind us. We'll figure it out then.

In late afternoon, Joe turned onto a more traveled, long winding road that seemed to lead to eternity. He was looking forward to a change, no matter what the change would bring. However, he couldn't help but wonder what or where the next circle in their lives would lead them?

Studying the land in front of him, he found a new strength in his dreams. He'd started something and was determined to finish it.

CHAPTER THIRTEEN

Early Winter 1852

Joe carefully led the mules, who'd made the trip better than he'd expected, through the muddy streets of Vicksburg, onto the main boulevard. The only bank he could see was just ahead. He wanted to cash in a little of the gold so he could buy Johnny and Horse some clothes.

He didn't like having to leave the two of them in the woods, but it was safer that way. At least 'til they could dress more like a white man and maybe be accepted more easily.

"Wow, Joe, I ain't never seen nothin' like this 'cept in pictures."

"Yeah, I know, Carl, me neither." Joe was in awe of the modern buildings lining the streets. Proper signs on every business told the names of the establishment.

"Musta rained recently. I'm glad we missed it." Charles said.

Carl slugged Charles on the arm. "Me, too, but a little rain might have made you smell better."

"Shut up, little brother, you don't smell too good yourself."

"Okay, boys let's not make a scene, I've got business to take care of.

Joe stopped the wagon in front of the bank and watched a steady line of people going in and out. Fine ladies escorted by well-dressed gentlemen passed the wagon.

Carl burst out laughing then put his hand over his mouth in a vain attempt to stifle the sound. Joe raised his eyebrows at his brother. "Carl." He drew out his younger brother's name in a warning manner. Then he heard Charles snigger and knew exactly what they thought was so funny.

Wiping a tear from his eye, Carl quieted and said, "Those people that just walked by called us Hillbillies. Did you see that man holdin' up that lady's dress so it wouldn't get in the mud?"

Charles replied, "Yeah, can you imagine what that lady would do if she saw Horse and Horn sittin' here in their almost nothin' bear hides. Hell, she'd probably run so fast she'd get across the Mississippi without touchin' the water."

Joe smiled at the thought. "That fine gentleman would probably pass her, boys." With his brother's laughter, he stepped out of the wagon. "Y'all wait here. I'll be right back." He started toward the bank entrance then glanced over his shoulder at the two. "As I said, don't cause a ruckus to draw any more attention to us then we've already got."

Satisfied at their positive nods, he approached the door and hoped when he got inside no one would ask questions. He wasn't in the mood to have to explain much or make up stories.

He got in line with the rest of the customers and felt everyone staring at him. Cigar smoke was thick burning his nostrils and eyes. He kept his gaze to the floor hoping his eyes wouldn't start to water then didn't realize it was his turn until he heard a man's voice.

"Well, come on up son, there are plenty more people waiting. If you don't have business, then get out of line."

Joe stepped forward and studied the bald headed man behind the barred window. His heart beat hard in his chest. He'd come to the bank to get money for his coins, so it was now or never.

Glancing around as he placed one of the large coins onto the counter. He circled it with his arms so onlookers might not notice. The clerk stared at it with amazement grabbed it then quickly closed the counter window. At first he didn't know what to think about the man's actions. Then a door opened that led behind the counter and into another area.

"Come with me, son."

The room he entered was small, held two simple desks and a large safe. There was another man working on books at one of the desks.

"Mr. Williams, will you take care of the customers at the window while I help this young man?"

"Yes, sir," Williams answered.

Joe nodded to the man as he got up. Williams acknowledged then opened the counter gate. Joe then met the first clerk's gaze.

"What's your name, boy?"

"Names Joe, mister."

"Johns," replied the clerk. "Winfield Johns."

"Nice to meet ya'"

"Same here." The man pulled a pair of spectacles from his vest pocket, placed them on his nose, then under the yellow light of a lantern, studied the coin. "One question though, where the hell did you get this?"

Joe watched the older fellow. Should he tell him the truth? Actually he didn't know what to say, but he had to say something. "Well, they were handed down through the family." That wasn't really a lie, but... "I've only got three."

"Three, hmmmm." The man glanced up. "I'm an honest man, Joe, meaning my bank has to make a little money if I buy these from you, but I won't be unfair."

He didn't know Winfield Johns, but he had to take him at his word. "I understand, sir."

"Tell you what. I'll give you a full hundred dollars for all three."

A hundred dollars! Damn! He tried to talk, but couldn't find his voice. The amount kept going over in his head. A hundred dollars! Damn! He saw a smile cross the clerk's face and felt the man's hand on his shoulder.

"Are you alright?"

A hundred dollars! Joe put the other two coins on the desk, then cleared his throat and forced himself to speak. "Y-yes, sir. I-I'm just not used to all this cigar smoke, that's all." Winfield chuckled and counted out one hundred dollars into his hand. Hell, he'd never even seen that many bills and gold coins together before, much less held them in his hand. He folded the wad of money then placed in the chest pocket of his overalls.

Johns reached for the door knob but stopped and turned toward Joe. "May I give you some advice young man?"

"Yes, sir."

"There are a lot of very nice people in Vicksburg, but lurking in the shadows are some really bad ones. Men and women alike so don't let people see your money. You hear?"

"I here ya, Mr. Johns, and thank ya. I'll take heed."

"Very well."

Winfield opened the door and it was all Joe could do to stop himself from running out, but he stayed calm until he closed the outside door behind him. Then he took off down the wooden walk and made a jump for the wagon, almost knocking Charles off the seat.

He grabbed the reins and whipped them against the teams' backs. "Let's go mules." Glancing over at Charles he saw anticipation in the younger boy's eyes.

"Well?"

He could hardly contain himself. "Well what?" Charles squinted at him with annoyance and he couldn't hold back his laughter any longer.

"Come on, brother, spit it out. What happened in there?"

Patting his chest pocket he replied, "Right here, next to my heart, I got us one hundred dollars."

Charles said, "A hundred dollars?"

"No kiddin'?" Carl chimed in.

"Yep, but we have to be careful. That banker said not to let people know we got it, so don't tell anybody. Swear." He heard their answers in unison.

Carl leaned forward from the back seat. "Where we goin' now, Joe?"

"I think we oughta find Aunt Estelle. I've never seen her, but if she's anything like Ma, I'm looking forward to it." He noticed a store keeper cleaning the mud from his porch. "Hey, mister, you know a lady named Estelle Rainwater?"

The store keeper stopped what he was doing and walked over to the wagon. Joe didn't like the look on the man's face. It was like he wasn't happy about what he was about to say.

"I knew Estelle for years. She was a fine Indian lady. Her

two sons moved off. After that, she went down real fast. You boys know her?

"She's our mother's sister." Carl answered.

"I see, Well, you'll find her house is out south of here 'bout a mile. That is what's left of it."

Joe studied the man's grim face. "What do you mean by that?" He wasn't sure he wanted to hear what the storekeeper had to say.

"It burned a while back with her inside, poor thing. It was a big loss for our city. Everyone liked that sweet lady. Barn's still standing, though. Mighty fine barn it is, too."

"Damn, Joe, we didn't even get to meet her."

"Carl, watch your mouth." Joe watched the store keeper start to sweep again. "Mister, where's that house again?"

"You'll know where it is. When you come to the fork in the road, you can't miss it."

"Thanks for your help." He put the reins down, got off the wagon and approached the store. "You got any clothes to fit big people? I need to buy some."

The man smiled. "I've got most every size. Come on in and take a look."

Joe followed his brothers into the store, the storekeeper to the clothing. He fumbled through the pants and shirts then heard the man say.

"I might be able to help you if you give me an idea of how big you're looking for."

How could he describe his friends? He stretched his arm high above his head. "They're about this tall."

"That looks like maybe six foot five or so." He shook his head. "I only have a few that size and they're right over here."

After looking for a while, Joe picked out some clothes for Horse, Johnny and himself. He also had Charles and Carl pick out a few things.

"Hey, Joe?"

"What Carl?" He noticed the youngest of them had picked up a very tall top hat.

Carl laughed. "This looks like somethin' Johnny One Horn should have. I'd like to see the look on his face when I tell him to put it on."

"I don't think you can tell Horn anything," Charles said with a snort. "You must not want to keep that pretty hair of yours."

"Know what, Charles?" The boy scoffed. "I always thought I'd look good bald."

Joe always enjoyed it when they all three laughed together. This time was no different. He paid the store owner, they took their leave and loaded the newly bought items into the wagon.

When they all took their seats, he whipped the reins. "Get up." The wagon creaked and squeaked when it took off. He knew it was a task for the mules to pull in the mud. "Y'all know I had to pay nine dollars for them clothes? I guess we needed them though."

"Hell, Joe," Charles said, "If you got a hundred dollars for only three of the coins, we must have a few thousand dollars-worth in the bottom of the wagon."

"Yeah, we need to get another wagon and team. One that's not so rickety. That way we can share the weight between the two and this one won't be so hard for these poor old mules to pull. There's got to be a livery around here that will sell us one. But first, I want to find Aunt Estelle's place."

Charles pointed. "But there's the livery right there. Let's stop while we're here so we don't have to double back."

The younger man had made his point. Joe pulled over to the livery and stepped down to the soggy street. "I'll be right back. If they know of somethin' we'll take time to buy, if not, we'll move on."

Joe went into the dim light of the barn-like livery and was greeted by a young man about his age.

"What can I do for ya?"

"Was wonderin' if y'all might know of a wagon and team for sale. Need one pretty bad." The man took off his hat, scratched his head and shook it from side to side. Joe already knew the answer.

"Sorry to say, I don't. Ya never know, though, maybe in a couple of days."

Offering the owner a handshake Joe replied, "Thanks, but we ain't got time to wait. Maybe somethin' will come along."

Joe went out and climbed in the seat of the old wagon.

"Nothin'."

His siblings didn't respond as he led the team out of town. He enjoyed the companionable silence between him and his brothers during the ride. It was only a couple of miles when the fork in the road came into view. Carl's arm shot forward almost hitting Joe in the side of the head.

"There it is!"

"I reckin so, Carl. Let's walk over there." The remains of the homestead rested not far from the road. The smell of burnt wood was still evident in the air even though the charred ruins were long cold.

Charles stepped closer. "Damn, there's just about nothin' but ashes left."

"Yeah," Joe said, "and somewhere in there is our aunt."

Carl took a step back. "You mean they just left her here?"

Joe squatted and ran a finger through the ash. "I'd imagine there wasn't anything to bury. I suppose they had some kind of service or somethin'."

Glancing at the sky Charles remarked, "Looks like rain."

"Yeah, it sure does." Joe stood and brushed his hand on his pant leg. "Bow your heads, boys." He still wasn't good at praying, but it was the least he could do before they left.

CHAPTER FOURTEEN

When they got back on the road, he was sure Horse and Horn were close by. The men would follow, but stay out of sight until it was safe.

It wasn't long 'til Joe saw another wagon coming toward them. He figured they were heading for town. The closer the wagon got, the better he could see the scruffy old man driving.

"Hey there," the man greeted.

Pulling off the road somewhat, Joe saw the old man do the same. "Howdy. You from around here?"

"Could be. What is it yous a needin'?"

"Is there a livery up ahead somewhere where we might buy a wagon and a team?"

"Nope, nothin' that I know of. You say you wanna' buy a rig?"

Joe nodded. "That's right."

"Well, boy, this is your lucky day. This 'en right-cheres jess happens to be fer sale. Twenty-five dollars for the whole kit-n-caboodle's what I'm askin'."

The thing didn't seem to be in two bad of shape and the mules looked pretty good, too. "Mind if I take a closer look."

"Not a'tall, my friend, not a'tall."

After assessing the rig and animals, Joe met the old man's faded grey eyes. "Okay, mister, we'll take 'em."

"Just how do you whippersnappers plan to pay ole Bobtail anyways? Huh?"

A stream of tobacco spit flew from the old man's mouth and Joe moved his foot just before it landed on his shoe. "We've got the money." He handed the old man the twenty five dollars in gold coins."

The man studied the gold. "My, my. Little rich boys. Just how much of this here gold do you-uns have?"

Not at all liking the way the man was eyeballing the wagon and their things, Joe could have climbed into a hole when he heard Carl's sarcastic voice.

"A whole lot more, mister, not that it's any of your business."

Charles jabbed Carl with a finger to the ribs. "He's just playin' games. That's just about all the money we have."

"Oh, really?"

Joe noticed the sly look on Bobtail's face and knew it was time to leave. "We gotta go, so you'd better get the things you want outta this wagon. It's ours now, so anything that's left belongs to us."

After the codger grabbed a few things, he reached deep beneath the straw and pulled out a large buffalo gun and tucked it under his arm. "Maybe we'll be seeing you later." He then turned and started down the road.

"Yeah, maybe so." The distance between them grew farther and farther apart then the man veered off the road. Joe was glad there hadn't been any trouble, but wondered why Bobtail hadn't headed on into town instead of into the brush. "I've got a strange feelin' about that ole coot."

Shaking his head Charles patted one of the new mules then checked its teeth. "Ah, hell, he's just an old man. He'll probably go to the nearest saloon and stay drunk for a week on our money."

"Don't be so sure. I didn't like the way he looked at us." Unable to shrug off the uneasiness in his stomach Joe shivered. There was something, he didn't know what, but he was sure enough ready to put some distance between them. "Charles, you drive the new wagon, but first let's put everything in it except the gold and the straw. Maybe folks'll think we only use this old rig to sleep in."

Carl climbed in the new wagon next to Charles. "You've

got it all figured out, don't ya, Joe." Charles turned the rig around to follow Joe.

"Doin' the best I can, little brother." He reined the team back on the road and glanced over his shoulder to see if he could get a glimpse of the old man. Nothing.

It was funny that Joe hadn't noticed how creaky the old wagon was until they'd gone down the road a ways. The new one hardly made any noise; then again, he didn't have his brothers rambling on beside him either.

"Hey, Joe."

He turned around to look at his youngest brother. "What?" Carl had a big smile on his face and was pointing at something ahead of them. Joe turned to once again face forward and saw them. Johnny and Horse had stepped out into the road ahead.

Carl yelled, "See the new wagon and mules Joe bought? Nice ain't it." He paused. "Hey, where'd y'all come from anyway?"

They stepped out of the way, as Joe pulled up beside them. He noticed Little Boy Horse had a rifle under his arm he hadn't had before.

"The woods, little man, where did you think?"

Carl hopped down from the wagon. "Don't be a smart ass, Horse. Hell, I'm damn near sixteen!"

Joe squinted at his little brother. "Watch out. You might get yourself in a pile of trouble."

Johnny One Horn stepped toward the wagon. "Speaking of watching, we've been watching you boys ever since you left town. Strange people live there. That old man, he followed you after you paid him."

Joe met his big friend's gaze. "I was wonderin' about that. I don't know. I just had a feelin'."

"Your feeling was right. As he crawled through the brush, he pointed the big gun at you."

"What happened to him?" Carl asked.

"He will not bother any of us again."

"Where is he, Johnny. I want to know what happened to him!"

Joe placed his hand on Carl's shoulder. The boy was getting taller every day. "Just shut up, Carl, leave it alone." As he watched Little Boy Horse slide the rifle under the straw in the old wagon, Joe recognized it to be the old man's. One thing was for sure, he never wanted to get on the bad side of his two Indian friends. There was no telling what they'd done to that codger, but he'd bet the man deserved it. "I don't think any of us really want to know."

He reached behind the seat of the buckboard and grabbed the clothes that were tied in a stack with string and tossed them. "Here, put these on." Horse caught the garments. He and Johnny looked at each other as though their mother had just spanked them. Joe forced back the laugh that fought to get out.

Horse studied the clothing. "Why?"

"We're gonna be around lots of white folks and we don't want to draw attention."

Horse shook his head. "This will make us look very funny."

Carl retrieved the gift he'd gotten for Johnny One Horn and handed it to the man. "Here, after you put those breeches and a shirt on, you can put your hair under this. It'll look real nice. "

The look on the big man's face was one of determination. Joe knew there was going to be an argument, but he wanted to put a stop to it before it got started. "Y'all want us to be safe, don't you?" His two friends nodded in unison. "Well, in order for us to travel, go into towns and be seen together, you have to look more like us."

"You are too pale. We are too dark."

"Okay, I'll give you that, but you two know I'm right. You at least have to have clothes like us. Don't you?" He saw them glance at each other, then watched the men head toward the trees.

Charles stood beside Joe and chuckled. "They sure are grumblin' a lot amongst themselves."

"Sure are," Carl added with a snigger.

Joe all but laughed out loud and checked the rigging on the wagons. "Yep, and they're gonna look a lot different when they come back out here. If you boys want to laugh at 'em face to face, then go right ahead and when they whup ya for it, I'll just have to stand back and watch."

A cold rain started to fall. Joe looked into dark sky. It burdened him that it would soon be full blown winter. Now that

Estelle was gone, he wondered where their little crew would stay until spring. It was as if Carl had read his mind.

"Joe, I'm chillin' some. Where we gonna stay when it really starts to get cold."

"I was just thinkin' that myself, Joe." Charles pointed toward where they'd just come from. "How about we camp in Aunt Estelle's barn for the winter? At least we'd have shelter. We could build us a pretty good fireplace between now and the real cold."

The more he thought about what Charles said, the more he liked the idea. From the size of the barn, the wagons, animals and all five of them could stay comfortably. "You know, that's not such a bad idea. After all, town's right there close and we can get supplies when we need 'em."

"Really, Joe?"

He smiled at Charles. "Yep."

Johnny and Horse stepped out in their new clothes. He saw Carl's hand fly up to cover his mouth. The boy was trying his best not to laugh. He knew the two big men would be glad to know they could go through winter wearing their leathers, but come spring Carl would probably have to stifle another laugh.

CHAPTER FIFTEEN

THE RIVER

Early Spring 1853

Joe was pleased how well staying in the barn had gone. It provided all they needed to survive. However, now it was time to move on and he was glad to be on the road again. The trees were leafing and the days were warm, it was the perfect time to travel toward the waters of the Missouri.

Little Boy Horse put his hand up. "Stop," he said, "I hear people talking ahead and also the sound of the big river we need to cross."

Joe slowed the wagon then stopped to listen. He heard the voices, too. "When I was in line at the bank, I heard someone talkin' about a ferry on the Mississippi. I bet we're gettin' close." He turned toward the Indians. "Horn, you and Horse don't talk lessin' you have to. Hear me?"

He accepted their acknowledgement and pulled forward. It wasn't long until he saw people scurrying around up ahead. Most of them stood on the ferry and were working on the cabin. Pulling up next to a man he asked. "Mister, does the ferry go across the river here?"

The man pushed his worn hat to the back of his head and looked up. "Used to, but right now, as you can see, it ain't. Had some damage that has to be worked on."

Damn, no ferry, what were they going to do now. He couldn't panic yet, he needed more information. "Is there any other way to get across?"

"Depends on where you're goin. If you want to go to St. Louie there's a steam barge type riverboat that runs off the point." The man pulled a pocket watch out and glanced at it. "But if you want to catch it today, you'd better hurry. It leaves in about an hour."

An hour? Joe hoped the point wasn't too far. "How do we get there?"

"Follow the river road for about a half mile. You can't miss it."

"Guess we'll be gettin' along, then. Grateful for your time." There was a look similar to concern on the stranger's face and when the man spoke again, Joe understood why.

"Just to let you fellow's know, it's probably going to cost you about twenty dollars to ride with both wagons. Ain't that much room on it."

Joe nodded his appreciation unwilling to tell them man they could afford it. Hell, they could probably buy the barge if they wanted. "Get up mules."

"Thanks, mister!" Charles' voice rang over the sound of the rigs in motion. "Hell, Joe, half mile ain't that far. We'll make it for sure."

It wasn't long after they made their first turn through the woods, then back toward the water, Joe saw the point in the distance. The Mississippi was a mighty river. He'd read about the powerful waters, but in real life, it more than impressed him.

Charles stood and held onto the back of the wooden seat. "Man, I never saw so much water in all my life." He pointed. "Look, Joe, you can barely see across it! And, damn, look at the size of that boat."

Carl remarked from the back. "It looks like it's on fire. Where's all that smoke comin' from?"

It was hard for Joe to hide his excitement. He felt like a boy again. It was all so magnificent. "That's not smoke, Carl, its steam, remember, it's a steam barge." He thought his heart would leap from his chest. Life was good and he was pleased he could enjoy this experience with his brothers. "Woo-hoo, looks like it's gonna be a hell of a ride."

When they approached the barge, Joe saw two men coming toward them. He figured them for deck hands. "Howdy," he greeted.

"Howdy. You men going to St. Louis?"

"That's right, sir." Joe didn't like the amusement that filled the man's eyes when he glanced at the other worker and smiled, then turned his attention back to the wagon.

"Hope you've got money. It's going to cost you twenty dollars to get across the Mississip' today, and we only got two more places left."

"I got money." He reached into the chest pocket of his overalls and pulled out twenty dollars in paper money. "I think this should cover it." He handed it to the man and the chiding look in the stranger's eyes disappeared. It was as if the money had gained Joe the man's respect.

"Mighty fine, son, mighty fine. Now, when you pull the wagons on, keep them to the right." The man pointed. "In that empty spot."

Joe studied the steep ramp. It was going to be hard for the mules to pull the weight of the gold up and onto the barge even with the other supplies in the new wagon. When he started up the incline the strain on Shadrack and Seemo was evident. "Pull," he whispered under his breath, "pull." Finally when the animals made it to the top of the ramp, Joe let out the breath he was unaware he'd been holding when one of the deck hands spoke to him.

"Damn, for a minute there I didn't think you were going to make it. That wagon don't look that heavy."

Charles pulled the second wagon behind the first, jumped down then stepped forward. "It's the mules. They're old and have had a long trip. They're just tired, that's all."

That seemed to appease the man, but Joe noticed the way the rest of the men aboard gawked in awe at Johnny and Horse. Then he became aware that one of the more curious hands was going to speak to Johnny.

"Hey, bigun, what's your name?"

Joe had to hide his smile when he saw the way Horn glared at the man. If looks could kill, at that moment, everyone would have seen it firsthand.

The man took a few steps back. “I-I guess that’s none of my business.” He turned and in a fast pace, walked away.

Things were quieting as everyone got settled. The crew pulled up the big ramps and the barge rocked and rolled slightly as it moved into the current. When the rear paddle started thrashing, Joe heard the sound of water cascading over the large scoops and enjoyed the peacefulness of it all.

He glanced at Carl and Charles who were both sound asleep in the straw covered bed of the old wagon. He knew they were exhausted, hell he was, too. He couldn’t understand how Horse and Johnny just kept on going. It seemed like they never tired.

His two friends were propped against the wagon wheels and took turns keeping watch. They had told him they were wary of their new found acquaintances. Riverboats weren’t the safest way to travel, but he had no choice. It was the fastest way to St. Louis.

Johnny One Horn’s hand rested on the handle of one of his two huge Arkansas Toothpick knives, while Horse whittled a piece of wood he’d found floating in the water with one of his. Behind him Joe heard the conversation of two of the crew members.

“Damn, what a knife. Look at that Tom. They both got one.”

“Listen, them people paid their way. You’d better mind your business and let things be. You can bet them big Injuns know how to use those things. There’s a buffalo gun layin’ in the back of one of them there wagons, too.”

“Reckin what they’re carrying that needs guardin’ like that?”

“Hell, they ain’t guardin’, they’re Injuns, they don’t trust nobody. Nope, I think when we get to St. Louie we oughta gladly let them go on their way.”

“Yeah, Tom, you’re probably right.”

Joe was pleased the two crew members had the good sense to leave well enough alone. He couldn’t imagine what Johnny and Horse did to that old man. Anyone else that crossed them could, and probably would, meet the same fate.

He watched the banks pass as the big barge slid through the

muddy waters of the Mississippi. It was strange that something this large could be pushed, not pulled. Hell, everything on land had to be pulled.

The sun became hidden by the horizon and dusk drifted in. Until now, Joe had been wide awake and watched the surroundings with caution, but the urge to lie down and close his eyes became stronger by the minute. He felt himself nod off but quickly lifted his head up and opened his eyes. Johnny and Horse sauntered toward him.

He straightened and cleared his throat, hoping the two hadn't seen his moment of weakness. "What's up?"

Johnny leaned against the wagon. "It's going to be a long night, Joe, you need to get some rest."

"I'll be fine. Don't worry about me."

Little Boy Horse smiled. "Yes, we see how fine you are. You were almost sleeping only a moment ago."

Joe raised one eyebrow. "Okay, so you caught me." He wondered if they were going to give him heck and was surprised when they didn't. He noted a bit of stress in Johnny's voice when he spoke.

"You sleep tonight." Johnny glanced at Horse. "We will keep watch. Neither of us will be able to rest in this strange environment. All of these changes are much for us to handle."

"I know." Joe patted Johnny on the shoulder. "I appreciate y'all and everything you do for us. It's good to have friends."

Horse said, "We'll wake you at first light."

"Thanks." He saw the two big men nod as they walked away. It was going to feel real good to actually lie down and sleep.

Chapter Sixteen

The sun cast a bright red glow that covered the eastern sky. Joe felt the warmth of the hand that had wakened him, on his shoulder. He sat up, rubbed his eyes and gazed out over the water. A somewhat transparent fog hovered over the river.

Johnny One Horn dropped his hand. "Look." He pointed.

Joe followed his gesture and in the dim shadows of morning saw numerous figures standing together against the side of the boat. Horse stood silent, and Johnny's voice was quiet when he spoke.

"Those men are watching us just as much as we are watching them."

"Why?" Joe's eyes began to adjust to the light and he could see the onlookers' faces more clearly. Each one of them looked as if he was staring at a rattlesnake ready to strike. "What's wrong with 'em?"

Horn met his gaze. "They are scared of us. This white man's land is a place they think we don't belong. Nobody trusts us here. I traded one of my knives to the one they call Earl Stockman for this bottle of whiskey. Good medicine if you get hurt or snake bit."

"Well, hell, we don't trust them either. Let's just bide our time. They ain't gonna bother us, you can count on it. Not with you and Horse and them Toothpicks of yours." He glanced at the large knives on the Indian's sides, then looked at them and smiled as confidently as he could.

He was greeted with his friends' toothy grins and was glad for the lighter mood. Stirring noises came from the other wagon and he glanced over to see his brothers waking up. "Damn, y'all decide to join the livin'?"

"Shut up, Joe, I gotta pee." Carl wiped the sleep from his eyes.

Horse laughed. "Carl, fifteen and still sleep like baby."

"I ain't no baby, Horse."

Rubbing Carl's hair Little Boy Horse teased, "You better hurry to side of boat before you pee pants."

"Why do you have to be so mean?"

"Mean? Not mean, just say truth."

Joe almost laughed himself when Carl got up and all but ran to relieve himself and Charles wasn't far behind. He looked at his friend. "You know Horse, he's gettin' pretty big. Like I said before, one of these days he may just whup your ass."

That brought a belly laugh from Johnny. "I want to see that."

The same man that greeted them when they first approached the barge drew near. Joe slid from the wagon and stood. "Howdy."

"Howdy. Just wonderin' if y'all are hungry? Old Levi's a pretty good cook and he'll whip you up some breakfast for a buck."

Joe reached out to shake the man's hand. "Thank ya, mister. We'll probably take ya up on that." He looked at the others in his party. "What do ya say, boys?" They all nodded their response so he reached into the front pocket of his overalls and took out a single gold dollar. "Let's go, then."

Joe was the first to reach the cook. The old man had kind eyes and when he spoke, his voice was raspy. Instantly, Joe liked the man.

"Name's Levi, what'll ya have fellers?"

"What do ya got?" Joe met amused looking eyes.

"Actually, I ain't got nothin' but salt pork and eggs, but I always ask anyway."

A sense of humor, Joe liked that, too. "Got plenty for all of us?"

"Sure 'nough."

"Then we'd be obliged." When Levi smiled, Joe noticed that most of the man's teeth were missing.

"Comin' right up!"

It didn't take long to whip up the meal and put it on wooden plates. Joe inhaled a big whiff of the salt pork. It somehow reminded him of his mother, God rest her soul. "Mmmm, this smells like home."

It was almost embarrassing how fast he and the others wolfed down the food. He handed the plate back to the cook. "Sure was good." He observed as his brothers, Horse and Johnny gave up their dishes, too.

Levi took the dirty utensils. "Damn, you boys must've sure 'nough been hungry."

Charles wiped his mouth with the back of his hand. "Mister, you don't have any idea. That was wonderful."

"Glad you got your fill; now scoot along so I can clean up."

Later that afternoon, Joe saw Levi sitting on a whiskey barrel, whittling. He didn't understand why he'd instantly taken a liking to the old man, but something in his blue eyes said the fellow was honest and could be trusted. Could it be Levi reminded him of O.C.?

He didn't think Levi was that old, the gray hair and beard is what made him look that way, but Joe felt the man was wise for his years. Could the man add his experience to Joe's task at hand?

When he approached, Levi stopped working with his piece of wood. Joe pulled his hands out of his pockets. "Howdy."

"Hey there, young feller, have a sit down."

Joe hopped up onto a barrel and met the man's gaze. "Levi, how long you been workin' on this boat?"

Levi chuckled. "Hell, boy, I don't work on here? I just get on now and again to make a trip to Vicksburg to see my brother."

"But I thought…"

"Naw. They let me cook for 'em to make me a little extra money." He started to whittle again. "Don't really know what I'm gonna do now, though. My brother died last week and he was my only livin' kin. My last job was cookin' for a cattle drive, but that was a few months ago and I used the last money I had to bury my brother." He took a deep breath and let it out slowly. "Guess I'll go to work in some eatin' place in St. Louie. Long as it ain't too fancy." He laughed.

Joe felt bad for the man. He seemed so lonely. "I'm sorry about your brother."

"He drank himself to death. He lost everything in a fire some years back. His house, wife and a little girl. He ain't been right since."

"So you've been taking care of him?"

Levi nodded. "Much as I could."

Joe made a spontaneous decision and hoped his brothers and Horse and Johnny would accept it. They didn't know of his dream to own cattle and horses either, but they would in due time. "Levi, I have an idea. Why don't you come to work cookin' for us? I'll pay you a fair salary."

"Pay me? With what?" He blurted.

Joe put his hand to Levi's mouth and glanced around to see if anyone had heard. "Don't talk so loud." He took his hand away. "Nobody can hear us. I mean it."

"What are you up to, boy? Somethin' illegal like?"

"No, nothin' like that, but I can pay you what you need and maybe more." Joe wondered what was going through the old man's head. Would he accept the offer or go off and tell someone about it? He hoped he hadn't made a mistake. No, he trusted Levi. Finally the man spoke.

"Where y'all goin' that you need a cook?"

"I wanna buy some cattle, maybe some horses and start a ranch out west. Well, we've kind of drifted northwest, but that's still my plan. That's all I can tell you right now. When we get to St. Louis, I'll give you your first month's pay in advance."

Levi jumped off the whiskey barrel. "By golly that's a good deal."

"Yep, anything else I can do for ya?"

"That's purtnear enough, but I could use a new bedroll and a horse, or mule."

Joe thought for only a moment. "Tell ya what, I'll throw in a bedroll, a mule and your own wagon to live in and cook from while we travel."

Levi stuck out his hand. "Son, you've got yourself a deal."

Accepting the old man's handshake, Joe said, "Glad you decided to join us." He saw Levi look in the direction where Johnny and Horse stood.

"Those two big guys, the Indians do they travel with y'all all the time?"

"They're friends,"

"Where'd they come from?"

Glancing at them he smiled. "Deep in the Mississippi swamp, but I don't want to go into that right now. When we get off the boat, I'll explain a little more to you, for now, let's keep this to ourselves."

"You're the boss." He nodded, turned and walked away.

Joe liked Levi's attitude and questioned his fondness of the man when he barely knew him. Again, he thought of his father. Why did Levi spark the memories? Was he as good of a man as O.C.?

Sometimes he was in disbelief of what he'd set out to do, take his brothers through some of the roughest territory in the country and for what? To buy cattle and horses? Make them rich? Hell, they were already rich.

He took a deep breath. Anything was better than rotting in the swamp. Anything. But could he carry through with the plan? Was he man enough? Did he have the guts?

If his pa knew the thoughts that were going through his head, O.C. would give him a good lickin'. No, doubting himself wasn't an option at this point. He could do it, and would do it, with the help of Horse and Horn, Carl, Charles and now Levi, they would succeed. O.C. would expect no less.

Resting his arms on the outer rail of the boat, he leaned over and watched the reflections of darkening clouds above float against the water below. The wind had picked up and waves white capped against the shore. Thunder clapped above and the sky opened up in a torrential downpour. He heard Carl's voice in the distance.

"Come on Joe!"

He turned and ran toward the wagons as lightning flashed ever so close. "I'm comin'," he called back. Now was as good of a time as ever to talk to them about his plan.

Scurrying across the deck, he joined his siblings under one

of the wagons for cover. "Hey, I got somethin' I want to tell y'all." When he was sure he had his brothers' attention, he continued. "I've been thinkin' that we oughta start us a cattle and maybe horse ranch when we get to where we're goin'. It would be a good thing to sink our money into."

Charles glanced at Carl then back to Joe. "We've been talkin' bout the same thing, Joe. Looks like we're all readin' the same book, and you've done a good job gettin' us this far, so whatever you say, that's what we'll do."

Smiling, he shook each of their hands. "Alright then, we're off to be cattle owners. Pa would be proud."

The sounds of the storm lulled him to relaxation. Listening to the heavy pity pat of raindrops against wood, Joe circled his legs with his arms and rested his chin on his knees.

What had happened to O.C.? It was so unlike him to just abandon his family and walk away to never come back. Would he ever see the man again? Was he really dead, or had he found another woman to love and… no, he wouldn't allow his mind to think those kinds of things. It was better just to think his pa forever graveyard dead.

CHAPTER SEVENTEEN

HELL'S GATE OPENS AND THE JOURNEY BEGINS

Late Spring 1853

The sound of keys and the crashing slam of the huge doors leading to the containment area woke O.C. He wiped salty liquid from his forehead and upper lip. Realizing he lay in a pool of sweat, he got up. The sound of the guard, Big Jack Tunnie, was the next thing he heard.

"Wake up, you mangy rats! Nobody gets to sleep all day around here. What the hell do you think this is? A home for the old?" The keys rattled as the man opened a cell door down the hall. "We've got a million cacti to plant out there!"

The work detail was something O.C. didn't want to think of. Sometimes it consisted of pulling cactus from the ground in one spot and re-planting it in another, then another, then another. It was a never-ending, agonizing job that meant nothing, had no purpose and he hated it.

O.C. listened as the sounds of other prisoners stirring in their cells filtered across the stale air. Had anyone died in the night? It seemed to him that somebody almost always did.

There was no end to the job of digging graves. Unfortunately, he'd had that duty many times, but he'd rather do that than uselessly move those damned cacti. He often wondered about the men he buried. Where were they from? What did they do for a living? Did they deserve to be there in that hellhole? Did they have families?

Thoughts of his own family crossed his mind as they so often did. Were they okay? Hell, they could all be dead for all he knew.

Big Jack, one by one, opened the cell doors down the dirty corridor toward his cell. O.C. retrieved an old fork he'd stolen years ago, then put another mark on the wall. Another day alive.

The big man didn't take to too many prisoners, but for some reason he treated O.C. almost like a friend. O.C. was glad for the private conversations they had when others weren't around. He knew Jack felt for him and his situation.

At last count, he had spent thirteen hundred and eighty three days in the living death trap of an Arizona prison. That was nigh on three and a quarter years. Almost four years for a crime he was unaware he committed.

The conditions were extreme, worse than anyone could ever imagine. He had never known about places like this. In a way, though, he considered himself lucky. Many men died before their first year was complete. He prayed every night to live through 'til the next day. To consider the possibility of a future beyond that had long since been abandoned.

Jack unlocked the door to O.C.'s cell and stepped inside. "What are you doing, marking another day?"

Putting the fork back in its hiding place, O.C. often wondered why the big man had never said anything about it. After all, a fork could be used as a weapon, he supposed. "Another day, another month, I don't really know anymore. All I know for sure is it's another mark."

"Judge Kramer wants to see you this morning."

O.C.'s heart fell to his feet. He closed his eyes and tried to catch his breath. The judge only came to the prison once a month and had never asked to see him before. What was going on?

Big Jack unlocked the chains on his ankles. It was the first time they'd been off for months and it felt good. He was surprised at how his voice broke when he asked, "Am I gettin' out?"

"I don't know. Maybe so. There's always a chance."

As Jack led him down the hallway to the main yard, other

prisoners whispered while under the watchful eyes of other guards. Did they know something he didn't? Surely not.

Once outside the cell block, O.C. couldn't help but ask Jack one question after another. "Why does the judge want to see me? Maybe I did something wrong. Am I gettin' out? Do you know?"

Jack smiled. "Hold on, O.C. It might just be a review or something. I know you don't belong here. I knew it the first six months you were here and I've told the warden that. For God's sake I hope you're getting out. I truly do."

O.C. let out the breath he didn't realize he'd been holding as they walked into the small prison courtroom. Two wooden chairs sat in front of the desk. A shiver raced through his body and goose flesh rose on his skin. The wood felt cold and hard when he took a seat.

The judge didn't even glance up at him. The man just sat there and rustled through some papers. An extreme quiet filled the room. Why wasn't Judge Kramer looking at him?

Two territorial federal marshals stood on either side of the judge. One of them was Joe Cloud, the tracker who arrested him so long ago. A man he hated with all of his being. This couldn't be good.

The judge cleared his throat. "Jack, I hear this is your last day here."

O.C. looked at his friend. Last day? Tunnie had never even mentioned it. Why?

Jack tipped his hat back. "That's right, sir, twenty five years is long enough."

Judge Kramer smiled then nodded his agreement. He then turned toward O.C. "So, this is the hide-cutter and cattle rustler O.C. Armstrong, huh?"

Blood rushed to O.C.'s face and he felt hot and flushed. Why did the man have to say it like that? He started to stand, but felt the warmth of Jack's restraining grasp on his arm and heard his whispering voice.

"Take it easy. He's just testing you."

O.C. realized he'd almost made a big mistake. He didn't know what this was all about, but didn't want to make the situation worse by annoying the judge. Inhaling a breath, he relaxed back into the chair. Kramer looked over the spectacles that sat low on his nose, directly into O.C.'s eyes. O.C. returned the man's gaze with as much confidence as he could muster.

"Armstrong, it states here you've been incarcerated almost four years. Is that right?"

"Yes, sir."

"Cattle rustling alone is ten years. You ain't even done half of that, however, it seems Jack Tunnie thinks you're an honest man. Because I have a great deal of confidence in his opinion, and because the evidence against you was a bit sketchy, I'm going to release you into Jack's custody. That is, with one non-negotiable stipulation."

O.C. tried to grasp what he'd just heard. Was he really going to get out? He swallowed hard. "Thank ya, sir. Thank ya. I'll do anything you ask."

Judge Kramer looked at O.C. long and hard, "The stipulation in that you leave the Arizona territory for at least the remainder of your sentence, which is six years."

His heart was in jeopardy of hammering right out of his chest. He was getting out.

"Do you agree with these terms, Mr. Armstrong?"

"Yes, sir. Yes, sir, I surely to God do!" The smile that creased his face was one of pure joy. He didn't remember when he'd ever felt this happy.

Laying his glasses atop the desk the judge said, "My advice to you, O.C., is to go home. Back where you came from. I understand you have a family in Mississippi. A man like you don't have any reason to spend his life in this prison system." The judge gathered his papers. "Jack, take Mr. Armstrong to the main quarters and return his belongings. Whatever they may be, and Armstrong, I wouldn't spend too long in this town. The townspeople don't take kindly to ex-jailbirds."

Kramer stood, picked up his papers and addressed Marshal Joe Cloud. "Do you have anything to say to Mr. Armstrong?"

O.C. saw contempt in the marshal's eyes. He remembered the day he was arrested and how brutal Cloud had been.

Joe Cloud glared at O.C. "If I ever catch your hide-cutting ass in my territory again, O.C. Armstrong, I'll personally hang you myself!" He paused. "Do you understand?"

To O.C., the man was a cold blooded killer. "I understand

very well, Mr. Cloud. You'll never see me again after this day." He'd damn sure better pray about that, for it wouldn't bode well for Cloud if they met again. He wasn't afraid of Cloud, but his evil was backed up by the power of the law.

Judge Kramer rapped the desk with his gavel. "Court adjourned."

Jack took O.C.'s arm and led him outside. O.C. couldn't contain his happiness as they stepped into the main yard. He turned toward Tunnie, reached out and grasped the man's hand. "You'll never regret this, Jack, I promise you that. I'm grateful to the bone."

Big Jack laughed and returned the handshake. "That's good O.C. One of the reasons the Judge agreed to release you is the fact that I'm going the same direction you are, and he asked me to make sure you get out of the territory. Anyway, I figured you'd be wanting to head home."

O.C. followed Jack to the place where they held his personal belongings. He almost didn't want to touch the items of clothing and especially his boots. Dried mud and blood still caked the bottom of them from the night he was arrested. His heart weighed heavy, even over his happiness. Not wanting to think about it, he pushed memories of that night out of his mind.

Jack shut the door to the small holding room. "I have an extra horse. I'll bring it with me when we meet. You can use it, or buy it from me later."

For the first time ever, O.C. couldn't think of a thing to say. He'd walk out of the prison for the last time in only a few minutes. He'd be damned if he'd look back at this nightmare of a place. His hands trembled when he pulled on the crusty boots, but he forced himself to push his foot inside. It seemed Tunnie knew what he was thinking.

"When I go into town, I'll pick you up something else to wear and some new boots."

O.C. breathed a sigh of relief. Thank God he didn't have to keep these cursed clothes on much longer. However, they were better than the prison uniform he'd worn the last four years. "I appreciate that, Jack."

"When we leave here, you head south, away from town. I'll go into town and get what we need. We'll take it one day at a time."

Jack escorted him to the main gate. O.C. blinked back a tear of joy that threatened to spill from his eye; he wouldn't allow that. He was a free man, a proud man, and he would hold his head high when he walked out of that place.

"Well, O.C., this is what you've been waiting for." Tunnie smiled. "Remember, go south to those hills. I'll be there sometime tonight." He handed O.C. some matches and a canteen of water. "Keep a fire burning and I'll find you."

O.C. shook Jack's hand, pulled his old battered hat snuggly on his head, then walked through the gate into the brush and cactus covered desert. It took everything he had not to shout his joy at the top of his lungs. He was a free man. Thanks to Jack Tunnie.

Tunnie. O.C. was grateful to the man, but did he really know Jack Tunnie? His thoughts went back to the private conversations he'd had with Jack and to one in particular. Should he have told the guard about the gold? Was that why he'd helped him get out and was going east? He pushed the doubt out of his head.

Jack Tunnie was a good man and he trusted him, he had to, there was no one else to turn to. In the four years he'd known Tunnie, he'd seen nothing but an honest man.

Slowing to a stop, he closed his eyes and took in a yawning lungful of the morning November air. A light breeze whistled through the sagebrush and cactus. His prayers had been answered; he was on his way home to his loving wife Martha. He missed her badly, and longed for the day he could be with her and the boys.

He had kicked himself in the butt more than once for not keeping out some of the gold before they buried it. What had he been thinking? One gold piece and all of this could have been avoided, but he was scared. Scared to take it to a bank, scared someone might take it away, scared to keep even one coin. Now he realized how stupid it was to have hidden every piece.

A quick glance over his shoulder at the hellhole he had lived in the last few years spurred him to walk quickly toward the hills again. Damn that cattle rustling Don Boggs. He hoped Boggs would rot in hell for all of his lies.

He reached the base of the low mountains and found a comfortable spot. It was too early and warm yet to build the fire, so he settled back on a soft mound of dirt. Drifting off to sleep, he reveled in a freedom he had once taken for granted. He vowed not to lose his independence again.

Chapter Eighteen

Dusk was just around the corner when O.C. awoke. He got up and climbed to the top of the hill. Out there somewhere was his destination. His rest gave him a clear mind, and a clear mind is what it would take to plan his route home.

The sun burned a distant golden orange with patches of radiant clouds surrounding it. It was peaceful and hard to think of its torture in the scorching summers past, and his back breaking tasks under its relentless rays. However, now it was over at last and there was no need for him to dwell on it.

He gazed at the horizon. It had been a long time since he'd seen a sunset and this one had to be the most beautiful one ever.

The autumn chill of the desert night was beginning to make itself known. Tunnie would come soon and he had to get the fire started.

He gathered dead grass, twigs and sticks; the fire blazed fairly quickly. It had been way too long since he'd experienced the warmth of a campfire on his face. He rubbed his hands above the flame. Life was good, but it would be better when he got some clean clothes and started home.

The blaze was burning well and dark descended quickly. O.C. made his way to the hilltop once again and stood looking north toward the town of Yuma. A full moon loomed in darkened sky. It had been years since he'd seen the moon. He stood for a few moments, lost in the magic of its splendor.

Somehow, he remembered the Mississippi moon being

bigger. Thoughts of home seized his heart as he peered at the sky, and prayed. "God, I hope everything is all right back there. Keep everyone safe until I see them again. I know you've heard this all before, but now I know for sure I'm going home. Oh, thanks for that, too. I'd say that after gettin' me out of hell, I owe Ya. Amen"

Freedom was a wonderful gift and he would never take advantage of it again. In the bright moonlight, he scanned the skyline for some sign of Jack Tunnie. He could make out the gruesome shadow of the prison in the distance. It was a wonderful feeling to be out where coyotes howled, desert crickets sang, and, at the same time, it was quiet. He'd never be able to lock even a wild animal in a cage ever again.

Was that the sound of horse hooves? He listened harder. It was. He lit a small piece of brush to be sure Tunnie saw where he was. Closer and closer the horses came until finally he saw the silhouette of Big Jack Tunnie.

"Hey, O.C., I'll bet you're missing your old prison bed about now and that good home cooking they fed you, huh?" He chuckled.

"I don't think so, Jack. The only home I'm missin' is 'bout fourteen hundred miles from here."

"I hear you." He shifted in the saddle. "I've got some beans and coffee. Why don't you build up the fire a little and let's put a pot on."

It was the first time he realized he hadn't eaten all day. "Sounds damn good to me."

Jack handed the reins of the extra horse to O.C. "It'll take a couple of hours for the beans to cook. I'll try to scare us up a rabbit." He smiled. "I brought us a bottle of whiskey, too."

The man turned and was gone in a flash, leaving O.C. thinking about the whiskey he'd made long ago. It had been years since he'd had a swig of the stuff. Hell, it had been years since he'd done anything but be locked up. He wondered if the jugs he'd filled were still in the old barn. That stuff was truly rotgut, but it was good at the time.

He tied the horse, unsaddled it then started the pot of beans. It wasn't long until he heard a gunshot. Soon after, Jack rode back into camp.

"These things are thick as fleas on a dog's back in the light of the full moon." Jack tossed a rabbit to O.C. then dismounted. "Say, you're a pretty good camp builder."

O.C. skinned the rabbit put it over the fire, then laid down and propped himself up against the saddle he placed on the ground. He stared at the flickering flames while Tunnie settled in.

"Want some of this?" He held up the bottle of whiskey.

"Sure." O.C. took the bottle and lifted it to his lips, and stifled a choking cough. The liquid went down anything but smooth. However, it wasn't long before his shoulders started to relax. He took one more nip then handed it back to Tunnie.

"O.C., tell me again how a man like you ever got mixed up with a sorry bunch of men like Don' Boggs' gang."

"Hells bells, Jack, I don't want to go over that again. You've heard it all before. I just wish I'd have known they were wanted men and Joe Cloud was on their trail." He accepted another shot of whiskey and rocked back against the saddle. "Joe Cloud is a dangerous man. A cold blooded killer if you ask me." He thought back to the horrifying night he was arrested.

"I've known Cloud for years at the prison," stated Tunnie. "I've seen the way he's brought in prisoners and often wondered what kind of man he really is. Hell, some of the men were beaten so bad you didn't know what they really looked like for several months."

Sickening images of that fateful night went through O.C.'s mind. Joe Cloud's likeness and the crazy look in his eyes were the most clear.

"You know, Armstrong, this country's rough and untamed. I think it probably takes someone like that to handle the job."

O.C. slowly looked up at the man sitting across from him. His stomach rolled and bile came up in his throat. He loathed the marshal. "If I ever run into Joe Cloud again, I'll probably shoot him where he stands." The whiskey went down easier with every swig. "I've seen that man kill six people in cold blood. Two of 'em women."

Tunnie's mouth flew open. "Women? You never told me that. What happened?"

He shook his head. He'd never told anyone, it was a

nightmare of a memory. "Boggs brought two Mexican women from town for the men to have fun with. Kind of a bonus it seemed.

"There was a storm comin', but I had to relieve myself, so I left camp and went over a hill." He nodded his head. "Those hide-cutters knew how to hide a campsite. Hell, I learned a lot from them about stuff like that, but that night they didn't hide it good enough.

"The wind blew and rain came down somethin' fierce. I did my business then hurried to get back to camp but I stopped in my tracks when I heard gun shots. I crouched down and watched it all from the hilltop overlookin' the camp.

"Cloud started shootin' through the tents, not even knowin' who was in there. He shot 'em all dead." O.C. shook his head from side to side. "Killed those folks just like that."

Tunnie scowled. "How did he find you?"

He stared into the fire and thought about the mistake he'd made that night. "Well, the rain had let up. I didn't know what to do, so I stood up to run the other way and through a flash of lightnin', the marshal saw me. He took a pot shot at me and missed, but I stopped. I knew he had a horse and I didn't. He'd be able to catch me either way. He hollered at me to come down."

"Why didn't he kill you when you got to the bottom?"

"I thought he was goin' to. His eyes were crazy, but he just laughed and said he had work for me to do when daylight came. The rain stopped and I slept on the wet ground. I wasn't gonna go into the tents with all those dead bodies.

"When mornin' came, he made me bury every last one of 'em. Then he arrested me and you know the rest." O.C.'s stomach churned at the memories of the last four years. "You know, Jack, I think that bastard'll probably come lookin' for me. He knows I know he killed those women."

"Ah, hell, if he was going to do that, I think he would have killed you in the first place."

Settling back, O.C. stared at the silent stars above. "He didn't think I'd ever get out. You saw to it that I did." He wondered what was going though Jack's head. "He'll come after us."

O.C. lay there listening to the sounds of desert and night hawks darting through the sky. He pushed the morbid thoughts of the years past out of his mind and drifted off to sleep imagining his sweet wife in his arms.

Wide awake just before the light from the rising sun began to show, O.C. was up. He stoked the fire, made a pot of coffee then woke Jack.

"Hell, man," Jack blurted. "We have a far piece to travel and a lot of time to do it in."

"Tunnie, I'm a man that's waited a long time to travel that long way so let's get with it." He didn't care how much grumbling the other man did. He was ready to see his family so he would push hard until they reached the Mississippi swamp land he called home.

The coffee in the old tin cup steamed as he handed it to Jack. When he took a sip of his own, it went down smooth. It had been four long years since he'd had a good, morning cup of coffee. He took only a minute to enjoy it before he got up and started to saddle the horses. He wanted to make some time today.

Tunnie sat and watched O.C. work. "What route do you think we should take?"

O.C. tightened the last of the straps on his horse. "I think we should head southeast. That way we can avoid some of the bad weather across the New Mexico territories high desert."

"Where's that lead?"

"It will take us to El Paso then we'll go straight east from there."

O.C. was surprised when Jack helped to break down the last of camp. He saddled up and took the lead. It was still cool, so he pushed his horse a little harder than he should have, but he wanted to get home. Tunnie didn't seem to mind, he followed close behind.

****

The sun beat down on O.C.'s shoulders. In the last several days they'd traveled his shirt had done little in the way of stopping the hot rays from penetrating the fabric. Somehow he and Tunnie managed to find just enough water to keep them going, but now his lips were parched, his canteen almost empty and he'd agreed to slow the pace so the horses wouldn't drop dead under them.

At night he was cold and in the day, he burned up. Damn when were they going to get through the desert! "You know, Jack, a man don't seem to notice things like hot and cold in that hell on earth place where you were one of my keepers."

Tunnie stayed at an even gate beside him. "That almost seems threatening. Should I watch my back, O.C.?"

"If I was gonna take you out, hell, I'd of done it the first night we left. You snore loud as a mule's yaw!"

A laugh escaped Jack's throat. "Yeah, I guess you could have."

O.C. noticed the uneasiness in Tunnie's voice. Out of the corner of his eye, he caught a glimpse of the man reaching into his saddlebag. What the hell? O.C. started to dismount so he could be ready for any attack.

"Whoa, O.C., settle down. And I thought you scared the hell out of me. I'm impressed with myself for getting your dander up."

He'd heard the man's words, but still he cautiously watched Jack Tunnie take his hand from the bag. What was he really doing? Was there going to be a confrontation? He saw sunlight reflect off of a long shiny blade then recognized it. His own knife.

Tunnie pitched it to him butt first. "I decided I'd give it back to you as soon as I felt it was safe."

The weapon felt comfortable in his hand. It was like holding an old friend. "I see. In other words, you thought I might cut your throat, huh?"

Jack nodded. "Yeah, something like that. Where'd you ever get a knife like that anyway?"

He relaxed again and thought of the knife maker. A smile crossed his face. "It's the hardest steel I've ever seen. It was made from a sword or somethin'." He saw the other man nod his agreement.

"Sword, huh?"

"Yep." He paused. "Ya know, we're not makin' any time

havin' to go so slow on these horses."

"As long as we're going, I guess that's all that counts." Tunnie chuckled. "O.C., you have a way of avoiding questions. Did you make that knife or did somebody else?"

O.C. lifted the corners of his mouth. "I guess I do. If you really want to know, an Indian boy made it for me. That little feller ain't a kid now. Matter of fact, he's a mountain of a man. They call him Little Boy Horse."

"That's a hell of a name."

"He's a hell of a man, but when he gave me this knife... well, it was a long, long time ago." He gazed into the distance. Little Boy Horse's small face appeared in his mind's eye. A long time ago? Hell, a lifetime ago.

O.C. caught hold of the saddle horn when his horse started acting up. The tired horse reared, lunged and acted like he wanted to run. "Whoa boy, whoa." He pulled back on the reins.

"What's wrong with him?"

"I'm not for sure, but I think he might smell water. Let's give 'em their heads and see what happens."

His horse broke into a fast lope first, then Jack's mount followed. O.C. pointed ahead. "They're headed for that canyon up there. That must be where the water is."

When the horses entered the box canyon, their hoofs hitting the hard dirt floor echoed like thunder around them. The horses slowed when they reached a small group of trees.

"There's your water O.C."

"Water it is! Clear and clean." He dismounted and let his horse's head go. "We can't let them drink too much too fast." He got down on his knees, cupped his hands and drank the cool beverage of nature he'd captured. Damn! That was the best stuff he'd ever tasted. He glanced at Tunnie who was doing the same.

The water ran down his neck and back as he splashed the liquid over his head and face. A shiver raced through his body, goose flesh rose on his skin. Was it the coolness of the water or something else? He couldn't quite put his finger on what he was feeling. Jack's voice drew his attention.

"Did you hear that echo, O.C.? Hell, I ain't never heard anything like that. Have you?"

He shuddered. "No, and I don't like it. Somethin's strange."

Glancing around, he commented, “It don’t feel right here.” Every word he said echoed violently back at them.

Even the clank of the empty canteens came back at them three fold. The wind blew eerily through the tops of the trees and dust stirred on the canyon floor.

“The horses are done.” O.C. corked the last of his canteens as he studied the area. The trees thickened as the creek widened. Huge rock boulders towered toward the unending sky. “Spirits are strong here. We’d be better off if we take our water and move on.”

“I’m with you.” Jack placed the last leather strap of his water cans around the saddle horn. “Let’s go.”

Silent, O.C. sat in his saddle and took in his surroundings. The tall rock walls reminded him of the walls of his cell, but these walls he would eventually escape. At least he planned on it. They wound their way through the canyon. He was glad for Jack’s company. It was a strange place. Even being a man, it was intimidating.

“Cliff dwellers.”

The sound of his friend's voice gave him a start. “What?” He glanced up ahead at the holes and caves in the tall rock walls. “Cliff dwellers?”

“Yeah, those are Indian ruins up there.”

“What’s a cliff dweller.”

“I don’t exactly know, O.C., but I’ve heard stories that some type of Indians used to build their homes up here in these rocks. They were trying to get away from something or somebody. Probably something.”

The way Jack slowly raised his eyes and looked at him sent a chill up his spine, then he started to laugh. “Wouldn’t it be somethin’ if we’ve lived the lives we have, then be scared to death by a spook?”

Jack cackled. “Sure would.”

O.C. took a deep breath and continued to laugh. “God, it feels good to laugh. I don’t know how long it’s been.”

Suddenly, Jack got quiet and stopped his horse. O.C. didn’t like the look on the man’s face as he stared straight ahead. He knew he didn’t want to see what Tunnie was looking at, but he forced himself to turn his head forward. “What the hell?”

"My God, O.C., what is it?"

He couldn't quite make out what was in the distance, and wasn't sure he wanted to. Three poles stood in the middle of the canyon floor with animals hanging from them. "I don't know. Let's get closer."

"Something's amiss here."

Keeping his horse at a steady gate, O.C. said, "It sure is, but what are we gonna do, go back?"

"Guess not." Tunnie stayed at O.C.'s side.

After only a few more yards, his breath caught in his throat, his stomach churned and threatened to spill itself on the hard dirt below. He pulled back on the reins, stopped his horse. It wasn't animals; it was three people impaled on the tall spike-like trees.

Chapter Nineteen

The bloated, battered bodies all seemed to stare back at him. O.C. felt like someone was staring a hole through his back. He turned and glanced behind them. Nothing. When he looked forward again he asked, "What are they, Jack? You know this country and its people better than I do, don't ya?" He watched Jack swallow hard, his face lost all color and his voice trembled when he spoke.

"They look like Mexicans, but I'm not sure."

The minutes of silence, while he studied the dead bodies, seemed like hours. "Why would someone do this?" Jack just shook his head. O.C. knew the other man didn't have the answer either.

"What do you think we should do with them?"

O.C. heart sank to the pit of his belly. "Leave 'em right where they are and get the hell outta here."

Jack met his gaze. "Just like that? Leave them?"

"That's what I said. We've got problems of our own."

"It don't seem right."

The hair stood up on the back of his neck. "You forget, Tunnie, I buried those folks Cloud killed and I was on burial detail at the prison. I'm tired of putting bodies in holes." He meant it, too. Tugging the reins to the right, he turned his horse around. "There's a trail there going out of the canyon."

He led his horse up the trail. Slowly he made his way toward the top of the gorge with Jack following close. The gruesome sight below left behind.

"Man, I never saw anything like that in my entire life, O.C."

"Forget it. That's the only thing we can do." It was easy for him to say that, but he knew he'd carry the sight in his mind forever.

When they reached the top of the canyon, it seemed he could see forever. It was a vast expanse of land.

"O.C., that might be Texas. At least it should be."

The hills and valley below were a beautiful sight. Even a few trees dotted the landscape to the southwest. He stared across the land. It was as though he could see all the way to the Mississippi. He envisioned his family. Tears threatened to well in his eyes and the lump in his throat felt like it would last forever. He was getting closer.

He spurred his horse into movement. "Let's put some distance between this place and where we camp tonight. I don't think we're in a very hospitable place."

Down the side of the hill they rode. He loped his horse whenever he could. They traveled on. The trees and brush had gotten thick and the terrain slowed them. As darkness approached, he figured it had been about five hours since they'd left the canyon behind. His back was aching, he knew the horses were tired and he could use a good cup of coffee and something to eat.

"Jack, you ready to set up camp?"

"Yeah, I'm wore out. There's a big tree. Let's set up there. Looks like a good place."

"No, not the trees. Let's get in that heavy brush." He pointed to the spot he meant.

"Hell, we can't even hardly get through there."

"That's just the point. No one else can either." As they dismounted, he was glad Jack didn't argue. Leading the way, they waded through the thick underbrush until he thought they had reached a safe place. "No fires tonight. We don't want any company. Especially from people who put folks on sharp sticks. If anyone comes through this brush, we'll hear 'em.

"We'd probably better leave the horses saddled, too. Just in case we have to leave in a hell of a hurry."

"I gotcha. I'll grab the bed rolls." Jack returned with the

gear in hand. "You really think someone's following us?"

He took his bedding from Jack. "Yep."

"How'd you get so good at this, O.C.? How do you know someone's out there?"

O.C. laid his bed on the ground. "I don't know how I know. I just know."

"Seems like you have a sixth sense or something."

"Did you ever play hide and seek when you were a kid?"

"Yeah, I guess I did."

"Ever play it with an Indian?"

"No," answered Jack.

"Then you've never played it at all."

"Holy, shit, O.C."

O.C. chuckled, but he knew their situation wasn't a laughing matter. He made himself as comfortable as possible. The thin bed roll didn't do much to keep the ground's roughness away from his back side, but it would have to do.

He dozed, but it seemed like he was sleeping with one eye open. Once in a while the shriek of a night hawk made his blood run cold. Then in the distance, he heard something. What was it?

Placing his ear to the dirt, he listened. Yep, he was right. He reached over to wake up Jack. "Horses are coming. You're snorin'. Wake up 'til they pass, but don't move."

They lay motionless until the sound faded away. Barely able to relax, he waited for the sun to come up. Dammit, who were the riders, and were they looking for him and Tunnie?

At the first light of dawn, O.C. watched the skyline for movement. Anything at all that was unusually different. He jumped when Jack broke the silence.

"See anything?"

"Hell's bells, Jack, don't talk so loud." He took a deep breath to settle his heart to a slower rhythm. "Not yet. But one thing's for damn sure, we had company pass by. I just wish I knew where they set up camp. It'll be our luck they stopped at that tree you suggested yesterday."

Man, a hot cup sounded good, but with no fire that was impossible. O.C. slowly made his way just outside of camp to relieve himself. The orange glow of sunrise gradually turned to daybreak and in the distance he studied the big tree. His hunch was right, there were half a dozen horses standing under it, he assumed the riders were on the ground asleep. He'd be damned if he'd go out of this world like those poor SOB's they'd seen in the canyon.

He crawled back to Jack and started to roll up his bed. His voice was just above a whisper. "Come on, they're under the tree like I suspected. Let's slip the hell out of here before they wake up."

Jack readied to leave. "How many?"

"Six or seven I'd say." By the time Jack returned from his morning duties, O.C. had the horses ready to go. "They got here real late. I figure we can get a couple of hours head start on 'em."

"Wonder who they are?"

O.C. grabbed the reins of his horse. "I don't have any idea, and I ain't waitin' around to see. I can tell you one thing for sure, they ain't Indians."

Jack finished tying his roll onto the back of his horse then started to mount. O.C. grabbed his arm. "Let's walk the horses out of this brush. Soon as we get to a clearing, we'll make tracks."

"Sounds damn good to me."

The brush was thick and O.C. figured it took them about twenty minutes to get through them. He was relieved to see the clearing ahead. "We'll go a couple hundred yards into the clearing before we mount." Jack's nod told him the man understood.

As soon as he thought they were out of hearing distance of the visitors, he got in the saddle and they rode east as fast and hard as they could without tiring the horses too fast.

The pace he'd set lasted for more than two hours. The sun was well in the sky before they slowed. The horse Jack had given him was strong and he was thankful for that. When they reached their destination, he'd make sure the horse was well rewarded for his hard work.

"O.C.?"

"Yeah."

"How do you know those people weren't Indians?"

"If they had been the kind of Indians I've always known,

we'd be dead right now. Simple as that. Swamp Indians scout the area before they set up camp. They would've found us."

"I don't know who they were," Jack remarked. "But they set camp up real quiet. Like they were hiding from someone, too. They also left their horses saddled. They must have some kind of experience, except they camped under the tree I wanted to camp under."

O.C. nodded. "They made one hell of a mistake there. I figure if it's Indians that are on their trail, they won't get far."

"I don't see how you're so sure they're not Indians. I mean, they wouldn't be swamp Indians out here."

"Swamp or prairie Indians, I never seen a lot of them rich enough to buy saddles, or even wanted one for that matter."

Jack laughed. "That makes me feel awful dumb. But you're right. You're damn sure right."

Chapter Twenty

"Damn, Joe, would ya look at that!"

Joe followed Charles' awe struck gaze. Towering buildings stood like giants in the skyline of St. Louis. People of all shapes, sizes and colors bustled along the waterfront as the barge slowly rocked its way into port. "Ain't it somethin'."

The creaking of the ramp being lowered caused uneasiness in the animals on deck. He turned his attention away from the view of St. Louis and focused on tasks at hand. "Charles, grab the mules. They might bolt any second and we can't handle that."

"Whoa, Shadrack, it's alright boy," Charles said grabbing the mule's bit.

"Carl, make sure everything's secure in the wagons. We're gonna be the first ones off and ain't nobody gonna wanna wait on us." Joe turned toward the rest of his party. "Johnny, Horn, y'all ready?"

"Yep," Johnny answered.

"Levi?"

"Yes, sir."

The apron ramp was settled on the ground and the way was open for them to disembark. Joe was thankful the angle of the ramp was level with the dock so the mules wouldn't have the weight of the wagons pushing them along. "Let's go then."

Joe got in the driver's seat of the old wagon, while Charles manned the other. The mules' hooves clickidy-clacked against the wood beneath them and the wagon wheels squeaked in protest of needing grease. Joe made note of it in his mind and realized how glad he was to be leaving the barge.

Unlike being gawked at onboard, no one on the streets of St. Louis looked their way, or seemed the least bit interested in his two big Indian friends. The less people that paid attention to them, the better and more at ease he felt. It was good to be on solid ground again.

"Hey, Joe, look at all them guys wearing the strange looking hats," Carl said. "Think you can buy me one?"

"What's with you and hats, little brother?" He glanced over at Johnny one Horn who proudly wore the top hat Carl had insisted on getting him.

Carl shrugged. "I don't know, but can I have one?"

His little brother's enthusiasm brought a smile to his face. Hell, Carl wasn't little anymore; he was as tall as Joe now days, so younger brother would probably be more appropriate. "We'll see. Maybe after we get everything else we need. A wagon and team of horses for Levi, and travelin' supplies come first."

From the looks of things, the rush to the west was in full swing. Wagon trains were being organized, but he had already decided they wouldn't join a train. They would make this trip alone and on their own time.

Levi walked up beside the wagon. "Boss, these folks will try to sell you everything under the sun. Just tell them no and they'll leave you alone."

"Okay. Hey, tell me somethin' Levi, do many wagon trains leave from St. Louie?"

"Some, and some leave from St. Joe, but most of 'em leave from the town of Sedalia, Missouri."

Joe nodded and took in his surroundings. He'd never seen the likes of the goings on in this city. Panhandlers everywhere begging for anything they could get, women sitting on balconies waving at them to come up and join them, music from surrounding saloons mixing in a jumbled mess in his ears, and drunks staggering from side to side.

Making their way through the streets, he was glad to finally get a little further into town and away from the immediate riverfront.

A well-dressed man and woman came out of a dry goods store and Joe took the opportunity to ask them some questions. "'Scuse me, sir, you from around here?"

The man put his arm out for the lady to take his elbow. "Yes, why do you ask?"

"We're in need of another wagon, and was wonderin' if you might know of one."

"No, I don't believe I do, so move along, please."

"John, wait," the woman said. "That man inside the store, I think I heard him talking about prairie schooner, or... something." She shrugged.

Meeting Joe's gaze, the man said, "I don't know, but you might go inside and see."

Joe jumped to the ground and watched the two walk away. "Wonder if everyone in St. Louis is that uppity?" He shook his head when he looked at his brood of travelers. Everyone needed a bath, haircut and some clean clothes. No wonder those folks snubbed them. "Y'all watch the rigs, I'll be back."

"May I help you?"

A woman with a white apron folded some material on a table beside the door. Her eyes were kind and Joe felt at ease talking to her. "Yes, ma'am, possibly. I heard there was a fella in here needs to sell a wagon."

"Why, yes, that would be Bill Adams. He's right over there talking to my husband."

He followed her gaze and saw the two men. "Thank you much, ma'am."

She smiled and nodded. "You're welcome."

Approaching the store keeper and the other man, Joe stayed quiet until they finished their conversation, then he asked, "Sir, you got a wagon for sale?" The well-dressed man looked at Joe like he'd said something wrong.

"Yes, but she's not just a wagon, she's a prairie schooner, fully dressed with a water barrel, jockey box, iron wheels, supply boxes on the outside as well as the inside and more. She's big, too."

"How'd you come about getting it?"

"Wife and I were going to make the trip west, but she fell ill and now we can't go."

"Can I look at her?" It seemed strange calling a wagon she and her, but if that's what the man wanted, that's what he'd get.

"Son, I need to get two hundred dollars for that schooner. Maybe you should look at something else; I don't think you can afford her."

Joe reached to shake the man's hand. "Name's Joe Armstrong, mister, and I got the money." He watched a questioning glance travel between the man and the storekeeper.

"Robert Foster." He accepted the shake. "She's a heavy rig and it takes six mules to pull her. They come with it."

"Sounds good to me."

"She's right out back. We can look at her now."

Following Foster down the stairs to the street, Joe saw anticipation on his crews' faces. The storekeeper's wife stood on the porch straightening goods. "Ma'am, would you watch our wagons while we take a look at the schooner?"

"Of course, y'all go right ahead."

It pleased Joe to know everyone in St. Louis wasn't like the couple they'd encountered only minutes earlier. They rounded the corner of the back of the building and there she stood in all her glory.

Charles ran his hand down the long side panel. "This is the biggest wagon I ever saw!"

"Me, too," Carl said with awe.

"Levi, what do you think?" Joe asked.

"It's everything we'll need and more. Why, hell, it's brand new."

Joe met Robert Foster's gaze. "Looks like we'll take her."

"You sure kid? Like I said, she's two hundred dollars and I can't come down on that price. That's what I paid for her."

Two hundred and some dollars was all Joe had left from when he'd cashed in for the first three gold pieces, but he knew there had to be a bank close by. He reached into the top pocket of his overalls and pulled out the bills. "Two hundred it is."

"Damn, you really do have the money."

Joe counted out the currency into the man's hand. "Did you think I was lyin' to ya?"

"Well, no, but…" He scratched his head. "Where'd you get this kind of cash?" The man put his hands in the air and shook his head. "Never mind, it's none of my business."

"It's okay, Mr. Foster, we saved it up to make the trip, that's all." His answer seemed to appease the man's curiosity and that eased some of Joe's tension about the question. He knew he'd have to be careful spending money because it would arouse too much suspicion.

"The mules are at the livery. I'll go fetch them for you." Foster placed the money in his pocket and took off toward the front of the building then to the west.

"Mules?" Charles asked, "I thought we were gettin' horses."

Levi stepped forward. "I've made trips like this before, not as long, but just the same, they's hard on livestock. Horses ain't strong enough." He bent to look under the schooner. "Sides, I talked to a mountain man on the barge, his name was Earl Stockman. He said the same thing while he was admirin' the two horses on y'all's wagon up front."

Joe knew the man Levi was talking about. He saw a knowing look in the cook's eyes. Did Levi know something about the team that he didn't? "Go on."

"Stockman said he recognized those horses. They belonged to an old man they found dead a few miles from the ferry towards Vicksburg. Had his throat cut from ear to ear."

Looking around quickly to make sure neither Carl nor Charles said anything. The look of horror was etched across the two younger men's faces. They both stared at Horse and Horn.

Levi continued. "From what I understand, the man was an old cutthroat himself. Mountain man said y'all was lucky to still be kickin' after dealin' with him. His name was Cross and he was wanted by the law, dead or alive so ain't nobody lookin' for who killed him."

With a hand on each of his brother's shoulders, Joe leaned forward to make sure he wasn't overheard. "It's done and over. We don't need to be askin' any questions. Pa used to say, it's survival before anything else. Remember that, you might come up on a situation yourself and you don't know what you might have to do."

"So much dyin'," Carl said. "Everywhere we go people are dyin' or gettin' killed. It just don't make no sense."

Joe put his arm around Carl's shoulder. "This ain't our little cotton farm back home, brother, this is the world and it ain't all nice. It's life, that's all." He gave his brother a reassuring slap on the back then said, "Now, Charles, let's go get the other wagons and bring 'em back here."

When he approached the front of the store, the nice woman watching their wagons sat on a rocking chair, the sun kissed her face with its rays. His ma came to mind and his heart ached with missing her. He took the bottom step and stood in front of her.

"Ma'am, you think it would be okay if we lead these wagons to the back where there's no traffic. We'd like to arrange stuff before we take out."

She got up and walked to the edge of the porch. "I think that will be just fine."

He stepped down and grabbed the lead to one of the teams while Charles got the other. "Thanks." Her voice brought Joe's attention once again and he met her pleasant gaze.

"And young man."

"Yes, 'am?"

"There's a barber shop and a bath house right up the street. I think if you can afford it, you should all give it a visit. If you have clean clothes, they'll even wash your dirty ones for you, so you'll be nice and clean to start your trip."

Her smiling eyes told him she meant no harm. It was nice to have some motherly advice for a change. Laughing was something he hadn't done in a long time, but he couldn't help but chuckle at her statement. "We'll do that, ma'am, thank ya."

Joe led the wagon, heavy with gold, to the back of the building. He would have to get coins from their hiding place so he could get more cash from a bank. There was absolutely no other traffic behind the store, but Foster would be back soon with the mules, so he'd have to hurry.

"Johnny, you and Horse take watch up front. Carl, you and Charles watch back here. If you see that anyone's coming at all, let me know, but don't yell, we don't want to draw attention."

It was time to let Levi in on the secret. Joe's heart jumped to his throat. Was he really going to tell this almost stranger of the gold? Yes, he trusted the man. Why he didn't exactly know, he just had to go with his gut feeling. However, he was glad that all of the gold wouldn't be exposed when they opened the hidden hatch, only a few coins.

"Levi, come over and help me."

"What's this all about?"

"You'll see, but we gotta be quick. Jump up in the wagon and move that barrel in the center then dust the hay from where it's sittin'."

Levi did what he was told. Joe pulled up on the piece of rope knotted into the hole and lifted the trap door. Sun glistened off of the shiny gold and he heard the older man draw a deep breath. He knew exactly what Levi was feeling. He'd done the same thing the first time he'd seen the riches.

"Damnation, boss, that there's g-gol–"

"Shhhh, somebody might hear ya. I gotta take some out to go get some money from the bank." Joe took out a few pieces of the treasure then shut the door back. "We need to cover that up, fast."

Without Joe having to say a word, Levi put the straw back into place, then situated the barrel atop it. "Perfect, Levi, thanks. Now, I know you've got questions, and I'll answer 'em all, but not 'til we get outta earshot of the towns people."

Quick footsteps behind him made Joe turn. Johnny One Horn stood tall in front of him. "Horn?"

"The man with the mules comes."

"It's okay, we're done. Send him on back."

"Horse, you and Johnny should probably get into the schooner. We don't want any more attention than we have to have and folks can't see you from out here. The two did as he asked and it made him feel older in some way. Was he really the 'boss' as Levi called him? Pride surged through him. Maybe he was growing up after all.

CHAPTER TWENTY ONE

The bank was bigger than any Joe had ever seen. To him the ceiling looked sky high and it was painted. "Don't that just beat ya."

"Excuse me?"

He turned to see a law man of some sort standing next to him. "Huh?"

"You said something and looked like you might be lost. Is everything okay?"

"Y-yes, sir, fine."

"I'm one of the bank guards here, they call me a door man. I have to check everyone to make sure you ain't got a gun. There's been lots of robberies as of late so tell me, what's that bulgin' in your pockets?"

Joe saw the man's hand grasp the fire arm on his side and quickly pulled his hands out of his pockets. He stared up at the bank door man unsure of what to say. The guard's look turned suspicious and he took a step toward him. Joe gulped down a breath. "It's ah." What was wrong with his tongue? It wouldn't let him talk.

"Maybe I'd better take a look."

Placing his hands protectively over his pants pockets he forced himself to speak, "Not here, sir, please. You got a room or somethin' we can go in?" He remembered the teller at the first bank had taken him behind the teller's desk.

The tall man pointed. "Right over there."

Once inside the small cubical, Joe pulled out one of the gold coins and lay it on the table. He watched the bank guard's eyes grow wide.

"Holy sakes." He squinted his eyes and studied Joe. "Where'd you get that?"

"It was our mother's. She passed away last month. Me and my brothers are tryin' to move on and we need regular money. We want to buy cattle, maybe some horses." He swallowed hard and tried to still his racing heart. He'd told the man the truth, surely he'd let him go.

"Mercy, kid, you'll go a long way with that much cash. You'd better keep a watchful eye. Anyone finds out you got money like that they'll be out to cut your throat and take it."

"Yes, sir." The bank guard led the way to a teller's booth and stood there while Joe cashed the coins. He felt as if the man were lending his size as a shield so that no one would see the transaction, but in the open space of the bank, it was impossible for no one to see.

At the window, he placed the coins on the counter in front of the cashier. Surprised the man had no more reaction then he did, Joe said, "I'd like to cash these in, please."

The clerk behind the cage nodded. "I'll be right back, I have to weigh this."

Joe waited and studied the building. How could the ones who painted the ceiling of the bank have gotten up that high? It baffled him to no end. One thing was for sure, he'd never seen a ladder that tall, and wouldn't have wanted to be the one standing on it.

The teller cleared his throat. "Sir, your money."

"Sure, sorry." He rested his hand on the counter, palm up, and waited for the teller to count out the booty.

"Do you have something to put this in?"

The stuffy teller eyed him with distaste. He was sure now a bath and haircut would have to fit into the plan somewhere. "My pockets."

"No satchel or bag of any sort?"

"Nope."

"Very well, but you're going to need something other than just your pockets to hold everything. Let me see if I can find you something."

In a moment, Joe saw the man approach with what looked like a potato sack only smaller. His mind raced. Just how much were those few coins worth in weight? Had he been taken in Vicksburg? He watched the man put gold coins and paper money on the counter, then he began to stick it in the bag.

"Now, there is three hundred in twenty dollar gold coins, fifty in ten dollar coins and seven hundred in Union Greenbacks."

Joe looked at the stacks of money. More than he'd ever seen. He was experiencing a lot of things for the first time in his life, and realized he liked it. However, he didn't trust the greenbacks. They might not be any good where he was going, but gold would be good everywhere.

"Ummm, if you don't mind, I'd like it all in gold coins. No paper."

The man shook his head, turned and went back to the safe, taking the bills with him. When he returned, he put many more gold coins onto the counter. By this time, Joe was aware that people around him were beginning to whisper. When the teller pushed the bag toward him, he was glad the guard still stood beside him.

"Thank you, sir. Next!"

Escorted by the door man to the exit, Joe kept a watchful eye around him. Once outside, he noticed two men following him. He'd seen one of them inside the bank, but not the other. From the looks of the rifles they were holding, the second man must have been outside holding them. He was almost to the wagon when one of the men caught up and touched him on the shoulder.

"Mister," the man from inside the bank said. "We seen that big wagon and only these two boys and that old man around, and you of course. We was wonderin' if you might need some hands to help ya get where you're goin'."

The second man stepped forward. He was the shorter of the two. "We're right handy with these buffalo guns. Carryin' all that money, you might need protection."

Movement came from the front of the schooner. Joe watched the tarp open in the center just enough to slip the barrel of a buffalo gun through. He met the first man's gaze.

"I see you already got help, but believe me, we wasn't the only ones to see all your money. There are some bad people in these parts."

Joe was comfortable with the protection of Johnny and Horn, but he would need more hands as they traveled and bought livestock. Two more guns wouldn't be bad to have either. He studied the strangers. "What's y'all's names?"

The taller man stepped forward. "I'm Nate Wilson, this here's my partner Bull Carry. We know this part of the country pretty good. Tell ya what, we'll work for a month for food. If after that you think we're worth it, you can pay us trail wages."

Considering his options, Joe couldn't see not giving the men a chance. After all, if he didn't want to keep them, he didn't have to, but he realized he should feel them out a little more before making his decision.

"You boys ever been west?" Joe asked, the rifle still leveled steady on them. He could tell Nate was the spokesman for the two.

"Been across Kansas and a ways into Colorado. Went buffalo huntin' there. Wrong thing to do. It's a dangerous place to travel through. The Sioux are mad as hell over the buffalo slaughter. A white man can lose his hair pretty damn fast if you don't watch out."

"I see." Joe nodded. He liked getting this kind of helpful information. "Go on."

"The smart thing to do is buy enough grub to cross the territory without havin' to kill anything. If they see you kill as much as a single turkey, you might find your party scalped."

Nate seemed knowledgeable enough, but Bull hadn't said much. However, they both looked physically fit and able to help with most anything. "You two sure you want to try a month with no pay?" They looked at each other and he saw them give an affirmative nod and knew their answer.

"Just one more thing you oughta know." Joe gestured toward the schooner. "Under the bonnet of that prairie schooner are two men you don't wanna cross. They're like my brothers, but make no mistake, they're not yours." Joe was sure to make eye contact with the pair, if nothing else, to make his point.

"Take heed in what I say. Don't look either one of 'em directly in their eyes like you are me now, unless they are talking to you. I'm tellin' ya, if you cross one of 'em the other one will probably kill you so fast you won't know you're dead 'til the next day. They'll do that for me and my brothers, too."

Both men bobbed their heads up and down as if they understood. Levi had accepted the same speech as truth, but Joe couldn't be certain about these two. Nate seemed to be the smarter one, Bull, he wasn't sure of. He did know, though, that he had to be sure these men were not going to try to double cross him.

"They're Indians, they're big, and they're like ghosts in the night. It's said they can track a spider, so please watch your asses. It might save your lives." He cleared his throat, still clutching the bag of gold in his hand. "So, you still wanna go?"

Bull announced, "We ain't never seen a man yet that we're afraid of. I figure we can hold our own."

Joe saw the questioning look Nate shot Bull and knew the man didn't speak for his partner. It pleased him to know Nate had listened to him.

He walked over to the wagon and kept his eye on Nate and Bull to see what their reactions would be. "Horse, Horn, come on out." Pride ran free when the mighty Johnny One Horn and Little Boy Horse stepped from behind the covering and glared at the two men.

Fighting the urge to smile, he heard his younger brothers snicker when both of the cowboys paled and quickly averted their gazes to the opposite side of the street. Joe glanced up at his two friends and winked. Now he felt okay about adding them on as hands and was even more affirmed when he heard what Nate said to his partner.

"Bull, if those big Indians are friends with this young man and his brothers, then I'd say they're probably pretty good boys. Let's lend a hand to get the schooner over to the supply store and help get her loaded."

Joe handed the bag of gold to Johnny. "First, we're all gonna go to the barber shop and get cleaned up. I'll pay for it. After that, we'll go back to the general store where we got the schooner to get what we need."

"I don't want a bath, Joe."

"Stop whinnin', Carl, you look a sight and smell even worse. You ain't gettin' out of it and neither is anyone else."

Carl smiled. "Even Johnny and Horse?"

He heard a low grunt. Joe knew it was a weak protest, then he heard Johnny's voice.

"Little man, Carl, if it will make you smell better, we will do it."

Sneering, Carl said, "Hell, Horn, you don't smell like perfume yourself. They probably won't even have a tub big enough and you'll have to take your bath in a dirty ole horse trough."

Joe started laughing when Johnny One Horn lunged at Carl and the boy took off down the street like lightning. "Y'all grab some clothes and let's get bathed so we can get the hell outta here."

"Why, you clean up real nice." The storekeeper's wife made a circle around Joe. "What a handsome young man you are."

"Thank you, ma'am." Heat rushed to his face and Joe hoped no one noticed he was blushing.

"Where are your folks, son?"

He thought of his ma and pa. He missed them something awful. "Far as I know, they've both gone on to be with our Maker. Least Ma has for sure."

She put her hand to his cheek. "You poor dears. You mean you're not sure about your pa?"

"No, ma'am, he went away one day and just never came back. Ma passed and we decided to go west through Kansas and Colorado. Maybe start a cattle ranch."

Patting his face she said, "You have high expectations young man." She lowered her gaze then looked at him again. "I had a son who would have been just about your age, but he drowned in the Missouri."

The sadness in her eyes tore at Joe's heart. "Sorry to hear that."

"It was a long time ago." She cleared her throat and swiped a finger under one of her eyes. "Well, now, y'all be careful out there. It ain't very friendly country." She met his gaze. "What's your name?"

"Armstrong. I'm Joe, and my brothers are Charles and Carl."

She smiled. "Well, Joe Armstrong," she stuck out her hand. "Myrt Rogers, it's nice to meet you. Now, you'd better get your supplies so you boys can get on the trail."

He didn't remember ever shaking a woman's hand before, but it was small and soft in his hand. "Nice to meet you, too, Mrs. Rogers." He turned to see everyone staring at him and the woman. "What are y'all lookin' at? Charles, get a couple sacks of tators. We'll need blankets, bacon, beans and… hell, Levi, get that new bedroll you wanted, finish getting what we need while we start loadin'."

One thing Joe didn't like was being embarrassed. He didn't know why the woman's affection toward him made him react like that when everyone was looking at him. Maybe he missed his ma more than he thought, and he was afraid his friends and family would think him less of a man for it. It didn't matter. He was who he was and that was all there was to it.

Bull turned to Nate, picked up a bag of flour and loaded it into the schooner. "You sure we want this job? Those two Indians are about the meanest looking men I ever seen."

"Damn, Bull, we need this job. I need this job and want it, too. If you don't want to go, don't."

"But we're partners."

"Yeah, and you know I've always wanted a horse ranch. I think Joe and his brothers are just the answer."

"How are they gonna help you by just payin' you trail wages?" Bull heaved in another flower sack.

"When I said I think these boys are good boys, I meant it. If I'm right, they've got more gold than they're letting on about." Nate, put a container of lard in the wagon. "Anyway, I'm not after what's theirs, I just think they're fair and I intend to become just like family to 'em. After all, I ain't got no family."

Shaking his head Bull replied, "Ok, but I seen death himself sittin' in back of that wagon when them Indians showed themselves."

"Yeah, well, like Joe said, you don't cross 'em, you ain't

got nothing to worry about."

"Humph!"

"Howdy, names Levi. I'm the cook of this here outfit. Didn't get to say much to ya at the barber shop, but reckin we'll get to know each other real good before this trip's over."

"Speakin' of that, where are we travelin' to?" Bull asked.

"Don't rightly know, exactly. West is all I was told. I think they's wantin' to kick up a ranch or somethin'. Maybe somewhere on the plains, but I'm just guessin' on that."

"Guess that's good enough, long as we get our money when it's time."

Levi shook his head. "I don't think you'll have any problem with that. Everything Joe's told me he'd do, he's done. He's an honest man."

"We'll need some shotguns, shells, pistol's, bullets, holsters—"

"You plan on running into trouble do you?"

"Mr. Rogers, I just wanna be prepared if somethin' does come up."

"I understand. With all the supplies y'all got, and these weapons, you've just about bought me out." The storekeeper smiled. "That's more than I'd sell in a month around here. I mean, we have people buy supplies for the wagon trains, but they can't afford anything like this." He stuck out his hand. "I really appreciate it."

Joe shook the man's hand. "Well, we appreciate you and the Mrs." Carl's voice came from behind and Joe turned to see what he was talking about.

"What do they call those hats everyone around here's wearin'? The ones like those up on the wall?"

Mr. Rogers took a hat down. "They're sometimes called 'Boss of the plains'. Mostly cowboys wear them. The tall crown provides insulation and the wide brim gives you shade. It can also keep the rain out of your eyes. They're mostly waterproof. Folks going west also wear top hats and derbies. These are mostly worn by riders on horseback and are sometimes called trail hats, but generally the ones who actually wear one call it the cowboy hat.

Remembering when they first got off the barge Carl had asked if he could have one of these hats, Joe decided to get them all one. "Mr. Rogers, give us seven of them cowboy hats. One for each of us."

"Only seven? But there's eight of y'all."

Joe nodded, the man was right. "Yes, sir, but you see, my brother Carl got Johnny a top hat. It fits his personality pretty good, so he don't really need one."

"Fair enough," said Rogers, "Let's get y'all fitted. What's the purpose of your trail drive?"

"We're goin' west to start a cattle ranch. We ain't got no cows or bulls yet. I figure we might pick up a few on the way, or just wait 'til we get to where we're goin'."

The storekeeper chose another hat and placed it on Carl's head. "Too big, we'll find one don't worry." He glanced at Joe and kept trying to fit Carl. "I heard they have completed the railroad from Selina to Abilene Kansas. There are a lot of cattle drives coming into Selina now. You could probably buy some of those trail cattle straight from a drive. Anyway, makes sense to me."

It sounded logical to Joe and was damn strong advice. "That's good information. I'll take it into consideration."

Mr. Rogers patted the top of the hat he'd put on Carl's head. "There, now that's a perfect fit."

Myrt Rogers approached. "Now, you make one good looking cowboy young Mr. Armstrong. You'd better hurry out of town before some young lady tries to snag you for sure."

Carl's face turned red and Joe was sure he was about to say aw shucks or something. When he simply turned and walked outside, Joe joined the others in laughter. "That was priceless ma'am. He'll be watchin' out the corner of his eye for girls comin' after him now. By the way, which is the best way out of town, Mr. Rogers?"

He listened closely to what the man said as the others went out to the wagons. "You've been mighty helpful. Thank you, sir."

Joe walked out liking the way the cowboy hat felt on his head and feeling, in some way, tougher. "We all loaded up, men?" It boosted his self-esteem to hear the hired help say yes sir. He walked to the back of the prairie schooner and looked inside.

Even though the wagon was fully loaded, it still looked big. Everything from tin cups and plates, guns and ammunition to extra saddles, was in its proper place. A couple of chairs sat on the floor and there was plenty of room for them all to be able to get in out of the weather if need be.

Pleased with the way everything had fallen into place. Joe climbed onto the driver's seat of the gold wagon. He glanced around at everyone. "Y'all ready?" Everyone nodded their willingness and Joe glanced up at the sun and gauged it to be about one o'clock, time to get started. "Then, let's go, boys."

Chapter Twenty Two

THE PRAIRIE

The road out of St. Louis was well-traveled and Joe was pleased that through the afternoon they made good time. Light was getting lower in the sky and it would be dusk in a couple of hours. They needed to stop and settle before dark.

Trees formed a line not too far ahead. Joe pulled his team to a halt and waited for the rest to catch up. "It's time to stop for the night." He pointed toward the trees. "We'll go over there, there's probably a creek or somethin'."

Carl squinted into the late afternoon sun. "There ain't too many trees on these plains is there. Not much cover if you're tryin' to stay outta sight."

"I'm thinkin' the same thing Carl is. You're right, Joe, that would be a good place to make camp. At least we could run into the trees and bush for cover if we needed."

"Well, let's get movin' then. The longer we sit here talkin' about it, the longer it's gonna be 'til I get supper started and I'm gettin' hungry."

Levi slapped the reins and went to the head of the train. Joe waited for him to pass and wondered why he was in such a hurry. They were all hungry, but he was almost trotting the mules.

He glanced around and saw Johnny One Horn walking up to his wagon. It was the first time he'd been out of the schooner since they left St. Louis.

"Joe, I want to ride with you. We need to talk."

"Come on up, Johnny." The old wagon creaked under the man's weight when he stepped on the side board then sat down. Joe felt short next to his Indian friend, even though he was over six feet tall himself. "Is somethin' wrong?"

"On the way out of town, while me and Boy Horse were in the wagon, we were watching."

"What were y'all lookin' for?"

Johnny nodded. "Trouble. I think we were not the only ones keeping a sharp eye."

"What do you mean?"

"There were men with Buffalo guns watching us. They didn't follow us right away, but they are probably on our trail."

"How many men?" Joe hoped they wouldn't have trouble this soon after leaving town, but from the look on the big man's face, he feared the worst.

"Many were looking, but only two we believe were no good."

"What do you think we should do?" Joe wanted to be prepared to keep everyone safe. He had faith in Horse and Horn to help him, but if there was something they thought he could lend a hand with, he would do it.

"We'll be okay until dark, then me and Horse will watch. The men did not see us looking out at them. They do not know about us, they think only six are here. The old cook saw them, too."

Levi had been on cattle drives and no telling what else he had done in his lifetime. Joe knew the man was savvy to the goings on of the trail. It explained why he was in such an all fired hurry to make camp.

"Thanks for havin' our backs all the time, my friend. I don't know what we'd do without you two."

Johnny One Horn winked at Joe then jumped off of the moving wagon. "Probably be dead by now," he yelled from behind.

The man was probably right and Joe knew it. This trip would have come to a halt long ago if it were only him and his brothers. Hell, they would most likely never have gotten the gold either. No, there was no probably to it, the gold would still be at the bottom of the swamp if not for the Indians.

Levi stopped the schooner and immediately started readying camp. He directed Joe to put the wagons in front and the creek would be at their backs. Joe liked the idea that camp would be between the two. It made for more protection.

"Biscuits and gravy with dried beef sound okay to you fellers?"

"Sounds good to me, Levi," Carl answered.

"Me, too," added Charles, "Hey, Joe, what do you want to do with the horses?"

"Take 'em creek side so they can get a drink. We'll settle them in for the night in a while."

"What the hell?"

Joe turned toward Bull's voice and forced himself not to laugh when Horse leaped out of the schooner. The huge man must have scared the daylights out of Bull. His eyes looked like they were about to pop out of his head.

"Holy crap, Nate, is he gonna kill us?"

"Kill us? What you got in your breeches, Bull, fire ants? I ain't never seen you so jumpy."

"Well, look at the big son of a bitch; he's lookin' at us like he's goin' to murder us."

Joe recognized the humor in Little Boy Horse's eyes, but was sure it looked like a death glare to the others. It amazed him at how powerful Horse was and at the same time how kind he could be. It didn't bother him to cut someone's throat; however, he'd help a motherless fawn get to its feet.

"Of course he's not gonna kill us. Settle down."

Approaching his two hired hands Joe asked, "Y'all doin' alright?" He wondered if they noticed he was grinning.

"Other'n gettin' the bjesus scared out us?"

"Shut up, Bull. No, sir, we're doin' just fine." Nate turned out his bedroll. "Last time we were out this way, there was Buffalo everywhere. Guess hunters cleaned them all out. Damn shame."

Looking across the great, flat expanse surrounding them, Joe agreed. "Sure is."

"Where'd y'all put the safety matches? I can't find 'em and

I gotta get this fire started if we're gonna eat before dark."

Joe turned toward Levi, saw Charles jump in the schooner then emerge with a large box of matches. It still surprised him how whatever was on the end of that match stick could light up by being struck against something. His stomach growled as he watched the dried grass beneath the wood ignite.

Johnny One Horn stood beside one of the horses they'd gotten with their second wagon. Joe walked up beside him and watched as Johnny petted and rubbed the large animal's mane.

"I would like to have this horse. He likes me."

The horse's neck felt warm under Joe's hand when he patted him. "Looks like he's big enough for you to ride."

"He's smart, too. I've been watching him since the day you got him." Horn looked down at Joe. "What do you think?"

There was no question in Joe's mind as to the answer. He didn't think Johnny realized he owned as much of that horse as the rest of them did. "I'd say as soon as we get a mule to take his place on the wagon, he's all yours, and if Boy Horse wants the other one, he can have him." He saw Carl walk up.

"Better watch him, Johnny." Carl ambled out and around the horses head. "He tried to bite me a couple of times."

Horn frowned. "Really? Where'd he try to bite you?"

"Right on the butt, I was too fast for him though, so he just got me by the coattail."

"You were not too fast. Like I told Joe, he is just smart. Knew your butt would taste bad. Missed on purpose."

"Funny, Johnny, real funny." Carl hopped up, sat on the back of one of the wagons and swung his legs back and forth. "So, what are you gonna name him, Smart Ass after you?"

Joe heard sniggers from the others and waited for Horn's response. He'd always been amused by the way the Indian and Carl constantly bickered at each other, but knew the love between them was strong.

"No, not Smart Ass." Johnny placed his hand to his chin and stared into the sky then a smile came over his face. "Coattail."

Laughing with the rest of the crew at the way Horn said the words, Joe realized he didn't hear Little Boy Horse's hearty chuckle. Through the dim light of evening he made a quick head count then glanced at Johnny when the laughter quieted. “Where’s Horse?”

Johnny studied the darkening horizon. “There.” He pointed.

Unable to see anything but prairie, Joe was sure Johnny knew exactly where Horse was. The Indian was watching for the two men from town. Hoping the men were smarter than to follow them, he could only imagine what would happen to the men if they did.

“I don’t see anything.” Carl said stretching his neck, peering into the grassland.

Horn dropped his hand to his side. “He is there, you look right at him. He will be out there all night. If he is not there, I will be.”

Carl glanced at his brother and jumped off the wagon. “You know, Charles, I still can’t figure how those two can disappear into thin air.”

“Yeah, I know. I wish I could do it. But I can’t, so may as well just go get some grub.”

“Here, I’ll go with ya.” Joe fell into step with his brothers. He was glad neither of them knew of the danger that might lurk in the distance.

CHAPTER TWENTY THREE

After Carl helped Levi with the supper clean up, and Johnny disappeared into the night, Joe enjoyed visiting with his brothers around the camp fire. He noticed Bull hitting the whiskey bottle pretty good and the man was getting wobbly on his feet.

Joe heard night bird sounds, only he knew they weren't birds. They were signals between Horse and Horn. Something was wrong. He sat up on his bed roll more alert to the things going on around him. Were they in danger?

Bull picked up a stick and drunkenly poked it at the fire. Joe heard a hissing noise from behind Bull but the man didn't pay attention, he just continued to stoke the flame.

Turning, Joe saw Johnny standing just at the edge of the light. He was trying to motion Bull to get down and away from the fire. Bull finally turned toward Johnny and squinted into the darkness.

The high pitched scream of a bullet ripped through the silence of the night. It hit the cowboy in the chest then Joe heard the echo of the rifle fire. His heart beat wildly as he watched Bull drop like a limp rag. One hand fell into the fire and Joe heard the flesh sizzle and wanted to retch at the smell. He knew the man was dead and there was nothing he could do.

Horse yelled and ran through camp. "Get up, get to cover. Now!"

Joe grabbed his gun, scrambled to his feet, crouched and ran, while watching Johnny grab Carl, almost carry him to the tree line. Charles, Levi and Nate ran for the trees and bushes, but Joe didn't know exactly where they were.

Sitting with his back to a tree, he stared out into total darkness. He put his hands to his mouth and made the sound of a nighthawk. Surely Carl and Charles would remember the game they used to play with the young Indian boys in the swamp.

The call of a Whippoorwill drifted through the night, then the hoot of an owl. He breathed a sigh of relief, his brothers remembered and they'd be back together soon. He stayed in place and sent his signal again, this time the others responses were somewhat closer.

Noises of Carl and Charles crawling through the bush toward him was music to his ears. They made their way to his side, sat up and leaned against the tree next to him. Then a third rustling sound came from the other side. Joe put his finger on the trigger of his six gun. "Who is it?" He whispered.

"Levi."

He'd been so worried about his brothers, he'd all but forgotten about the cook. "Where's Nate?"

"Ain't sure."

The moon had risen high enough in the sky that a silver glow waived in the prairie grass and reflected softly across the water of the nearby creek. Joe's eyes were beginning to adjust to the dim light and he searched the ground for Nate. "There, there he is hunkered down in that brush pile."

From out of nowhere, Joe saw the huge shadow of a man. Horn moved quick and silent toward Nate and with lightning speed put a hand around the man's neck and put a finger in his face warning him to stay quiet. Seeing Nate's slight nod, Joe knew he agreed and Johnny released him.

In moments the two of them joined him and the others at the tree. "What's goin' on, Johnny?" His voice was barely hearable to his own ears and he wondered if he'd even said it out loud, but he didn't dare speak again.

Once Nate got settled, everyone was quiet. A ground owl made a faraway screech and frogs croaked around the water's edge, then Johnny squatted down in front of him, his voice low.

"There are two of them."

Johnny turned his head and glanced around the tree as if he

heard something from the prairie beyond the camp. Joe felt Carl scootch a little closer to him, then the Indian cupped his hands around his mouth and made the sound of a night dove.

The blood chilling scream that came from the darkness behind them sent shivers up Joe's spine. Carl shuddered next to him and Joe saw tears glisten in the moonlight on his brother's face. He placed a hand on Carl's and patted it, but knew it was little reassurance. A deep moan emerged from the same place the scream had come from moments earlier.

"Now there is one," Johnny said.

Joe knew Little Boy Horse was alone in his feat to stop the intruders and was confident the man could do just that. He was also aware of the fact that Johnny had stayed behind to protect the rest of them. He would never cease to be amazed by the two and said a prayer of thanks for their friendship.

A rustling sound then a sharp crack shot through the night, gurgling, then a deep moan then nothing. Johnny stood and Joe looked up at his towering frame.

"They are no more." He reached for Joe's hand. "We should see about the man by the fire, but I know he is dead already."

Johnny One Horn's hand engulfed his and the strength Joe felt radiate through the man when he helped him up, was raw power. Nodding his agreement, Joe brushed off his backside, and turned when he heard Nate running into camp.

Nate kneeled next to Bull's lifeless body, turned him over and pulled his charred hand from the now dying embers. Joe walked with the rest of the crew to stand beside Nate. Blood covered the ground and the flesh of Bull's hand was burned to the bone. He heard Carl run, then lose the biscuits, gravy and dried beef they'd had for supper.

"Holy crap, Bull." Nate looked at Joe. "I've known this man for ten years. I never thought he'd end up like this."

Joe put his hand on Nate's shoulder. "Nothin' you can do. Bull was just in the wrong place at the wrong time."

"But I—"

Joe knew what the man was thinking. "It could have been any of us. It was his own decision to come on this trip, it wasn't your fault. Let it go. We'll bury him once the sun comes up."

The sound of horses approaching took Joe's attention and

he saw Nate pull his gun, stand and turn. When Johnny knocked the gun away, Joe wondered if he broke Nate's hand. Fear crossed the cowboy's face then realization.

"That's Horse." Johnny announced picking up the pistol. He handed it back to Nate.

Little Boy Horse led two horses up to camp. Over his shoulder hung two gun belts and strapped to the side of one of the saddles were two buffalo guns. Joe went over to Horse and watched him tie the reins to a wagon wheel.

"Those are men from town. Bad hearts. They wanted what was yours, ours. I gave them chance to go, but they fought and died. I saw scalps hanging from their horses. They weren't from white men. They needed to be dead. Very bad men."

Joe nodded. He couldn't find the words to express his gratitude. Hell, he never thought he'd be grateful to someone for killing another human being. It was a life lesson he'd keep with him forever.

Johnny and Nate wrapped Bull's body in an old wool blanket. Joe watched them put the dead man in the back of one of the wagons and cover him with straw. Joe felt bad for Nate, but the man seemed to be okay. He didn't have a choice, life went on.

So much had happened in just one day, Joe was spent. He walked back into camp wanting to check on Carl and Charles before they bedded down. Would he be able to sleep? He didn't know, but he was damn sure going to try.

Joining the tired brood at the campfire Levi got started again, Joe took a deep breath and rubbed the back of his neck. "What a day!"

Charles said, "Joe, what if the law comes after us for killin' them men? I mean when somebody finds their bodies."

That was something he hadn't thought about. Joe watched Nate skirt around the blood stain that had soaked into the ground.

"I don't believe they would come after us. Those bastards bushwhacked us. They killed one of us and deserved to die." Nate answered.

"Their bodies will never be found. Coyotes will take care of that. It's why we have to bury the cowboy deep or they will have him, too." Johnny squatted on his haunches then stoked the fire.

"What if there's more of 'em out there?" Carl lay on his bed roll.

"No more," Boy Horse said. "You can sleep. I saw other tribesmen in the brush; if I had not killed those men, they would have. The tribesmen took the scalps. I believe they were those of their people. Those Indian's will not bother us, they are grateful the bad hearts are dead."

Carl covered up with his blanket. "I don't know if I'll ever sleep again after what I saw tonight."

Johnny stood, gathered his bedroll and moved it next to Carl. "You will sleep, Carl, I will be here."

Joe knew his little brother was growing up fast. He was slowly but surely becoming a man, but sometimes the little boy still cried out and Johnny was always there for him. If O.C. were there, he'd be the one beside his youngest son.

"I guess we all should try to get some rest." Joe went to his belongings and lay down in the same spot he had been before the night's happening. "We have a long day ahead of us tomorrow."

****

The fire crackled and the smell of frying bacon drifted on the air as Levi was preparing breakfast. Joe went to the creek side to relieve himself and saw Charles doing the same. "How's our little brother this mornin'?"

"I don't know he was just startin' to stir when I got up."

"I bet he rested good thinking Horn was beside him all night. Did you get much sleep?"

"I slept okay. You?"

"Enough, I guess." That was a lie; he had hardly slept all night. The sounds of death kept playing over and over in his head, and in the distance he heard coyotes fighting over the dead men's flesh. It had been all he could do to lay there.

Why had those men come after them? Had they seen him in the bank? Did they see him and Levi take the gold out of the wagon? He followed Charles back to camp, got a cup of coffee and stared at his reflection in the dark liquid. It didn't matter if the pair had seen him get the gold or not. They would never bother them again, thanks to Boy Horse.

Taking a sip of the steaming hot coffee, he figured as strong as it was, Johnny had probably made it even before Levi got up. Java was one thing Johnny loved. It was the first thing he'd have in the morning and if at all possible, the last thing he put in his stomach at night.

"Breakfast smells good, Levi."

"'Bout ready, too."

Joe put his cup down and tied up his bedroll then tossed it into the schooner. He saw Nate in the distance digging Bull's grave. Grabbing a shovel he took another drink of coffee then started toward the man. He hoped this would be the only grave they'd have to dig on their way west.

"Let me give you a hand, Nate."

"Sure would appreciate it." Nate stopped digging, rested his hands on top of the shovel and leaned toward it. "You boys weren't kiddin' when you said those big Indians would kill someone that messed with you, were you?"

Remembering the warning he'd given Nate and Bull Joe shook his head. "Nope."

"They were gone when I got up this morning just before dawn. Haven't seen hide nor hair of 'em, either."

Throwing a scoop full of dirt onto the pile, Joe glanced out at the prairie. "They're out there somewhere. Watchin'."

Nate began to shovel again. "I'm tellin' ya, I sure wouldn't want them two after my ass. Mercy! But I'm uneasy about those other Indians."

"If Horse said they're gone, they're gone. Me and my brothers are at ease because we trust him with our lives. Stop worryin'."

"Soon as we get your friend buried, we'll head on out. Horse and Horn will know where we are, we just won't know where they are."

The hole was dug. Joe followed Nate back, ate then helped break camp. He didn't like the idea of putting Bull in the ground without even as much as a box around him, but the circumstances were out of his control. He was sure it wouldn't be the only time during the trip. Matter of fact that had already been proven; now he just had to learn to live with it.

Everyone helped cover the cowboy's body with dirt then

pile rocks on top. Carl made a makeshift cross out of a couple of sticks and hammered it into the ground at the head of the grave.

Joe placed his hat over his heart and bowed his head. "Dear Lord, we hope ole Bull found his way to Ya okay. See us all safe on the rest of our journey across this wonderful land You made with Your own hands. Amen."

Carl stepped up to the wood cross and hung the man's new cowboy hat on top. Tears poured down the boy's cheeks. Joe joined his brothers and started back toward the wagons.

"Little brother, you sure got a soft heart. Why, you didn't even really know that fella."

"It's not that, Charles. Like I said before, there's so much killin' all of a sudden."

Charles put his arm around Carl's shoulder. "There's always been killin' Carl. You've seen a hell of a lot of things for your age, killin' just ain't been one of 'em 'til now. None of us have ever seen a lot of the things we are seeing at this point."

Carl's voice cracked. "It just makes me wonder what's there."

Joe followed Carl's gaze toward the west. The vastness of the prairie spread out in front of them seemed to go on forever!

Chapter Twenty Four

The rains on the plains came in and out from one summer storm to another. The wagon trail was difficult from time to time and the amount of mud would vary from one day to the next, but Joe was determined to push forward.

"Nate."

"Yeah, Joe."

"I'm gonna take Little Boy Horse and scout ahead to see if we can find one of those cattle drives. You stay close around the boys. Keep on the trail, we'll meet up with you later."

Nodding Nate asked, "How long you think?"

"I guess y'all travel for two days then make camp. Hold there 'til we get back." He had really taken a liking to Nate, and had gained a lot of respect for the man and his kind heart.

"It's a plan, boss."

Joe rode up beside the wagon and listened to Levi's complaints. Something he'd grown accustomed to, since it seemed to be all the old cook did.

"I sure hope to hell ever where we end up there ain't none of them damn skeeters. I hate them blood suckers."

Carl sniggered. "That man in St. Louis said skeeters grow big as birds in Nebraska."

"Well, which way is Nebraska 'cause I'm a goin' the other way."

Carl and Charles laughed and Joe joined in. He'd never seen a grown man so afraid of bugs, especially spiders, but he guessed every man had his fears. He broke into the conversation. "Levi, Horse and me will catch up to y'all in a couple of days."

"Where you goin'?"

"We're goin' ahead to do some scoutin'."

"I'll do my best, but these boys won't be much help if we get bushwhacked."

"You worry too much, Levi. Johnny One Horn is staying. He'll be watchin' after things."

"Hell, I'm just as scared of him as I am the damned ole bushwhackers."

Laughing at the old man's toothless grin, Joe turned toward Boy Horse. "You ready, my friend?" Horse nodded and Joe took the lead as they rode ahead.

Levi climbed down from the schooner. They'd traveled a day and a half since Joe and Horse left. "Boys, I hear some squeekin' goin' on back there. Bring the middle wagon up here. We're gonna pack those bearin's. I ain't wantin' to lose a wheel out here in the middle of nowhere."

Charles pulled the second wagon to a stop. "How long did Joe say they'd be gone?"

"Should be seein' 'em tomorra'."

"I am going hunting." Johnny One Horn stated, "I saw some turkeys a while back. I will see if I can get some for supper."

Levi glanced up from what he was doing. "Nate said if the Indians around here see you killin' anything, they'll kill you."

"I am not afraid old man."

He shook his head. "No, don't 'spect ya are." He pointed at Johnny's mount. "You know, that damn horse of yours tried to bite me again this mornin'. You need to keep him tied or somethin'."

Johnny raised his eyebrow. "I think Coattail is part snake. The kind with the shaker on the tail, that's why he likes to bite you."

"Yeah, well, rattlesnake or not, do me a favor and keep him away from me. And I been wonderin', don't ridin' on that damn trouble maker's back chap your ass? Looks to me like a saddle'd be more comfortable."

Johnny shook his head, turned his horse around and headed

back the way they came. "Do not worry about my ass. You have one ugly ass of your own to fear." Johnny's laughter trailed off into the distance as he rode away.

A half hour later, Johnny returned to camp with two turkeys. They swung from the horse's shoulders by a rope tied to their feet; he walked in front leading his mount.

Levi wiped grease from his hands. "What did you do there, Johnny, run those turkeys down and ring their necks? I didn't hear no gun shots."

"Did not use a gun." Johnny slipped his Arkansas Toothpick out of its casing and held it in the air.

"My God, it's unbelievable somebody can throw a knife like that and hit their mark."

Nate approached them. "You done with those wheels, Levi."

"Yep."

"Good. We need to find a place to camp soon. Maybe there's somethin' not far ahead." He glanced at Johnny. "Those turkeys will make some fine eatin'. I'll ride on, find a place and start a fire."

Johnny mounted. "No."

"I know how to build a fire, Johnny."

"No." He shook his head. "I will go."

Nate nodded. "If that's what you want, I guess that's the way it should be."

"Yes, you make too much noise. I will be waiting. You watch after the boys."

Carl hopped into the seat of the prairie schooner. "We'll be okay, Johnny. You just make that fire a big one, 'cause I want some of that turkey meat. I'm so hungry I could eat a bear."

Shortly after Johnny cleaned the fowls and got the fire built, the rest of the party rode in.

"I'll put them birds on," said Levi, "while y'all make camp."

Charles took his bedroll out of the wagon. "Looks like it's gonna be a nice night. Listen to the frogs and crickets. They're just singin' away."

"Yes, this is a good camping spot. We should wait here for

Joe and Little Boy Horse."

Nate placed his belongings by the fire. "I agree."

A day later, Joe and Horse rode into camp about sun up; just in time for breakfast. Joe was pleased to be back with his friends and family.

He happily took the plate of biscuits and salt bacon from Levi. "Y'all have any trouble?"

Charles stood next to his brother. "Nope, just the old man here, gripin' about Coattail bitin' him, that's all."

The cook shot Charles a warning glance and Joe suppressed a grin. Poor Levi caught hell from everyone. "That ain't nothin' new." Joe took a bite of biscuit.

"What'd y'all find out?" Charles asked.

"There's a town a couple days' ride from here. Abilene, Kansas, just like Mr. Rogers in St. Louis said. There were lots of cattle. The drives came and left almost continuously."

Nate joined in the conversation. "I've been to Abilene before. They've got a big stock yard there."

Joe met Nate's gaze. "Knowin' you'd been in these parts, Nate, I reckined you'd be familiar with it. We just got close enough to see the drives from a distance. Damn lot of cattle."

"I can lead you right to the yard. No problem and we can detour round the bulk of the crowds."

"Sounds good."

"What are we gonna do then, Joe?" Charles asked.

Joe was confident about his decision, and smiled. "We're gonna get us some livestock, little brother."

The evening they arrived Joe picked a campsite a few miles outside of Abilene, and they settled in. Nate had said the town was a rough, tough, cow smelling place that lived up to its wild reputation in every way. He took the man for his word and didn't want any kind of situation to arise.

He prepared his horse, got a canteen and some dried beef. "Everyone that's staying in camp, I want y'all to stick pretty close to each other 'til we get back. Understood?" Watching nods and hearing yes sirs, he was satisfied.

Johnny rode up beside him. "There are many cows not far from here. Guards with riffles are all around them."

He smiled up at the towering figure atop the horse. "That's okay, we're not gonna steal them, my friend, we're gonna buy them. Tell Nate where you found them. He can lead us there." Johnny nodded. Pulling the strap tighter under the horse's belly, Joe shouted, "Nate, you and Charles saddle up! We're gonna pick us out some beef!"

"Yes, sir!" Nate looked at Charles. "Come on, young man, you're going on your first cattle drive."

Charles threw his saddle on his horse's back. "Is it hard? You know, driving cattle?"

"Naw, most of these cattle have already come a long way and they're used to it."

"Good." Charles mounted.

Joe waited for Johnny to finish talking to Nate. "Levi, you cook us up some good grub for this evenin'. We'll probably be wore out time we get back, and I'm sure we'll be real hungry."

"Don't you worry, boss, ole Levi'll take good care of ya."

He looked at Nate and Charles, who had ridden up beside him. "Let's go, boys."

They had been riding a little over an hour. Joe wondered just where these cattle were. "How much farther, Nate?"

"Well, Horn said a ways past the second creek we cross. We've crossed the first one, and by the looks of that row of trees ahead, I'd say that's the second one."

Charles said, "Funny how there's no trees on the plains 'cept those around a creek or waterin' hole of some kind."

"That it is." Nate pointed. "There's smoke in the trees? Looks like that might be a camp. Pretty big camp fire, they must be cooking one of those cows."

Joe laughed, but the humor didn't last long once they got close enough to see what the smoke was from. He swallowed the lump in his throat. "That ain't no campfire, boys."

Charles slowed his horse's gait. "Looks like someone's wagon caught fire."

As they got closer, heart pounding in his chest, Joe saw the grim truth. Two men and a boy, maybe fourteen, hung from two different trees. He grabbed the handle of his revolver. "Get your guns out. Now."

Nate pulled his weapon from its holster. "My God, look,

there's two more dead over in the brush."

"This couldn't have happened long ago, or Johnny would have seen it earlier." Joe dismounted and noticed Nate and Charles did the same. He walked to the bodies, his friend and brother beside him. "Oh, hell, two women."

"Looks to be mother and daughter." Nate bent closer. "Their throats are cut."

Joe looked over at his brother. "What devils could ever do such a thing as this?"

Charles put his hand to his face and rubbed his eyes. "What the hell is this country anyway? Life means nothin' round here. I'm ready to hightail it back home.

Seeing the true look of despair on Charles' face, Joe knew the younger man really meant what he said. "There ain't nothin' to go back to, Charles."

"Ma's there."

"What, her grave? You want to go back to a burned out shack? A flooded swamp?" He put his arm around his brother's shoulder. "No, brother, memories are the only thing left there."

Nodding, Charles relinquished, "You're right. I'm sorry. I guess I wished we were still boys on the farm, instead of men learnin' 'bout life."

Joe dropped his arm. "I understand." He knew what his brother was talking about. It wasn't that long ago he'd dreamed of being back in the safety of his childhood. Everything seemed to be right back then.

He was determined to make things right again, in the near future, but now there were other things at hand. "We're too close to town to just bury these folks. I think I need to get the law out here. I'm sure they'll have a preacher that can give them a proper send off to the Lord."

Nate stood to his full height. "Marshal's name's Hickok. He's a pretty tough hombre. Don't argue with him, Joe."

"Don't intend to. You and Charles stay here. Watch your backs while I go into town to find the marshal." He glanced at the hanging men. "Y'all cut those poor men down. I'll be back soon as I can."

CHAPTER TWENTY FIVE

A half hour later, Joe was riding down the main street of Abilene, Kansas. To his surprise, the town was pretty quiet. He noticed a sign in the middle of the street that read, Check all guns in at the marshal's office – Bill Hickok

Not only had Nate told him about Hickok, but he'd heard the name from other people along the trail, and knew the man was no one to contend with.

He made his way to the marshal's office, dismounted and went inside. Two men sat at a table playing cards while several prisoners were behind bars. He closed the door behind him. "Marshal here?"

One of the men spit tobacco into a spittoon. "Don't you know, boy, you might get shot for interrupting a man's poker game?"

"I'm sorry, sir, but I came to check my gun and talk to the marshal."

"What about?"

He wondered if the man doing the talking was Hickok. "My group came across some people that have been killed."

"Yeah?" The man nodded toward a table. "Put your guns over there and I'll tell you where to find the marshal."

Joe placed his pistol and rifle on the table with all the others. "How will you know which ones are mine, when I get back?"

"Don't worry. We, that is Deputy Swartz and me, hang

people for stealing. Nobody's gonna take your precious firearms. Now, if you want to see Marshal Hickok, he's over at the saloon playing some poker. If I were you, I'd walk up to him real slow, or he might just shoot you dead.

"I'll do that." Joe walked out of the office, then crossed the half cow manure filled dirt street. He guessed cattle that came through were driven right down Main Street to the holding corals of the stockyard.

The saloon was dim and smoke hovered in the air along with the smell of sweat and stale beer. He barely got in the door when a saloon girl touched his hind end. He jumped at the forwardness of her action. Then she came around front and ran her finger down his cheek.

"Hey, cowboy, I'm Molly Good Time. Are you ready for a..." She smiled, "...good time?"

He'd love to have a good time with a lady, since he'd never had one before, but that would have to wait. "No, Miss, I just need to talk to Marshal Hickok." Her interest immediately disappeared and she pointed toward a man who sat in a far corner with his back to the wall.

"That's him over there. I guess if talk's all you want, talk's all you'll get."

"Thank you, ma'am." He started toward Hickok, who didn't take his eyes off him. The man had long hair, a mustache, wore a light colored buckskin shirt and had a perfect view of the door and the entire saloon. Joe's heart skipped a beat when he met the man's penetrating gaze and heard the marshal's deep voice.

"What do you want kid? You're holding up my game."

"Names Joe Armstrong, Marshal. We came across some people down by the creek that was killed. Looks like a whole family."

"Who's we?"

"Me, my brother and a hired hand."

"I see." He looked back at the cards in his hand. "Well, it'll be dark in an hour or so. Nothing we can do tonight. Go back to the office and give those lazy assed deputies of mine directions. We'll be there first light."

"Mornin'? It's only a couple of miles from here. Those people have been killed. It won't take that long to get there." He couldn't believe he'd just said that. Especially when he saw the man slowly put his cards face down on the table. He knew from Hickok's measured movements, he was aggravated. The sound of his voice only confirmed the man's irritation.

Hickok glared at Joe. "Armstrong, don't argue with me."

"No, sir." Damn, why had he questioned this man? He knew better.

"I said we'll be there in the morning. This town starts getting riled up about this time of day and I'm not leaving. Did you hear me that time?"

"I guess I heard it right, Marshal." He spun and started toward the entrance. The last thing he wanted was a confrontation with Bill Hickok. Just before he pushed through the swinging doors, he heard the man's voice again and turned to face him.

"If I find out you had anything to do with these killings, I'll hang you for sure."

Thankful Hickok hadn't gotten out of his seat, Joe tipped his hat toward him. "I didn't, so you won't have to." Joe figured the marshal was mocking him when he tipped his hat, too.

"First light."

Joe arrived back at the sight of the murders. Nate and Charles had lined the bodies up next to each other. He sat atop his horse and stared down at the pitiful sight. "The whole damn family."

"Yeah," Nate took off his hat. "Appears to be a man, his wife and kids, then maybe his brother, can't tell for sure." He glanced up at Joe. "Is the marshal behind you?"

"No, he said he's too busy. Busy playin' cards and drinkin' whiskey, if you ask me. But he said someone would be here by first light." Nate turned and looked across the plains. Joe followed his gaze. The orange glow of dusk was breathtaking amid the loss of life.

"Damn, nobody seems to care about anybody."

Joe climbed off his horse. "You're right, Nate, not even the law."

Charles walked up beside them. "Are we gonna just leave 'em here?"

"No, I suspect we should stay for the night, maybe a few yards away, and wait for the marshal. We don't want any varmints to eat at 'em. When we don't show up at camp, Horse or Horn will come lookin' for us."

"I wish they were here right now. I sure would feel a lot safer." Charles turned toward Joe. "What if whoever did this comes back?"

"They ain't comin' back. They got what they wanted and are long gone." Joe led his horse by the reins and walked in front of him. "Come on, let's eat a bite then bed down and try to get some rest. I have a feelin' tomorrow's gonna be a long day."

The sun broke over the horizon. Joe sat up, ran his hands through his hair and scanned the distance for any signs of approaching riders. Nothing.

He was surprised neither of his Indian friends had checked on them. Hell, for all he knew, Horse or Horn were out there right now watching them.

Lying back down, he waited for the others to wake. There was nothing they could do until the marshal came.

A few minutes later, he heard Nate stir, then Charles. It was almost daylight now and he peered across the plains again.

"Any sign of the marshal?" Nate asked.

Joe stood and tried to stretch the kinks out of his back. The ground was double hard without a bedroll beneath him. "Not yet."

"I thought he said first light."

"He did, but maybe he had to sleep off some of that whiskey."

Charles got up off the ground. "Damn, I sure wish I had a cup of Levi's good, strong coffee."

"Me, too, brother, and if I hadn't told Hickok we'd be here when he got here, I'd send you back to camp."

Shaking his head, Charles replied, "I ain't goin' anywhere by myself." He pointed to the dead bodies. "Not after seein' that."

"I don't blame you," Nate commented. "It ain't a pretty sight."

Joe wondered if they were waiting in vain. Maybe the

sheriff wasn't coming at all. Maybe he'd been toying with him. Hell, it was a pretty good piece after dawn. Then Joe glanced up at the sound of Charles' voice.

"Two wagons comin'."

Once they got close enough, Joe recognized the two deputies from the day before, each one driving a flatbed wagon. He walked over to where the bodies were and they pulled right up to him.

"Mornin', deputies, this here's my brother Charles and my friend Nate." He watched them exchange handshakes, then saw the men put their attention on the dead family members.

"Marshal's about five minutes behind. How about you fellows help us get these bodies loaded before he gets here."

Joe gave an affirmative nod to Nate and Charles. Just as they placed the body of the young girl in the wagon, the marshal rode up.

Hickok studied the situation then met Joe's eyes. "So, you say you just rode up here and decided to help these people?"

"That's right, sir." Joe saw the marshal shift his gaze to Nate and watched his squint in a questioning manner.

"Don't I know you friend?"

"No, sir, I don't think so. Unless you've seen me in Springfield, Missouri, that's where I'm from."

Hickok shook his head. "I never spent too much time in Springfield. I did stop there one time and played some cards. Some crook won my watch."

Charles smiled. "Won your watch? Must have been better than you, huh?"

Unable to believe Charles had made the remark, Joe nudged his brother with his elbow and kept a watchful eye on Hickok. Amazingly, the man made no move to scold the younger man.

Taking a deep breath, the marshal replied, "I think he cheated. Don't really matter. I shot him the next morning in a fair gunfight. Might have been a good card player, but the old boy was too slow with his six shooter."

He shifted in his saddle and brought his attention back to Joe. "You boys need to steer clear of Abilene. The town is full, and no place for your kind."

Joe wondered what their kind was. He stepped forward to

stop the marshal from leaving. "But we're looking to buy some livestock. Cattle and horses."

"Then go to the stockyards. Most of the dealing is done there, not in Abilene. Remember what I told you about going into town. The cowboys around here are a mean bunch. You can see that from what happened here."

The marshal tipped his hat, like he'd done at the saloon. Joe had thought the man was mocking him, but maybe he was just being polite. Somehow he knew that Hickok meant 'inexperienced', when he said 'your kind'.

"Get those wagons rolling, deputies. I've got a card game to get back to." Marshal Bill Hickok turned his mount and started back toward town.

"It just don't seem right, Joe." Charles got on his horse. "We've always been farmers. I can't fathom ownin' cattle."

"I never liked bein' a farmer, did you?"

"Guess I never knew no different. I didn't like the Mississippi mud we had to trudge through gettin' the crop in, but sometimes I sure do miss that Mississippi moon."

"Yeah, me too. But cattle ranchers we're gonna be, brother." Joe would make sure they heeded the Marshal's warning. He mounted up then faced Nate and Charles. "Let's go back to camp. Tell 'em what happened and get restocked on dried beef and biscuits. Then first thing in the mornin', we'll go to the stockyard and buy us some livestock."

Chapter Twenty Six

Little Boy Horse watched from the underbrush of a hilltop a short distance away. When he saw the two wagons and the rider carry away some bodies, he knew Joe and the others would be alright. He'd been close by most of the night watching.

The party of three reined their horses back toward camp. He turned to follow, but he had something to take care of first. Through the night, he'd noticed a child in the brush not far from the sight of the murders. He'd left him be, but now it was time to get him. The little one would die out here alone, or worse, be murdered like the others.

He heard the rustle of the bushes ahead, so he dismounted and slipped through the brush. The slight whimper told him he was nearing his prey. Within moments, he was standing in front of... a girl? A small Indian girl; her brown eyes were filled with fright.

Holding out a helpful hand, he gently grasped her arm, but her fright quickly turned to fight and she began to kick and claw. She kicked him in his man parts, and while he fought to catch his breath, he still held her.

Once he could breathe again, he tried to calm her in his native tongue, but when she didn't seem to understand, he tried the white man's language. "Stop, I am not going to hurt you." Unlike she had already done him. "I am here to help, little hell cat!"

When she quit her rebellious behavior, he saw the sadness

in her eyes. Where had she come from? Was she traveling with the ones who had been murdered? Satisfied that she was going to remain calm, he picked her up, mounted his horse and sat her in front of him.

To his surprise, she began flailing again and he wrapped his arm around her little body and pinned her legs beneath his. He almost laughed when she tried to bite him, but he knew she was safe for the time being, even if she didn't realize it.

Apparently the sight of the camp ahead and the boys calmed her and finally she stopped her protest. He was pleased because his man parts had taken quite the beating. First from her kick, then from her constant squirming and bouncing. Slowly, he let her arms go, then her legs. She sat still as a day without a breeze.

Joe sat back eating his stew and listened while Charles told the story of the murdered family they had found. The smell of death would forever stay in his mind. Most of his dinner was eaten, but suddenly, he lost his appetite.

"Those women had their throats cut from side to side. It was terrible."

"I sure am glad I wasn't there. I hope I don't have to see another dead person for a long, long time." Carl sat beside Charles on the ground.

"Me either, Carl." Joe stood and threw the remainder of his stew into the weeds. He heard a commotion and looked up. Shading his eyes from the early afternoon sun, he saw Little Boy Horse riding in. "What the hell?" Was that a child? He met Horse as the man rode into camp.

"Damn, what do ya have there, Boy Horse?" Levi asked.

"You can see what I have, old man. She's wild as a coyote and kicks like that mule horse Shadrack! The pain in my balls can prove to it!"

The girl had thick black hair that was tangled to beat hell, dirt marked her face and though she was clearly Indian, she was dressed like a white girl. Joe's heart went out to the little thing. "Here, I'll take her." Joe reached up and the girl held her arms out to accept his help. He set her on the ground and Carl bent to look at her.

"Little girl, what are you doing out here? Where's your ma

and pa?"

Little boy horse dismounted. "She understands some white man's words, but I do not know how much."

Joe took the girl's hand and watched the big Indian wince when he shifted his privates into a more comfortable position. He stifled a smile and glanced down at the child. "It seems you gave our friend here a good fight."

"Humph! I have been hurt worse."

"But not by a little girl!" Carl mocked.

Joe laughed out loud when Boy Horse lunged at Carl, who took off like a flash. "One of these days he's gonna get you, little brother."

"I bet she's hungry, ain't cha little girl?" Levi filled a bowl with rabbit stew and after Joe led her to a spot to sit, he handed it to her.

"Dang," Carl came back out of breath from his run around camp. "She's just eatin' that with her bare hands, and fast too. I hope she don't puke."

"She ain't gonna puke, Carl, get her some water." Joe noted that by the time his brother got back with the cup of water, the girl had eaten every ounce of stew and was licking her fingers clean. She gulped down the water like she hadn't had any for days.

"Wow, she was starvin' and thirsty, too."

Joe nodded. "Seems that way, little brother. We'll give her more later. I bet she needs some rest." He turned toward Levi. "She can sleep in the second wagon. Put some blankets in there, would ya? Maybe she can rest for a while.

Before they could get the wagon ready for her, she'd lain down on the ground and fell fast asleep. Joe moved away while Horse picked her up like she was a feather, then carried her to the wagon and put her little body on top of the covers. Joe studied her face. "She's a pretty little girl."

"I think she has been through much, Joe." Horse propped her head on a folded blanket.

"You're probably right. I hope she don't try to run away in the night."

"Do not worry, she will probably sleep through the darkness until daylight. If not, me or Johnny will hear her."

"I know you will." Joe was feeling the pressures of the last couple of days and tomorrow was going to be a long one. "I think I'll turn in pretty quick myself." He looked back at the child. "I'll figure out what to do with her another day." Damn, being the man of the camp was getting more complicated every day they were on the trail.

Daybreak was just around the corner and Joe was up and saddling his horse when he heard the cook beating a pot with a spoon. He knew it would have scared the dickens out of the girl if she hadn't already been awake. He'd given her his ma's brush so she could get the tangles out of her hair. She'd washed up and looked much better than she had the night before, but it seemed she didn't want to leave the wagon for any length of time.

"You men gonna sleep all day?" Levi clanged the pan once more. "You've got cattle to buy."

Joe made sure his saddle was secure, then headed toward the fire. "He's right boys, let's eat us some of that left over stew of Levi's then it's time to go." He took a bowl from the old cook. "Levi, I want you, Carl and Charles to take the wagons and settle into camp just North West of town, that's the way we'll be headin' the cattle."

Charles' head jerked up. "I'm goin' with you and Nate, Joe."

"Not today. I want you to stay with Levi."

"But why?"

He didn't want to take a chance of putting his brother through any more than he'd already seen. If there was more trouble, he and Nate would have to deal with it. "Don't argue, Charles. It's better this way."

"How the hell are you and Nate going to herd the cattle, just the two of you?"

"We'll manage. You need to keep an eye on that girl. Make sure she doesn't cause trouble." The look on his younger brother's face told him Charles was none too happy about the decision, but he wouldn't argue any more.

Just about daybreak, Joe watched Johnny One Horn enter the camp area. He'd been out on the prairie all night standing guard and didn't know about the girl. He sat in silence and listened as Horse told Johnny the story behind the little girl.

Johnny nodded. "I see. Your father Gray Wolf told me of the ways of the great people of the North."

"Yes, he once stayed with them before I was born."

Pointing at the girl Johnny said, "The little one ties her hair like he described their women did, yet she dresses like a white child."

"This I have seen myself," agreed Horse.

"What do you plan to do with her?"

"I do not know yet."

Charles approached the wagon. "Well, for now, she's here, however good or bad that might be."

Joe would let the matter go until they could figure out something, but today's task was now at hand. "Johnny, I need you to scout north west for open land with grass and water. That's the way we'll be headin' and we shouldn't be too hard to find."

"I will find something."

"Thanks, and I'd appreciate it if you'd put on the white man's clothes I bought for you. They'll cause less of a stir if someone sees you." Johnny gave him an affirmative nod that assured Joe the man would do as he asked.

Minutes later he saw the big Indian emerge dressed in the new clothing and wearing the tall top hat. That was something that would definitely draw attention, but he had to admit, Johnny looked good in it. "Ummm, maybe you'd better not wear that hat, it's a might too showy. Maybe Horse will let you take his cowboy hat. He never wears it anyway. Why don't you ask him?"

"I will do that, Joe, but I will take this one that young Carl bought me along also. Maybe it carries good luck!"

Joe smiled. "Whatever you need to do my friend. Take what supplies you need, too."

"One blanket and some dried meat is all. Other than that, I will live off the land. I don't plan to be gone more than a few days."

He watched Johnny grab his supplies and mount Coattail. Soon his friend gave a hand signal goodbye and left the camp sight. Joe heard Carl sniff from behind and turned to see the younger man wipe a tear from his cheek. "What's wrong? You look kind of pale, little brother."

"I'm alright, Joe, I just thought he'd say somethin' before he left. Especially to me because we're such good friends."

Joe smiled and walked over to Carl, who had always had a special bond with Johnny One Horn. "If he really meant goodbye, it would have been different. You should know the sign he gave us meant he'd see us soon. He's left before and you never acted like this."

"I guess so, but with this country being so bad, and people dying all the time, you never know if you're gonna see a person again."

"Oh, he'll be back, Carl, I'm sure of it. Now, y'all help Levi break camp and get on the trail." Joe turned toward Nate. "You ready?"

"Yep."

"Then let's head out." Joe couldn't tell Carl he agreed with him about never knowing if you'll see someone again. Hell, he didn't know if he, or anyone else in his party, might have seen their last sunrise. It was something he wasn't going to dwell on, though. Today was a new day, life would go on, and whatever happened, the Lord would see them through.

Chapter Twenty Seven

The stockyards hustled with cowboys cutting cows from herds and separating the livestock for the buyers. Joe had never seen the like and was in awe at the way things were handled. He needed to go to the buyer's bank with some of the coins so they could purchase with cash. He was sure it would be more than he had left from what he got in St. Louis.

"Nate, you know how to pick the livestock, so I'm gonna leave that to you, while I go to the bank. Buy a herd of a hundred, and if you think we should hire a couple more hands, then do that, too. I trust your judgment."

"Thanks, boss. I'll do my best."

Joe knew that was true and was comfortable with it. He made his way to the bank and inside the place was bustling with buyers and sellers of all kinds.

He approached the teller's window and handed him some of the gold coins. To his surprise, the man didn't act surprised. "You ever seen gold coins like that before?"

"Nope, can't say I have, but we get everything form paper notes to gold dust around here. We pay by weight in gold. I assume that's alright with you?"

"Yes, sir." This place was sure different than anywhere Joe had been. Most places, except in St. Louis, the people were shocked by the coins. He watched the man go back to weigh the gold then disappear into the vault only to return with paper bills.

"You have five thousand and two hundred dollars in return

for your gold, sir."

The man behind the desk looked at him over spectacles that rested half way down his nose. He was a funny looking fellow with hardly any lips and no chin at all.

"Thank you, Mr. Armstrong. Come back any time."

Joe walked out of the crowded building. He was getting used to having money on him, but was glad the paper wasn't as bulky as gold. It made him feel safer in a way.

He got on his horse and went to the holding yard where he searched for Nate. He finally saw him and two other men putting cows into a pen. He pulled his horse to a stop at the pen and dismounted.

"Hey, Joe, glad you're back."

"You hire these two fellas?"

"Yes, sir, and I had the blacksmith make you a brand. It's a circle with a double A. Hope you like it."

The Armstrong family had never had a brand of its own that Joe knew of. "It'll be fine."

"Good. Let me introduce you to the guys. They're brothers, but you'd never know it. One's a little guy and one's a big one. Soon as you approve, we'll start branding the stock. I've been watchin' them and they're right good at what they do."

Joe followed Nate to where the new hands were. He stuck out his hand to the one, who couldn't be over five foot tall, for a shake. "Howdy, I'm Joe Armstrong."

"Shorty's the name. Purtty glad to be in your company, Mr. Armstrong." He shook Joe's hand. "I'm a little guy tryin' to make a livin' in a big world, if you know what I mean. This here's my birthday present, I turned thirty today."

The man didn't look any older than Joe, but if he said he was thirty, he had to take him at his word. "Happy birthday, friend."

"Thank ya kindly, sir."

Nate pointed to the other man. "This here's Pete, Joe."

"Just plain ole Pete, that's right, got the name from my granddaddy." Pete accepted Joe's handshake. "Heard all about you from Nate when he hired us."

"Glad to meet y'all and welcome to our crew. Nodding Joe replied, "I'm just learnin' the trade, and until I do, Nate's your boss, I'm just one of the boys." Pete stood at least two heads taller than his brother. He was a man almost as tall as the Indians. It would be interesting to see them standing side by side.

Joe joined the other men and through the hot afternoon, they succeeded in getting all hundred animals branded and ready for the drive. He'd wondered why Shorty seemed so jumpy and when he asked why the man was nervous, he had to stifle a smile at the little man's reply.

"Well, when you're my size, somebody's always wantin' to beat your ass, so I have to stand ready at every turn. You just get tired of bein' picked on, that's all.

He could only imagine what the man had to deal with over his stature. "I understand, Shorty, and I'll warn you now, if there's any one of us that will give you heck, it'll be Levi. He's our cook, but he don't mean no harm, he's just an old man who likes to rib."

"Aw, funnin' like that don't rile me none. I know when someone's bout to try to whup up on me, that's when I get peeved."

"Good, then you and the old man will get along fine."

By evening Joe readied his horse to make the trip back to camp. "Nate, I'm gonna go get Carl and Charles to help us. You stay with the livestock and don't go into town."

"I ain't goin' anywhere near town, and neither will Shorty or Pete." He laughed. "Hell, Shorty already had a run in with Hickok and he don't want nothin' else to do with the place."

"Good. I'll be back in the mornin'. We'll ride out then."

"We'll be waitin' for ya, Joe. You be careful out there."

Joe rode toward the North West, keeping a watchful eye out at all times, not only for their campsite, but for anyone who may try to ambush him. After about four miles, he spotted the wagons and headed toward them. He'd be glad to sit and rest for a spell. Branding cattle wasn't the easiest job he'd ever done, but he felt it would be one of the most rewarding.

Just knowing he and his brothers were the owners of the livestock made him swell with pride. Hell, they were well on their on their way to being ranchers. It was a far cry from working their pa's tenant farm. But thinking about that now, somehow he wished he was back there. It was a happier time.

He rode into camp, dismounted and unsaddled his horse. "Hey, Levi, a cup of java sounds good."

Levi grabbed the pot and poured a cup. "Just happen to have one, Joe." He handed Joe the steaming liquid. "How'd y'all do?"

Taking a long drink, Joe savored the flavor. "Ahhhh, that's good." He saw the pleased look on the old cook's face, then answered the man's question, "We did great. I think Nate managed to hire two more good cowboys and we bought a hundred head." He glanced at his brothers. "What are y'all smilin' about?"

Charles took a drink from his own cup. "Seems like we've had bad things happenin' for some time now."

"Yeah," Carl said, "but things are startin' to look up."

It was true, things were only going to get better from here on out. The one thing that would bring everything together was if they could see their pa one more time. If only Joe really knew that was possible, but it was probably only a dream. The man was most likely dead, so he had to get the notion out of his head.

"They sure are, brothers, and guess what?" He saw the sparkle of expectation in his youngest brother's eyes.

"What, Joe? What?"

"Carl, you and Charles are gonna ride with me in the mornin'. We're gonna leave at sunrise."

"Really?"

"Yep. You'll be helpin' to drive the herd back here then farther to where—" Suddenly, he thought about Johnny scouting for them a place, and Horse and the girl. "Hey, where are Horse and the little girl?" Joe watched Levi shake his head and raise one eyebrow.

"That big Injun is carryin' on like an ole' mother hen with a baby chick. I swear he won't get away from her. He's out there teachin' her the way of their people, but I spect she needs to know it."

"Did he find out her name?"

Levi stoked the cook fire. "Yep, it's Wind."

"Wind? Just plain old Wind?" Why should he question what her people named her? It was none of his concern. "I guess that's a good name. It sounds peaceful enough."

Chuckling, Levi stepped to the supply wagon. "Yeah, but Little Boy Horse calls her Kicking Wind because she wounded his man parts when she was fightin' him after he found her."

"He even made her a bow and showed her how to make her own arrows." Carl said, laying out his bedroll.

As long as Horse didn't put teaching the little girl the ways of her people above keeping their little party safe, he didn't care. He knew the man well enough to know that wouldn't happen. "That's all well and good. Kicking Wind can stay with us if she wants."

A child's laughter and two sets of footsteps coming into camp told Joe the man and girl had returned. He nodded an acknowledgement to the pair then laid out his bedroll. "We'd better get off to bed now. It's gonna be a long day tomorrow."

Sunrise came early and Joe heard the others milling around in camp. He must have been more tired than he thought. He started to get up and realized he hurt in places he didn't know he had. Branding cattle was hard on a man, but he could handle it. However, he'd be damn glad to get a place, get settled and sleep in a real bed again.

"Well, lookie there fellers, seems sleepin' handsome himself is wakin' up." Levi handed Joe a cup of coffee.

Handsome? The few days' growth on his face, need of a bath and clean clothes made him feel anything but good looking. "Thank ya, Levi, I didn't know you thought I was handsome." A grunt was all the old man mustered and Joe turned his attention to his brothers. "Looks like y'all are anxious to get started. You've got the horses saddled and everything."

Charles gave Joe a plate of biscuits and gravy. "Sure are. We want to see the herd and meet the new hands."

"I guess we'd better go then." He shoveled down his food and handed the plate and coffee cup to Levi. The java made him think of his old friend. Glancing out over the prairie, he wondered if Johnny One Horn had found a place for them yet. This was a large expanse of country and he was worried just how hard it would be to find the man.

At the same time he knew Horse and Horn had a special bond, and Boy Horse would probably be able to find him with no problem. That was something he wasn't going to worry about. Now, he had some cattle to drive.

Charles and Carl had already mounted, so he made way to his horse. "Time to head out."

Carl shifted in his saddle. "How far is it to the stockyards, Joe?"

"Just a few miles."

"Okay."

He glanced over at Horse who was teaching the Indian girl how to ride. Little Boy Horse waved at him and Joe smiled. The man had a good heart and he was glad they were friends. He prayed most of their hardships were behind them. At that moment, life was good.

When the stockyards came into view, he reined his mount to a stop. "Okay, my brothers this is it. Y'all ready to herd some cattle?" He heard their voices in unison.

"Yes, sir!"

Riding beside his brothers into the stockyard was something he'd never dreamt of doing, but he was proud they were there today. He took the time to introduce them to Shorty and Pete.

They all listened intently while Nate gave him, Carl and Charles instructions on what to do with the cattle. When they figured out who was doing what, he heard Carl's voice behind him. He turned and followed the young man's gaze into the wilderness.

"Wonder where Johnny is today?"

"Don't know, but he's out there somewhere looking for the place where we're gonna settle."

"It'll be the best place ever, Joe, I can feel it."

"I hope you're right, Carl." He spurred his horse into motion and led the way as they drove the herd into the wide open spaces of Kansas.

****

MEETING THE ENEMY

O.C. was pleased with the time they'd made. At least it was

as good as two men on horseback probably could. He was also thankful that the hours had passed uneventful. He was still trying to get those men on spike poles out of his mind.

Tired as hell, all he needed was a good night's rest, some good food and a cup of coffee. The sun was getting low in the sky and soon it would be time to stop for the night.

Jack spotted something on the horizon. “See that, O.C.?”

He squinted into the sunset. “Yep, a wagon. Looks like a hunter or trapper. I’d say it’s a buffalo hunter.” As they got closer, he saw the man who’d been driving the wagon, but had now set up camp. He could tell by his long gray beard he was no spring chicken.

It wasn’t too much farther until the old man spotted them. O.C watched the old man jump to his feet and draw up a buffalo gun. “Hold on there, fella.” O.C. held up his hand. “We don’t mean ya no harm. We’re travelin’ through and our paths have crossed. That’s all.” He stopped his horse so they wouldn’t get the old guy’s dander up any more than it was.

The old man kept the gun pointed at them. A few seconds passed before he spoke, “What’s the matter don’t your partner know how to speak English?” He looked at Jack. “Cat got your tongue?”

Jack’s voice was strong when he spoke. “I speak a hell of a lot better when I’m not staring down the barrel of a fifty caliber Hawkins.”

The old man chuckled. “Boy what a difference it makes when a man looks ya straight in the eye.” He began to laugh, spit tobacco juice on the ground then lowered the rifle. “Come on over. I got some fresh deer and a jug of whiskey that’ll separate the men from the boys.” He raised an eyebrow. “You men wouldn’t be boys in disguise now, would ya?”

When Jack looked at him and chuckled, O.C. allowed his guard to go down somewhat and dismounted. The smell of beans cooking wafted across the prairie air and the sweet aroma of roasting meat floated into his nostrils. He was hungry as a bear after hibernation.

The old man grabbed a leather bag from the wagon and drew out a bottle of whiskey like a gunfighter draws his gun. O.C. was surprised the old codger was able to move that fast.

"Sit down," the buffalo hunter said as he spread a blanket on the ground. "What brings you siblings out here in man's country anyway? Looking for gold?"

O.C. thought he heard a sneer in the man's voice but he let it pass. "No, we're not lookin' for gold, ole buddy. We've been workin' out here, so to speak and now we're tryin' to find our way back to Mississippi."

"You're a hell of a long ways from Mississippi. I know, I've been there." He handed them each a cup of coffee after he poured some whiskey it. "What makes you think you two will ever get across this territory without losing your pretty little curls, anyway?"

Laugher bubbled up through O.C. and escaped about the same time Jack and the old fellow began to laugh. He didn't know why the comment had struck them all so funny, but he laughed so hard his side hurt, then laughed some more. Finally he caught his breath and watched the old guy stoke the fire.

"They call me Stockman. Earl the pearl Stockman. Why, I used to be the toughest man west of the Mississippi. Maybe east of it, too. You know boys, I've chased a mountain lion down runnin' on my feet just to see the look on his face. Just so's he'd know he'd been bested. "

Doubting what Earl said hadn't crossed O.C.'s mind. He could just imagine in the man's younger days, him doing just what he'd said.

Earl nodded toward O.C.'s knife. "Where'd ya get that toad sticker?"

He'd noticed Stockman eyeballing it. What was his interest in it? He made a note to keep it well protected in case someone tried to steal it. "You mean this?" He asked, pulling his toothpick from his belt.

Stockman nodded. "I mean that." He pulled the chaw out of his mouth and threw it into the fire. "You know redneck, I thought you might be lyin' to me 'bout Mississippi a while ago, 'til I seen that blade."

"You've seen somethin' like this before?" O.C.'s curiosity was peaked when Earl walked to the wagon and pulled an identical knife from the inside. However, it wasn't an Arkansas Toothpick, or was it? His jaw dropped when he looked closer and identified the weapon for sure. "Where the hell did you get that, Earl?" He took it from the man and studied it. "It can't be."

Chapter Twenty Eight

Earl retrieved it from O.C.'s hand. "Oh, but it is. Got it from an Indian."

"From who?" His teeth hurt he had them clenched together so hard waiting for an answer. "A big ole Indian. Traded some whiskey for it. Can't remember his name, though."

O.C.'s heart leapt into his throat and he forced himself to swallow. Surely, this wasn't… "Was it Horn?"

The older man placed the knife back into the wagon. "Yeah, yeah, that's it. Some kind of Horn."

He couldn't believe what he was hearing. This was for real. He gazed off into the far away sunset that seemed so close. The pink, purple and gray colors were brilliant and mixed to God's perfection. He was getting closer to home. "Johnny One Horn," he said, before turning back toward Stockman and Tunnie. "That's where you got the knife. Well, I'll be damned." He couldn't stop the smile that lifted the corners of his mouth.

"Let me ask you a question, Earl. How long ago was it?"

"Hmmm." Earl rubbed his chin. "Don't seem like it's been that long ago. A few months, a year, maybe two, maybe not that long. I ain't for sure."

"Was anybody with him?"

Earl looked up, his brow furrowed. "Why all the fuss about that Indian? Some relation of yours?" A smile crossed his face then and he began to laugh.

It was no laughing matter to O.C., but he let the man have

his humor. "You might say that, but please, was there anybody with him?"

"I'm tryin' to remember. Give me a second, redneck." Earl continued to laugh and took a gulp of whiskey. "I think there was another Indian, and two or three white boys or half breeds with him."

Was his heart going to pound right out of his chest? White boys? "These boys, did you hear any names called? Where bouts did you see 'em?"

After sitting still for a couple of minutes, Earl took a shot of whiskey. "No, redneck. I don't remember hearing any names. But I do remember where I seen them. On the barge goin' to St. Louis."

"St. Louis? What the hell were they doin' there?"

"Now that I can't answer. But to be swamp Indians, looked like they were doing pretty good. Had some fine horses and nice duds."

O.C. turned and walked away from camp. The boys must have gotten the gold from the swamp. That had to be it. Joe found the gold! They must have gone to Vicksburg to buy supplies and horses then moved on to St. Louis. He rushed back to camp. Maybe, just maybe… "Earl, did you hear them say anything about their mother? Or, anything at all that you can remember?"

"No, I didn't." He met O.C.'s gaze. "I'll tell you what. If I ever run into 'em again, I'll ask 'em all those questions for you. How's that, redneck?"

Blood rushed through O.C.'s veins and warmed his heart. It was the first time in four years he'd talked to anyone that knew somebody he did. Damn, it was good to hear. It was a wild story, but not all of it could have been made up. Hell, there were too many things old Earl knew that he couldn't have unless it happened. And his toothpick, that was more evidence. Even if Stockman wasn't telling the whole story, it made him feel good anyway.

He got comfortable around the fire, watched the flames and listened to Earl and Jack talk. It was good to relax and his stomach was ready for food. By the looks of the deer carcass on the tripod Earl rigged up, it wouldn't be long.

Earl handed the whiskey jug to Jack. "Have a snort. It's better without the coffee."

Jack shook his head. "We wouldn't come into a man's camp and drink all his whiskey."

A loud belly laugh escaped Earl. "All who's whiskey? I got half a wagon load. How do you think I get through this God forsaken country? The Indians like whiskey. I trade it for furs and safe passage through the territory. Hell I know all them Indians." He laughed again and turned the jug up again.

It was enjoyable to O.C. to listen to the other men's banter. They were kidding around like young boys would likely do. He got in on a little of it, but he had a serious question. Fortunately, he didn't have to ask it, Jack beat him to it.

"Hey, Earl, if you know all these Indians, then you must know the ones who impale folks on sticks and dangle them up in the air."

"Yeah, that's Tom Crow and his bunch. Meanest band of cut throats you could ever imagine. Tom Crow's a half breed, 'cept he's half Mexican half Apache. If you seen anybody stuck on them poles, it would be sure Crow had somethin' to do with it."

"Know anything else about him?"

O.C. was glad for Jack's questions. He wanted to learn all he could about the man. It might save his own life in the future.

"He's kind of a chief or somethin'. Dresses like an Indian but wears a Mexican flat hat. You'll know him if you see him."

"How come he does that to people?"

"You see, the Indians around here like Mexican women, so they go across the border and steal 'em."

Jack took the jug from Earl and swigged it before he asked, "Damn, don't some of those girls and women have family somewhere?"

"Yep," Earl replied. "When their people come lookin' for 'em, they are too inexperienced to deal with the likes of Tom Crow so they usually end up with those sharp sticks up their butt. Like the one y'all seen."

This time O.C. grasped the whiskey jug when it was passed to him. How the hell did this Crow fellow get away with murder like that? He lay back and continued to listen.

"Good God, man, that must hurt like hell."

"It's a terrible way to die. The more they move around the deeper the stake gets until they can't stand *not* to move, then death comes fast."

After Earl told the gruesome story, Jack listened to so intently; O.C. spoke to Tunnie, "Mexicans." It looked as though Jack had just awakened from a bad dream. "Mexicans," he repeated. "Those six tree campers that were following us. They probably thought we were some of Tom Crow's bunch. That explains why we're still alive. It explains their lack of tactics."

Stockman stirred the beans and checked to see if the meat was done. "You boys probably done those poor Mexicans a favor, 'cause if they'd found that bunch, they would have been dead, maybe you two as well."

It intrigued O.C. at how this man had lived so long in this territory. He wondered if there was something, other than providing whiskey that the old man wasn't telling them. "Earl, do you know this Crow fella?"

"Yeah, I know him. Know him well. He lets me go through here without any trouble." Earl's lip curled and his brow furrowed. "He trusts me, but one day I'm gonna kill him. When I get a chance. I've been waiting for the right time for a long time." He spit tobacco juice into the fire. "He would've killed me already if I hadn't supplied him and his bunch with whiskey. He don't pay for it, neither. Just takes it. Don't he know I have to make money, too. Yeah, he knows, he just don't care, that's all. I'm waitin' for my time. It'll come."

The faraway look in the old buffalo hunter's eyes let O.C. know the man was in his own world. Dreaming of how to kill Tom Crow. "What do you plan to do? Sounds like he's a pretty bad hombre." The focus came back to Earl's eyes as if he'd had a revelation. O.C. met the man's gaze and saw the reflection of the wheels turning in the old fellow's mind. He didn't get a chance to ask what Earl was thinking before he volunteered the information. Brown tobacco spit stained the corners of Earl's mouth as he broke into an evil grin.

"Say, if you men would help me, I'd be able to do it. But, I warn you, every man Crow's got with him is bad. If you decide to do this, you might get yourself stuck up on one of those poles."

O.C. didn't interrupt and when he saw Tunnie start to speak, he just shook his head and Jack sat back. It wouldn't hurt to hear what Earl had to say, even if he and Tunnie didn't want to go along with it.

"I've got a plan. Have had for a long time, just been waitin' for the opportunity. Anyways, Crow is supposed to meet with me tomorrow in the high plains north of here. He usually brings me a couple of Mexican women to trade for whiskey." He shook his head in disgust. "He thinks I take them to the cattle herders up north, but I try to get those poor gals back to Mexico to their families where they belong."

By now, Stockman had earned his trust. O.C. listened cautiously as Earl went on in detail about the plan he'd worked so long to put into action. It was well thought out and he was sure that something had to be done about the crazed outlaw Tom Crow.

One thing for sure he didn't want to get himself or Jack killed now that he was on his way home. Still yet, he could hardly believe the bazaar stories Stockman told them about Crow. If he hadn't seen some of his grisly handy work himself, he would have thought it was all made up. How could a man be so cruel and heartless?

He knew Earl Stockman was a smart old coot. The preparation the man had done to get rid of Crow made it clear he was determined to carry it out. One way or another. He listened while Earl talked.

"We have to separate Crow from the rest of his men. I'll tell them that I met these two Texas rangers, that's y'all, and that you're lookin'. for Tom. Knowin' him like I do, he'll send his men after you to bushwhack you. Probably at night when you're sleepin'.

"You two need to lay a false trail for them to follow. Lead them on a two or three day wild goose chase, then double back to the original camp. Think you can do that?"

Of course they could. He learned tricks from the swamp Indians, and even more from the cattle rustlers. "Yep."

"Good. Once his men are gone, I'm gonna get old Tom Crow drunk and when the time's right take advantage of it. I'll get him secured. Tie him up and tie him down, whatever I have to do so's he can't move, then I'm gonna take him to Mexico. I'll turn him over to the Mexicans. I think justice will surely be served there. If I can take him alive, I will, but if I have to kill him, I'll do that, too.

O.C. didn't like the idea of Earl taking such a big risk. "I wouldn't want the SOB alive and at my back in the wagon. Tied up or not. You'd better kill him first then take his body to the Mexicans."

"Yeah, you're probably right." He nodded his agreement. "By this time, Crow's men will be thoroughly confused, give up the chase, realize something's amiss, panic and try to find their boss.

"If y'all can keep them occupied that long, it will give me a couple days to put some distance between them and me."

Knowing he would go along with Stockman's plan, he couldn't assume Jack would. "What's on your mind, Tunnie? Want to help old Earl the Pearl get this bastard?"

"Sounds risky, but damned if I'm not for it if you are."

O.C. offered Earl a handshake. "We're in."

Chapter Twenty Nine

PERILS OF FREEDOM

Heavy cloud cover hovered in the sky. There was a faint smell of rain in the air and a slight wind out of the north. O.C. knew the whole plan could fail if it rained. There would be no tracks to follow.

The popping sound the toe of his boot made when he kicked the saddle beneath Jack's head brought the man to a startled awakening. "Get up. Time to make time."

Jack sat straight up. "What the…Damn, I thought I'd been shot."

"You ain't shot yet, but you might be if we don't get outta here soon. Ole Tom Crow might decide to show up early."

Tunnie studied the sky. "Sure's hell looks like rain."

"Yeah, Dammit. I just hope it holds off. I want to leave a clear trail, at least for a little while." Earl had been quiet. O.C. figured he was thinking of what the day might bring. "Hey, Earl you alive this mornin'?"

"Well, I am this mornin', I only hope I am tomorrow mornin'!"

O.C. joined in the laughter, but it wasn't really funny. The old man could in fact die today. He sensed, as Earl threw his bedroll in the wagon, that the mountain man was unsure of what he was going to do.

"Stockman, Dammit, don't take any chances. You can

always back out if it don't feel right. And there's no need to worry about me and Jack; we've been through too much hell already to be killed now."

"I bet you have, boys. Nope, I'm gonna get this done. I've been waitin' a long time to get that sorry cuss and it's time for him to pay for the wrongs he's done."

All O.C. hoped was that the old man accomplished his goal without getting hurt. He and Jack stood beside their horses, reins in hand waiting, for what he didn't know.

Earl approached them and pointed. "You fellas' just lead them east. Play around with those bastards for a few days then lose 'em. Then y'all can keep goin' where you're goin'."

Jack mounted. "I don't feel good about us leavin' you to handle whatever might happen after we're gone."

The campfire still smoldered. Stockman walked over and kicked dirt onto the embers. "Jack, I've planned this for years now. I know what I'm gonna do. You men head for the high plains, I'll do the rest. Whatever you do, don't let those cutthroats catch up to you. You'll wish you'd never seen me."

O.C. knew that was true but they were committed now. He couldn't change his mind, even if he'd wanted to. He took his place atop his horse and for a moment, just sat there watching Earl pack up the last of his supplies. When he was finished, O.C. met the older man's gaze. He saw determination in Earl's eyes. He nodded his head as to say goodbye. Earl nodded back, and without another word, he and Jack rode east.

The sloping hill leading out of this canyon wasn't at all like the last one they'd had to climb, though it was still steep. O.C. hoped the trail they were making was good enough for the outlaws to find. He led the way as they rode the canyon wash, then up the hill to the top of the plateau.

He looked back over his shoulder and saw Earl and the wagon below on the canyon floor. He looked like a piss ant down there, yet O.C. could still make out his movements. The wind had picked up and the smell of rain was stronger. "I guess we'd better hold up here, Jack. If we get too far, they won't be able to follow us."

"How far do you think we've come?"

"Don't know. A mile, maybe farther." He glanced around at the terrain. "Let's wait behind that big ole rock over there. No one can see us there 'cept the Man above."

They dismounted and a slight sprinkle of rain dotted the surface of the rock. "This is what I was afraid of. Let's just hope they show up soon."

Two hours passed. O.C. had just sat down from taking his watch on the canyon floor. Thankfully, the rain hadn't come yet, and their trail was still fresh. He heard Jack whisper his name.

"O.C. there they are, right on time."

He peeked over the rock at the scene below. His heart skipped a beat. Something was strangely familiar about one of the riders. The one riding the paint. "There's something not good about this."

The riders dismounted by the wagon. One walked up to Earl and have him a hi sign from the chest. "That's probably Crow. He's checkin' it out, ain't he?"

Jack kept his voice low. "Hope he don't suspect anything."

A half hour went by before the men started looking toward the rim of the plateau. Earl had set the plan in motion and it would soon be time to get moving.

"Let's go," Jack said.

"Not yet. We need to see if they take the bait." He squinted into the distance. "Looks like they're havin' an argument."

Tom Crow stood up and shot one of the men. From the looks of it, he was instantly dead. "Damn, how'd ya like to work for him?"

Jack shook his head. "Not me."

The second man in Crow's gang took his hat off and motioned what looked to be a 'come on' gesture to the top of a small nearby knoll. In a flash a fourth member of the gang appeared. He heard the anger in Jack's voice.

"There's the women. No telling what they've been through to get this far."

"Probably anything to stay alive." The women were bound at their wrists with a rope that was tied to the saddle horn of the man's horse. Poor things.

"Hell, O.C., he's dragging them with the horse!"

He felt Jack's movement and grabbed his arm. "Hold on,

you can't go down there. I don't like this anymore than you do, but we ain't changin' the plan now." His heart went out to the Mexican women. Jack was right the horseman was purely dragging the two toward the wagon.

When the man on the horse reached the place Crow and Earl stood, he got down. Crow cut the ropes just above where they were tied and with the help of the other man, threw the women in the back of the wagon. Dirty SOB's anyway. Nobody deserved to be treated like that. The bastards would get their due. He, Jack and Earl were going to see to it.

The man on the paint never left the saddle. O.C. didn't like the way he kept staring at the rim. It was almost as if he knew exactly where they were. That was impossible. Nobody knew where they were. Still, his spine tingled. "There's somethin' about that man on the paint. I just can't figure it out." Jack didn't answer.

In a flash, Crow's man mounted, the other lay dead on the ground, and no one seemed to care. Crow stood beside Earl while the man on the paint and the other outlaw started a fast gallop up the wash.

"That's it." O.C. got on his horse. "They fell for it. Let's ride."

He spurred his horse. The wind in his face refreshed him and the adrenalin of the chase rushed through his veins. He was living dangerously and after those four years behind bars he felt alive again.

Looking toward Tunnie, he hollered over the beat of the horse's hooves, "We'll keep up a fast gallop for a while, then we'll slow down. Their horses aren't as fresh as ours so I doubt they'll be able to keep up."

The more he thought about the man on the paint, recognition crept into his mind. He envisioned the outlaw and saw his face as clear as day. "Jack! That fella' back there on the paint stallion."

"Yeah?"

"It's Joe Cloud. The son-of-a-bitch is a cutthroat outlaw."

Jack frowned. "Cloud, what makes you think that?"

"I feel it. I know it in my bones. If it is, we'd better be good at what we're doin'"

"What the hell's he doing in Texas?"

"Chasin' us, dammit, chasin' us!"

They ran the horses almost to the point of exhaustion before O.C. thought it was safe to slow. Thunder rumbled across the sky and dark gray-black clouds hovered above. A slight sprinkle started to fall as he and Jack came to a running dismount behind some mesquite trees. The rest was well needed, and he was glad for it, but rain pounded like a hammer on the dry desert sand. "We might lose them if this keeps up."

Jack wiped his horse's head with a handkerchief. "Not likely. Cloud can track a man, I've heard, at night on solid rock."

Looking down the plateau, the pounding rain with the wind of the storm stirred a dust cloud. The dirt would continue to kick up until the ground was soaked. O.C. once again got on his horse.

"Let's ride until sunset."

Jack nodded. "Cloud will pace his horse, but he'll keep coming, you can bet on that."

"We'll pace our horses, too. They're workin' hard for us, and they don't need to die doin' what we ask 'em, too." The rain began to lighten when they started to travel. O.C. couldn't keep his mind off the outlaw marshal. "You know, Jack, I made Joe Cloud a promise that I'm damn sure gonna keep."

"I remember."

"I hope we live to see that promise through, my friend, I really do."

"This looks like a good place, Jack."

"Good place for what?"

"Good place to camp."

"Camp! Looks like a good place to get our throats cut."

O.C. scouted their surroundings. To the left were the remains of a cliff dwelling. Many fires had burned inside its walls. It would be the perfect place to attract a bug like Cloud. "Gettin' our throats cut is not quite what I've got planned. Let's see if we can find some dry brush." He glanced up at the sky. This rain is gonna make it difficult, but there might be some near the mouth of this place. If we find anything to burn, we'll make a fire in there."

"What are we going to do, put a light in the window?"

"Somethin' like that." He met Tunnie's questioning gaze. "Jack, you're gonna have to trust me. Remember, I know tricks learned from the swamp Indians. Now, these ain't just a couple of outlaws like we thought we could shake at the beginning. This is Cloud and I guarantee he ain't gonna give up 'til he gets to us."

Tunnie bobbed his head up and down. "Okay, O.C., whatever you say. Just tell me what to do and I'll do it."

He knew his friend felt vulnerable. The man had lived his life working inside the Arizona State Prison and never had much experience outside its walls. Jack was damn sure no match for the real Joe Cloud. O.C. was thankful for his own upbringing, his years in the swamp, friendship with the Indians and, though he never thought he'd appreciate it, what he learned from the Don Boggs gang.

"First, let's get that fire built." He helped gather as much dry sage as he could, stacked it and lit it. "This may take a while to make a blaze, but it will.

"Now, let's gather some of these tumble weeds, stack 'em best we can then we'll wrap our coats on 'em sos from a distance, they look like men standing out there." He pointed. "I figure if we get ambushed, it'll be from that clump of heavy brush. And, if you want to know the truth, I don't think Cloud is too far behind us. He'll be here soon."

He grabbed the two long rider coats Jack had provided then moved the horses out of sight. They stacked the tumbleweeds, hooked them together with their barbed branches then placed the long riders on them. It took some doing, but he was pleased that the figures looked as real as they did.

"Put your hat on it, too, Jack. If he just falls for it for a minute, it might give me the time I need." He watched Jack place the last item on the makeshift man. "Okay, get your rifle and get in the ruins. I'm gonna take my chances out there." The concern on Jack's face was evident.

"Out where?"

"Just out there." O.C. said then left the abandoned dwelling.

Chapter Thirty

Things were getting serious now. O.C. strained his eyes to see through the pouring rain. Minutes seemed like hours as his adrenalin began to flow. He made his way to the heavy brush then stripped off his clothes. The rain was cold dripping into his eyes; the cool night wind brought a welcome chill. The mud he smeared over his body did little to insulate the cold, but he had to be completely covered.

He thought back at how the swamp Indians taught him to move through the underbrush like a ghost in the night. Waiting, watching, stirring nothing, while he moved from bush to bush to bush, making no more noise than a whisper.

In the distance, the figures he and Jack made reflected off the canyon walls, silhouetted by the fire. Damned if he himself didn't think they looked real.

To his right, a sound in the brush. He squatted down not feeling the least bit vulnerable in his nakedness. The mud would hide him in the dark light of night. Maybe this was it. His heart raced. There it was. The shadow of a man moved between him and the flickering firelight at the mouth of the ruins.

The intruder crouched in a kneeling position and unsuspecting he raised his rifle. O.C. quietly moved in behind him. The crack of the buffalo gun rattled the canyon walls and one of the tumbleweed figures blew apart.

Apparently the man knew he'd been tricked and stood to run. O.C. couldn't allow that. Revenge welled in his heart and bubbled out in an Indian yell. With the speed of a deadly swamp viper he plunged the razor sharp Arkansas Toothpick through the outlaw's throat.

O.C. made sure the man never saw it coming nor did he see who did it. He staggered a few steps then fell to the ground. A high pitched choking noise came from his throat causing an eerie echo between the canyon walls. In the blink of an eye, the interloper was dead.

Staring at the body for only a moment, O.C. walked to the person who now lay face down in the mud. With his bare foot, he turned him over. Why wasn't he surprised at who it was?

"Well, Cloud, my enemy, you sorry bastard, I promised you wouldn't see my face again. You never did." He put his foot on Cloud's lifeless chest and extracted the knife.

Hatred drained from his heart, relief riveted through him and he gave a silent thanks to the Lord for letting it be over. Maybe now he could have safe passage home.

He gathered his clothes and headed back to the cave. "Hey, Jack, it's over! I'm comin' in!"

As he moved toward his friend, he saw the look of disbelief on his face as he watched his muddy figure come into the firelight. He was so calmed he could have almost laughed when Jack spoke.

"Man, what the hell happened to you?"

"Nothin', and this mud is why."

"You get'em?"

"Yep, I got him."

"Him? Only one?"

"Yep, and I was right, it was Joe Cloud."

"What about the other one."

O.C. dropped his clothes on the dry floor of the ruin. "I don't think we need to worry about him. If I'm right, that fellas dead. Cloud left no witnesses, remember? He probably cut that guy's throat when they were barely out of sight of Earl and Crow.

"Wonder how Earl made out with that?"

"Don't worry about him. I'm sure he got the job done. He's smart and has been around this old world a long time. I told him not to take any chances and I believed him when he said he'd be alright. Now, I gotta get some of this mud off me."

The rain had all but stopped, however, like a water fall its remains plunged from the cliff making the perfect spot for O.C. to bathe. It felt good to get clean. It had been a long time since he'd washed.

He ran his clothes through the water then hung them to dry across rocks on the inside of the cave. Jack did the same. Cleanliness and safety made for a restful night. One O.C. welcomed.

* * * *

A week of hard riding behind them, O.C. recognized the Pecos river. Somehow on their journey from El Paso they had veered farther south east than they intended. He figured Fort Stockton, Texas wasn't far from where they were. Hell, a few miles was nothing compared to what they'd already traveled.

The next day, they walked the horses down the main street of Fort Stockton. Jack glanced around. "This sure's hell isn't much of a town."

"Yeah, I've been here before. It's peaceful enough though, the soldiers keep the place pretty well in line. Besides, we ain't gonna be here long enough to make friends." O.C. glanced around. The town's folk stared at them as they rode by.

"You know, Jack, these people probably think we're outlaws. With dust covering us from head to toe. This big old knife strapped to my side don't help nothin' and neither do these buffalo guns we're carryin'."

Jack smiled and patted the Army Colt hanging from his belt. "Damn, O.C. for all they know we're a couple of Preachers from St. Louis bringing glory and salvation."

"There's the general store. Let's get our supplies." He tied his horse to the hitching post, stepped up onto the walkway and was greeted by the local marshal. The man tried to stare Jack straight in the eye, but Jack was a big man and stood a head taller than the lawman.

"I'm Marshal Bob Tibbs. Howdy."

"Howdy," Jack replied.

"I'll get right to the point. People around here don't like

buffalo hunters. Just get what you need, with no offense, and get out of town."

O.C. stepped forward. "We'll only be here long enough to get our supplies, sir. We're not lookin' for trouble of any kind."

"Good. Get what you need then go."

"Yes, sir." O.C. heard a disturbance across the street. He glanced over to see an Indian arguing with two cowboys. He turned back toward the marshal. The younger man tipped his hat to him and Jack, then walked across the street.

"Jack, if you'll watch the gear, I'll get the things we need. I wouldn't want any of the good people of this grand town to run off with our horses."

The ruckus across the street became more violent. One of the cowboys knocked the Indian to the ground and started to beat him up. O.C. wanted to help the Indian, but it wasn't any of his business. However, he couldn't understand why the marshal was standing by letting it happen.

He clinched his jaw and forced himself to go inside, but when he returned with the supplies, the situation hadn't changed. "What the hell's goin' on over there?"

"They've been beating him since you left."

He tossed the cloth bag of goods to Jack then walked straight across the street. The marshal was still standing idly by. He pulled his pistol just before he got there and left it at his side. "Y'all stop right now!" The men looked up at him. "You men tell me what this man has done and I might help you."

"Who the hell are you?" One of the cowboys scoffed.

"That didn't answer my question." He pointed his pistol at the man. "I said what did he do? If I don't get an answer, I'll let this forty four ask the next question."

Tibbs stepped forward. "I thought I told you to get out of town."

He turned the forty four on Bob Tibbs. "Wrong answer. Now, care to try again, Marshal?"

The man looked down the barrel of the pistol. "This drunk spilled whiskey on one of my friends here."

Out of the corner of his eye, O.C. saw one of the cowboys easing his hand toward his gun. Tunnie appeared out of nowhere and nudged the man in the back with one of the buffalo rifles hard enough to knock the breath out of him. Nobody, not even he saw the big man come from behind.

He kept his pistol trained on the marshal. "Any one man can whip a drunk. Jack, help him up." With his left hand, he grabbed the reins of a paint. "This his horse?"

"It's his," Tibbs said. "Why don't you men take your drunken Indian and get out of town before someone gets killed."

"I think we'll do just that."

The Indian man was unsteady on his feet, blood dripped from his nose and oozed from his mouth. O.C. saw Jack walk behind the marshal. What was he up to? In an instant he grabbed the man around the neck with his elbow resting under his chin. He'd seen Jack use the grip before when a prisoner got out of hand.

Tunnie put his knife to the man's throat. "I'll tell you what. You're no lawman. I was a lawman before you were born. You're supposed to respect the law and the folks in your town. Indian or not! Don't come after us or you'll be dead. You understand?"

O.C. knew Tibbs didn't hear a word. He was passed out on his feet. That was a hell of a hold Jack knew. Worked every time. The outlaw of a lawman crumpled to the ground like a rag when Tunnie let him go.

Jack put his knife away and picked up his rifle. "You men stand back. We're going to ride out now. If you come after us, I might let you have a little taste of this buffalo gun."

The two men backed toward the saloon door. Jack helped the beaten Indian across the street while O.C. took his horse. He kept his pistol trained on the men as he backed his way to the other two steeds.

Literally, Jack threw the Indian atop the paint then mounted. O.C. placed his pistol back in his belt, got on his horse and rode to the end of the street. He looked back over his shoulder in time to see the two cowboys help the sheriff off the ground. The man's pants were wet in front where he'd peed himself.

O.C. grinned. "I don't think they'll be after us, Jack. We scared the pee waddin' out of 'em."

Jack laughed and spurred his horse into a lope.

****

"This is Fort Stockton." O.C. got off his horse and bent down for a drink. The Indian was still behind them. He'd followed them as if he wanted to join their cause. Soon he caught up and without speaking, got off his horse and began to wash off the dried blood.

"What's your name?" O.C. stood and approached the man.

"I'm called Big City."

"Well, that's quite a name." O.C. smiled at him. "You speak good English." Jack stepped forward and O.C. listened to the men's conversation.

"I was a scout for the Army once."

"You know this territory?"

"I know Texas very well."

"What were those men picking on you for?"

"I won most of their money playing cards. I guess they were embarrassed to be beaten by an Indian. I'm glad you came along."

"What were you doing in that town in the first place? Not that it's any of my business."

"No matter. The Army told me they didn't need me anymore. My people kicked me out of the tribe for scouting for the Army, so I had no place to go. I've just been traveling from place to place. After the card game, I knew I should get out of Fort Stockton, so I went outside to leave. They followed me out. I was not drunk."

"No?"

"Well, maybe a little."

O.C. saw a glint of humor in Big City's eyes. "By the way, I'm O.C. Armstrong and this is Jack Tunnie. I'm sorry to hear about what your people did to you."

"I hope to go back to them one day, but right now, it's impossible."

"Tunnie, I don't know about you, but it's okay with me if Big City here stays with us if he wants."

"Suits me," Jack agreed.

Big City nodded his thanks. He wasn't a big man, and didn't look like he could whip a rabbit, but O.C. liked him.

"We're goin' to cross Texas to find a place called Texas Bay. We plan to catch a ship there and eventually make our way to Gulfport, Mississippi."

He got his canteens down to fill. "I have a home near there. Or, I used to. Hell, it's been so long since I've been there, I don't know whether I do or not." O.C. put the lids back on the containers.

"Why have you been gone so long?"

"Big City, that's a hell of a long story. One of these days I'll tell it to you, or you'll find out yourself." He stood up, put his canteens away then started to gather wood for a fire. He noticed Big City stared to the east across the Pecos River.

"I would not build a fire, my friends. We're not too far from a Kiowa village. They don't like white men so much. Don't like other tribes either. We should travel a while longer before we camp.

"Dammit!" Shouted Jack. "I've never seen anything like this damn Texas. Seems everybody in this place is out to shoot you or peel your head like an apple!"

O.C. mounted his horse and smiled at Big City. "Don't pay any attention to him. He used to be a school teacher."

Jack grunted when he got on his horse. "The hell I did!"

Big City took the lead and O.C. followed. He could hear Jack behind them still grumbling as they eased their way across the river. He'd make it a point to tell their new friend the truth about Tunnie, but for now, he'd let the man stew.

"You know this place where you are going is far away."

"I know, but I'm determined to get there, No matter what it takes."

It was beginning to get dark and O.C. figured their last stop was about five miles behind. In the quiet of night, he and the others built their camp.

He lay on his bedroll and thought of his family. Had the boys really found the gold? Hell, he didn't know why he still thought of them as boys. They were men now. If his years were right, Joe would be close to twenty one, Charles nineteen and little Carl would be almost seventeen. Damn he missed them. He sure hoped he could find them again someday.

Martha's sweet face came into his mind. Was his precious

wife still alive? He knew his leaving took a toll on her, and he could only imagine what she thought when he didn't come back. Hopefully, the boys took her with them and when he got there, he'd find her at her sister's. He prayed for that at least.

At first light, his travels would begin again. It had been quite a journey so far and he had a lot farther to go. The nights seemed to get shorter and the days, hot and long.

He closed his eyes, took in a deep, calming breath and whispered to a night hawk overhead. "By damn, I'm gonna see my family again if it's the last thing I ever do."

****

ABILENE TEXAS

O.C. glanced over at the short Indian. "Comin' this far north sure drove us off course. I didn't think Abilene'd be this much out of the way."

"It was out of the way for a reason."

"What reason's that?"

"You still have your hair, and you may not have if we'd traveled further south."

Tunnie rode up beside O.C. "I, for one, sure am glad we kept our hair." The man turned toward O.C. "You don't have that much hair to worry about anyway, Armstrong."

"Kiss my ass, Jack." O.C. welcomed the laughter his statement brought. I was good to be in a town and not in the wilderness. "Didn't realize this was such a big town."

"Me neither," said Tunnie. "Hey, O.C., that old man… Earl… he said he saw those boys of yours on the barge going to St Louis. If he was right, maybe they're still there. You know it doesn't make sense for them to go back to that cabin in the swamp you talk about."

"S'pose you're right, but my bet is they ended up back in Vicksburg. St. Louis is a pretty big place. I don't think they'd like it there." Maybe it was a dream, or maybe hope, that they would settle in Vicksburg. Getting to Vicksburg didn't seem out of sight, but what would he do if he couldn't find his family? He'd have to go on with life, that was all there was to it. His heart skipped a beat and hope started to seep in.

"Probably find your wife there, too." Tunnie shook his head. "Rough trip any way you go, but Vicksburg's pretty much a straight shot from here."

The man was right; where to go had been on his mind, too. Matter of fact, it had been all he could think about. "Let's go on to Vicksburg. If they're not there, then maybe we can pick up their trail and find out if they went back to the swamp, or moved on somewhere else." He'd had big dreams for his family, always wanting to get them out of the swamp, but never reaching his goal. Maybe, just maybe, they had done it themselves.

Tunnie slapped O.C. on the back. "Let's get some supplies and see if we can make some time today."

Laughter bubbled up inside him once again. "Damn, I'm gettin' excited. Just hope I don't fall dead before we get there." O.C. noticed even Big City, the man of few words, chuckled.

They had left Abilene two days earlier and O.C. was tired of the saddle. He was ready to make camp. "Hey, boys, if that sign back there was right, looks like we're about fifteen miles from Fort Worth. We'd better camp here then make the rest of the way tomorrow.

Tunnie got off his horse and unstrapped his saddle. "Sounds like a plan."

O.C. dismounted and noticed Big City sat firm on his horse. "You gonna sit up there the rest of the evening?"

The Indian met O.C.'s gaze. "I am going north now. Some of my people are up past the Canadian border and maybe I will find my family."

"A man's gotta do what a man's gotta do, I reckin." O.C. reached to shake Big City's hand. "Maybe we'll cross trails again. You make for good company, even if you don't talk too much." He chuckled but knew where the man was headed was serious business. "Remember, you're in Comanche country. Don't build any fires. If they come, you won't know 'til you're dead." He couldn't tell the man anything he didn't already know.

"Yes, thank you for your advice. I have traveled this country before and will do as you suggest."

O.C. felt Jack's presence beside him as Big City gave them

the farewell sign then rode away. “Jack, I’m gonna miss him.”

“Yeah, he’s a good man. I kind of wish he would’ve stayed around. He’s pretty damned smart, too.”

He had to agree with Tunnie, but still worried for the Indian’s safety traveling alone. He turned toward his horse and began to unsaddle. “Guess we’d better turn in. We’ve got a long trip ahead of us.”

The same as he did every evening, O.C. fell into a dream filled sleep. Dreams of seeing Martha at her sister’s, and finding the boys safe, with or without the gold, were so vivid behind closed eyes.

Chapter Thirty One

THE JOHNNY ONE HORN STORY

With the sun sinking in the west like a huge fire ball, long black shadows stretched over the landscape. Johnny One Horn topped the last hill before he reached the small lake he'd seen in the distance. He knew he'd drifted farther south than he was supposed to, but for some reason he was drawn in this direction and now only a thicket of brush lay between him and the inviting water.

He dismounted and started toward the brush, but stopped dead in his tracks when he heard voices from the other side. Women? It couldn't be. He got on his knees, slipped through the thicket and slowly parted the brush to take a look.

Two very large women stood bare-ass naked only a few feet from him. One of them saw him and let out a blood curdling scream. How could he have been so careless? Nothing like this had ever happened before. Maybe he was losing his edge.

He watched the bigger of the two grab a double barreled shotgun that was resting against a tree. Damn, she was going to shoot him! He jumped up and started to run through the brush, but he heard her words loud and clear.

"I'll teach you, you peeping tom bastard!"

He reached Coattail and jumped on his bare back just as the thunder of both barrels firing at the same time sounded. It was like a cannon going off and echoed through the rocky cliffs surrounding the water. The horse spooked and Johnny found himself flying through the air. When he landed, everything went black.

"Damn, Ulla May, you killed him."

"I hope not. I shot almost straight up in the air so I wouldn't hit him. I just wanted to scare the hell out of him, that's all." Without putting her clothes on, Ulla May walked through the thicket toward the man on the ground. When she reached him, she glanced down.

"You think he's dead, Ulla May?"

"Naw, Pickles, he's just knocked out."

"He sure is a handsome devil."

Ulla smiled. "Yeah, he sure's hell is and I saw him first, so you keep your hands off him. You hear me?"

"You always get to have all the fun."

"Oh, stop whining and go get our clothes and the wagon. I'm taking this one home with me."

Standing guard, Ulla waited for Pickles to bring the wagon. She dressed, then put the shotgun in the driver's seat. "It's going to be hard getting him in the wagon."

"Yep, he's a big one."

"Well, I guess we'd better try."

Pickles grabbed under the man's arms. "He looks like a Mexican, but he's dressed like a cowboy."

Ulla took hold of his feet. "You know, we aren't going to be able to lift him all the way up. Maybe if we kind of swing him we can get enough momentum we can just throw him in."

"Let's do it. Start swinging and on the count of three, we'll let him go. Ready?"

"Yep… one, two, three."

"Damn, Ulla May, it worked. You know, he might be one of that bunch that's run up here from the border. The ones we've been hearing about."

After studying the man, Ulla climbed into the wagon seat. "Well, Pickles, that would be just our luck. Or he could be a marshal or some kind of law man. Hell, we'll probably be the first fat women to get our asses hung. We'd better take him to Garden City and get him patched up and find out who he is."

Pickles moved the gun over and took a seat. "You really

think they'd hang us?"

Ulla chuckled. "Probably not, but we'd have to give it up to ole Marshal Nash and his dirty deputies forever!"

The sun was just beginning to go down when Ulla May pulled into the alley behind the saloon she owned and ran. She reined to a stop at the bottom of the steps where a man who worked as her handyman, was sleeping. "Jo Bo Hatton, you drunk again?" She laid the reins over the seat and climbed down. "Why is it every time I leave town, I come back to find your ass drunk as hell?"

Fighting to wake up, Jo Bo whipped out his knife. He tried to focus on who was talking to him.

"Don't you pull a knife on me, you old coot. I'll stick it right where you don't want it to be."

"I'm sorry, Ulla. What's goin' on? You scared the hell out of me." He stood on unsteady legs and glanced into the wagon. "Who's that?"

"Just shut up Jo Bo, and help us get this bear of a man up the stairs. You didn't try to have your way with any of my girls for free, did you?"

Jo Bo rubbed his eyes with the back of his hands. "No ma'am. I learnt my lesson last time." He pointed to the man. "What's wrong with him? Is he drunk?"

"No, *you're* drunk; he fell off his horse. Got a hell of a bump on his head. Now, quit jawing and let's get him upstairs and in a bed."

Finally in the bedroom, Ulla wiped sweat from her forehead. " Whew! Damn hard work getting him up here, but look at that fine hunk of a man, would you?"

"He don't do a thing for me," Jo Bo said.

"Oh, hell, not you, Jo Bo, I was talking to Pickles. You run along and get Doc. Young. See if he can come attend the big man, while we take off his clothes"

"Suits me fine, I don't care nothin' 'bout lookin at another man naked, that's for sure." He turned and left the room.

Pickles placed the last piece of clothing on the back of a chair. "Taking off all those duds was hard work, wasn't it?"

"Sure 'nough, but just looking at him made it all worth it!"

"Woo wee, don't believe I've ever seen a man with all them muscles tight in his belly like that. And his man parts, damn! You're just lucky you saw him first. I don't know if I could keep my hands off him whilst he was sleeping."

"Soon as he's well, I'll tell you all about it." Ulla got a rag and went to the water bowl. "Place downstairs sounds like its hopping. Why don't you go and see how things are going, I'll stay here and wait for Doc."

With that, Pickles left the room and closed the door behind her. Ulla washed the blood from the man's head, pulled the covers over him and sat in the chair next to the bed. In a few minutes a knock sounded at the door.

"Come in, Doc."

The door opened and Jo Bo walked in. "Doc ain't comin'. He's drunk."

"Damn, is everybody drunk today? What am I supposed to do now?"

"I told him what happened and that you wanted him to come attend this feller. He handed me this ointment, said it would fix him up for sure. Then he slammed the door in my face."

"Probably thought you had the bed bugs again." Ulla took the jar from Jo Bo and opened the lid. "Damn, this stuff stinks. Are you sure he gave you the right ointment?"

"That's what he said."

"Well, alright, I guess it won't hurt to try it." She dipped her fingers into the greasy substance then rubbed it on the man's head. "Damn this stuff stinks!"

Johnny One Horn reached his hand up and rubbed his head. It throbbed, and when he tried to open his eyes, everything was blurred. What the hell was that in his hair? Did he fall into something? "Smells like a polecat." It sure wasn't any of *his* medicine.

His own voice startled him full awake and he sat up in bed, ignoring the pain in his body and head. He felt like he'd been dragged through rocks, but more important, he realized he was in a real bed and the two fat women were sitting beside it while an old man stood gawking at him. "Who are you?" He glanced from one to the other.

"Why, hello darlin'. I'm Ulla May, this is Pickles and that over there is Jo Bo Hatten."

He studied the room around him. "How did I get here?"

"You fell off your horse," Jo Bo said.

"Coattail, where is he?"

"Just don't you worry about that right now, we need to get you well." Ulla looked at Jo Bo. "You go on home now. Me and Pickles are going down to see what's happening at the bar." She looked at Johnny. "Big man, you get some sleep and we'll see you tomorrow."

Johnny lay back and pulled the covers up over him. The woman was bossy, but she was right. He was weak and he knew it. It shouldn't take long for him to get back into shape if he just rested. He nodded to the three, closed his eyes and heard the door click shut.

Was his mind playing tricks on him, or had he seen those two women naked by a lake? No, he knew exactly what had happened. The one called Ulla May tried to shoot him! Well, now it seemed like she was nursing him back to health and he appreciated her for that, but he wished he had his medicine bag. Then maybe he could get out of here faster.

His thoughts briefly went back to Joe and the boys, but memories of the two fat women running around without clothes kept haunting his mind. Thankfully, blissful sleep finally overtook him.

Johnny awoke, sat up on the side of the bed and glanced out the window. The position of the sun told him it was midday. How long had he been out? He saw his clothes, clean and laying on the chair. Reaching for them, his mind raced. He had to get back to Joe and the boys. They were counting on him to find them some land, and he hadn't done that. He needed to tell them what had happened.

When he started down the stairs, he realized he wasn't as steady on his feet as he should be. He knew he had hit the ground hard, but this was ridiculous. He was supposed to be tough.

He studied the bar below as he made his way down. Girls were everywhere; some came up the stairs to meet him, pulling at his clothes and laughing. It was nice to get the attention, but soon he found himself backed into a corner then he heard Ulla May's voice and saw her bustling through the crowd.

"Big man, what are you doing down here? You're not well enough to be out of bed yet." She turned and shook her finger at the other women. "Keep your hands off. I've got dibs on him."

Pickles shouted out, "You don't even know his name, Ulla May."

"You shut your face or you'll be plucking chickens for a living." She put her hands on her hips and looked at the women. "You girls get back to work!"

Johnny was amazed at how the girls cowered down and hustled back to the bar. He was also surprised at how little clothes they had on. Their shoes had high heels and their stockings went clear up their thighs to hooks of some sort. It made him want to see more but Ulla May's persistent pushing wouldn't allow him the pleasure.

"You get yourself right back up there in that bed, now."

The pressure of her hands in his back and forceful shoves sent him on the move, but it didn't stop him from glancing over his shoulder at the beautiful girls down below. He'd never seen anything like it, then in no time, he was back in his room and Ulla shut the door behind them.

"Now, you get back in bed. You'll be well soon enough. When that happens, I've got some work around here I want you to do."

Work? He didn't have time to work for this woman; he had to get back to Joe and the boys. They'd be wondering about him. "How long did I sleep?"

"Bout three days."

"Three days?" He started for the door. "I have to go. Where is my horse?" She blocked his passage with her large frame. He had never been disrespectful to a woman and he wasn't going to start now. Though she was the cause of his injury, she had indeed taken him in and helped him.

"Oh, no you don't. I've got too much invested in you to just let you go on your way. You owe me that much, big man."

What was he going to do now? He didn't have any idea where his horse was, it was for sure he'd taken quite a lick on the head and he wasn't up to full health yet. He watched her slowly retreat through the door, then she stuck her head back inside.

"What's your name anyway?"

"Name?"

"Yeah, you're damned name! What is it?"

"Name is Johnny One Horn! Johnny One Horn!" He wouldn't let her get away with yelling at him. He wasn't one of her hired help. Then she looked at him and smiled and he couldn't help but smile back. She was pretty for a fat woman.

"The hell you say. That sounds like something out of one of those story books. I like it."

He had no idea what she was talking about and more than that, he didn't care. Focusing on getting back to one-hundred percent is what he had to do now. It had already been almost a week since he'd left his friends in Kansas. This was not good.

****

Joe sat beside Little Boy Horse by the campfire. The sun was setting in the west and the night critters sang their songs. "Where do you think he is, Horse? Hell, it's been over a week since we've seen him. I thought he'd be back by now."

"I do not know where he might be. I am concerned, yet I know Johnny One Horn can take care of himself."

"But what if something happened to him? What if he's layin' out there somewhere hurt?" This reminded Joe of when O.C. left the farm and never returned. He had the same feeling inside as he'd experienced then.

What ifs can go on forever, Joe. No matter what, we have moved on already."

His Indian friend was right, but it didn't make the worry go away. "I know, Horse. It just seems like it's slow goin' that's all."

"Did you think driving cattle would be a quick undertaking?"

"No, I'm just whinin' I guess. I was hopin' Johnny'd be able to find us a place to stop. Let the cattle rest and graze for a while." The real reason was Johnny was his friend and he didn't want to think about him never returning.

"If he is not dead, he will return sooner or later. If he does not, there will be good reason."

That was true enough. Joe knew Johnny One Horn wouldn't abandon them unless something out of the ordinary happened. He nodded his agreement, looked off into the distance and said a silent prayer that one day he'd see his friend again.

Chapter Thirty Two

"Here's you a change of clothes, Horny."

Johnny opened his eyes and saw Ulla May standing over him. "What time is it?"

"'Bout six o'clock in the morning. Time to get up. I've got things around here for you to do."

He glanced at the clothes and saw a top hat. Was that his? It had been with his other things on Coattail's back. "Where is my horse?" He threw back the covers and stood to his full height, unfazed that the woman was ogling his nakedness. "My horse, where is he?" As if she'd been slapped, she looked into his eyes instead of at his privates.

"I don't know. He ran off. Probably half way to Texas by now."

"Did you buy this?" He pointed to the top hat.

"Sure did, Horny. Thought it would look good on you."

At least she had good taste. "My name is Johnny, Johnny One Horn." He put on the breeches and fastened them then grabbed the shirt. The hat made him think of Carl, but now wasn't the time.

"I don't really give a damn what your name is, long as you do good work. Finish getting dressed and come with me."

He fought to keep from smiling at the lustful look in the big woman's eyes as she watched him dress. She wanted him and he knew it. It amused him to see her lick her lips when she stared at him. He flexed the muscles in his stomach on purpose so he could see her reaction. He liked this woman, but not enough to fulfill her fantasy.

Buttoning the last button on his shirt, he sat on the edge of the bed and donned his boots. "I am ready." He followed the woman down the stairs and watched the girls come alive when he reached the bottom. He noted the sour look on Ulla's face when she tossed him a handle with strings on the bottom.

"You can smile at the girls later. You've got to pay for your keep. I suppose you know how to mop."

"Mop?"

"Yeah, you know, clean the floor. With this... it's a mop."

She pointed at the gadget he held in his hands and he looked down at it. He'd never used one of the things before. "I want coffee first." It had been a long time since he'd had a good cup of coffee. He was sure this woman's wouldn't be as good as Levi's.

"Well, get you some then do a good job mopping."

"I will try." Ulla seemed satisfied with that.

"Good. I'm going to send Jo Bo out to see if he can find your horse. If he can't, I'll let you work here until you can afford to buy another one."

He worried about the horse being loose for the last few days, but the stallion was smart and would survive. He was sure of that.

The coffee went down smooth and his energy was renewed. He took the mop in hand. Swishing the pole with the strings on the end of it was harder than he'd thought. It was all but impossible to keep from bumping into things. He banged it into a cowboy's chair, who was playing cards.

The man jumped to his feet and turned around. "Watch out you crazy fool."

Johnny stood there, unmoving. Who was this man calling a fool? He squinted at the short fellow making the man shudder then slowly, deliberately, pulled out his Arkansas Toothpick and held it steady by his side.

"Ah, t-that's okay, big man. Anybody c-can have an accident. I'm just go-gonna sit back down here."

Sometimes silence had a bigger impact than action. This was one of those times. You could have heard a pin drop throughout the saloon. The man took his seat and after a moment, Johnny put his knife back in its sheath, then continued to mop. He heard Ulla and some of the girls giggling in the corner, then heard the big woman's voice.

"By God, I finally got me a bouncer."

The girls were clambering around him, gawking, but none of them touched him. He enjoyed flirting with the pretty little things when Jo Bo came through the swinging doors.

"Pickles, give me some whiskey."

The woman slammed a shot glass on the bar. "Get outside and dust yourself off, you ass. There's enough dirt in here already."

Jo Bo went outside then came back in. Johnny walked to the bar where the old man drank his whiskey down. "You find my horse?"

"Matters-a-fact, I did. Iffin' he's yours, the crazy bastard's at the stables right now. He's a paint, right?"

"Paint?"

"You know, brown and white on his butt, and around."

"Yes, that is him." Johnny dropped the mop, made for the door and ran to the livery stable. He wanted to see a familiar, friendly face.

When he entered a scruffy man was trying to give Coattail some water and Johnny saw that look in the horse's eye. It was too late for a warning by that time, the man had already been bit.

"Yow! You sorry bastard!" The livery owner grabbed a horse whip. "I'll teach you to bite me in the ass, you ornery buzzard."

Horn couldn't let the man land a blow, and in moments he grabbed the hand that held the whip. "You hit my horse…" He pulled out his Toothpick and saw the man's eyes widen in fear. "and I'll skin you with this."

"I'm not going to hit him, big fellow. I was just a little mad."

"You just a little mad, then I just skin you a little." He smiled and holstered his knife for the second time that day.

"Damn, don't scare me like that. I'm too old and I might've just fell over dead!" The man studied Johnny. "You use that knife like an Indian. Are you an Indian or Mexican, big fellow."

One Horn thought for a moment. He remembered what Joe had said about the ways of the white man in this land and knew what he had to do. "Neither, I am French, but I lived close to Indians for a while. They are very good people." He noted the questionable look on the stable man's face, but let it pass.

"Name's Bill Brooks."

"Johnny One Horn." He turned toward his horse. "I will clean up Coattail now." He turned from the man, hugged his horse then began to groom him.

Johnny was pleased to see his personal belongings lying on the floor in the hay. Jo Bo must have put them there. He was a good ole drunk, no matter what Ulla said about him.

After washing, brushing and feeding his faithful companion, Johnny patted him on the side of his head. "I'll see you in the morning, my friend. We will leave soon, but now, I want coffee."

The next morning the sun peeked over the horizon when One Horn opened the stable door with a loud bang. "Bill Brooks, I am here. I am going for a ride." Johnny was surprised to see the old man rustle out from under a pile of hay. Did he sleep there? Well, he'd slept in worse places himself.

"You'd better come back. You owe me for board and eats on that snappin' turtle of a damned horse of yours."

"I know that. I will be back to pay you." In time, he would also pay his debt to Ulla May for her care and help. If he had money now, he would do it, but when he saw Joe again, he would get some of the gold.

"You'd better or I'll send Snatch after you."

He smiled at her nick name for the sheriff. Johnny knew Nash was too lazy to even come looking for him, but he wouldn't have to worry about that. He vowed to pay his debts to the people of Garden City.

He mounted and without looking back, spun Coattail around and rode out of town. It took two hours to reach the lake where he'd run into Ulla and Pickles. He smiled at the memory. What a turn that day had brought to his life.

But now he had to reach the boys. It would take him another eight hours in the saddle before he would get to the last place he'd left them. If they were there waiting for his return, he would be pleased, but if they weren't he'd have to make the decision of whether to go on, or come back and pay his debts.

He pushed Coattail pretty hard, but was sure not to tire him too much. It had been a long day for both of them and when he saw the area where he'd last left his friends, it was clear they'd left. "Damn, Coattail. They probably think I am dead."

Though he couldn't put his mind around exactly how long he'd been gone, he knew it had been more than a week maybe two. "They would not wait that long for us, my friend. They have moved on." He checked the fire pit. "It has been a few days, too. I will build a fire and cook the rabbit I shot a while ago." He gathered wood started the fire and got ready to camp for the night.

The rabbit was over the fire and Johnny was ready for rest, but he had to take care of Coattail first. "If they travel thirty miles a day, they could be a couple of hundred miles ahead of us already." He brushed his mount, proud of the way he cared for the horse. "That would be a long way for me and you to go to catch up." Putting the brush in its proper place, he walked toward the fire. "I will not decide tonight. We will rest. Morning is soon enough."

Johnny awoke before dawn. The fire was merely embers and it was time to figure out what he was going to do. He wished he had a cup of Levi's stiff coffee, but all he had was his water bag and some dried beef. Damn how he missed his coffee.

In order to go after Joe and the crew, he would need more supplies. If he went back to Garden City he could work off his debts and save enough money to get what he needed for the long trip North West.

He poured some of the water into his hand and gave Coattail a drink. "It seems we will go back to Ulla May's, friend. Little Boy Horse will take care of the others; they do not really need us." When the horse had his fill of water, Johnny broke his small camp and mounted.

"Someday soon we will see Joe Armstrong, our little friend Carl and the rest. A few weeks of work and we should be able to go after them."

Coattail snorted and bobbed his head as if he understood what Johnny was saying. "You are a smart one. I just hope I am doing the right thing." He got on the stallion's back and started his trek. In his heart, he knew he would see the others again, but for now, he had to go his own way.

****

"Joe, you think Johnny's ever gonna catch up with us?" Carl pulled the brake in place on the flatbed wagon. "I miss the hell out of him."

The bond between Carl and Johnny had always been strong, and Joe knew the boy was telling the truth. "I think so. If he's able bodied, he'll find us again someday."

"That's what I thought about Pa, and he's never come back. What if Horn is dead like Pa?"

"First off, Carl, we don't know that Pa's dead."

"We don't know he ain't, either."

Carl's words hit home and stabbed at Joe's heart. "You're right, little brother. We don't. But, like Horse said, if Horn is alive, and he don't come back for a while, he'll have good reason. Same goes for Pa. We just gotta keep thinkin' we'll see them both again."

"I suppose you're right."

Joe smiled and from atop his horse, ruffled his little brother's hair. "Now you'd better get caught up with Levi's wagon. I see a stray over there I need to round up." He rode away with doubts riddling his mind.

CHAPTER THIRTY THREE

Lights flickered through windows, while darkness covered the land. Johnny One Horn rode to the stable then after taking care of Coattail, made his way back to the saloon. He slipped up the back stairs and into his room. He was disappointed he didn't find the boys, but someday he would find them. Now he just wanted to rest. Worn out from the long day's ride, he was asleep almost before his head hit the pillow.

The morning found him rested and he was anxious to get to his duties in the bar. None of the girls were up yet and he was pleased at how much easier it was to mop the wooden floor when the place was empty. He would make a habit of doing it this way.

He would work hard to make the money for the supplies he'd need to get out of town. Already, he liked a lot of the folks he'd met here, but one woman in particular had caught his eye. She was a proper lady, and pretty, too. One day soon he wanted to meet her. Could she be the real reason he came back? Ulla's voice drew his attention from his thoughts.

"Where'd you go, One Horny? We missed you around here."

"Does it matter? I am here now to work and pay off my debt."

"By golly, big man, I knew you were a man of his word."

He watched the woman ready the bar for the day and was pleased when she brought him a cup of coffee. Customers started to filter in early; Johnny continued to do his chores throughout the day, then in the afternoon he saw Bill Brooks from the stable enter and walk toward him.

"Hey, One Horn, saw snappin' turtle in the stall. Knowd you'd be back. Let's have a drink."

Drinking the white man's crazy water was something he was reluctant to do. Grey Wolf had warned him about the effects it could have on a man, and he'd seen it with his own eyes as well. "I do not think so. I like coffee."

"Ah, hell, one ain't gonna hurt a big guy like you. Come on, I'll buy."

He was big and surely only one little shot of the stuff wouldn't hurt. "Alright."

Bill waved at Pickles. "Hey, beautiful, bring us a shot of your best rotgut!"

Horn watched the woman pour the honey colored liquid to the brim of the small glass. He picked it up and put it to his nose.

"Don't smell it, man, just drink 'er down."

Johnny put the glass to his lips and turned it bottoms up. He frowned and fought the urge to cough as the burning went all the way to his belly. He took a deep breath and welcomed the cooling air on his throat.

Bill patted Horn on the back. "See there? It ain't that bad. Now, wanna play some poker?"

"I have never played cards before."

"Ah, go on," Pickles urged, "You've done all your chores for the day. Relax and have fun. I'll bring y'all a bottle and a couple of glasses."

Nodding he agreed and followed the livery man to a table. He was surprised at how fast he caught on to the game and that he liked it, too. Bill poured them shot after shot as they sat playing throughout the afternoon.

"Damn, One Horn, you sure catch on fast and you're good at this. Are you sure you weren't pullin' my leg when you said you never played before?"

"Yes, I am sure." His head was feeling funny and he didn't know if he liked it or not. One thing he did know was that he liked cards. When he stood up, he wasn't too steady on his feet. "Ulla May, I want to buy this bunch of cards."

The large woman laughed. "It's called a deck, and I'll put them on your bill."

He smiled, proud of his purchase and swayed back and forth on his feet. When he sat back down, he realized he couldn't focus on the spots of the cards anymore. Everything was blurry. "Bill Brooks, I believe I am drunk. I will take more of your money another day, but now, I go to bed." With that he stood again and carefully made his way to his room.

Two weeks had passed since Johnny had gotten drunk, and learned to play poker from his new friend Bill. He got a kick out of the game and his talent for winning hadn't gone unnoticed by local cowboys who left often without their money. He looked across the table at the owner of the saloon.

"I've never seen anyone learn poker so fast, Horny. I'll tell you what, you can play poker for the house and I'll give you half the winnings. How's that sound?"

"Not too good."

"Why not?"

"It seems I can keep all of the winnings if I play for myself." The mischievous smile on Ulla May's face said she had something in mind.

"Well, big guy, I've got a better offer than that. How about you don't have to mop and clean around here anymore, but I will still give you your wage, on top of the winnings. All you have to do is play cards."

"What if I lose?" This was sounding better all the time, but he'd be damned if he'd pay half the losings.

"Hmmm, well, I hadn't thought about that because I've never seen you lose, but... I'll pay all the losses, but if you lose, you will only get your regular wage. Nothing over and above. In other words, I win you win. You lose, I lose but you still get paid.

No more mopping floors, and losing someone else's money, now that offer he could live with. "Shake and it is a deal." He stood, stuck out his hand and the woman grasped it firmly. "I will start today!"

He sat at the house table and waited for his first challenge. It wasn't long before two dusty cowboys pulled up a chair. Horse started to shuffle the cards and noticed one of the men only had one eye, the other was covered with a patch.

The man with both eyes looked toward the bar. "Can we get a bottle of whiskey over here?"

The men put their money on the table and Ulla May poured their glasses full then sat the bottle on the table. Horn refused the brown liquid. He didn't like the way it made him feel, being out of control was something he wasn't used to. "I will have coffee."

In the course of a couple of hours playing poker with the men, Horn was pleased he'd only lost one hand. However, the two looked at each other, they were anything but happy, then one of them slammed his cards down on the table.

"Hell, you can't tell me that someone's that damn lucky. You've won almost every time." He slid his hand under the table. "I think we've been railroaded!"

Horn reached for his Arkansas Toothpick, but the man froze in place at the sound of a shot gun being cocked. It was hard to keep from smiling at the look on the cowboy's face when he turned to see Ulla Mae pointing a ten gage at him. Johnny relaxed back; this might be a good show.

Ulla leveled the weapon and pointed it at the pair. "I know you, Hoots Barnes, and you, too, One Eyed Bill Pritchard, but don't be pullin' any guns in here or I'll blow you through that door."

"But Miss Ulla, this feller done won fifty dollars off us."

"I'll give you credit 'til next month, if you want to stay and drink, but I don't want any trouble from you. Now, what will it be?

Johnny didn't trust these two. He'd just as soon them leave, but Ulla was the boss and if she wanted to give them credit to drink, that wasn't his business. His hand on his knife, he watched the two slowly rise, pick up the bottle of whiskey and walk to the bar.

Hoots put the bottle on the bar. "I still think he cheated and I hope the bastard chokes on our money."

Horn wasn't going to let him get away with that. He stood. "I do not cheat!" He felt more than saw some of the saloon girls surround him, but stayed focused on the man until Pickles voice drew his attention.

"They're just blowing off steam." She approached Johnny and whispered. "Watch them, though, they'll shoot you in the back if they can get away with it."

If they thought they scared him, they had another think coming. He took a step forward and felt one of the girls' hands on his chest. Raising his voice to be sure the two cowards heard him, he said, "I told you, I do not cheat. If you say I do to anyone, I will skin you both then hang your balls over the saloon door for everyone to see. Understand that!"

Barnes looked at Pritchard. "By God, I think we better get the hell outta here. I never seen a man look that mean before."

The one eyed man opened his mouth to speak, but Johnny was glad to see Barnes had enough sense to stop him. He'd just as soon kill the bastards as look at them.

Barnes grabbed Pritchard's collar. "Damn, man, there'll be another time. Somethin' tells me he means what he says."

Johnny's heart began to slow and the tension gradually left his shoulders as the men walked out. If he was going to have to deal with players like that, he wasn't sure playing cards was what he needed to do.

"Horny!" Ulla May stood at the bar. "You can't threaten to cut your customer's balls off just because they disagree with you."

"That man was rude. If I had my way, I would cut more than his balls."

Ulla shook her head and smiled. "I just bet you would, big man."

Johnny sat back down and shuffled the cards trying to calm down. He was glad when the saloon quickly went back to normal and more players sat down.

****

Walking out of the store wearing his top hat and a new suit, Johnny puffed on one of the best stogies money could buy. He didn't understand how a man could enjoy smoking cigars as much as he did.

He liked this new life he fell into, and the money he made playing and winning at poker. It just bought him three new suits, a Sharps fifty caliber rifle and two forty-four caliber Colt pistols. His buffalo gun was back at the hotel where it stayed most of the time. These smaller guns were less noticeable.

The first thing he wanted to do, though he was confident in his shooting, was some target practice with his new guns. He needed to sight the pistols in until they were perfect. If he had a moving target, he'd be sure to hit it.

Through the next few days, he took care of business at the saloon, then did his target practice. Today, he found himself at the lake. He felt like being the old Johnny One Horn, so he took off his city clothes, put on the one's of his people, and painted his face.

Coattail barely spooked when Johnny let out a whoop at the top of his lungs. He knelt beside the water and looked at his reflection. It felt good to be him again. Though he had grown accustomed to his life in Garden City, he missed the Armstrong boys and his great friend, Little Boy Horse.

Why was it that every time he thought about going to find them, when he got on his horse, he turned back to town? What strange hold did this place have on him? He had to admit at first he liked all Ulla's girl's fighting over him, but lately, he was tiring of them.

He smiled at the thought of the young school teacher he'd seen in town at times. She watched him when he walked by, and smiled at him when he met her gaze.

He glanced at his surroundings. This would be a good place to bring the pretty schoolmarm. Maybe it was time to get away from the saloon girls and ask the teacher to go for a walk. After that he would introduce her to the thought of coming to the lake.

Thinking about Pickles and what she'd said to him the night before, he had to laugh.

"Horney, you need to start paying for my girls like everybody else does."

"I quit doing that."

Jo Bo had slammed his whiskey glass down and busted out laughing. "I just wish I had your leftovers, Johnny."

Little did Pickles and Ulla know that the girls would sneak into his room and have their way. Now that he was really thinking about Miss King, playing with the saloon girls would have to stop. If she found out, she probably wouldn't have a thing to do with him.

He did his target practice, then washed the paint off his face and dressed once again in his city clothes. Mounting Coattail, he put his top hat on, lit his cigar and started back to town.

****

"Dammit, Hoots, that dang Injun took most all my month's earnin's."

"Mine, too, Bill."

"What are we gonna do?" One eyed Bill Pritchard put a whiskey bottle in front of his partner.

"Hell if I know. I can tell you one thing for sure. I don't like this rat hole of a saloon, but I'll be go-to-hell if I step foot in Ulla Mae's place again."

"You got that right." Pritchard glanced out the window. Ulla Mae's place was cattycornered across the street. "There he is, Hoots. Smokin' his big cigar, wearin' his fancy suit."

Hoots stood and followed Pritchard's line of sight. "He's probably comin' back from the lake by the rim. I heard he rides out there sometimes. When the time's right, we'll watch for him to leave town. That's where we'll bushwhack him."

"We'd better be quick when we do. I hear he's pretty damn good with them there pistols of his."

Hoots sat back down. "There's plenty of brush 'round there. I guarantee he'll never see us. We'll dig his grave first, then shoot his sorry ass and throw him in it."

"What a plan. You've been thinkin' 'bout this, ain't ya."

"Yep. One of Ulla Mae's girls, Big Ruby, is a might sweet on me. She's gonna keep us informed. All we have to do is wait for the right time."

Johnny saw the pretty young teacher leaving the small school house and fell in step beside her. "Ma'am?" She jumped at the sound of his voice then met his gaze. She was beautiful when she smiled, and it warmed his heart.

"Why, Mr. Horn, walking me home from school is becoming quite a habit."

"I like being with you and telling stories about my little buddy Carl Armstrong."

"I'm pleased, and I enjoy your company, too. Every day for the past week you've shared the afternoon with me, and I love your stories. They make me laugh. All of your friends sound wonderful and Coattail biting folks so funny, but Carl must be special to you."

"He is a good boy. Almost grown now, more a man than boy." Johnny's heart skipped a beat when they reached Sue's house and stopped at her door. He was sure not to ever go inside. People watched them closely and he wouldn't do anything to tarnish the woman's reputation.

She stood with her back to the door and gazed up at Johnny. "I think you should take me riding Sunday after church."

A woman had never affected him this way. The thought of being alone with her made him giddy, but he was pleased she wanted his company. "Riding?"

"Yes."

He loved the way her brown eyes sparkled when she looked at him. She was something special for sure. "Where?"

"People will talk if they see us leave town together. I'll meet you at the lake where Miss Ulla Mae and Pickles found you."

"You mean where they attacked me." Johnny smiled down at the beautiful little thing in front of him. She'd suggested their meeting at the lake before he did. That meant she trusted him. "How do you know of this place?"

"My father used to take me fishing there when I was a little girl. I've been there many times and would like to go again. It will probably bring back some old memories. Please?"

Her plea was something he couldn't resist. "I will be there."

"After church, right?"

"You go to church; I will go to the lake early and wait for you." He wanted to kiss her, but people bustled by and he knew it would be inappropriate. Maybe at the lake. She turned the knob and disappeared into the house.

"See you then," she said, then closed the door completely.

Chapter Thirty Four

Saturday night brought little sleep to Johnny One Horn. He couldn't stop thinking about being with Sue, and now that the sun was coming up, he could get out of bed.

He washed up, then dressed, ate breakfast at the café and headed to get Coattail. The church bell was ringing just as he walked in the door of the livery and saw Bill Brook scowl at him.

"I'm going to charge you more for boarding that snappin' turtle horse of yours. He bit two more of my customers and one of them was the Mayor."

Johnny almost laughed, but knew it wouldn't help the old man's mood. "Hmmm, not good Coattail. You need to settle down."

"He sure better or he'll be finding another place to bunk."

"There is no other place." Johnny mounted Coattail's bare back. He couldn't make himself use a saddle. That was one part of his past he wanted to keep.

"Well, I-I guess you're right." He forked another chunk of hay into a stall. "You're just lucky he don't bite me anymore. I'd be skinning him for sure."

Johnny nodded to the old man and reined the horse toward the door. "I will be back before night." Bill mumbled something under his breath and Johnny thought it was damned varmint, but he didn't stop to find out. Laughing he patted the varmint on the neck. "Good boy, Coattail."

He picked up speed, wanting to get somewhere and stop before he reached the lake. It would be nice to surprise Sue ahead of time and ride with her the rest of the way.

A short distance out of town, he found the perfect place. He could lose himself in the trees and if anyone happened by, they wouldn't see him.

Dust kicked up from the wagon wheels on the dirt road not too far away. Johnny's palms began to sweat and his stomach fluttered. What was it this woman did to him?

When she was close enough he could see her face clearly, he stepped from behind his cover. A wide smile lifted the corners of her lips and he wondered, for the hundredth time, what it would be like to kiss them.

She pulled the wagon to a stop. "Somehow I knew you were going to surprise me. I've been watching for you, hoping I was right."

"It is good to see you." He traced her face with his finger and her skin was soft beneath his touch.

"Thank you. It's nice seeing you, too."

She shivered and he wondered why. It was a warm day. "You are cold?"

"No." She smiled. "Your gentle touch did that to me. You're such a big man, yet a kind soul."

If she only knew of all the men he'd killed with the very hand he was touching her with, she'd be sickened by him. The person who knew him best, Little Boy Horse, was the only one who knew, or ever would know, everything about his past.

Would this woman be his reason to choose not to go back to the Armstrong boys? Would her soft skin and beauty tempt him to settle down and marry? He dropped his hand from her cheek not wanting to dream of a future he was not sure about. "Shall we go?"

"Why don't you tie that biting horse to the back of the wagon and ride up here with me."

"Yes, ma'am."

"Oh, and Johnny, that knife you wear, it scares me. Would you take it off and put it in the back of the wagon?"

He was never without his Arkansas Toothpick, but for this one time, he would do it. He laid the weapon close to the back of the seat, the wagon squeaked under his weight when he joined her on the bench. He looked down at her small frame. Her dark brown hair glistened in the early afternoon sun and he longed to touch it.

Sue slapped the reins across the two horse team's back. "Get up." She glanced at Johnny. "I don't think any of the busy bodies in town will catch on that we met today. I drove out the same way I do every Sunday for my ride, then doubled back."

"You are smart, Sue."

He put his arm around her shoulders careful not to hold her too tight. "I hope you can drive good, too." Her laughter filled the air and his spirit soared. "You are pretty, and so tiny I fear if I hold you tighter, you might break."

"You are a big man, Johnny, but you won't hurt me. Matter of fact, I think I would like it."

Johnny pulled her closer and enjoyed the ride the rest of the way to the lake. They pulled to a stop and he jumped off the wagon, went around and put his hands around her little waste. She was light as a feather when he lifted her down.

"Thank you." She straightened her dress. "There is a blanket and a picnic basket in the back if you'd like to get it."

He nodded and did as he was told, then led the way through the thicket to the water's edge. "We will sit here."

"This is perfect." Sue sat on the blanket and began to pull things out of the basket. "You say this lake is where Ulla Mae and Pickles found you. Tell me what you were doing here and where you were going?"

"My friends I told you about sent me to scout for open range so they could settle the cattle they bought. I had been riding for a long while." He glanced up. "It was there, where the lake meets the hill, I saw this place." He pointed in the direction, remembering how inviting the water looked. "I came down to refresh myself and..."

"Well, don't keep me waiting, what happened then?"

A smile lifted the corners of his mouth at the memory. The scene was etched in his mind. "I got off of Coattail and started to the water when I heard women's voices. I crouched and made my way through the bushes." Trying to make the scene more dramatic, he did a reenactment of the day.

Sue's laughter warmed his heart as he told her of the naked fat women, Ulla Mae and the shotgun, Coattail getting spooked and throwing him. He took his seat beside her once again and watched her wipe tears from her eyes.

"That is the funniest thing I've ever heard."

He nodded. "It is funny now, but then I was not amused. When my head hit the ground it knocked me out. That is the last I remember until I woke up in a strange bed. I was used to sleeping on the ground." Sue met his gaze. Her eyes were the color of his people's, with added flecks of gold and green. They filled him with happiness, then he watched her smile fade. What was wrong? Had he done something?

"Johnny, where did you come from? Originally, I mean."

"My grandfather came from across the great ocean when he was a boy. Saved by warriors after a shipwreck, he was raised as an Indian. He taught the people to speak the white man's language. He was mostly French, but his mother had English blood, too. Grandfather spoke English well. He taught the people so they could trade with the whites. I do not speak the native tongue anymore unless I am alone, or with Horse." He realized it had been months since he'd spoken his language out loud.

"That explains why you speak our language so well and why your skin is lighter than most Indians and mostly tanned by the sun." She smiled. "You're such an interesting man, Johnny." She met his gaze. "Why did you leave the swamp, your people?"

He thought back on his journey. How much did he want to share with this woman? Though he liked her more than he wanted to admit, would he ever really settle down and have a family? Make her the most important thing in his life? These were questions he knew the answers to. He admitted to himself he knew where the future would eventually take him.

"Johnny?"

"Grey Wolf went with the Great Spirit. Some of our tribe members went separate ways. Me and Little Boy Horse did the same. By the swamp's edge was a family named Armstrong. O.C. Armstrong, the father, went away and never returned. Grey Wolf traded with O.C. and our people became friends with the family.

"Carl, I tell the stories of, is the youngest of the three boys.

Their mother was half Chickasaw. Though she lived like a white woman, we had much in common. The people learned much of the white man's ways from the Armstrong's.

"When we reached the Armstrong farm, many things happened. I cannot tell it all to you now, but we joined the boys in their quest to find their father and start a ranch."

"That's fascinating! Did the boys find their father?"

"I do not know." He had said enough, she needed to know no more. It was time to tell her his plans. "Sue." Turning toward her he took her hand. "I will leave to meet my friends. I have to go back to them."

Sue shook her head and looked down. "I knew this was too good to be true. I will miss you, even though I haven't known you all that long."

"Do not worry, Sue King, I am not going to leave now, but in time. The boys are not alone, they have Little Boy Horse and they are also growing into men."

"So we'll have more time together before you go?"

"Yes, we will come here, to the lake, many times before I leave. Does that please you?" Her smile tugged at his heart.

"It does."

"That is good. I have time because I know Joe Armstrong bought many cattle. They have probably already found land and have settled. I will just get to see them from time to time. I like dealing cards and have made a lot of friends here." He lifted her chin so he could look directly into her pretty eyes. "But most of all, I like you." Was that a tear in her eye? Why would she cry?

"I like you, too, Johnny One Horn, but I fear you have made some enemies, also."

Was she concerned for him? It pulled his heart string a little tighter knowing she really cared.

"Barnes and Prichard are dangerous. They're not to be taken lightly."

"I think they are cowards."

"Just watch them, that's all I ask."

He nodded. "I will, but now I am hungry. What do you have in that basket?"

CHAPTER THIRTY FIVE

Just outside of Garden City, Hoots Barnes went to the door of his shack. "Hold on, I'm comin'. Damn, don't break down the door."

"Hurry up, Hoots, I've got something to tell you!"

Pritchard stood. "It's Big Ruby, Hoots."

"Sounds like it. Maybe we'll be gettin' our man soon." He opened the door.

Ruby barged in. "Them two are meeting somewhere, and this won't be the first time they've left town like this. It happens every Sunday after church. If you want Horney, I don't think they'll be hard to find."

Hoots smiled. "Which way do they go?"

"The Indian goes one way and she goes another, but if you ask me, I'm betting they both ended up at the same place."

"Stop beatin' 'round the bush, Ruby. Where do you think they're goin'?"

"I've been watching them talk and listening when they didn't know. I'd say they've been meeting at the lake."

"Thank ya, darlin'. You done a good thing this day. We'll find 'em, if they're out there." He put his arm around Ruby's waist. "Now, honey, if anyone were to ask about us, you just tell 'em we went down to Texas to work, 'cause we may be gone for a while."

Prichard scratched his head. "They'll believe that, that's what we always do." He grinned. "Good thing we done dug that grave."

Hoots jabbed Bill in the ribs with his elbow. "Stop funnin', One Eye."

Ruby cast the two a glance. "You're just gonna rough Horn up, right? You're not gonna really do anything bad, are ya, Hoots?

"No, darlin'. Don't you worry your pretty little head, we're just gonna get our money back, and run that big son-of-a-bitch out of town, that's all. He's gonna be mad as a hornet, so we'll need to hide out for a while."

"Okay, so you're not gonna hurt Sue or anything like that, right? I mean, there's not any lost love between us, but I don't wish her any harm."

"We ain't gonna hurt her, but if she decides to run off with that red-skin, there's nothin' we can do about that."

Ruby leaned into Hoots' embrace. "I suppose not." She rubbed his chest. "Hootsie, you're gonna miss me, ain't ya?"

"Mmm-hmmm. And I got somethin' special for you when I get back. If you know what I mean, darlin'."

"I'll be looking forward to it."

Hoot's dropped his arm. "Let's get goin, One Eye. We need to beat 'em there and get in position."

Big Ruby got in her wagon and drove back to town while Hoots rode behind Bill toward the lake. "One Eye, let's get into the brush on the east side."

"Where the sandy beach is?"

"Yeah." He slowed his mount. "That's where most folks go when they visit the lake." He saw the area ahead, stopped and dismounted. "Let's leave the horses here. Hoot's jumped off, tied his horse and grabbed his buffalo gun. "We'll get in amongst the thicket, settle down and wait."

Johnny stopped the wagon at his and Sue's favorite place at the lake. There they could be alone with no prying eyes. "I like it when you hold onto my arm like that, and put your head on my shoulder." Sue's eyes sparkled when she glanced up at him. Bending, he kissed her. Her lips were like satin beneath his and she tasted sweet.

"I do too, now let's eat. I'm hungry."

She had prepared food each time they'd done this. He enjoyed her cooking. He jumped to the ground went around and lifted Sue off the seat. She laughed when he twirled her in the air and he joined in.

"You act like I don't weigh anything. Like I'm no heavier than a rag doll."

"You are light as a feather, woman." He put her down but held her a little longer than he should. "And you are beautiful in the afternoon sun."

"I'm amazed by your strength, but I fear you need spectacles." She turned and got the blanket.

"My eyesight is perfect. I know what I see." He longed to kiss her long pretty neck when she threw her head back in laughter.

Grabbing the basket out of the wagon bed, One Horn almost put his knife in the sheath on his side where it belonged, but he didn't want to frighten Sue. She didn't like guns either, so he never brought one on their treks. Still he felt something was out of sorts, but that was stupid, they hadn't seen anyone since they left town. No, he shook the feeling then followed the woman he loved to their favorite spot.

No sooner had they sat down 'til the hair stood up on Johnny's neck. Sweat, he smelled human sweat. Someone, besides them, was there.

"And I–."

"Shhhhh." He heightened his senses. Something was wrong, very wrong. Sue, he had to get her to safety, and get his gun and knife. How could he have let himself be so careless! In the blink of an eye he grabbed the woman, picked her up and ran toward the wagon.

"Johnny! What are you doing?"

"Something is not right. We must go. Now!" He reached the wagon and put Sue in the seat. Just as he reached for his weapons a shot rang out. Pain shot through his head and the world went black.

"Johnny!" Sue jumped from the wagon and knelt down beside Johnny One Horn. "Johnny! Talk to me." Tears streamed down her face. Blood seeped into the ground beneath his head. "Oh, no! Johnny!"

One eye Bill Prichard jumped into the air. “Woohoo, we got the big man Hoots!”

“Let's go grab the girl before she gets her wits about her, gets on the wagon and takes off.”

Hoots ran out of the brush, dove and knocked Sue away from Johnny. “Get outta the way, girl. I wanna see for myself he's dead.” He kicked Johnny in the side as hard as he could, but One Horn didn't stir. “Hahahaha. You bastard Injun. Now who's gonna skin who?”

Bill looked at Sue who lay behind the wagon. “What are we gonna do with the woman, Hoots? She saw the whole thing, we can’t just let her go.”

“I slammed the hell outta her. Small as she is, it probably killed ‘er.”

“Look again, Hoots, she's breathin’”

“Hell, I guess we'll take her with us.”

“We gonna have our way with her?”

“That bridge will be crossed after we're clear of here, and get to the hide out, but I'd say we can have a little fun with her before we finish her off. Nobody will be able to find us at the old Justin cabin, that’s for sure. Now tie her up.”

Bill grabbed her hands. “She's limp as a wet rope.”

“Throw her over the horse that's pullin’ the wagon, while I unhitch it.”

“What are we gonna do with the Indian's horse?” He hoisted the unconscious woman over the other horse’s back.

“I’ll tie her in place, Bill, while you get him. I'm sure we'll be able to sell a good paint somewhere.”

Prichard walked to the back of the wagon, and untied the horse's reins, but before he could turn around, it bit him in the back. “Ouch! Damn, scoundrel got me from behind.” The paint rose up on his back legs, kicked, whinnied, and no sooner had Bill covered his face, the horse was back on all fours and it took off.

“Shoot him, you fool!” Hoots wrapped the rope around Sue's body.

“Don't think I can hit him. He's fast.” Bill pulled his gun and fired a shot. “Don't know if I hit him or not, but I betcha he won't be back."

"He bit ya good. Drew blood."

"Damn mean bastard!" Prichard glanced at Johnny. "We gonna put him in the hole?"

"Hell no. Just leave him there. With all the coyotes and wolves around here, he'll be gone by tomorrow."

One eyed Bill Prichard leaned down and took Johnny's money. "We sure 'nough got our money back, and more. There's almost five-hundred dollars here."

"We can talk about our riches later. Let's go."

"Are we going to just leave the wagon here?"

"Let's roll it into the lake. The water's pretty deep, nobody'll ever find it."

Once the wagon was hidden in the water, Bill mounted his horse then took a bottle of whiskey out of his poke and gulped down a swig. He pointed at Sue. "I've been watchin' her for a long time. I'm gonna enjoy my time with her for the next few days."

****

Johnny rolled over onto his back and put his hand to his forehead. Dried blood? Damn he had a headache! He wiped away some of the crust then slowly opened his eyes. How long had he been out? From the position of the sun, he figured about four hours.

He ran his fingers through his hair and found the deep gash across the back of his head. The sandy dirt had helped to stop the bleeding, but the wound was still seeping fresh blood.

His vision was blurred, but he made his way to the water's edge and stripped off his soiled clothes. The cool liquid felt good when he stepped into the lake to clean himself. He splashed his face, washed the blood away and cleaned the gash in his head.

Water dripped from his hair and body when he walked onto the bank. His heart fell to his feet once his head began to clear. Whoever had done this took Sue. Coattail was gone as well. Sleepy, he was so sleepy. His stomach turned upside down and he lost its contents on the ground. He felt like he needed to sleep.

He sat on a mound of soft grass. When he woke up, it was

dark and he realized he'd passed out. No matter how hard he tried to stay awake, it was impossible.

Something woke Johnny, and the sun warmed his bare skin. Morning. He'd slept through the night. No matter how bad his head hurt, he had to move. He forced his lids open and was pleased with what he saw. Coattail stood a few feet from him.

Staggering to his feet, he hugged the animal then noticed dried blood on the side of paint's head. "Someone shot you, too, my friend." There was a bullet hole through Coattail's ear. "Do not worry, we will find them.

He studied the area and saw the wagon's tracks leading to the lake. Was Sue down there? Had they taken his knife? His head cleared more each minute. He had to dive into the water to find out if they'd overlooked the only weapon he had with him. "Stay here, boy, I will be right back."

His heart thumped hard in his chest. He hoped he wouldn't find the woman tied to the wagon, drowned. If she wasn't dead, and he could get to his knife, he vowed to kill whoever had done this.

Johnny inhaled a deep breath and dove into the lake. He swam almost straight down to find the wagon resting about fifteen feet below the water's surface. Sue was nowhere to be found. That meant at least he could *hope* she was still alive. He spotted the Arkansas Toothpick he'd made with his own hands, resting right where he'd put it. The Great Sprit was looking out for him at that moment and he said a silent thank You.

After he got out of the water, he put the knife on the ground long enough to clean Coattail's ear. Then he dressed in the native clothing he'd had tied to his horse, and placed the Toothpick in the sheath at his hip.

He was worried about Sue and what she might be going through. Was she being tortured? Or worse yet, raped by the scoundrels? How had he let his guard down so completely? It was something he would never do again.

Coattail stood still while Johnny mounted. It felt good to be on his back, dressed the way he was accustomed. "Now it is time to track our enemies, my friend." He patted the horse's neck while he studied the ground, then heeled him in the direction the hoof prints led.

If the situation wasn't so grave, he would have laughed at their vain attempt to cover their trail. "They do not know that even their trickery to cover their tracks does not fool me. It will not stop me from finding them."

The sun peeked over the horizon, bringing the old log cabin in the distance into better view. Johnny studied the area while cautiously making his way through the trees. No horses stood or moved around the place. "They have gone, Coattail. I fear we are too late."

Johnny stepped out into the open and quickly, but silently, moved to the entrance of the small, rickety homestead. He pushed the door open and peered into the dim interior. His worse fears crept up from the hollows of his stomach and gripped his heart. "No!"

He ran to the wooden bunk where the woman lay strapped down and covered in blood. "Sue!" She didn't responded even when he untied her restraints.

"Sue, wake up!" He swallowed hard and gasped for air. Why had they done this to her. She didn't deserve to have her clothes torn off, left naked and bleeding in this place. She was innocent! Even if he had his bag full of medicine, there was no cure for what had been done to her. Fury consumed him. He would see the people who did this dead.

"I will help you." Though he knew in his heart she was close to death, he ran to get a bucket of water from the well he'd seen outside. He re-entered the cabin, covered her body with what was left of her tattered dress, then used a piece of the torn cloth to wash the blood from her face.

Her breathing was labored when he took her in his arms. He glanced down at her battered face and could only imagine what she'd been through over the last few days. "It is okay, Sue, you are free to go to the Great Spirit now. No one can hurt you when you are in the heavens." He rocked back and forth while he held her, and in minutes, she was gone.

Gently, he laid her back on the bunk and went outside. Arms held up toward the sky, his pent-up frustration bubbled from deep inside, made its way up and escaped in a scream he couldn't suppress. The shriek of a madman echoed back to him from the surrounding hills and his hatred chilled him to the bone.

He stood for a long moment with his eyes closed. Slowly he brought his arms down, inhaled a deep, calming breath then opened his eyes.. The bastards would die, but now, he had to figure out his next move. Sue deserved to be buried by her people in their Christian way. Yes, he would take her body back to town, then he would go on his quest for revenge.

CHAPTER THIRTY SIX

Through the darkness, Johnny rode into Garden city and went straight to the back door of Ulla Mae's saloon. He dismounted, gently pulled Sue's form from the horse and cradled her in his arms.

He took the steps to the entrance and knocked. It didn't surprise him when Pickles opened the door then screamed at the sight of the dead woman's partially exposed, battered body. "Calm down and move so I can bring her inside."

Pickles backed away allowing Johnny to enter. "My God, Little Sue King! What happened?"

"Someone killed her."

"Obviously!"

"We were out by the lake and two men ambushed us." He went into his room and put the woman's body on his bed, glad they didn't meet anyone in the hallway.

"How do you know how many there were?"

"I tracked them. There were two riders, but three horses. The third was the one that had been on Sue's wagon. It was the one they tied her to."

"My goodness."

"I was shot in the head. They must have thought I was dead, or close to it, so they left me where I lay. When I woke up the first time, I saw that Sue was gone, and so was Coattail."

"Oh, Johnny, that's terrible. How did you find her?"

"I slept for many hours, waking from time to time. The last

time I awoke, Coattail stood nearby. My head cleared and I knew she was in danger, so I followed their tracks to an old cabin." The memory of what he saw when he entered the dwelling tore at his heart. He would spare Pickles the details. "She was close to death when I got there, then soon after, she was gone."

Pickles covered Sue's body and face with a blanket then turned toward Johnny. "Let me see your head."

He sat in a chair and realized how tired he was. The last few days had been some of the hardest of his life. Pickles' large frame stood over him and she began to run her fingers through his hair trying to find the wound. When her hand stopped searching, and pain shot across his scalp, he knew she was in the right spot.

"You're lucky to be alive, Big Man. That is an awful gash. I'm going to send word to Sheriff Nash. I'm sure he'll have lots of questions." She walked toward the door.

"No, do not get him yet. Let me leave first. He will think I did this and will throw me in jail, or hang me."

"Nash is hard, but everybody knows you and you wouldn't do anything like this."

"This I know, but I cannot take the chance." He stood, retrieved the Colt forty-fours from the place he had hidden them, and took the buffalo gun from the wall mount. "Everything else will stay here. I have all I need."

He pulled back the blanket and gave Sue one last kiss on the forehead, then covered her back up. "I'm going now. I will remember you always." Walking past her, he hurried down the stairs, got on Coattail and rode away without looking back.

****

Realizing in his anger he was pushing Coattail too hard, he slowed until he reached the lake. The full moon reflected gold hues off the tranquil water. It was beautiful, but knowing he would never view it again with Sue King the serenity only held emptiness. Just as his heart. Damn the men that did this.

Coattail drank from the water. Rest. He needed rest, they both might drop from exhaustion if they didn't stop for a while. When his mount had his fill, Johnny found a mostly hidden area, and lay on the ground. Sleep would do him good, and would lead to a fresh start with a clear mind.

Just before dawn, Johnny awoke. By the way he felt, the break had done him good. The morning air was cool and Coattail seemed in better spirits, too. "We have work to do, boy." The horse neighed and threw his head back as if he understood. "I am ready, too."

Johnny gathered his weapons, jumped on Coattail's back then headed toward the cabin. The ride went faster than he'd expected and soon the log house came into view.

In the distance he saw storm clouds. He had to push past the dwelling and stay focused on the tracks. If it rained, he would lose them, and he vowed that would not happen. He would find the men before they had time to reach the next town.

Along the trail, he found empty whiskey bottles, this was good. The men would be traveling slower than usual. "Coattail, we must hurry. Maybe they have not broken camp yet. They are stupid white men who do not know me. I will make them pay for what they've done, and it will be today."

He heeled the horse to a trot and it wasn't long before he noticed smoke from a campfire drifting up through a group of trees. "This is it, boy." He reined his horse out of sight of the camp, then jumped to the ground and laid the reins across a bush. "You stay here. I will return."

Making the rest of the way on foot, Johnny kept to the shadows and approached the sight. What he saw, told him his heart had been right. Beneath a tree, by a huge log, were Hoots and One Eyed Bill.

Anger reared its head in Johnny's chest when he saw Sue's blood on the bastards' clothes. The two men were passed out. This made his plan even easier.

He cut the reins off of their horses and bundled the leather in his hands. Neither horse made a sound, they just walked away. After grabbing appropriate sticks to make stakes from, he entered the camp without notice. How could they know he was there, they were dead drunk.

After he planted the stakes into the ground, Johnny bound the Hoots' and Bill's hands and feet to them. How could these people be so stupid? Their guns were haphazardly lying on top of the log. He grabbed them, took them into the bush then hid them beneath some brush.

Gathering dead limbs and twigs, he got all he needed. He knelt and put them on the smoldering embers of what was left of the campfire. The charcoal around the fire had cooled and he put the black powder on his fingertips then slowly, deliberately, he made lines on his face with it. He then dressed the streaks of black with bands of red clay.

When he returned to the camp, the two men started to stir. The fire was getting high and hot and Johnny enjoyed watching them squirm, not yet knowing they were imprisoned in leather straps.

He held One Eyed Bill's big buffalo knife in one hand, and whipped out his Arkansas Toothpick with the other. He placed the blade of his knife in the blue flames. The smell of whiskey drifted to his nose when he heard a man's voice.

"What the hell?"

Turning, he watched the men struggle, trying to get free. Johnny knelt and began to cut One Eyed Bill's clothes off.

"Hey, that's my knife. What are you doing?"

Sue's blood streaked the man's pants and shirt. This made his own blood boil and he imagined what the poor woman had gone through. These two would get what was coming to them, he would make sure of that.

"Are you gonna kill us? Hoots, talk to him."

Johnny threw the clothes in a pile, pointed to them, then went over to Barnes. What he really wanted to do was plunge the knife into their chests, kill them quickly and leave them for the buzzards, but that's not what they did to Sue. They made her suffer, and they would feel her pain, but it would do little to heal the pain in his heart for losing her.

One Eye pulled at his tethers. "Why are you doing this? Please, Injun, don't kill us, we ain't done nothin'. We're just passin' through. We didn't mean what we said about you cheatin' in cards. Please."

Johnny slit the material of Hoots' shirt and yanked it off his body. Then he cut one leg of his jeans and threw it into the pile.

"Horny, what is it you think we done?" Hoots met Johnny's gaze.

Johnny glared at the man while cutting the other leg of his pants off. He ran the knife up and down the blood that stained the cloth, then piled it with the others.

"What? That's deer blood? We killed a deer, they ain't nothin' wrong with that."

Their lies and pleading did nothing but kindle the fire of his anger. The two sorry men now lay naked on the ground in front of him. Their constant talking was getting on his nerves.

"Damn it, man, we killed a deer so's we could eat. What the hell's wrong with you?!"

Johnny reached down and got a handful of sandy-dirt. He refused to listen to their pleas anymore. Prying Hoots mouth open, he sifted the dirt into the man's mouth. The gagging and coughing sounds didn't stop him from doing the same to the other man.

One Eyed Bill tried to curse and beg at the same time. He stood, and while the two men spit and sputtered the dirt out of their mouths, he went to get Coattail. He heard Bill when the man began to talk.

"He weren't dead, when we left him back at the lake, Hoots. You said he was dead!"

"I thought he was!"

"Well he ain't and he's gonna kill us for sure. Did you see the look in his eyes?"

"You snivelin' dumbass. He don't know nothin' for sure, but if you keep talkin' about it, he will."

Johnny walked Coattail into camp. Hoots was still coughing and spitting. It was hot by that fire, and the sun beat down on their bare skin. After the night of drinking the two had done, he was sure they were real thirsty.

Bill raised his head and looked at Johnny. "Are you really gonna kill us?!"

The fear in the man's voice didn't change his mind about what he was going to do to them. "Yes."

"No, please." A tear ran down One Eyed Bills face.

"But before I do, I'm going to peal your skin away with a hot knife."

Bill looked at Hoots. "He's gonna skin us alive. We shouldn't have done that to that girl."

"Shut up, you damn fool!"

If Hoots had been free, Johnny was sure the man would land a fist to Bill's face. They knew what they had done, and now they knew they were going to pay.

He threw Bill's knife into the brush, wrapped his hand in a piece of the tattered clothing and picked up the Toothpick. The blade was red hot. He walked over to the crying, begging excuse of a man, One Eyed Bill. Johnny glared at Hoots. "Watch Barnes, I want you to know exactly what you're going to get."

He stuck the blade against Bill's face. The scream was blood curdling and Hoots paled. "Yes, it's torture, just different than the kind you did to Sue."

"We're sorry," Hoots said. "We thought you were dead, you bastard."

"No, you killed only part of me. Something in here." He pointed to his chest. "Now you are going to wish you would die, many times before you do." He put the hot knife against Hoots' thigh and listened to the sizzle as he moved it slowly toward the man's knee.

"Ahhhhhhhhhhhh!" Hoots jerked at the leather bindings.

The men thought he was going to skin them alive, but he'd changed his mind. That would kill them too fast. The places he burned would make blisters and then sores. The wounds would be even more painful exposed to the heat and elements.

Johnny listened to the moans of the men after what he'd done to them. The night had gone by slowly and he'd been on his knees for hours asking the Great Spirit for forgiveness and knowledge. His anger had lessened, but he didn't feel sorry for the scoundrels. Not after they had killed his Sue.

He dozed, and with the dawn, what he had to do, came to him in a dream. Coyotes howled in the distance, and the wounded men moaned when he got up and mounted Coattail.

"Please, give me a drink."

"Yes, please."

"Okay." Johnny dismounted and picked up one of the whiskey bottles that still had some of the brown liquid in it. "Have a drink on Sue."

First Hoots, then Bill screamed in pain as he drained the contents of the bottle onto their raw, burned flesh. Bill was the first to speak.

"Shoot me, Injun. Kill me now."

"Yeah, One Horn. Don't just leave us here."

"No, I will not kill you. The buzzards and Coyotes will do that."

He reined Coattail Northward. The new life he'd thought he'd found was behind him. Now it was time to find Little Boy Horse and his other true friends, the Armstrong boys.

CHAPTER THIRTY SEVEN

FINALLY IN VICKSBERG

Thunder rumbled and the wind whistled down the main street of Vicksburg, Mississippi. O.C. fought to keep his horse under control when lightning struck not a hundred feet away. It was all he could do to rein the spooked mount through the stable doorway.

He glanced over at Tunnie who was having the same problem. "Jack, you okay?" His friend nodded. O.C. dismounted when the stable keeper closed the big wooden doors behind them.

"Damn glad to be inside. Don't think I've dried out in a week."

"Maybe you'll smell better."

"You're such a smart ass, Armstrong. One thing about all this rain is it makes these southern towns a lot greener. They look a damn sight better than the dried out desert towns."

O.C. had to agree. Mississippi was beautiful country, lots of green grass, tall trees and flowers. "You're right about that, my friend."

"I hate to admit it, but you were right about something, too. Takin' that ferry saved us some time."

The stable keeper secured the doors then approached O.C. "How long y'all stayin'?"

"Not sure. Probably be leavin' soon, but can you take care

of our horses while we're in town?"

"Yep, it'll be fifty cents for two nights."

Tunnie pitched the keeper the change. "That's reasonable."

Vicksburg was a pretty big town, but O.C. wondered if this man might know anything about his family. It couldn't hurt to ask, maybe he'd get lucky. "Hey, Mister, do you remember three young men that came to town a few months back? Might have had a woman with 'em, too. Their name is Armstrong. Their aunt lives here; her name is Estelle Rainwater. You know her?" He saw the solemn look that suddenly cast over the man's face.

"I did." The man looked O.C. in the eye. "She died in a house fire a couple years back. Terrible thing."

He hated to hear about his wife's sister, but wondered about his family. "How 'bout the boys?"

"Can't say as I remember no boys or young men. Try askin' over at the general store. Almost everybody that comes through town stops there for supplies or somethin'. Owner's a nosy old coot, and if anyone would know, he would."

"Thanks for your help." O.C. handed the man the reins, turned and walked back outside into the rain, leaving Tunnie behind. He'd come too far not to find out all he could, fast, and knew Jack would understand.

He wiped what mud he could off his boots then went inside the store. Rain still poured outside. The man behind the counter glanced up from some paperwork. "Afternoon, what can I help you with?"

Was his heart going to stop beating? Just the notion of actually learning something about his wife and sons had him all wound up inside. "Sure hope so. I'm lookin' for three boys, well, young men that might've come through a few months back." A thoughtful look crossed the man's face piquing O.C.'s curiosity. They man knew something; he could read it in his eyes.

"Three young men, huh? What are you looking for them for?"

"Well, sir, they're my family. My boys." His patience was growing thin, but at the same time he was pleased the man was being cautious. "Did you see 'em?"

"I saw them. They asked about the riverboat and mentioned goin' to St. Louis."

"Was a woman with 'em?"

The man shook his head. "No, no woman. If their ma's who you're talkin' about, they said she died. They were lookin' for their aunt Estelle. I had to tell them Mrs. Whitaker was dead, too. They didn't take the news too well when I told them about her house burnin' down with her in it. I showed them how to get to where the place was."

O.C.'s heart went out to his sons. Not only did they probably think he'd abandoned them, their precious mother went to meet her maker, and when they got to Vicksburg they found her sister had passed, too. "You said they were headed to St. Louie?"

The man met his gaze. "I can't promise that, but that's what they were talking about."

A Missouri trip might be in his future, but first he felt the urge to head back to their cabin home. Maybe the swamp was down and he could dig some of the gold. He was so confused. His mind was going around and around. He decided, for now, he just wanted a drink. "You got a bottle of whiskey?"

"Sure do." He put the bottle on the counter. "That'll be a dollar."

After pitching the dollar on the wooden topped cabinet, he grabbed the whiskey and went out the door. If Martha had passed while they were still in the swamp, she would be buried nearby. He needed to say goodbye and pay his last respects.

The rain had let up, but the street was still full of mud, and the sky threatening. He glanced down the way, noticed a small church then stepped into the muck and made his way to the peaceful looking white building.

Once he reached the place of worship, he walked onto the covered porch. He took off his boots, opened the door and entered the chapel. There was one other man sitting in a pew.

"Welcome to our little town church, Mister."

He wasn't in the mood for conversation. Peace, quiet and...whiskey was what he needed. "Thanks." O.C. sat on a bench as far away from the stranger as he could, and pulled the cork out of the bottle.

He knew he'd left Tunnie waiting for long enough. It was

time to leave. O.C. put the cork back into the half empty bottle and left the church knowing the first saloon he came across is where he'd find Jack.

He stepped inside the dim lit, smoke filled business, saw Jack at a table and made his way over. A lady approached as he sat down.

"Can I get ya somethin' hon?"

"No, ma'am, thank you."

"Well, if you decide you want a drink or… anything, you just let me know. My name's Kat."

Nodding, he watched her walk away, then turned back to Tunnie and took the full whiskey glass that sat in front of the man. "My wife's gone, Jack. She died. I should never have left her alone."

Tunnie shook his head. "Sorry to hear that."

O.C. slammed down the brown liquid, slapped the empty glass onto the table and stood. "Let's get the hell outta here. I don't know where, but I gotta go." He turned, and started to walk toward the door. He heard the legs of Jack's chair scuff against the wood floor and knew the man was behind him.

"Armstrong, I got some news on your boys."

Not sure he wanted to hear what Tunnie had to say, he walked out the door and started down the wooden sidewalk. "I hope it's better news than I heard about their ma."

"Slow down, O.C., I think you'll want to hear what I found out."

He stopped and looked at his friend. It wasn't right for him to take his foul mood out on Tunnie, the man hadn't done anything but help him and he was grateful. "I'm sorry, Jack, I just can't believe I'll never see my Martha alive again."

"I understand."

"What is it you know of the boys?"

"I was playin' cards with some fellas and told them we were lookin' for three young men named Armstrong. A man said he'd run across them in St. Louie. They were buying a lot of supplies, even bought a big old prairie schooner. Said there were some other men with them, and two big, scarey lookin' Indians."

He smiled knowing exactly who those scary looking Indians were, then nodded his head. "That would be Johnny One Horn and Little Boy Horse." Earl said they were with the boys, too. This helped solidify the fact.

His hopes started to rise again knowing they had for sure gone to St. Louis. At least now he had true direction and didn't have to guess, but something was drawing him to the cabin first and he didn't know why. "Let's hit the trail. I want to go home before we head to Missouri." He felt Jack's hand on his arm.

"Now, O.C. I know you want to hurry and all, but I could use a good hot bath and some rest. Let's take a couple of days, sleep in a good bed and relax. Hell, we've been dodging bullets, knives and been travelin' non-stop for weeks now."

"I don't know, Jack." He wanted to trudge forward, but after he thought about it, his friend was right. They needed to rest, although he wasn't sure he'd be able to relax. What the hell, Tunnie hadn't asked for anything on their journey; O.C. felt he owed the man a couple days to take it easy. "Aw, hell, okay, but only two days."

Tunnie started to laugh. "Two days is two days, my friend. Let's get us a room and start unwinding."

O.C. had to admit that Tunnie was right about needing a rest. After the haircut, shave and bath, he'd felt better, but now, the closer they got to the cabin the louder the familiar song of the swamp became and the heavier the cloud over his heart hung.

The boys had left, Martha was dead, and would rest alone here for eternity. She'd be surrounded by birds singing, frog sounds, crickets and critters of all kinds. They were all things his beloved cared for, and enjoyed hearing. Now she'd be able to hear them in heaven. He'd miss her, but God would take care of her 'til he joined them.

Tunnie rode up beside O.C. "Good God, this place is alive! Everywhere you look there's somethin' movin'."

"The place is alive alright. Never was a problem catchin' somethin' to eat out of the swamp until it flooded so bad." He looked around at the tall Cyprus, green surrounded them. He had to admit he loved this part of Mississippi. "It grows on you, but it can be a hell of a place, too." O.C. cleared his throat. "I don't know what we're gonna find when we get there, Jack, it almost scares me."

"Yeah, but you gotta know, just to ease your mind."

It wasn't too far now, and O.C.'s heart started to race. "We're less than a mile from the cabin. I can see the water already. Damn, it's never been this high." He questioned if the cabin was under water by now.

O.C. rounded the last corner. He wanted to stop, but he kept riding. "The house is burned, Jack, and most of the barn. Wonder if that's what killed my Martha?" His heart jumped to his throat and tears welled in his eyes. He didn't want to think his wife had gone through the hell of burning alive. No, he didn't need those thoughts in his mind. The boys wouldn't have let that happen. They were strong and would have saved her.

Once they reached the burned out cabin and partially burned barn, O.C. couldn't bring himself to dismount. He couldn't believe the sight surrounding him and glanced back and forth trying to pick up any clue as to what might have happened.

It was almost more than he could bear when he saw the grave marker on the top of the hill. Then he noticed a second marker, a cross. Did that mean two of his family members were buried there? How could that be when all the folks he'd talked to said there'd been three boys? Something was amiss. It took everything he had to get off his horse and climb the mound.

He made the trek to the top and stood before the larger marker. His heart broke into a million pieces as he ran his fingers across the top of it and read the words carved out of the wood. Our Mother, Martha Armstrong, rest in everlasting peace. We love you.

His knees hit the ground with a thud. All the strength in his body had been pulled from his core and left him too weak to cry. Questions raced through his mind. Why had he left? Why didn't he take his family with him? Would things have turned out different if he had? Did the Lord think he'd ducked his responsibility so He took it out on his family? Why had his Martha died so young?

Anger ate at his insides and blood pumped through his veins returning his strength. Too many questions and no answers. Why? Why? Why?! He looked toward the heavens and raised his arms feeling a scream of agony make its way up. Like a living entity it pushed past his heart, his lungs and finally tore from his throat. He opened his mouth and the cry escaped, loud and long, over and over. He couldn't stop himself even when he heard his own voice, more haunting than the wisp, echo through the swamp.

Breathless, he dropped his arms and bowed his head. Life would never be the same, but he'd known that for some time. It was time to move on. "Lord, grant me the strength." He looked toward Martha's headstone. "Darlin', I'll see you again. I promise. I know you'll be waitin' for me. I'm gonna find the boys, I promise that, too. You help the Good Lord guide me. I love ya."

Now tears flowed steadily down his cheeks. He wiped them with the back of his hand, then touched the cool wooden surface bearing Martha's name one last time. It was the first he'd noticed that Indians had left things at her grave as a gesture of love and respect. Something they did for all of their buried loved ones. He was proud they'd done that for his Martha.

He stood, then sniffed and blinked a few times to clear his vision and turned toward the small cross. He couldn't see what was on it so he bent to read the three simple letters sliced in the surface. "W I T, what the hell is that?" Trying to think of someone he knew with those initials, he shook his head. It meant nothing to him. Maybe it was a dog they'd gotten after he left. He didn't know, but it was time to leave this all behind and move forward to find his sons.

When he turned to go he saw Tunnie studying the surroundings with great interest. O.C. could only imagine what the man must have thought when he cried out. It didn't matter; he needed to cleanse his heart of questions he'd eventually get answers to. A weight had been lifted and he could live on.

O.C.'s hat lay on the ground beside his feet; he picked it up, put it back on his head then headed toward Jack. Tunnie looked down into the water as if in a trance. O.C. followed the man's gaze. "What do you see?"

Tunnie jumped and reared back his fist, then stopped short of O.C.'s nose. "Dammit, man, you scared hell out of me. I thought one of those gators out there or maybe a gar sneaked up behind me. Shit!"

His emotions all over the place, O.C. almost laughed at

Jack's expression. It was good, maybe this visit was just what he'd needed. "Never heard a gar talk before…gator, neither."

Jack pointed into the water. "Them's the biggest gar's I ever seen."

"Yep, some are nearly big as a gator."

"Do ya eat 'em?"

"Can. Ain't that tasty."

"I think I'd lose my stomach if I tried. Just thinkin' how ugly they are would make me puke." Tunnie pointed to the edge of the swamp some feet away. "Looks like them boys of yours made a hell of a raft. It's over there, O.C., go take a look."

O.C. move toward the manmade water craft. It was big, looked like it would carry a lot of weight. Maybe that's how they got the gold, but maybe not. "There's no proof this belonged to them. High as the water is, it could have drifted in from somewhere. Look at all the damage it has from crashing with the waves."

"You could be right. Don't look like it's tied to anything. Just kind of free floating."

It didn't matter. "There's nothin' left for me here, Tunnie, let's head to Missouri."

"I'm with you, friend."

Mounting his horse, O.C. took one last look around at the ruins of his longtime home, then his gaze stopped at the hill where his wife was buried. One big piece of his heart would always be here in the Mississippi swamp. "I love ya, Martha."

He reined his horse around and started up the overgrown road. Glad for Jack's silence, O.C.'s memories flowed freely as he thought back on his life. Some of it was a blur while other things were clear as a bell. Like the day Joe was born.

He smiled when he remembered how beautiful Martha had been when Estelle handed the little bundle to her. She glowed with pride. He'd never loved her more than at that very moment. It was the same with each of the boys. They were all special in their own way. He loved them and couldn't wait to see them again.

The image of Joe sitting on the back of the wagon the day O.C. left came to mind. What a strapping young man he was then. He could only imagine what the last few years had done for the boy's maturity. That had been a hard day in O.C.'s life. Leaving his family behind, trusting Joe to know when it was time to go after the gold. "That's it!"

"What?"

"That's it, W I T." O.C.'s heart started to pump energy into his veins. That Joe was one smart man and he was proud of him. He turned his horse back toward the cabin.

"W I T? What the hell are you talkin' about?"

"The cross on the mound, it said W I T. When it's time."

"Have you lost your mind?"

O.C. heeled his mount into a gallop. "Come on, Jack, we got us a little diggin' to do." He heard Tunnie follow behind. It was a miracle they weren't farther away from the cabin before he recognized the message Joe had left. Martha and the Lord were already looking out for him and he was grateful.

At the bottom of the burial mound, O.C. dismounted and ran up the hill. He took out his Arkansas Toothpick and began to dig under the cross. "Come on and help me, Jack."

"I ain't puttin' my hands down there. Not the way you're hackin' with that big ole knife. I'm liable to lose a finger."

When O.C. had cleared about a foot of dirt, he saw some leather. When the hole was big enough, he reached in and pulled out a saddlebag. The weight of it told him his guess was right. Joe had left some gold behind for him. He placed the bag on the ground.

"What the hell's goin' on, O.C.? What's in that thing?"

Sitting back on his heels O.C. said, "Take a look."

Jack reached over and opened the top of the leather pouch. "Good God Almighty! I never seen anything–"

"Gold, my friend, pure gold coins from the French!" O.C. closed the saddle bag, stood, put it over his shoulder and started down the hill. He stopped and turned back toward Martha's grave. "Thank you for lookin' out for me, darlin'." He faced forward again and realized how proud he was of how Joe had made the best of a bad situation. His oldest boy had grown to be a smart man.

At the bottom of the hill, he put the saddle bag in place. He couldn't help but smile at the dumbfounded look on Jack Tunnie's face. "Now, let's go to Missouri and find my boys!"

Chapter Thirty Eight

O.C. was glad the trip to St. Louis had been uneventful except for a small number of thunder storms during a few nights of the voyage. He'd found it peaceful to watch lightning finger across the sky, followed by a low rumble. The sound of rain hitting the water relaxed him.

Rejuvenated and feeling more hopeful than he had in years, O.C. took the lead when he and Jack led their horses off the barge. The boardwalk to the street above the Missouri River was filled with travelers who'd reached their destination, and those waiting to board.

St. Louis was a huge city. He studied people of all kinds, hustling through the streets. It had been a long journey, but he began to see light at the end of the tunnel now. If he could find someone that had seen the boys, life would be good.

Then something caught his eye, and it was just what he'd been looking for. "Hey, Jack, there's a general store." It was the first store he'd seen after coming off the boat, and he prayed he was right in the assumption it was the same for the boys. "I bet you almost anything the boy went there for supplies."

"I hope so. Want to head over there O.C?"

"Sure 'nough." The sooner he could find something out the faster he could be on his way to his family.

He walked into the store and up to the counter. A friendly looking man stood beside the cash box. "Sir, could you tell me if you happened to see some young men passing through here?

There might have been a couple of other men with them." O.C. noticed the inquisitive look on the clerk's face.

"What's your name, mister?"

O.C. pointed to Jack. "This here's Tunnie, I'm Armstrong. O.C. Armstrong." He saw the slight smile that lifted the corners of the man's mouth as the clerk raised his eyes to meet O.C's gaze. The look gave him hope. "And you?"

"Burl Rogers." A woman walked up beside the store keeper. "And this is my wife, Myrtle."

"Pleased to meet you, ma'am." He tipped his hat to the lady, then looked back at Rogers. "Now about my boys? It's important to me; I've been lookin' for a spell."

Rogers glanced at his wife. "Myrt, you remember those boys that came through a few months ago? The ones that bought the cowboy hats?"

"I sure do. They got seven hats and they bought two sets of clothes that were too big for any of the three of them."

"Well, this here's their pa."

Myrtle smiled. "The Armstrong boys' daddy? My, goodness. Those are some fine young men you raised, and handsome, too."

"Myrt took to those boys right kindly, Mr. Armstrong."

"I sure did. They were very well mannered."

"Thank you, ma'am. It's been a mighty long time since I've seen 'em. Are they still in town or did they say where they were headed? Were they okay?" He was throwing a lot of questions at these folks, but Dammit he had to find out. Knowing they bought the big clothes was yet more confirmation Horse and Horn were with them.

"Mr. Armstrong." Myrt came from behind the counter and put her hand on O.C.'s shoulder. "They seemed to be doing just fine. Why, they bought almost every gun Burl had, plus enough supplies to last a month or more. They had hired a couple of hands and were moving on."

Burl stepped forward. "The two men they hired looked like buffalo hunters from the way they were dressed."

Nodding Myrt added, "And they had taken on a cook they met on the steam barge from Vicksburg. He was an older fellow, but seemed to know what he was doing."

Jack Tunnie stepped forward. “Ma'am, you said they were moving on, did they by chance say where to?”

Mrs. Rogers busied with folding fabric. “Said they were going towards Abilene. It seems they wanted to connect with a cattle drive.”

The first thing that came to O.C.'s mind was the mistake he'd made by joining a cattle drive. It was what landed him in prison all those years. His heart sank to the soles of his boots. “They want to go on a cattle drive?”

Laughing, Burl said, “No, sir, they wanted to buy some cattle of their own. Those boys are looking to start a ranch.”

A ranch? That would explain why they'd hired a cook and a couple of hands. O.C. glanced back at the woman. “When you say Abilene, are you talkin' Kansas?”

“Yes,” she replied. “I told them Kansas is a rugged place, but that oldest boy, Joe, seemed very capable.”

Rogers put his arm around his wife. “Yes, and those two big Indians with them couldn't hurt, either.”

“You met these two big men?”

“No, I didn't actually meet them. I got a glimpse of them out the back window of the store when they were loading supplies into the prairie schooner they bought.”

O.C. knew he was on the right track. Everything they'd learned so far was true. “Thank you for the information, folks.”

She looked at O.C. “They said their ma passed, but they weren’t sure about you.”

He could only imagine what his boys thought had happened to him. “I intend to find them. Hopefully they’ll find out soon that I’m alive.”

Mrs. Rogers smiled. “They’ll be right happy to know it, too.”

“Like Myrt said, Kansas is rough but I noticed that the boys, and the hired help, were very conscience of what was going on around them.” Rogers dropped his arm from his wife's waist and went behind the counter.

“That's good.” Jack walked out the door and O.C. thought about what he and Tunnie had come through to get this far. Hell, Kansas would be a piece of cake. “I hope to catch up with them soon.”

Myrt smiled. "It's been some months since they were here, but with those wagons and all, they'll be traveling much slower than you men can." Myrt Smiled. "Don't you worry, you'll meet up with them." She joined her husband. "Now, you're going to need supplies. Let us take care of you before you leave town."

O.C. hadn't gone to the bank to exchange the gold, but he had some money in his pocket and agreed they would need things for the coming trip. "Yes, ma'am, I'd appreciate that."

When O.C. came out of the store he saw Jack sitting on a barrel. "You ready?"

"What ya got there?" Tunnie gestured toward the supplies.

Lifting the burlap bags O.C. replied, "If the boys are headed to Kansas, and that's where we're going, I figured we'd need some provisions. Ready to get started?" Jack stood and O.C. didn't like the expression on the man's face.

"My friend, I don't think I'm going."

He wondered what had changed Tunnie's mind, but he would go on alone if he had to. "Like I told Big City, a man's gotta do what he's gotta do, Jack."

"I'm sorry, O.C. I've never told you this, but all those years at that hellhole I dreamed about coming to St. Louie. I'm going stay, eat at some fine places, have fun with the ladies. This place is buzzing and I want to experience it."

O.C. would miss the man's company, but he understood that Tunnie wanted to live a little. "Hell, Jack, can't say I blame you. You worked in that dungeon and spent many more years behind those walls then I did."

"Glad you feel that way. Now that you know where they're going, you will catch up in no time. I won't be tagging along to slow you down."

He stepped down to the street, went to his horse and put the supplies in their proper place. "Ah, damn, Tunnie, you never slowed me down. Looks like I'll need to buy a mule to help tote this stuff." He laughed knowing full well he wasn't going to do that.

Jack stepped up beside O.C. "I hope you understand."

"I do, Tunnie." He took Jack's hand in his for a shake. "I do." O.C. turned back toward his horse and removed another bag then faced Tunnie. He was excited to share his fortune with a man he knew would be a lifelong friend and one who'd saved his life more than once.

O.C. held out the bag to Jack Tunnie. “I want you to have this. It will help you enjoy things…for a while, at least.” Jack took the sack from him and O.C. smiled when Jack's eyes grew large and his arm dropped from the weight.

“Is this what I think it is?”

Glad the man had the wisdom not to say the word out loud, O.C. glanced around at the passersby then nodded and looked back at Jack. “It is. I split it up earlier. Had the feelin' this time might come.”

The man stuck the hidden coins out to O.C. “I can't take this.”

“The hell you can't! You're a great man and someone I consider a friend and a brother.” Tunnie nodded and O.C. swore he saw a tear in the big fellow's eye.

“When I get tired of St. Louie, I'll come find you.”

“You do that.” O.C. mounted. “I still have some daylight left. Oughta make a few hours down the trail before dark.”

“I suppose. Be safe, brother.”

O.C. rode a few feet, then a glimpse of the past few years raced through his mind. The prison, the impaled men, Sheriff Tibbs, the entire journey this far. “My God.” He stopped and looked back to see Tunnie watching him. O.C. shook his head, faced forward and heeled his horse to a trot.

Chapter Thirty Nine

O.C.'s bones ached after riding the dry, hot plains of Kansas all day. It had taken a toll on his horse as well and O.C. figured it was time to stop and get some rest. During the day, he'd dropped some of the supplies he'd bought to lighten the load on the horse. He'd had enough for him and Jack, so he didn't need it all anyway.

He glanced around and realized a fire was out of the question because Sioux, Kickapoo and other Indian tribes might be in the area. He dismounted from Boy and wondered why he'd never given the horse a proper name. He patted the steed's neck. "It's just me and you now, Boy."

There wasn't a lot of water left in his canteen, but the wetness of the warm liquid felt good when he swallowed. He poured some into a tin plate and shared with Boy. "I'm gonna try to sleep a bit. You'd best do the same. Mornin' will be here before you know it and we'll be on the move again.

He pulled the saddle from Boy's back, put it on the ground, got the gold and put it beside him then made himself as comfortable as possible. His lids grew heavy as he thought of finally getting to see his boys.

He didn't know how long he'd slept when he was awakened by his horse stirring about. Opening his eyes, he raised his to take a look around. A strange orange glow illuminated the distant horizon. "Oh, mercy." He jumped to his feet. A dreaded prairie fire was headed his way and he needed to get to his horse.

After he gathered his things he ran for the horse, but Boy spooked and took off like a bat out of hell! “Boy, come back!” Boy!” The stallion was out of sight in the darkness. “Damn.”

He picked up the saddle and the gold. The lighter items he'd left on boy’s back in case they had to make a hasty retreat. Little good that did, now that the horse had run off. He hoped the poor thing didn't meet its death in the fire.

With only the help of the half moon, it was hard to see if there was any shelter. He walked fast at first then broke into a run as the fire got closer. It was hard to tell exactly how close it was, but he knew for sure he had to find somewhere fast.

Though he hadn’t noticed it when he looked for a place to camp, he saw a small creek where a few small trees lined its border. Studying his options, he realized that if he could find a stand-alone tree to climb, he'd be safer. Trees in a clump would burn higher and hotter. He picked out the only choice he had, dropped his saddle and the gold in the shallow water, drenched himself, filled his canteen then climbed as high as he could.

The fire was only a few hundred feet away and moving fast. Wind whipped around him as he saturated his bandana with the water from his canteen and put it around his face. Smoke was thick in the air now and he struggled to breathe. He closed his eyes from the burning, black wretched stuff. “Dear God, please don't let it end like this. Please not yet.”

He held on for dear life. The noise was so loud… and hot, it was so hot. He knew the fire was only a few feet from the base of the tree. Flames lapped upward and the intensity of the heat was almost unbearable then a burning pain hit his right side. He screamed trying to withstand the agony, the sound of his voice overtaken by the roar of the raging fire beneath him.

The flames raced by, but the seconds it took seemed like hours and the pain was almost intolerable. Fortunately, it passed so fast the tree was left smoking, but not burning. It was important he stay where he was until the ground cooled. However, he wasn't at all sure he could hold on to consciousness for that long.

Time passed and the air cooled. Before he passed out, he had to get down. Pain shot through his side when he moved and a groan escaped as he fell to the ground. Darkness overtook him.

***

O.C. opened his eyes. That turned around feeling of not knowing where he was, or what he was doing there, passed over him. He tried to sit up then pain overtook him and he remembered the fire. But where was he? He moaned, he couldn't help it, the pain was too intense.

He stared up at the dome over his head. Where the hell was he? A rustling sound drew his attention. Someone pulled the flap at the opening of the Dwelling and walked inside. He couldn't see clearly, but could tell it was a woman. She carried a bowl of some kind and kneeled down beside him.

Who was she and what was she going to do? Still half out of his mind with pain, instincts took over and he reached for his pistol. It wasn't there. His knife? Gone!

"Be still. I will not hurt you."

Her voice was calm and soothing, and he relaxed back. Soon the cooling sensation, of whatever was in the bowl, started to quell the burn in his side. She was doctoring his wounds.

He blinked a few times to clear his vision. She was an older Indian woman with kind eyes. "Thank you, that feels good. You probably can't understand me, but I'm grateful." Saying it over and over again, he knew he was rambling, probably with fever. The woman pointed to herself and he listened closely.

"Rain."

Pointing to himself he replied, "O.C." He glanced down at his raw flesh that oozed with fluid, and realized it could have been much worse. Maybe the Lord had heard his prayer.

The flap opened again and a man, who appeared to be the chief, walked through. He watched the powerfully built Indian approach and give a hand wave from his chest. The dark skinned man reminded him of Horse and Horn. O.C. returned the gesture.

"Found you by creek."

"You speak the words of the white man?"

"Some."

Relief surged through him. He was going to be able to communicate with these people. "Are you the Chief?"

"I am Running Bear. I am in hunting party. Need food to

take back to main camp. When you get well, you will help."

It was the least he could do to repay their kindness. He nodded his agreement.

"Should have left you for dead, but the woman felt sorry for your bad fortune so we brought you here. You will repay this debt. Your life belongs to me now, that is our law. If you do not, I will tie you with raw hide and leave you for the coyotes."

O.C. would have been shocked but he knew the ways of the Indians well and wouldn't protest. There was no doubt the man would do just that if he felt double crossed. The pain was all but gone for the time being and his thoughts wandered to his family. He met the big man's gaze. "I've been trying to find my sons. They came across this land not long ago. They have two of your kind with them. Maybe not Sioux, but like you."

Running Bear glared at him. "Will you pay this debt you owe me? I grow tired of talking."

The man's body language said it was time to shut up. "I will pay it. Like you, I'm a man of honor."

***

A week had passed and it was his first day outside the dwelling. He helped the woman with her chores by boiling clothes. It was the least strenuous thing he could offer. The lady seemed to like him, but her communication skills weren't as advanced as Running Bear's so it was a slow process.

He did learn, however, that she was Running Bear's wife. She was the only woman allowed to join the hunting party. He wasn't sure what her duties really were. He assumed the real reason she was there was because Running Bear wanted her to be.

Several hunters and Running Bear walked their horses to where O.C sat. He stood with care and looked at the man in front.

"How are your burns?"

"It's still hard to walk and very painful, but they're gettin' better, Running Bear."

"Good."

He glanced at the back of the horses and his heart skipped a beat. "Boy?"

"We found your horse. He is uninjured."

"That's wonderful!" O.C. took a slow step toward the animal but was stopped by Running Bear's voice.

"I will take him for my own."

"But..."

"This was yours also." Running bear lifted O.C.'s rifle. "I will take it as well."

How the hell was he going to go anywhere or do anything without his horse or his rifle? One thing he knew for sure, he meant nothing to these men and he dare not argue. He would just have to prove himself to them and gain their trust.

"You have white man's yellow iron. I will let you keep it for it means nothing to our people. It is evil and only brings bad things." He threw the gold at O.C.'s feet. "These sons of yours, I know them."

O.C.'s heart jumped in his chest. His boys! "Tell me, please."

"My people watched them cross our land. I did not tell you because we did not know if you would live, or if we would kill you."

His stomach turned and bile rose in his throat. Had they harmed his family? "Are they alright?"

"We did not slay them. They have a young girl with them. She is from our tribe was taken first by our enemy but she ran away and another white family took her in. They became sick. That is when she was found by your people."

"So she's with them now?"

Bear nodded. "We would have taken her, but there is no place in this party for her and our hunting cannot be stopped. It is more important to take care of all of our people then it is to rescue one when we know she is not in danger."

O.C. wondered why the girl couldn't stay with Rain in the hunting camp, but the man must have his reasons, and it wasn't his place to question. Pride surged through him. His boys had rescued the young Indian girl and were taking care of her. "Go on."

"She is called Wind. We believe the big man watching after her is Horse. He is a fierce warrior."

"That he is. His father was a chief called Grey Wolf, the warrior's full name is Little Boy Horse."

"He knew we were watching him, but did nothing."

"You're lucky. He's like a wolf, very cunning. He could have killed your scouts if he wanted to."

Running Bear nodded. "We have respect for him. Because of this and him taking care of Wind, we let him and the others pass. However, one day we will get her back with our people."

It hurt like hell to keep standing, but O.C. knew that showing his pain would radiate weakness. He refused to do that. "I believe you will."

"They are north of here. Our scouts say your sons have many cattle and the number is growing." Running Bear dismounted and faced O.C. "You tell me why I should let you go. If the reason is good, I will. If not, you may not live."

O.C. had to choose his words right or it might be the end of him. He straightened, but ignored the stabbing pain in his side. "For one thing, I never did anything to you or your people. Everyone in the camp here's been very good to me and I appreciate it. I promised I would repay you for everything." Suddenly a thought hit him. "I'll tell you what; I'll take this yellow iron and buy cattle for your people. I'll bring them to you as soon as I get settled with my boys. I will bring you another horse if you will allow me to keep mine." He gave Running Bear the hand to chest gesture. "I give you my word."

"You will bring Wind with you?"

O.C. caught that this was as much a statement as it was a question. He had to make his answer count. It could be the difference in life or death, but he had to tell the truth. "I can't promise you I will bring her. All I can do is talk to Little Boy Horse and tell him after the hunt you're ready for her to come back to your people. The rest will be between you and Horse." He wasn't sure what the look on the man's face meant, but was relieved when Bear gave an affirmative nod.

"I will give you until the leaves turn color. Then your debt will be due. If you do what you say, all will be well. If not…"

"I'm a man of my word, but if something happens to me, I won't be able to follow through."

"We have many eyes on the prairie, you will be safe. Go at

first light to find your sons by the river on their new land."

****

It seemed like O.C. slept with one eye open, but somehow he felt rested. Most of the braves had left with hunting groups. They trusted him to do the right thing, at least that's what he hoped.

He packed his horse then walked slowly out of camp. Some of the Sioux women trailed with him to say goodbye. O.C. climbed onto his mount then looked down at the squaws. "I know you can't understand me, but I've never been treated so well." He smiled at them. "May your days be happy."

They all smiled back and he graciously accepted a Plains flower one of them gave him. With a nod, he gestured the goodbye signal across his chest, then waved, turned his back and road away. "Well, Boy. Let's go find my family and make a home somewhere."

CHAPTER FORTY

Joe glanced around the campfire at all the men he'd hired over the last few weeks. He knew they were trying to get used to each other and were doing a good job. However, some of them didn't want to accept that Nate was in charge. They wanted to disagree on how things got done. When he saw Nate walk into the middle of the group, the look of determination on his face, he knew they were fixing to find out who was the boss.

"Listen up! Now I've heard you men bickerin' amongst yourselves, and some of you even tryin' to argue with *me*. Let me tell you somethin', startin' right now, that all comes to a halt! No more, period! I'm the one runnin' this operation and I only take orders from Mr. Armstrong there."

Nate pointed at him and he stood. Joe knew with a crew this large, Nate would have to stay in control. "That's right, and I stand behind the trail boss one-hundred percent. We're all men here, so I'm askin' you to do your job." He sat back down, confident Nate could take care of the rest.

"That's right, and I'll tell you somethin', if I hear anymore, I'll hand over the pay that's owed you and you can be gone. That's the end of it!" Nate glanced toward Little Boy Horse. "Well, that's not quite the end." He pointed toward Horse. "See that big man over there?"

Joe watched the men steal glances in Horse's direction, and almost laughed when he noticed none of them would meet the glare he was focusing on them. He was putting on quite the show for Nate right now.

"Well, you know what? He don't like hearing all this foul language around his little girl there. So I suggest you tone that down, too. Trust me, you don't want to get him riled.

"Again, if you don't agree with what I'm sayin', just let me know and I'll give you the pay that's comin' to ya, and you can be on your way." Nate put his hands on his hips. "Any questions?" No one spoke. "That's what I thought."

Shorty sat down next to Joe just as Nate walked out of the circle of the firelight. Joe accepted a cup of coffee from the man. "Thanks, Shorty."

"He told 'em, didn't he?"

"Sure did."

"Joe, I got somethin' I want to talk to you about."

There was a bit of excitement in Shorty's voice and he was curious as to what was on the little man's mind. He took a sip of the dark hot liquid and nodded his agreement to listen.

"You've been waitin' for your other Indian friend for some time now. Not sayin' he ain't comin' back, or anything like that, but you need to find a place to settle. These cattle, and the men are gettin' tired of being on the trail. "

Johnny One Horn, and the situation of finding a place, had been heavy on his mind the last few days. He didn't want to think something had happened to him, but he also knew he had to make a move, one way or the other. "Go on."

"I been up around Great Bend before. There's some good land to be had around there. It's good cattle country, and I hear tell the railroad's movin' in there soon. It'd be closer to the cattle market and it's said the land can be bought for a fair price."

Knowing his brothers would like nothing more than to have a place of their own again, Joe took all of this into consideration. "We're headed in the wrong direction."

"I know, but I swear, it ain't no farther than a few days from here."

It was tempting, but he'd have to think about it. "We'll have to see. Now let's get some shuteye, morning will come quicker than we think." When Shorty got up to walk to his bedroll, Joe realized the man truly had best intentions in mind. "Hey, Shorty?" The man turned back to face him. "Thanks for tellin' me."

Joe lay down and closed his eyes but it didn't bring sleep. All he could think of was Shorty's words. Great Bend hadn't been a place he'd thought to settle, but Dammit, he had to do something. Horn had been gone a long while and Shorty was right, they shouldn't wait any longer, but before he made a decision to move the herd that way, he wanted to see the country for himself.

He got up and made his way to the little man's bedroll. Squatting down he whispered, "Shorty."

Shorty rubbed sleep from his eyes and sat up. "Yeah, boss?"

"You feel like makin' that trip to Great Bend?"

"Sure 'nough."

"At first light we'll gather our gear and be on our way, then."

"Yes, sir."

Unsure when sleep took over his thoughts, Joe woke to a gentle nudge on his shoulder. He looked up at Shorty then glanced at the horizon; in the distance the orange glow of the rising sun barely peeked out.

"Time to skedaddle, Joe. I woke Levi and he got us some grub together. All we gotta do is gather whatever else we need and we're ready."

The others wouldn't be up for at least another hour, and Joe didn't bother to wake Nate. He knew the man could be trusted with the hands and the herd. Levi could fill him and the boys in. It wasn't like he was going to be gone for weeks, only a few days.

After he gathered his bedding, he grabbed his saddle, put it on his horse, loaded his belongings and mounted. "Looks like we're outta here, Levi."

"Don't worry 'bout nothin'. We'll handle things 'round here. Y'all be careful and don't get scalped on your trip."

Joe had come to understand the older man's humor. He knew Shorty was still trying to get used to him, though, and Joe smiled when the short man pulled off his hat and ran his fingers through his hair.

"Damn, Levi, what kind of thought is that to put in a man's head."

"Hell, Shorty, we ain't gonna get scalped. Now let's go." Joe wished he could be sure of what he'd just told his hired hand. Truth was, there were no guarantees in these parts.

"Coffee smells good, Levi." Charles reached for a cup. "Ain't seen Joe this mornin'. Any idea where he is?"

Levi took the pot and poured Charles some Coffee. "All I know is him and Shorty left at daybreak and said they'd be back in a few days. We was told to stay here by the creek until they get back."

Charles took a sip. "Figures he'd leave us here where there's probably a Sioux behind every bush. Damn, I wish he wouldn't just ride out like that without tellin' me."

"No Sioux." Little Boy Horse walked up behind them, Kicking Wind by his side.

"Holy shit, Horse, you 'bout scared hell outta me!"

Horse smiled. "You scare easy, my friend."

"Everything in this country will try to kill ya, why shouldn't I? Damn." Charles turned his attention back to his coffee. "Sorry about the cussin' Wind."

Taking a cup from Levi, Horse squatted next to Charles. "The Sioux moved farther west. I see them often. They will not let you see them; they don't trust the white man."

"Can't say I trust them much either."

"You know, my young friend, they leave us alone because I killed two of their enemies. Even though they have moved, they are watching all the time. They say the great buffalo are disappearing, and we must not kill them."

"Why would we kill the buffalo, Horse?"

"Many white men have killed them."

"Yeah, but that ain't us."

"I know this, but the Sioux do not. You know they have warned that if we hunger, we must eat these cows. If we kill buffalo, they kill cows. They will do as they say, so you need to tell your men."

"I'll tell Nate and he can tell them. He's their boss and I think that after the talkin' to he gave them last night, they'll do what he says."

Horse stood. "That is good." Horse grabbed Kicking Wind's

hand, turned and walked away.

Charles watched the Indian's retreat into the distance. "Wonder why he didn't tell us he's been talking to the Sioux."

Levi put another log on the fire. "Ain't no surprise to me. Do you think we would of got this far, without gettin' scalped, if he hadn't been?"

"I don't know."

"'Member those two bushwhackers that killed ole Bull?"

"I 'member."

"Think about it, boy, they must have been the enemies of the Sioux that Horse was talkin' about. Makes sense to me. Hell, they had Indian scalps on 'em."

"Seems pretty quiet, don't you think, Joe?"

Joe looked down the main street of Great Bend, Kansas from the edge of town. "It's early yet. We don't even know what day it is, it could be Sunday."

"Might be, but I think you're right, it's just too early for folks to be millin' around."

"Lookie down there." Joe pointed to several men at the far end of the street. "Wonder what they're doin'?"

"Don't know. Lots of talkin' and hammerin' goin' on, though. Probably buildin' somethin'. What say we take a look see?"

Spurring his horse forward, he followed Shorty. When they got closer, Joe spoke to the first man they came to, "Howdy." The man stopped digging the post hole he was working and met Joe's gaze. A quick assessment told Joe he was an honest fellow.

"Howdy." The man wiped his brow with his shirt sleeve. "Y'all ain't from around here, are you?"

"No, sir, we ain't."

"Can I help you with something?"

"Maybe, if you know somebody that's got some land for sale." Joe noted a more interested look on the older man's face at the mention of wanting to buy land.

"Well, youngun, I might." He put the post hole digger down and reached out to shake Joe's hand. "Name's Billy Ray."

"Joe Armstrong and this here's Shorty."

"What exactly are you looking for, Joe Armstrong?"

"A place big enough to raise some cattle and horses."

"I've got to tell you the truth. There's not a lot to choose from unless you pay ten times what it's worth. Here a while back, you could have bought all you want, but when the big shots from out east found out the railroad is coming through here, they bought most all of it up."

The older man gazed off into the distance and Joe noticed a faraway look in his eyes. Something was on Billy Ray's mind but Joe couldn't read his expression. He decided to stay quiet, and maybe the man would speak his mind. Moments passed. Was that a tear in the man's eyes?

"Sorry, I was lost in thought for a minute." He looked up at Joe. "I've got a well-kept secret, Joe Armstrong. Hadn't wanted to tell it 'til now. No reason, I guess, but you seem like a nice young man."

"Thank ya, sir. What might that secret be?"

"Well, I had a great place once. Arkansas River runs right close and there are plenty of creeks. Yep, good water, lots of grass. Put many years in on it, but had to leave. Indians wouldn't leave me be." He looked to the hillside again. "I hear the house and barn are still standing and the corral's in pretty good shape. I haven't been back there in some time now."

Shorty shifted in his saddle and followed the man's gaze. "I've been in these parts many times. May have even been to your place once. I remember your wife and daughters, real sorry to hear about them dyin'."

"Yeah, seems like I remember you. That's been a few years back, though."

"Yes, sir, it has. These Indians you speak of, what'd they do to ya?"

Billy Ray chuckled. "They really didn't do much. Sometimes they'd take a steer or pig, maybe a chicken or two. Nothing I couldn't put up with. Then the fever took my wife and two girls. Seems after that the Sioux got more certain they wanted me to leave. Started getting a little more aggressive and I just don't understand...or never understood why. Hell, I was lonely, too. Figured coming back to town was best for me anyway. "

Joe couldn't be sure why after the ladies' deaths the Indians wanted the man to leave, he could only guess. "They must have liked your family. They are people just like everybody else. Must've liked you, too, or you'd probably be dead."

"Yep, that's what I figured." He leaned on the posthole digger. "Place is a little over a half a day's ride southwest of here. Tell you what, I'll sell the place to you, lock, stock and barrel. Just know you'll be the only duck in the pond out there, that's for sure."

Could this be what Joe was looking for? "Why didn't you sell to the railroad when the price was high?"

Billy Ray kicked at the dirt. "I didn't want those no caring bastards to get something I love. Hell, they'd just sell it for profit to somebody I don't know. I'd rather see it sit there and rot first."

Maybe it was too good to be true that the first person they'd run into had land for sale. "Tell me more about your spread, Billy Ray. How big is it?"

"It's mostly open range with a homestead deed of six hundred forty acres, but the closer you get to the house, you'll come to some hills. There's a nice river that runs straight through the property. The house sits in front of a rock bluff and has some wooded land close by. Joe Armstrong, keep in mind you may get killed or skinned."

Knowing he had to take everything into consideration, he wanted to look at the property before making any decisions. "How much?"

"For you, young man, my price is seven-hundred dollars." Billy Ray shook his head. "Never thought I'd sell it, but I'm too damned old to fight Indians…so be it." He pointed down the street. "The bank holds the papers on it. Talk to Tom Madden, he can help you. Tell him the deal I made you and give him the seven-hundred dollars. He'll take what I owe out of that and give me the rest. He's a fair man."

"That sounds mighty good, but I'd like to see the place. Think you could take us there? Show us around?"

"The Sioux gave me my warning. No, I'm not going, but Tom's got a map that will tell you how to get there."

Shorty touched Joe's arm. "That won't be necessary; I remember where the place is. He's right, though; there are Sioux all around there."

"We'll worry about them if we come across 'em." He looked down at Billy Ray. "Sir, I'm gonna go out and look at your property. If it suits me, we gotta deal and I'll come back and pay the bank."

"Sounds good to me, Joe Armstrong, I'm glad I met you today."

CHAPTER FORTY ONE

"Let's camp here, Shorty. We've ridden three hours now and it'll be sundown soon. I'm ready to get outta the saddle and I'm sure the horses would like the rest."

"Okay, Joe." Shorty dismounted and started taking the saddle off his horse. "I'm 'bout ready to bed down."

"Me, too." He helped the short man get the camp ready and gathered wood for the fire. "I'm gonna have a bite then see if I can get some shuteye."

The sun went down and it was all Joe could do to stay awake, but he couldn't stop daydreaming about what Billy Ray's land might be like. Could it be his, Carl's and Charles' new home? Shorty's voice drew his thoughts.

"You think the Indians know were here?"

"Yeah, they've been watching us for a while."

Shorty reached for his pistol. "That's what I thought."

Joe propped himself up on one elbow. "Put that away, Shorty. If they wanted to hurt us, they would've done it already. This is their land and they know every move we've made."

"Yeah, well, I think I'll just sleep with this right beside me. I don't feel like wakin' up dead tomorrow."

Laughing, Joe said, "Do what you have to do, man, but I'm tellin' ya, if they wanted us dead, we'd of been there by now."

Morning came and it was no surprise to Joe that they didn't 'wake up dead' as Shorty had said. He took the coffee pot off the fire as the sun rose. Shorty stirred and rubbed his eyes. Joe couldn't wait to see the man's reaction to what he was about to show him. "Mornin'. Sleep okay?"

"Better than I thought I would."

"Take a look behind you." Joe waited for Shorty to focus on his surroundings and gestured in the direction he wanted Shorty to see. "By your bedroll."

Shorty stretched and looked where Joe pointed. "Holy shit!" He jumped up and stared. "What the hell is that in the bush?"

"It's a rattle snake tied by his tail."

"For Christ sake."

"See that circle on the ground."

"What the hell kind of feather is that inside it."

"It's a turkey feather."

"What's it mean?"

Joe knew it was a cautionary statement, and he wanted to make sure Shorty understood the importance of it. "It's a warning."

"Hells bells, Joe, I've been here before, but just passin' through. You sure you want to settle in these parts?"

He'd lived around Indians all of his life. Hell, he had Indian blood in his veins, too. He would like to think he understood them, but he couldn't be certain about the Sioux. "We just need to be careful of what we do."

"How do we know what to do, or if we do something wrong?"

"Well, we just won't do anything crazy, that's all. We'll stay calm and mind our own business."

"Shit, you'd think I'd be used to this by now."

"I don't think life's somethin' you ever get used to, Shorty. There're too many twists and turns in it."

Shorty started to gather his bedroll. "I'll do whatever you say, boss."

For some reason, there was calmness inside Joe he couldn't explain. It was like he was supposed to be here. He hadn't had this feeling since he was a kid, and he liked it. "Let's go look at that land."

They'd ridden over open range for some time, then the foot hills started and Joe knew they were close. They rode over the last small hill and he studied the land. Large bluffs were to his right. The river Billy Ray spoke about ran close by and was lined by trees and brush. Straight ahead, the house, barn and corral were nestled where the bluff and woods met, just like the man described.

Was that smoke coming out of the chimney? No, that was impossible, the place was supposed to be empty. His heart beat a little faster at the anticipation of this possibly becoming his home. It was a beautiful sight in the middle of the flatlands of Kansas.

"There it is, Joe."

"Yep, I see it."

He also noticed between him and the house, there was a knoll that looked man made. The old man hadn't mentioned it and he figured he knew why. It might have scared them away. He urged his horse to go a little faster, and after a ways, he reined to a stop at the foot of the mound. "Hold it, Shorty. Let's go around this."

"Is it what I think it might be?"

"There are some markings on these rocks. I believe it's somethin' special to the Indians."

Shorty nodded toward the bluff above. "Look up there."

Joe cast a glance upward. A lone Sioux watched them from atop his rocky perch. "I see him."

"You think he's alone?"

"Probably not." Meeting the dark skinned man's gaze, Joe gave him the sign from the chest gesture. The brave gave no response, he turned and rode away. "That's all we can do, Shorty. Just steer clear of this mound at all times. We need to respect these people. It will help keep us safe."

"You won't catch me settin' one damn foot on that thing. Don't worry 'bout that."

A smile lifted the corners of Joe's mouth. He'd have to make sure to let all of his men know this sacred place was completely off limits, no matter what.

As they approached the house, Joe saw it was definitely smoke he'd seen coming out of the chimney earlier. He drew his shotgun from his saddle holster, dismounted, took the steps onto the front porch then banged on the door.

No one answered, so he grabbed the knob, turned it and slowly opened the door. He was promptly confronted with a naked old woman's high pitched scream, and a fire poker to the head. He fell to the ground, but was glad it didn't knock him out.

He watched her run around and around in circles toward the creek hollering a chant that made no sense, then he saw Shorty draw down on her. "No! Don't shoot her. Hell, she's crazy, just let her go."

Shorty holstered his pistol. "You okay?"

Joe picked himself up off the ground, took the bandana off his neck and held it to his head. "I'll be alright. The bleedin'll stop soon."

"That woman packed a hell of a wallop."

"Gonna have a headache." He glanced inside the house. "Hello?" Another surprise like that was something he didn't want. "Anybody here?" When his questions were met by silence, he went inside.

Shorty followed behind then glanced back out the front door. "Wonder where she went? It's like she just disappeared and did you see she didn't have on a stitch of clothes?"

"Yeah, that's somethin' you can't unsee, that's for sure."

"She didn't look too bad."

Joe shook his head. What was the little man thinking? "Shorty, I swear, you've been out on the range too long." He joined in when Shorty began to laugh, then made his way through the house. "Looks pretty good in here. Plenty of room." There were enough bedrooms that he and his brothers could have one each. That was something that they'd never had in their lifetime and he was excited to tell Charles and Carl the news.

"Let's take a look outside."

Joe followed Shorty outside, shutting the door to the house behind him. "The holding corral needs a little work, and the barn could use some, too, but overall, the place is in good shape. Livable."

"If everyone chips in on the work, it won't take us long to build a bunk house, either."

The land, house and surroundings pleased Joe more than he could have ever imagined. "Let's go, Shorty. I want to sign the papers on this place. It's a long way back to camp, too."

Shorty shrugged his shoulders and peered into the distance. "What about the crazy lady?"

"She'll probably be here when we get back. 'Til then I suppose she'll be fine. The Sioux won't hurt her, they stay away from crazies." He rubbed the sore spot on his head, then chuckled. "Yep, damnedest thing *I* ever seen!"

****

The dust on the busy streets of Abilene, Kansas almost made O.C put a handkerchief over his mouth to breathe, but that was the last thing on his mind. Knowing the boys might be buying cattle, he headed straight for the stockyards.

Once there, he went to the sales office. The clerk glanced up from some paper work and O.C. knew he'd come to the right place. "I'm wondering if you know anyone named Joe Armstrong."

"Why?"

"I'm his father. I've been lookin' for my boys for some time now. I'm feared they think I'm dead."

"And your name?"

"O.C. Armstrong. My boys' names are Joe, Charles and Carl." The grin that lifted at the corner of the man's mouth made O.C. smile, too.

"As a matter of fact…" He bent and took a piece of paper out of a file. "I remember Joe Armstrong. Nice young man. He had a couple of hired hands with him. Said they were headed north." He handed the paper to O.C. "He bought a hundred head. Wanted more, but some big buyers from St. Louie had claim on the rest."

He recognized Joe's signature right away. "Yep, that would be my Joe's writin' alright." He handed the sales slip back to the clerk. "Guess I'll be headed north, then. Thank ya for your time." He tipped his hat at the man.

"Ain't been that long ago, just a couple of weeks. You should be able to catch up real quick."

His heart soared when he walked away. "Thanks again." He closed the door behind him, glad the Sioux Chief had pointed him in the right direction. It shouldn't be hard to track the herd.

Buffalo were getting scarce and that would make the cows hoofing up the ground easy to follow. A hundred head would surely leave a wide trail. He'd get a good night's sleep then head out at daybreak.

****

Joe approached the teller window at the Bank of Great Bend. "Can ya tell me where to find Tom Madden?"

The man pointed. "Through those doors to your right. Mr. Madden don't like to be bothered by strangers, though, so don't talk long."

It seemed to Joe it was the teller that didn't want to be bothered by strangers. He was a grumpy ole coot. After he tapped on the door the teller pointed to, he heard a man's voice.

"Come in."

Joe opened the door and stepped inside, Shorty right behind. He was pleasantly surprised when he was greeted by an expectantly nice man.

"Come in, come in. Have a seat."

Taking off his hat, Joe sat in a chair on the opposite side of the man's desk, while Shorty remained standing. "Thank ya." He put his hat in his lap.

"What can I do for you, son?"

He might as well get straight to the point. "I've come to buy Billy Ray's place. He told me your bank holds the note."

"That we do." The man studied Joe. "I've held that note for a long time. How much did he say he wanted for it?"

"Seven hundred dollars."

The man cleared his throat. "That's a fair price for that property. The note is three-hundred dollars, the other four hundred we will deposit directly into Billy Ray's account. Now, that's cash only. I have my doubts a young man like you has that kind of money."

"I got it, sir." He stood and pulled the already counted roll of cash from his pocket, then handed it to the man. "I think you'll find it all there." The look on Madden's face was priceless. Joe pulled the other money out of his pocket then and put it on top of the desk.

Madden looked at the wad. “And what is this?”

“That there’s another five hundred dollars. I want to start an account.”

Tom Madden smiled and met Joe’s gaze. “I see. Well…ah…would you boys, I mean men, like some coffee? Got a fresh pot out in the lobby.”

Shorty turned toward the door. “I think I’ll go have me some while y’all take care of business.”

Joe was glad to have Shorty as one of his hands. Not only was the man good for a laugh, but he was savvy on many things, like when to take his leave. The banker’s voice drew his attention.

“Don’t believe I caught your name.”

“Joe Armstrong.” He offered the man a handshake.

Madden reached across the desk. “Nice to meet you, Mr. Armstrong.” He put his hand into a desk drawer and pulled out some papers. “You know Indians are something you’re going to have to deal with on Billy Ray’s place. You’ll have to make a good first impression because if you don’t, it might be your last.”

“I’ve lived around Indians all my life and I’ve found them to be more honest than any white men I’ve known.”

“You’re right about that. It’s a shame what’s happened to their people. I wish you well, my friend and hope you keep your scalp when you go out to the place.”

“Not to worry. I’ve already been there and I’m here to talk about it, so I don’t foresee any trouble with those people.” He thought about the crazy woman, now she might be a totally different story.

“You ready to sign some papers?”

Joe walked out of the office and didn’t see Shorty so he ambled outside. The ranch hand was standing by the horses. “We’re done here. Let’s hit the trail.”

Shorty nodded toward a couple of saloon girls leaning on a horse rail outside the tavern. “Reckin we might have a drink before we go?”

He knew what was on the other man’s mind. “Hell no.”

“That gal sure is purtty.”

“Yeah, I bet there’s a passel of pretty ones around here, but we've got cattle to drive. And we have a long ride ahead of us."

"Ah, hell, a man can't have no fun. No fun at all." Shorty mounted his horse.

Late into the night, the saddle was sitting hard under Joe's backside. "Guess we should stop for a few hours and give the horses a rest. They won't be no good to us if they collapse."

"We been pushin' 'em pretty hard, and besides, my ass is numb."

Joe laughed. "You're somethin' else, you know that, Shorty?"

"Just statin' the truth."

"This is as good a place as any to stop." He got to the ground, unsaddled his horse and patted it's neck. "Won't be long, and you'll be home. You'll have a barn and plenty of fresh land to graze on."

Late the next afternoon they rode into camp. Joe was never so glad to see Levi cooking a pot of beans, he was hungry as hell. Little Boy Horse was teaching Kicking Wind to use a bow. He swung out of the saddle. "Hey, Horse, how's she coming along?" He saw the little girl say something into the big man's ear.

"She says it won't be long before she can beat any of your cowboys."

Everybody laughed and Joe was glad to see Kicking Wind laugh, too. She was different now than she had been when Horse found her, and it was good to see her happy.

He tied his horse, took off the saddle then grabbed a biscuit. "Hey, y'all, gather round I have somethin' to tell ya." He waited for everyone to get settled then took his last bite.

Carl was the first to speak. "What is it, Joe?"

"We're leavin' in the mornin', first light."

"Where we goin'?" Charles took a sip of coffee.

"We're goin' home, boys." He grinned at his brothers and watched closely. Carl squinted at him with a questioning look.

"Home?"

"Yep. I found us a ranch!" He couldn't stop the laughter that bubbled up inside when both his brothers jumped up and gave him a big bear hug.

Carl sat back down first. "Tell us all about it, Joe. Hurry."

The two reminded him of when they were little boys and he'd tell them stories. They sat down next to each other, Indian fashion, just like they used to, and gave him their undivided attention.

Sometimes he missed those days back on the farm. He sure did miss his ma, and wondered whatever happened to his pa, but now wasn't the time to think about that. The Armstrong boys were moving forward.

"I've been there and it's real nice. Good water, big house, barn and plenty of room for a bunk house and stables." The look on his brothers' faces were ones of pure joy, especially Carl's.

"A real house, Joe? Where we can stay and live?"

Joe's heart soared with pride to be able to answer. "Yep, a real house, little brother. You even get to have your own room."

CHAPTER FORTY TWO

As they were closing in on the ranch, Joe rode beside Charles and Nate. He turned his horse and gave the signal for the hands to stop the herd, then led his horse to the center hoping everyone could hear him. "Everybody knows about the mound. Well, there it is." He pointed to the knoll in front of them. "I told y'all not to go near it, and that's what I mean."

He thought about the snake in the bush above Shorty's head, and the circle of rocks on the ground. "We've been warned already, and I for one know that warning was serious. Like Horse told us, that rattle snake was a death threat. None, and I mean *none* of you will test that warning!" He had to emphasize the point. "If you do, they'll kill us all! Is that understood?"

Glancing at the ridge of the bluff above, he didn't see anyone, but knew the Sioux watched their every move. He motioned for the men to get closer so he didn't have to raise his voice so much. He didn't know if the Indians could understand him, but he wanted to give the men more instructions.

Once everyone was close by, he shifted in the saddle. "We know the Sioux are watchin'. You men keep your eyes open, but don't shoot at anything or anybody. Is that clear?"

The men nodded their agreement and Joe realized he was actually, for the moment, taking charge. He suddenly felt like a land owner and it was good. However, there was one more problem he had to address before they went any further.

"There is one thing I haven't mentioned to any of ya." It

was best just to come right out and tell them. "There's a crazy woman livin' in the house that we're gonna have to deal with." Mumbles went between the men, glances shot toward the house, and he looked at Shorty then laughed.

"A crazy woman?" Charles pushed his cowboy hat back on his head. "That makes my day, Joe."

Carl frowned. "How do we know she's not a witch or somethin'?"

"Hell, Carl," Charles straightened his hat. "That old witch might turn you into a sack a taters, or even worse, a frog."

"That ain't funny, Charles."

Joe watched the banter between his brothers, but knew when Carl kicked at Charles, he had to calm them down. "Okay, that's enough, now."

"You're an ass, Charles." Carl turned his horse away and headed away from them.

"Joe," Charles said, "how do you know that lady's crazy?"

"If it tells you anything, brother, last time me and Shorty seen her, she hit me in the head with a fire poker. Then stark naked she ran toward the creek in circles, screamin' at the top of her lungs, then disappeared."

"How do you know she's still here?"

He pointed toward the house. "Smoke's comin' out of the chimney."

"Shit!"

Joe laughed at his brother until he saw the strained look on Nate's face as he approached. He didn't even realize the man hadn't been there until this very minute. He turned back toward Shorty. "Take the hands and y'all move the herd forward."

"Yes, sir." Shorty addressed the men. "Let's go."

Waiting until Levi pulled past him with the Schooner, he rotated to meet Nate's gaze. "What's wrong?"

"Was takin' a look around when I saw a wagon beside the river. It don't seem to be good, Joe. Appears to be people layin' around it. Dead folks. Maybe the Sioux killed 'em, I don't know, but we need to find out."

"Ah, hell, this is supposed to be a happy day." He didn't want to see any more death, but he knew they had to figure out what had happened.

Joe heard the river before the wagon came into sight, but there was no mistaking Nate's words.

"How the hell did he get here so fast?"

Bile rose in his throat when Joe saw Carl jump out of the back of the wagon holding some blankets. The young man's horse was tied to a low branch.

"Those look like Army blankets." Nate cupped his hands around his mouth. "Put those down, Carl! Put 'em down now!"

"What the hell, Nate?" Joe didn't know what the man was so riled up about. They were only blankets.

"They could be infected."

Joe swallowed hard when they got closer to the scene. "Infected?"

"Look at 'em." Nate pointed to the bodies. "They weren't killed by the Indians, they died of somethin' else. Maybe smallpox."

The corpses were still a good ways away, but Joe could see they were ghastly looking, and he didn't want to look at them. "I think you're right." He realized that the brush on the back side of the wagon had shielded the bodies from his little brother's sight. "Carl, back off! Get away from there!"

Carl glanced up. "Why, Joe? There's some good stuff on this wagon."

"There's some dead folks on the other side of the bushes there."

"Good God, more dead people?" Carl dropped the blankets. "Wonder who killed them."

"I don't think they were killed, Carl." Joe reined his horse forward, but before he could move Nate grabbed his arm.

"Don't go any closer, Joe; you could get infected, too. Matter of fact, I don't think Carl should go back to the ranch. He might already be infected himself."

"What the hell do you think he should do? I can't just leave him here."

"That's exactly what I think you should do. Just for a week or so, or at least 'til we're sure he won't get the pox."

Joe glanced over at his youngest brother. In good conscience, he couldn't and wouldn't leave him out there alone. "Dammit, Nate, he's my brother and I'm gonna stay with him."

Nate shook his head. "I wouldn't get close to him if I were you. I'm tellin' ya, that stuff spreads quick."

"I hear what you're sayin', but if I catch it, then I catch it. Bottom line; and I don't want to hear no more about it. Now, bring us some supplies and clean bedrolls. Tell Charles what we're doin' and why. I trust you to take care of things. He'll help you."

He knew Nate was a good man. God forbid anything happen to himself or Carl, but if the Good Lord decided to take them because of the pox, Joe was confident Nate would look after Charles.

"Okay, boss, I'll be back as soon as I can. If I were y'all, I'd move farther down river. Get away from of this place."

"We will."

"There's a sand bar a ways from here."

"That's where we'll be." He saw Nate's nod and he reined his horse back toward the ranch. Joe knew what he had to do. It wasn't going to be pleasant, but most things that happened in his life up 'til now, hadn't been.

He rode to where his younger brother was staring at the gruesome bodies. "Carl, we gotta burn these folks, wagon and all." He got off his horse and started to gather brush. Carl helped put the dried wood under and on top of the wagon then with the strike of a friction match, Joe lit the fire.

"I can't believe this is happenin'. We just found us a house, and now we can't even go there. What's next, Joe? Are we gonna die?"

"Hell, I don't know. If we do, I guess we do." The crackling of the fire filled the air while he put brush around the bodies. He pushed down the lump in his throat, then struck the match and threw it into the pile of dried timber. He backed away and saw that Carl was already on his horse, staring at the flames.

"I never thought we'd ever have to do things like this."

"I know, but it's life, Carl." Funny, the older he got the more he tended to accept things that happened without question. He figured it was all part of the growing up process. "It's never gonna change. Good with bad, and that's the way it is."

"What? I'm goin' out there."

"No, Charles, it wouldn't be wise for any of us to get very close. Smallpox is somethin' we don't want to mess with.

"So we just wait? That's all?"

"Yeah, that's all we can do. Wait and pray."

"If it ain't one thing it's another." He plopped down in a wooden chair on the porch. "How come you didn't stay?"

"I kept my distance. Didn't get close as Joe did."

"Why did this have to happen now? This is supposed to be a happy time." He took his hat off and sat it in his lap.

"I know it is." The foreman pointed at the smoke beginning to rise over the tree tops. "They're burning the wagon and bodies now."

Charles glanced in the direction Nate indicated. "Dear God!"

Nate continued to load supplies onto Shadrack. "I'm gonna take as many things out there as I can on this trip so's we don't have to go out there often."

"Maybe I should take it. At least I'd get to see them."

"Nope, ain't gonna happen. Joe's expectin' you to help me take care of things around here. We can't take the chance of all three of you gettin' sick now can we? We just gotta deal with this."

"I guess you're right, but that don't make me like it any."

"Don't 'spect it does."

Calling out, Nate said, "You men gather 'round!" The small group formed next to him. "I've got some bad news. Seems we might have come across a family down river a ways that might have died from the pox."

Levi stepped forward. "Damn, Nate, them pox are bad. I hope none of us get 'em."

"Me, too, Levi, but we can't all start worrying about dying. Carl was exposed so Joe's going to stay with him 'til we find out if he's gonna get it or not." Nate hoisted himself onto his horse. "I'm only gonna take this stuff so far, then they'll have to come get it. I don't want to take any more chances of getting sick myself. I didn't go close and I didn't touch nothin', so I'm confident I won't."

He reined his horse toward the river. "Why don't you cook us up some of the steer you and Shorty butchered? I'll be back directly and we'll eat and get better settled." He turned toward Pete. "These corrals are in pretty good shape, you and the men get the cattle rounded up and in them. I'll be back directly."

"Will do, Nate."

"It's gonna work out, men. Me and Charles will look out for things until Joe and Carl come back. You have my word."

Joe glanced up and saw Nate tying Shadrack to a bush about one hundred yards away, then hurriedly rode back toward the ranch. Carl walked up beside him and Joe saw terror in his brother's eyes.

"We are gonna die, ain't we, Joe. I don't want to die." Tears streamed down Carl's face. "I don't want them worms eatin' me like they was them folks we had to burn."

It was obvious Carl was about to get out of control. Joe's emotions were running high, too, but he didn't want Carl to get out of hand. He grabbed the younger man's shoulders and shook him. "Carl, if we die, we die together. But right now we're alive so let's do somethin' with ourselves instead of frettin'."

Carl sniffed and wiped his nose with the sleeve of his shirt. "Like what?"

"We need to build a shelter before rain comes. You build a fire, then start gathering things we might need for a lean-to, and I'm gonna to get Shadrack and the supplies." He forced Carl to look at him. "I'll be back in a few minutes, and later we'll cook some supper then throw a line in the river." Carl loved to fish and Joe was glad to see a smile cross his brother's face.

"Be careful goin' in there, Charles. That crazy woman is somewhere, maybe inside, and she put the hurt on Joe."

Charles turned the knob, shoved the door open then quickly stepped back. "Nobody's movin' in there, Levi. What say we go in?"

"You first."

"Sure." Charles couldn't stop thinking of his brothers. He prayed they'd be okay. He'd never lived a day without Joe by his side and wasn't sure what he'd do without him. He shook the thought and stepped inside the house. "Looks pretty solid. Clean, too. The crazy woman keeps a good house. Wonder where she is?"

"Probably saw us comin' and run off into the woods… Naked."

"Better watch out, Levi, when you go out to relieve yourself, she might jump out of the bushes and do ya."

"You know, I've never been easy, but right now, I could be had."

Charles shook his head, took his gun out and headed upstairs. "You're somethin' else, old man." He stopped in front of every opened door. "Somebody's livin' here alright. All the beds are made up proper and everything." Each one looked inviting and he couldn't wait for his brothers to get to see their new house.

"Yep and it looks like, since you're the only one here right now, you get to pick which room is yours!"

Indeed he did, but he would be fair. "I'll take that middle sized room, Joe can have the big one and Carl the smaller one."

"You Armstrong boys amaze me. Always lookin' out for each other in the best way. Sometimes I wish I had some family left."

Leading the way back downstairs, Charles stopped at the bottom. "Levi, you're part of our family now and that nice kitchen in there belongs to you."

"The hell you say. I got me a real kitchen."

Charles couldn't help but smile. "You might have to share it with the crazy lady."

Chapter Forty Three

FINDING THE BOYS

The cattle were indeed easy to follow. In the three days he's been tracking the boys and their herd, O.C. was gaining on them fast. He trailed the outskirts of Great Bend, almost able to taste the good steak the cattle town probably had, but he was determined to carry on.

In the distance, some miles out of the town, he saw a wagon. It resembled a buffalo hunter's wagon except it had a long pole attached to the back. It looked familiar. Was that feathers on the pole?

He got closer and saw Sioux trinkets hanging from the rod. Then he couldn't believe his eyes. "I'll be damned, Boy." He patted the horse's neck. "It's old Earl Stockman." It was unbelievable he'd see someone he knew right out in the middle of nowhere.

"That old man sure gets around." As he approached the wagon he rode up beside the driver in silence, glanced over at him then heard his familiar voice.

"Hell, redneck, I thought you'd be bald by now!"

"I thought you would be, too, you old buzzard!" It was good to laugh with an old friend. O.C. dismounted at the same time Earl hopped off the wagon. "Good to see ya, Earl." He offered the older man a handshake. "What are you doin' up here?"

Earl took O.C.'s hand. "Ran out of things to do down in

Texas. Thought I'd come north and do a little trappin'."

"Any luck?"

"Not yet, but I 'spect it'll come when it's time. Looks like you ain't had no luck findin' those boys of yours, either."

"No, but I can tell you they're only about a day or so from here. I've been trailin' them for a few days now and the tracks are pretty fresh."

"Well, hell, O.C., that's good news, heard in Great Bend they bought an old man's ranch."

Maybe he should have stopped in town after all. "Then I guess the ranch is where I'm headed." He couldn't wait to get their either, but seeing Earl was good as well.

"Hey, what about Jack?"

"He decided to stay in St. Louis. Wanted to stick around and live the city life for a while. Said he'd head this way when he's ready."

"He'd better hurry. Ain't none of us gettin' any younger."

O.C. had to agree. It would be good to sleep in a real bed and get some rest. The ground was cold and hard against his old bones. "Guess you're right about that."

Earl glanced to the back of the wagon. "S'pose I'd better be gettin' on. Although, I have a hankerin' for a cup of Joe."

"A cup of coffee would do me some good, too." A look of concern quickly passed over Stockman's face, then he smiled and sat straighter on the wagon seat.

"What say we go over to that stand of trees, build a little fire and do some visitin'."

It seemed something was bothering the man, but it was none of O.C.'s business. "That sounds fine."

The smell of hot coffee floated across the air when O.C. took the cup from Earl. "Thanks." He sat on the ground, relaxed back against a tree and sipped the brown liquid.

Stockman stoked the fire then sat at the foot of a tree across from O.C. "So, Armstrong, you know Johnny One Horn raised quite a stink in Garden City?"

"No. He's with the boys, isn't he?"

"He might be with them now, but a while back he was bushwhacked by a couple of women while he was scoutin' for the boys."

O.C. couldn't believe anyone could sneak up on Horn, much less women. "What?"

"It's a long story. I'm sure when he sees ya, he'll tell ya about it all, but bottom line, they shot at him, his horse spooked, he fell off and it knocked him out. The women loaded him up and took him to Ulla Mae's saloon. Well it's a whore house, too."

"A whore kidnapped Johnny?" It was sad and funny at the same time. What had he missed in the last few years?

"Yeah, and she told him he owed her for saving his life. So she put him to work."

O.C. knew Johnny was a man that would pay a debt if he owed it. "In the saloon, I suspect."

"Yep, Pickles said he cleaned at first, and had quite a time with the ladies, but he took to playing cards real fast and was good at it, so she put him to work dealin' poker for the house."

After taking a few more sips of his coffee, O.C. slung the cold remains out of his cup and poured some more. "Card player, huh? Wonder where he learned that." That big Indian would never cease to amaze him. "Then what?"

"Everybody seemed to like him, but he made a couple of old boys mad by winnin' their money, and they set out to kill him, so they set a trap. I guess Johnny fell for the local school teacher and they were secretly seeing each other. Those no-goods ambushed them, took the woman and left Horn for dead."

"Johnny must have sure been thinkin' about somethin' else to get bushwhacked twice. It just don't sound like him."

"Well, it happened and those no-goods killed that schoolmarm. When Johnny came to, he tracked them to an old cabin. The men were gone, but he found her body, took it back to town and left her with Pickles. Guess he knew they'd try to blame it on him so he left town. Sheriff said Johnny done the town a favor when he went and found those guys and... well, you know the rest."

O.C. was all too aware of what kind of torture Johnny One Horn probably put the men through. "Sounds like they deserved what they got. I just hope he's back with the boys."

Earl stoked the fire with a small limb. "I've heard rumor

your boys are rich. People are talkin' about it throughout the plains. I hope they're careful. There's a lot of bad hombres in this country."

"They're smart. They'll be careful." He didn't like hearing folks were talking about the boys' money, but he supposed it was inevitable. However, he knew them well enough to be confident they'd watch their backs, no matter what.

He glanced up at Earl and a thought occurred to him. "Say, why don't you ride with me? Then you can see, along with me, how the boys are doin'."

Shaking his head, then looking around, Earl replied, "Naw, better not. Wish I could, though. I got a good bottle of whiskey that ain't got a drop out of it."

O.C followed Earl's gaze toward the wagon and noticed movement in the back. Remembering the past, and knowing the man, O.C. had his suspicions as to what was in there but wanted to make sure. He turned his attention back to Stockman. "What you got under that tarp there?" He watched the man shift, give him a sideways look then squint, as if sizing up the situation.

Earl relaxed his eyes and nodded. "I know I can trust you, Armstrong. I figure you already know anyway with what we went through back when. It's some Mexican gals. They were bein' mistreated and wanted to get out of their country. They were all bunged up; I couldn't just leave 'em."

"That's what I figured was under there. Damn, Earl, you get around more than anyone I know." He shook his head and remembered how the man rescued the women from Crow. "You have a soft spot for those Mexican women. They gotta be burnin' up under there, Earl. Let's get them out, let them relieve themselves and have some coffee or somethin' to eat."

O.C. approached the wagon alongside Earl and was surprised to see three pretty girls all probably in their late teenage years. "They're kind of young for ya, ain't they?"

"They ain't for me. I'm too old and dried up, but they'll make good wives for some young men someday."

The girls were giggling, and O.C. thought he smelled alcohol on them. "Looks like they might have found that whiskey you were talkin' about." He could tell they were glad to be free of the cumbersome cover. They all kissed and hugged

Earl, then started toward him. He smiled at their show of gratitude and accepted their affection.

"It's been a long time since I've been hugged by a pretty young girl, Earl. I think you did a real nice thing saving 'em. They seem to think so, too."

"Yeah, I 'spect so."

O.C. sat back down at foot of the tree and got a fresh cup of coffee. "The offer still stands."

"What offer's that?"

"Ride with me to meet the boys." He heard the girls in the distance laughing and carrying on. He nodded toward them. "They're welcome, too."

Earl paused for a moment, then a grin lifted the corners of his mouth. "Aw hell, why not? Nobody's waiting for any of us anywhere." He laughed and looked around. "What say we go ahead and camp here tonight then ride on in the mornin'. The ladies can cook us up somethin' and we can get some good rest."

"That, my friend, is a plan."

Later in the evening, O.C. took a swig of what was left of the whiskey. "Looks like this stuff did the girls in. They're sleepin' like babies." He handed the bottle back to Earl. "Their stories were sad."

"They've been through a lot. I'm just glad I could help 'em."

"You're a good man, Earl the pearl Stockman, I don't care what anyone says about ya'."

The last day and a half's ride seemed like it lasted a week and O.C. woke Earl and the girls way before sunrise. He wanted to get started. His heart thumped hard against his chest at the thought of possibly being reunited with his boys by sunrise.

He studied the skyline in ahead as the sun broke over the horizon. A fading cloud of smoke loomed in the distance. He swallowed hard knowing at one time it must have been a lot of smoke; more than just a campfire or a chimney.

Earl pointed to the dissipating plume. "Wonder what's burnin'? Looks like it could have been a damn big fire."

Feeling sick to his stomach, O.C. shifted in the saddle. "I don't know, but I hope it's not the ranch house Joe just bought."

"Me, too, O.C. That would be a hell of a note!"

"You and the girls wait here. I'll go on ahead and see if everything's alright. If I'm not back in an hour it will mean you can come on."

Earl pulled out his pocket watch. "All right, I'll keep an eye on the time."

Chapter Forty Four

When he approached the ranch house, O.C. noticed men sleeping on bedrolls around a camp fire in front of the house. Some were rousing in the early morning hours. One man stood and sized him up.

The man put his hand on the butt of his holstered pistol. "Who are you, mister?"

O.C. saw an older man come out of the house with a shotgun drawn down on him. He knew better than to try to dismount, so he held his hands up to show them he meant no harm. He met the man's gaze. "Name's O.C. Armstrong. Joe, Charles and Carl are my boys. I heard tell this might be their outfit." The men were all standing now and focused on him, but he didn't see any of his sons. "Are they here?"

Lowering the shotgun, the older man jumped off the porch and walked toward O.C., then stretched out his hand. "Name's Levi, Mr. Armstrong. Nice to meet ya." He pointed to the man with his hand on his pistol. "This here's Nate, he's the foreman."

O.C. got off his horse and accepted the men's handshakes. "Nice to meet y'all, too."

"You know your boys think you're dead."

"I figured as much. It's been a long time that I've been tryin' to get to 'em. So, are they here?" The glance between the two men disturbed him. Something was wrong. "What's goin' on?"

"Well, no, sir, they're not here." Levi glanced at Nate. "Tell him."

Nate stepped forward. "What I got to tell you ain't good."

Was he too late? Were his boys dead? His heart sank to the pit of his stomach, but he had to know. "I'm used to bad news."

"Carl's been exposed to the pox. So has Joe. They're camped on a sandbar down river 'til we know if they're going to get sick. There was a wagon down there. Everyone was dead, but Carl didn't see the bodies, only the wagon. He started gathering blankets. That's when me and Joe found him. They burned the wagon, everything on it and the bodies."

"That explains the smoke we saw this morning."

"Yes, sir, it started burning yesterday, probably only smoldering now."

"How come you ain't down there? And where's Charles?"

"I'm not there because I didn't get close. Joe didn't either, at first, but he refused to leave Carl alone. He said if he got sick, then he just got sick. Nothing I could do. I tried to talk him out of it."

"That sounds like Joe. Always lookin' out for Carl."

"Joe made me promise I wouldn't let Charles go near them. Said he'd have to take over if something happened to him and Carl."

"Where is he, then?"

Levi met O.C.'s gaze. "He's up river doin' some target practice. He's real good with a gun, but I think he just needed some alone time. You can see worry all over his face."

"How would I find him?" About that time he heard a gunshot, then another.

"Just follow that sound. You'll find him." Levi pointed at something in the distance. "They with you?"

O.C. looked up to see Earl and the girls coming around a stand of trees. "Yep."

"Hells bells, is that old Earl Stockman?"

Looking at Levi O.C. nodded. "You know him?"

"You're damn tootin' I do. That some Mexican girls he's rescued?"

O.C. smiled, it was apparent Levi really did know Earl. "Yep." He heard another pistol shot. "I'm gonna go find Charles. Will you take care of Earl and the ladies for me? Make sure none of the men try to have their way with them?"

"We've got a pretty good bunch of hands. I don't think you'll have to worry about that." Nate took his hand away from his pistol. "Charles is going to be happy to see you."

He took off toward the river at a good pace then caught a glimpse of Charles setting up some rocks to shoot at. As he got closer, he noticed the young man seemed to hardly care that he was riding up on him, but it didn't surprise O.C. when instead of pointing his pistol at the target, Charles turned it toward him.

"Who are you and what do you want?"

The deep voice of the man in front of him was nothing like he remembered his son sounding like. "I was looking for a boy named Charles, but looks like I found a grown man that's pretty good with a gun." Some of the darkness went out of Charles' eyes and O.C. got off his horse then stood about twenty feet away, unsure of what to do next.

He saw tears roll down his son's cheeks and fought the urge to jump when Charles fired a shot. O.C. stood dead still when the bullet hit the ground right between his legs.

"You left us! Four years, Pa, four years we waited. Ma died of a broken heart. We buried her in the pouring rain then had to leave our home! All because you didn't care enough to come back! No letters, nothin'! Now you just show up! Now that we got us a new home, no thanks to you. Why?"

The gun was still pointed at O.C. and he didn't move. Charles' hand trembled when he wiped tears from his face. He couldn't blame the boy for being mad. Hell he'd be angry, too. "I'm sorry, son. I never meant to leave y'all like that. It's a long story. If you'll put the gun down, I'll explain." He was relieved when Charles lowered the pistol. The young man fell to his knees and O.C. ran to him, took him in his arms and held him. It felt good to embrace one of his boys. "I'm sorry. I'm so sorry."

Charles straightened, moved out of O.C.'s hold then holstered his pistol. He sat on a tall rock and O.C. met his questioning gaze. "After I left, I got a job on a cattle drive. At least I thought it was a cattle drive. Turned out they were rustlers and wanted by the law. No matter what I said, the Marshall wouldn't believe I was innocent. Stuck me in a hellhole of a prison in the Arizona Territory. That's where I spent those four years." He sat next to Charles. "God help me, son, if I could have come home, I would have."

Tears welled in Charles' eyes and spilled onto his cheeks again. "Dammit, Pa! I'm sorry I was so mad at you, I didn't know."

He hugged his son again. "It's over. I'm here now, we're a family again and everything's going to be okay." He pushed the young man back and looked him up and down. "God, you're all grown up."

"I missed you somethin' awful, Pa." Charles pulled a small flask out of his pocket and handed it to O.C.

"Have you taken to drinkin'?"

"No, sir, just thought this would be a good occasion to have a little nip."

Charles' smile warmed his heart. "Okay, I guess it's cause for a little celebrating." He took a swig then handed the container to Charles and watched him take a drink. "We'd sit and talk, but I want to go see your brothers, too."

"We can't get close or we might get the pox."

"That's what Nate and Levi told me, but I've gone through hell and high water to get here, so I'm gonna see 'em. Even if I have to keep my distance." He glanced around and noticed the trees were moving pretty good in the breeze.

"Then I'm goin' with ya." Charles stood, went to his horse then mounted.

"We'll stay upwind." He got on Boy and took the reins. "I think we'll be safe enough as long as this draft keeps up."

O.C. rode beside Charles. "How far is it?"

"Only a few minutes. Hey, Pa, where'd you get the scars on your arms and face?"

He glanced down at the marks on his body. "Got caught in the middle of a prairie fire. Did all I could to keep myself safe, but it wasn't enough. I would've died but some Indian's took me into their camp and saved my life."

"Indians?" Charles nodded. "They've been watching us. I think Horse talks to them some."

"It'll be good to see Horse."

"Don't know how much of him you'll see, he's stays awful busy teachin' Kicking Wind how to take care of herself."

O.C. remembered Running Bear's words. "You know those Indians I said saved my life?"

"Yes, sir."

"They are the girl's tribe. I feel like I know her already. The chief, Running Bear, said Little Boy Horse was taking good care of her. That's why they let y'all cross the land with no problems."

"Why haven't they tried to get her back?"

"They're on a hunt right now, so the hunting party is who found me all burned up. The tribe's further north. They're not havin' much success on the hunt, so Running Bear exchanged my scalp for some cattle, and wants Kicking Wind back when I deliver them so they can go home."

"Oh, pa, I don't know if Horse will let her go. He's taken a pretty good shine to her. Like she was his own little girl."

O.C. saw the smoke of a campfire and knew they were close to their destination. "She kind of is, Charles. Most of those people aren't like the white man. Oh, they have tribal differences, but they also seem to hold together. They have Great Spirits that run as one. Kind of like our Lord. I'm glad y'all have Indian blood running through your veins."

"Me, too." Charles stopped his horse and pointed. "There they are."

He couldn't believe they were barely more than one-hundred foot away and he couldn't touch them. If something happened to Joe and Carl, he still had Charles so he couldn't take the chance of getting sick by going closer.

O.C.'s heart soared with pride at how strong Joe looked when he threw the fishing line in the river. He'd missed out on so much of their lives and it hurt to his very core.

Charles sat forward in his saddle. "Joe, look who found us!"

A tall man with a face full of whiskers glanced up and looked in O.C.'s direction. "Joe?" His voice was a whisper in the wind, his oldest was truly a grown man.

"Who?"

"It's Pa!"

After dropping the fishing pole, Joe started to run toward them then stopped in his tracks. O.C. knew the young man remembered the situation he was in, but was happy Joe wanted to greet him close up. Joe's voice was lower and more mature than he remembered.

"You picked a hell of a time to show up, Pa."

"Seems that way, son." O.C. saw Carl come around the brush by the river. He was almost as tall as Joe, but that boyish face was still the same.

"Pa! I can't believe my eyes, is that really you?"

"It's me for sure, Carl!"

"Where you been all these years? We thought you were dead, why haven't we heard from you!"

The frustration was evident in his youngest son's voice. He wanted, more than anything, to gather all three of his boys in his arms and share the happenings of the last few years with them, but not this way. Not talking from a distance, but up close, and now was not the time. "It's a long story, Carl, but we'll get all caught up when this mess is over and I can be close to you."

Charles spoke from beside O.C. "I hope that happens. I've learned it ain't never going to be over. Seems to get better, then somebody else dies. I just hope it ain't Carl or Joe this time."

O.C. reached out and touched his middle son's shoulder. "All we can do is talk to the Good Lord about it. It's in His hands now." He dropped his hand and watched Joe back away. "You sure have grown into a big man, Joe. Hell I wouldn't have known you, if I'd seen you somewhere else, with that beard and all."

"It's been a hard row to hoe, but we're all grown now. Livin' like we have has forced it on us." Joe swiped at his eyes. "I missed the hell out of ya, Pa."

"I missed you, too, Joe. I missed all of ya. Sure would like to hug you boys, or at least shake your hands. We've waited this long, it'll wait a few days longer."

Carl walked up beside Joe. "How'd ya find us?"

"I've been tryin' to catch up with y'all for a long time. I had help from some good people. Y'all have made quite an impression on a lot of folks, even the plains Indians. Hell, most of them even know y'all's names, even though you don't know them."

O.C. took his sweat stained hat off and slapped his leg with it, knocking some of the dust from the brim. "Damn good to see y'all!" He watched all the happiness drain from Carl's face, and noted the crack in the boy's saddened voice.

"We might die, Pa, me and Joe. It's my fault. I handled some danged old blankets, but honest, I didn't know anything like that could kill ya!"

"Let's don't be thinkin' anyone's gonna die. Hell, I just got here; we got lots of good years ahead of us yet." O.C. gauged the wind and made a decision. "Tell ya what, I'm gonna make camp right here. If the wind keeps blowin' I'll be alright. If it stops, I'll go back to the ranch. I'm gonna ride this out with y'all."

"I'm gonna stay, too, Pa."

He glanced at Charles. "You're a grown man, you can do what you want, but I'd rather you go back to the ranch and be with your hands. The men up there need someone to run the place. Hell, you boys own it and as far as I can see, there's no use you stayin' here. You can come down every day and spend time."

Over the next few days, O.C. began to feel close to his boys again. He realized that not being able to get near Carl and Joe, didn't sever the bond between them, but was pleased he and Charles could share coffee by the fire every morning when the young man came to the camp.

On the third day, he noticed Carl wasn't as talkative as he'd been in the prior days. He wanted to think it was because the boy had hardly stopped talking in the days past, but something gnawed at his insides, something that just wasn't right. That night when he lay down, he prayed to God it wasn't the pox.

The sun peeked through the trees and woke O.C. up. He gathered some wood and started the fire. It was unusual for the boys not to be awake by now. He cupped his mouth with his hands. "You boys up yet?" Joe stepped out of the brush but O.C.'s smile faded quickly when he saw the look of dread on Joe's face.

"Carl's got a fever, Pa. He's been shakin' since way before dawn. I got him covered up real good, but it don't seem to keep him warm. He just keeps shiverin'."

He forced himself to swallow the lump that formed in his throat. Not now, not when they'd just been reunited. God, please don't let it be small pox. O.C. saw Charles coming over the small ridge toward camp.

"Stop right there, Charles."

"What's wrong?"

"Carl's got a little fever. I want you to go into Great Bend and see if you can find a doctor. Get him here as fast as you can." He watched Charles rein his horse around then head back toward the ranch.

No matter what the outcome, O.C. decided he needed to be with Joe and Carl. Hell, this might be the last few hours his youngest son had on earth.

****

Nate was saddling his horse when Charles rode up. "You're in charge, Nate."

"What's happening?"

"Carl's got fever. I'm goin' to town to find a doctor."

"Dammit! I was afraid of that. You go quick, but don't run your horse too hard, he'll never make it back."

"I'll try to be back by mornin'."

Nate nodded. "Watch your back, my friend, and good luck."

Charles couldn't believe he had to make this ride. He didn't want his brothers to meet their Maker. Not yet, they were too young. What would he do without them?

He pushed his horse as hard as he dared and when he rode into Great Bend, the mare was all but totally spent. He'd have to get a fresh ride from the livery, but now it was more important to find the doc.

The sun was going behind the horizon when Charles got to the doctor's office. He prayed that by the time they got back to the ranch, it wouldn't be too late. He jumped off his horse, tethered him to the rail, took the steps and banged on the door. "Doctor! I need a doctor!"

His knuckles ached from the pounding, but he heard nothing. Wasn't anyone here? A voice from across the street drew his attention.

"Hey, fella, the doc is at the saloon, but I doubt you'll find him sober."

Just his luck! He'd passed the saloon on the way in, so he

knew right where to go. “Thanks, mister.”

Charles ran down the street then burst through the swinging doors. Smoke stung his eyes and the stench of whiskey invaded his nostrils as he glanced around the room. He tried to talk above the buzz of the crowd. “Where’s the doctor?”

No one answered, but a saloon girl looked upstairs and gestured with her head that the man was up there. He took the steps two at a time and once at the top started to open every door, one by one, startling the people behind them. Every cowboy in the place probably wanted to blow his head off, and all the girls screamed fowl names at him. Finally, he found the right room. Then he heard pistols cocking from below.

He glanced over the rail and every man in the saloon had a gun trained on him. Dammit he had to think fast before someone shot him. “Hold it! I’m sorry, I don’t want no trouble, but I need the doctor. I got a brother with the fever, may be smallpox, we’re not sure. I’ve been ridin’ for hours to find someone to help him.”

It surprised him when the saloon got deathly quiet. Then the patrons began to holster their guns and started to head for the door. Did they think he brought the fever into town? He didn’t care what they thought, he needed the doc.

Turning he saw a half dressed woman on the bed holding a sheet to her chest. “Sorry ma’am.” A man buttoning his shirt stood in the room and Charles stepped toward him.

“Stay right where you are.” He picked a gun up from the bedside table. “I’m Doc Reed, son, but I can’t help you.”

What? Was this man for real? “You ain’t gonna help? But you’re a doctor.”

“I’m not going to take the chance of catching the pox. Just by coming here, you might have exposed the whole town.”

“Please, my brother needs medicine.”

“I feel for you, but you’re crazy as hell to think anybody in their right mind would go asking to get the pox. I’m sorry.” He pointed the pistol at Charles. “Now you need to get on out of town.”

“But…” The sound of boot heels on the floor below echoed through the silence of the large room, then a voice reverberated through the air and Charles’ gaze followed the sound.

“Son, I’m Sheriff Willard Young. He’s right; you should get

out of town. I know you're hurting for your brother, but you've got to understand, the good people of the town would like to help you, but they're scared to death of getting that devil's disease." He put his hand on the butt of his gun. "Now, you need to come on down."

Tears welled in his eyes when he glanced back at the doctor. How could he be so cold hearted? "Please?" The man's eyes softened and hope leapt into his heart. Was the doctor going to change his mind?

"I can't go, but keep him warm and make sure he gets plenty of water. Unfortunately, there's no cure or medicine for the pox, so that's all you can do. That, and pray."

The tears spilled onto his cheeks. "To hell with ya all!" He turned and walked down the stairs and knew the doctor followed a ways behind.

The sheriff stepped away from him. "I'm sorry, son."

Though the man's words sounded sincere, he couldn't help but hold contempt in his heart. As he walked toward the door, he heard the men talking.

"God help us Willard, I wish there was something I could do, but we can't take the chance of having to bury the whole damn town."

"I know, Doc, I know."

In his mind Charles knew they were right, but his heart said something different. He felt broken and helpless as he made the horse trade at the livery then rode out of town and into the dark.

CHAPTER FORTY FIVE

Cool, wet rags in hand, O.C. walked from the river to where Joe sat beside Carl's hot, shaking body. He hated seeing Carl sick like this, but at least they got to visit some before the boy drifted into this fitful sleep.

He handed all but one rag to Joe, and the young man laid them on a big rock. Wiping Carl's brow, he listened to his fevered mumbling.

"Joe, snowin'… never snows in swamp… cold, so cold."

"Pa, he's been talkin' about the swamp all night. He's out of his head with fever."

"I know. Maybe he thinks he's back there."

Joe glanced into the distance. "Wonder when Charles is gonna get here with the doctor."

O.C. continued to wipe Carl down. "Sun's comin' up. 'Spect he'll be here soon."

"I hope so." Joe wiped a tear from his cheek.

"Me, too. Dammit I wish I could have been here for you boys." He continued to bath Carl, but met his oldest son's gaze. "Joe, I spent four years in a hellhole prison in Arizona for somethin' I didn't do. That's why I couldn't come home. Your ma, you and your brothers were on my mind constantly. I wondered what y'all thought happened to me. Chained up, plantin' cactus, eatin' shit food, it was terrible" A odd look crossed Joe's face. "What is it, son?"

"Pa, I had a dream one time and I just remembered."

"What was it?"

"I heard chains rattlin', it stunk in there, Pa, stunk real bad. People were moanin' like they were in pain. There was a real long hallway."

O.C. recognized what Joe was talking about. "Go on."

"I saw someone at the end of the hallway. Well, I didn't really see who it was, but I knew it was you, Pa. You said, 'Wait for me Joe.' Then, an Indian chief made me follow him, then he was gone and a beautiful piece of land lay before me."

O.C. couldn't believe what Joe was telling him. Had the Great Spirit sent the boy a vision? "You're describing the prison I was in, Joe. Exactly."

The young man nodded. "I know that now, and I just now realized the land...it was this place, Pa. We're supposed to be here. I know it." He glanced down at Carl. "I'm just sorry about what this place has already brought."

"The Maker knows what He's doin', son." Joe's story amazed O.C. and he followed his son's gaze. Realization hit him. The rash of pus-filled blisters began to show on Carl's skin, and O.C. stood. "We need to stop touchin' him now, Joe. We've done all we can do at this point. He'll have to fight on his own 'til the doctor gets here." He looked at his oldest boy. "It don't look good."

As the hours went on, O.C. knew he was watching his youngest son die. There's been no sign of Charles and the doctor so his concern grew for his middle son as well. O.C.'s gut told him something had happened, but there was nothing he could do about it. He felt helpless all the way around. Joe's voice drew his attention.

"Pa, he's startin' to stir."

It was almost sundown, but O.C. could still see Carl's movement under the heavy cover. The tortured look on the young man's face seemed somewhat relieved. Though he didn't open his eyes, O.C. was glad to hear Carl's voice.

"Is... it... time? Oh... so... pretty."

Joe glanced at his father. "What's he talkin' about?"

"I don't' know. Maybe he's seein' heaven." Carl's breathing was short and sporadic. O.C. had seen death before but this was different. It was almost like Carl welcomed it.

"Yes... Sir... I'd... like... that..."

O.C's heart thumped hard against his chest. Was his boy talking to the Maker? Tears flowed down his cheeks, and found their destination on the hard ground, as the smile lifted the corners of Carl's mouth.

"Ma,... that... you?" Carl opened his eyes and looked toward the sky, then pulled his arm from under the cover and reached upward. "Yes... ma'am... I'm... ready..."

Putting his hand on Joe's shoulder, O.C. watched Carl slowly drop his arm, close his eyes and take his last breath. He and his oldest son were witness that the Lord, and Martha, had come to take their boy home.

It seemed like morning would never come, but finally the sun peeked over the eastern horizon and O.C. started to gather wood. "Never thought I'd have to burn the body of my own flesh."

Joe worked beside him. "Pa? Do you think Ma was really here?"

"I want to believe that."

"Me, too."

O.C. threw a stack of limbs into a pile. "Carl believed it for sure."

"Yes, sir. He loved life and hated death. Doesn't seem right that he'd be taken from this earth first, but I don't think he was cut out for this country."

"Maybe not." A horse appeared in the distance and O.C. recognized Nate.

"Mr. Armstrong, the doc isn't coming."

He stopped picking up branches and stood to his full height. "I figured. What happened?"

"Afraid of spreading the pox."

"Well, it's too late anyway. Carl died last night."

Nate pulled off his hat and rested it on his leg. "I'm sorry to hear it."

The hired hand was sincere and O.C.'s like for the man grew. "Thank ya, Nate."

Joe walked up beside his father. "Where's Charles?"

"That's what I came to let y'all know. He got thrown from

his horse on the way back from town. Broke his arm and got bruised up some, but he's okay. Levi's got a splint on his arm and has him in bed resting." Nate put his hat back on. "I think Charles likes the attention those ladies with Earl are giving him. They're doting on him something awful."

O.C's spirit lifted somewhat at the news. At least he knew Charles was safe at the ranch. "I'm just glad he's home."

"Y'all need anything?"

"After we burn Carl's body, we'll have to stay here a few more days. If you could bring us some more food and a fresh supply of blankets, I think we'll be fine."

"I'm real sorry that has to be done, but it's the right thing." Nate turned his horse toward the house. "I'll be back with what you need."

As Nate rode away, Joe began to pick sticks up again. "He's a good man, Pa."

"I know that."

"Been a real help to us."

"I know that, too."

"Earl's got ladies with him?"

"Three of 'em. Mexican woman he rescued." O.C. figured Joe would have more questions about the girls, but apparently his son knew that for now, taking care of Carl was the most pressing.

Silence filled the air over the next couple of hours while he worked beside Joe gathering the wood. He was proud of the man his oldest had grown into and hoped they'd live through the next few days.

The stack of limbs, branches and dried leaves was high enough to get the job done. He took a deep breath and looked at Carl's lifeless body wrapped in blankets. "You ready, Joe."

"Yes, sir."

He helped Joe hoist the body onto the burn pile. They placed the rags, and all other items that had come into contact with them or Carl, on as well. O.C. struck a match and held it to the kindling. Joe broke down, and turned his back on the blaze as it grew.

O.C. wanted to reach out to the young man, but didn't. He was dealing with his own grief and needed to get through it before he could help anyone else.

After he gathered his composure, O.C. stepped away from the heat of the flames. “Let’s go, Joe. I ain’t gonna stand here and watch this. I don’t think you want to, either. We need to see if Nate brought the supplies we need, then make a new camp.”

“Yes, sir.”

It was good to see the stack of fresh blankets, clothing, a bar of lie soap and a potato sack full of food. Seeing the supplies spurred a thought. “Let’s throw these old clothes on the fire, too, Joe. We’ll bathe in the river, put on the clean ones, then move camp.”

Joe started to take off his shirt. “A good bath sounds fine. Maybe it’ll wash some of this death and sadness away.”

Once they finished they moved to shore, then up river and made camp, O.C. took some food out of the bag and started a small campfire. His glanced down river to the spot on the sand bar where smoke lightly spiraled into the air. The deed was about done, and Carl’s body was gone now. Though his heart would ache for a long while, it was time to focus on Joe and him staying well. A meal under their belt would help.

“You ready for somethin’ to eat, Joe?”

“Yep, seems we haven’t eaten in days.”

O.C. found some biscuits wrapped in a cloth. “Levi sent us some good food.”

“He’s ain't a bad cook. We’re lucky to have him.”

“You boys done good for yourselves. I’m proud.”

“Thanks. Too bad Carl won’t be here to enjoy our new life, but maybe it was meant to be. Sometimes he’d just stare at the moon and listen for the whippoorwill’s song. When he didn’t hear ‘em, it seemed to make him lonely. He always wanted to go back to the swamp.”

“Sometimes I do, too.” He looked Joe in the eye. “I feel bad about bein’ gone. In all that time, all I thought about was getting back to you boys and your ma.”

CHAPTER FORTY SIX

It was close to the end of being two weeks since Carl passed, and O.C.'s heart was still heavy. Though he'd enjoyed the time he and Joe had spent building a small lean-to for added protection, and the many hours they'd caught up on life, he still wished he'd gotten to spend more time with Carl. That was something he'd have to do in heaven.

He figured it would be okay for him and Joe to go back to the ranch in the morning, but tonight it looked like a storm was brewing. That was good, rain would help wash away the disease. He only hoped there'd be a lot of it.

Lightning flashed then thunder cracked and it started to sprinkle small drops. "Looks like we'd better get inside."

Joe nodded. "I'll gather up stuff."

"Hope it comes a downpour. We might get wet, but the rain will do a lot to wash away the pox, if there's anything left."

The sun went down and the rain steadily got harder. Joe fell asleep and O.C. lay there listening to the storm. He thanked the Lord for the blessing that neither he nor Joe had any signs of being sick.

Every day, Nate had come to check on them and bring fresh supplies. O.C. appreciated the men at the ranch and all they'd done for his family. He was pleased they'd been there when he wasn't.

Sunrise came before O.C. ever realized he was asleep. The makeshift shelter had held up under the wind, without getting them soaked. Birds chirping and the early morning sounds of the woodland by the river reminded him of the swamp. It was going to be a good day.

He sat up at the sound of a horse snorting, then a large figure shadowed the front of the lean-to. Joe rustled beside him and reached for his gun. O.C. placed a hand on him. "Wait."

"O.C. Armstrong? I thought you were dead."

He'd recognize that voice anywhere. Standing over him was Johnny One Horn. He jumped up and hugged the big man. Joe wasn't far behind. "It's good to see you, friend."

"Horn! How long you been here?" Joe threw his arms around the Indian. "We didn't know what happened to you."

Johnny hugged Joe. "Sometime I will tell you." He pushed the young man away and grabbed at the whiskers on his face. "What is this? I do not recognize you." He got out his knife then held it out toward Joe. "Maybe you should make good use of this blade."

Joe reached for the Arkansas Toothpick. "Really Horn? You're gonna let me shave with this?"

"Yes, but be careful, I do not want you to get blood on it."

O.C. glanced at his son and smiled. It was good to hear Joe laugh for a change. "I'd like to see you without that thing, too. Go grab that soap and get to it."

"Yes, sir!"

He watched Joe run to the river then noticed Horn had brought Boy, and a horse for Joe. He walked over to the three equine. "This is sure a pretty paint." As soon as he reached to pet the horse's neck, the thing bit his arm. He was surprised it didn't break the skin right through his shirt.

Rubbing his arm, O.C. frowned. "Damn mean, though." He looked at Johnny who had a smile on his face. He'd missed his friend. "How'd you ever find us Horn?"

"I am a good tracker. You know that, O.C. Armstrong."

"That I do. I hear you've had a time of it." O.C. sat on the ground and Johnny did the same.

Nodding, the Indian said, "Yes, I went to find land for the boys. I came up on a lake and heard some women laughing. I stopped and looked through the bush." He looked at O.C. "Fat, they were very fat–"

O.C. began to laugh. "Yes, I hear they bushwhacked you kidnapped you then put you to work." The surprised look on Johnny One Horn's face made him laugh even harder.

"How did you hear this?"

"From Earl Stockman."

Horn thought for a scant moment. "I know this Earl Stockman. I traded him one of my Toothpicks for whiskey. He is a tough old man. I like him." He glanced at O.C. "Did he tell you I killed some men? A posse is probably looking for me now. I will be hanged if they find me."

"I don't think they're lookin' for you. Earl told me the Sheriff said those shit heads had it coming for killing that school teacher. You ain't gonna hang, my friend."

"That is good to know, but I will keep watching." Johnny pointed to the ridge. "I have been watching down on you for many days. It makes me sad what has happened. I will miss my friend Carl. Along with his mother, I am sure he's with the Great Spirit now. I hear his voice in the wind." Horn looked at O.C. "I do not do medicine anymore, but anything I might have put together would not have helped him."

Nodding, O.C. replied, "I know." The thought of Martha and Carl both being gone was something that would hurt his heart for a long time, but he had to live for the present. He still had two boys living. He'd been gone a long time, but he was here now and would make the best of it. "Why didn't you go on to the house?"

"There are many men that work for the boys now. I didn't want to scare them. Besides, I was not the only one looking down on you."

"What do you mean?" O.C. glanced around but didn't see anything.

"There were three Sioux. I did not know what they were up to. They are gone now. I don't think they mean anyone harm."

O.C. stood, he thought enough time had passed that he and Joe were out of the woods. They needed to join the rest of the friends and family at the dwelling.

He stuck his hand out to shake Johnny's hand. "My friend, I'd like to thank you for watchin' after my boys over the years. You and Little Boy Horse have done a good job."

Johnny accepted the shake. "You are welcome. Make no mistake, though, Joe and Charles have turned into men. They are both good with their guns and are not afraid to use them."

Joe approached rubbing his clean chin. "It sure feels good havin' that thing off there, I tell you."

What Horn said was true, Joe was a man now, but without the hair on his face, he looked more like O.C.'s little boy. "What say we head to the house, men?"

"Sounds good to me, Pa."

Johnny handed O.C. and Joe each a cigar. To O.C. it appeared to be a pretty expensive one. "Where the hell did you get these?"

"At the fat women's city. I won many dollars playing poker. I'm very good at it."

O.C. nodded, "Earl told me that, too. Maybe you can teach Horse" He turned and gathered the belongings he wanted to take with him.

Horn mounted. "Where is Little Boy Horse? Does he still have Kicking Wind?"

Johnny probably knew the answer to the questions already, but O.C. would respond anyway. "Yes, he does and I understand you can't pry them apart. When fall arrives, he needs to take her back to her people."

"This will make him sad. The leaves will start to change in only a few of weeks." Johnny glanced at the trees. "We have been blood brothers for many years. I will go with him on that journey. I have been cooped up in the city and am ready to live under the moon and the stars again."

"I don't blame you for that. I'll make the trip with you. I have a debt to pay." O.C. reined his horse toward the house. "I was locked up in a faraway place for four years. I don't like the walls much more than you."

"It is easy to get locked up in a white man's prison." Horn rode up beside him.

"It damn sure is, my friend, it damn sure is!"

Joe mounted the mare Johnny brought for him. "Yeah, but y'all are here now, that's all that matters, so let's go home." He heeled his mount into a run. "I kinda like sleepin' in a real bed!"

CHAPTER FORTY SEVEN

It had been over a month since Carl's death. Joe still couldn't believe he was gone, however with O.C. back, it seemed easier. Life was less demanding now that they were settled and were beginning to get into a daily routine.

The crazy woman came back now and then. Levi would put food out for her every day, sometimes they'd see her get it, but most times she snuck in without anyone knowing. However, when Joe heard her laughter, he knew she had taken the morsels. He didn't know where she was staying now that they were in the house, but where ever it was, apparently she made it work.

He heard footsteps behind him and turned to see Charles. "When are you going to stop milking that broken arm, brother, and get back to work?" Charles was not lazy and he knew the young man wasn't using his accident as an excuse for disinterest in the new ranch. Something else was bothering him. Joe thought he knew what it was, but Charles would bring it up if he wanted to talk about it.

Charles gave Joe a half smile. "I guess when the ladies stop helping me get dressed and stuff. It's kinda hard to do with one arm." He took his arm out of the sling and moved it around. "It's a lot better though. I'd say in a day or two, I'll be okay."

"You're just lucky it wasn't your neck." Joe went back to forking hay into Shadrack's stall.

The younger brother sat on the back of the wagon. "Hey, Joe, can I tell you somethin'?"

"You know you can."

"I think I'm losin' my mind."

Joe put the pitch fork down and sat beside his brother. "How come?"

"All I can think about is Carl. Y'all havin' to burn him and all. It goes over and over in my mind. I can't sleep or nothin'"

"I've heard you up and about in the night."

"Yeah, I just walk down to the river and sit for hours."

A thought came to Joe. "You think you can ride?"

"I think so."

Joe hopped off the back of the wagon and started forking hay again. "Let me get my chores done and I'll come get ya. We'll go down to where Carl died."

"I don't know if I can handle seeing his ashes all over the place."

"The ashes are gone. The rain over the last few days washed them away."

Charles nodded and smiled. "I knew you'd have the answer, Joe. You always do. Hey, you think we can put him up a marker. Kinda like we did Ma?"

A chuckle escaped Joe and he saw Charles' smile broaden. "Tell you what. I'm going to make that your job. You're about healed up and you have to have somethin' to do besides let the ladies dress ya'." He winked at his little brother and watched his face turn crimson before he turned and left the barn.

The sun was sinking in the west when Joe approached Charles. It had been two weeks since his brother had set Carl's marker. "Looking pretty good, Charles. How many markers are you going to put up?" Joe counted five with the words 'unknown' carved into them.

Charles sat in front of Carl's tombstone. "I think this is enough. I wanted to pay respect to those poor folks in the wagon. Wonder if they have family somewhere wantin' to know what happened to 'em?"

Joe sat beside Charles and gave him a hug. "That's somethin' we'll never know, brother." He straightened and reached into a bag he'd brought with him. "Here."

He handed Charles a bottle of whiskey. "I know you seldom drink, but it's time you pulled yourself together and get back to life. Me and Pa need your help running the place."

After he opened the bottle and took a swig, Joe handed it to Charles. "Drink." He watched Charles take first a small sip, then a big swallow of the brown liquid.

Charles coughed then caught his breath. "That's nasty!"

Joe laughed and patted his brother on the back. "It gets better the more you drink." He pulled a cigar out, lit it then took a long draw before he handed to his brother. "What's gone is gone. No matter how much you sit down here, Carl ain't coming back."

The younger man put the whiskey bottle on the ground, picked up a stick and began to make meaningless marks in the dirt. "Joe, have you ever thought we should have listened to Johnny and Little Boy Horse when they said gold is cursed?"

"Sometimes."

"I mean look at what's happened. Even Carl kept saying something was wrong with the things we are…or were doin'." He threw the stick into the river. "It bugs the hell out of me, that's all. Worryin' about being cursed and such."

"Look at me, Charles." Joe turned his full attention on his brother. "We ain't been cursed. It's the times, not the gold. I believe if we weren't meant to have the gold, it would never have been found." He gestured toward the ranch house. "Look, Pa's back, we have a new home that's better than the one in the swamp and we are raising cattle. Even though bad things have happened, it ain't a spell the gold has put on us, it's life. That's all."

"Yeah, I guess you're right." Charles turned his gaze back to the river. "Nate and Pete said the night Carl died they saw a strange light moving slowly down the river."

"Maybe the Wisp came to make sure his soul was carried home."

"Maybe. You know, until Carl died, I never heard a Whippoorwill in this part of the country. Now I hear them every night. They were the little guy's favorite bird, you know. It just all seems strange."

"I ain't heard no Whippoorwill, Charles."

"Well I have, but like I said, only since he died. Then the Wisp showin' up to take him to heav–"

Joe stopped his brother in mid-sentence. "I think Ma got here first."

"What do you mean?"

Joe picked up the bottle and took a swig. "Did I ever tell ya what Carl's last words were?"

Charles shook his head. "No."

Swallowing the lump in his throat at the memory, Joe fought back a tear and continued. "He said it was pretty."

"What was pretty?"

"I don't know. Heaven I guess. Then he said… 'Ma, that you?' Joe cleared his throat. He never thought it would be this hard to recall Carl's last moments, out loud. "Just before he took his last breath he very clearly said, 'yes ma'am, I'm ready'.

Tears streamed down Charles' face. "Ma's here, ain't she."

"I'd like to think that."

"I know now what I need to do."

It was good to see a genuine smile on his younger brother's face. Maybe this talk was just what Charles needed. Hell, he even felt better. "What's that?"

"I know her body's back in the swamp, but I'm gonna make a headstone for Ma and put it next to Carl's. They're together in heaven and they're gonna be together here, too."

Joe stood then mounted his horse. "That will make Pa proud. I think it's a good plan." Just as he reined his mount toward the house, for the first time since they'd been settled, he heard in the distance the lone call of a Whippoorwill. He smiled down at Charles when he heard him say.

"Howdy, Carl."

****

Mid Fall 1853

O.C. watched how good Joe and Charles were as they helped him gather the small herd of twenty head of cattle. He was damn sure proud of the way they'd both turned into men.

"You sure you don't want us to go with you, Pa?"

It wasn't much to his liking to leave them again, but it had to be done. "No, Joe, y'all need to stay here and take care of things. Like I said, I made a promise to Running Bear I'd repay him for savin' my life. These cattle will free me from most of that debt, and Johnny returning Kicking Wind will make good on the rest. As for the cows, I'm sure Horse and Horn can help me keep them inline if needed."

"We just hate to see you leave again, Pa." Charles rode up beside him .

They approached the house and O.C. saw his two Indian friends and the girl ready and waiting to leave. "Don't worry, son, I'll be back much sooner this time." He dismounted and checked his belongings to make sure he had everything he needed.

Charles jumped off his horse to the ground. "But what if something happens? What if..."

Joe joined his father and brother next to O.C.'s horse. "Stop it, Charles. Pa's gonna be fine. Hell, look how far we came with Horse and Horn lookin' after us. There ain't no better than them for watch doggin'."

O.C. placed his foot in the stirrup and hoisted himself onto the saddle. "That's right. Besides, you've got more than me to worry about." He pointed at the beautiful woman standing behind them. "Those ladies have their eyes on y'all as well as some of the other men on the ranch." He smiled and heeled his mount. "And life goes on."

"Feels like he just got here, now he's gone again. Why don't Pa just forget about that debt, Joe. "

Joe led his horse toward the barn. "'Cause he's a man of his word. That oughta be good enough reason."

"You're right, but aren't you the least bit worried about him."

"Nope, I've got other things to think about."

"Is everything okay with the ranch?"

"Yep. Hey, can you keep a secret?"

Charles followed Joe into the barn. "You done somethin' wrong?"

"No, but I am gonna meet pretty Miss Cindy down by the persimmon trees tonight."

The corners of Charles' mouth lifted in a grin. "I admit she sure *is* pretty. Maybe it's because she's half Mexican and half

Indian." Charles unsaddled his horse. "Joe?"

Joe heard concern in his little brother's voice. "Huh?"

"You know how Earl is about those girls. He might skin you if he finds out."

"No matter, I'm goin' to go anyway. We're gonna pick some persimmons and she's gonna make some cookies for us." Joe glanced at Charles and saw his toothy grin. "It sure is good to see you smile."

The cows grazed on the hillside while O.C. stoked the small campfire. He heard footsteps behind him but didn't become alarmed. He knew that if Horse didn't stir at the sound, it was probably Johnny coming back from his scout.

Horn sat down on a big rock and accepted a piece of jerky from Kicking Wind. "Good place to camp." He took a bite of the meat. "Many Sioux are to the north. I am not sure Running Bear is with them, but believe your friend knows we are here. I'm sure he will let his presence be known soon."

All they could do now was wait. It had only been a couple of hours, and O.C wasn't surprised when Little Boy Horse put down his cup. His voice was so quiet O.C. could barely hear Horse's words.

Little Boy Horse stood. "They are here."

O.C. noticed Wind put her arms around Horse as if she wanted his protection. Slowly, out of the darkness walked three warriors. Running Bear followed, but didn't make eye contact with O.C. Instead, the man gave the chest sign to Horse, who quickly returned it, then waited.

Running Bear broke the silence. "It is finally good to see and talk to you, friend. You are a good warrior. We have watched you cross the plains. You knew this."

"I did."

The chief pointed to Kicking Wind. "How is she doing? She hugs tightly to you."

Horse put a protective arm around the girl's shoulder. "She is dealing with the bad things that happened. I have helped her with this."

Nodding, Running Bear said, "What are your plans?"

O.C. knew Boy Horse would push his limits to get to keep

the girl. He only hoped there wouldn't be bloodshed. However, Running Bear seemed to be a fair man. The two Indians' gazes never faltered. They continued to look each other in the eye. O.C. saw tears well in Wind's eyes. She knew enough English to realize the men were talking about her.

"I planned to take her north to your people in the spring."

Bear glanced down at the girl. "If this is your plan, it is good. I can see where she needs to be at this time." He looked back to Boy Horse's eyes. "That is with you."

Kicking Wind's features relaxed. O.C. was glad the chief had enough common sense to let the girl get over her woes the best way possible. He saw Bear turn his attention to Johnny One Horn and give him the chest sign, which Johnny, too, returned.

"The man skinner. My scouts have told me many stories about the Indian that looks almost white. They say you are a fierce warrior, but a kind one."

"Thank you. I have heard many brave stories of you, too, Running Bear. I am proud to finally know you and call you a friend."

With a nod, Running Bear turned to O.C. "You have kept your promise and I will keep mine. From this day on, we will be brothers. The land where you make your home holds the mound where Chiefs before me are buried. You will make sure no one disturbs our forefathers?"

"Rest assured, it will be done." Bear was a man of his word, but O.C. wanted to secure the future so the boys could stay on the land after he was gone. "I would like to give you cattle every fall for the ability to freely use the other land around the ranch." He saw the wheels turning in the Bear's head.

"Twenty cattle every fall?"

"Yes."

"We have an agreement, but only if you do not kill the buffalo."

"No buffalo will be harmed." O.C. gave the chief the chest sign to promise his word would be kept.

Running Bear returned the sign. "We will leave now."

Just as ghostly as he came from the dark, the man disappeared into the dark. O.C. was pleased at the outcome of the evening. Just like Grey Wolf and his tribe of swamp Indians,

Running Bear and his tribe would be forever friends.

Chapter Forty Eight

Spring 1854

O.C. stood on the porch and looked out over their land. He was awed at how the ranch had grown in such a short time. With the help of the hands, the girls, Earl, Horse and Horn, he and the boys had built three cabins, a fairly good sized bunk house, added on to the main dwelling and enlarged the corrals. Earl had taken up with Rose, the oldest of the women and they'd built them a nice place down close to the river.

Thank God they'd had an easy winter, or they couldn't have done it all. O.C. heard the bawl of a calf and glanced in the direction where the hands were burning the Circle JA brand into their hides. The cattle buying trips to Abilene had paid off and their herd was growing rapidly. Life was good!

The only thing that weighed on him now was the fact that Little Boy Horse and Johnny One Horn would leave the next morning to take Kicking Wind back to the Black Hills and to her family. Tonight they would have a sendoff party to celebrate. Levi, with the help of the ladies, was cooking a side of beef at that moment.

"Hey, Pa, can we talk?"

O.C. turned at the sound of Charles' voice and met his gaze. The thoughtful expression on the young man's face said he had something serious weighing on him. "Sure, what's on your mind?" O.C. took a seat on one of the old wood chairs on the porch.

Charles sat beside his father. “I’ve been thinkin’.”

“What about?”

“Goin’ to school.” He cleared his throat. “I’ve studied off and on over the years, but I feel like I want to do some real learnin’. Maybe even enough to be able to go to law school someday.”

O.C. had never known Charles was interested in law. “That’s pretty high expectations, son, but if anyone can accomplish it, you can. What made you want to study law?”

“We saw some bad things on our journey here, Pa. I think I’d like to help some of the innocent people out there being hurt by criminals.”

Smiling at his middle son he said, “Or helpin’ to keep innocent ones out of prison?”

Charles laughed. “Yes, sir, that too.”

“I think that’s a mighty fine goal.”

“Thank you. I’ll probably leave the first of May.”

“That’s only a couple of weeks away.”

“Yes, sir, I’ll be goin’ back to St. Louie I suppose. I hear they got some real good schools there.”

“You’re a grown man now, Charles. If that’s what you feel you need to do, and that’s where you think you should go, I’m behind you all the way.”

“Thanks, Pa. I hope Joe will feel the same way.”

“He will.” A voice in the distance took O.C.’s attention.

“O.C. Armstrong, you sorry devil!”

He stood and saw two riders approaching the ranch house. It looked like man and a woman. “Well, I’ll be a son-of-a-bitch.” O.C. made his way down the steps and started walking toward the couple. “Jack Tunnie, you old bastard, I thought I’d never see you again!”

“You’re not that lucky, Armstrong!” Jack jumped off his horse, helped the lady down then turned to shake O.C.’s hand.”

O.C. took his good friend’s hand, pulled him forward and gave him a big hug. “It’s good to see ya, you ole cuss.” He turned to the woman. “And who might this be?”

Tunnie cleared his throat and put his arm around her waist. “This is, Amy. Amy Tunnie, my new missus.”

"Well, Good Lord, hon, I can't believe you saw somethin' in this fellow that was worth a good woman savin'." Her face flushed and O.C. liked her pretty smile.

Amy looked down to the ground. "Truth bein', he saved me from a life as a saloon girl."

"Yep, I know what you mean. He's good at savin' people from places they don't belong. Did the same for me."

"Yes, sir, I heard."

"Welcome to Circle JA Ranch, you two." He looked at Tunnie. "I'd be right proud to introduce you to my boys, Jack. Only have two left. Carl died of the pox right after I got here."

"I'm sorry to hear that. That must have been rough."

"It was. Real hard, but I'll see him and Martha again in heaven one day."

"I have no doubt about that, O.C. You're a good man."

O.C. was ready to change the subject. "Well, y'all have pretty good timing I'd say. We're gonna have a party tonight. Might even play a little music." The last time they'd played was back in the swamp. It was damned time they did it again. "Yep, that's just what we're gonna do."

Tunnie stepped forward. "O.C., we want to settle around here. Think you can put me to work doing something."

"Put you to work? Dang right! There's plenty to do around here. We built three cabins just in case our little operation grew bigger. You folks can use one of 'em." O.C. saw genuine love in Amy's eyes when she gazed up at her husband.

"Oh, Jack, this is just perfect!" She put her arms around O.C.'s neck and gave him a kiss on the cheek. "Thank you, Mr. Armstrong. I'll work right alongside my husband doing anything that needs done."

"Yes, ma'am, I'm glad this old coot found you and brought you with him. We're one big happy family around here and you'll fit in just fine."

Joe walked up to O.C. as everyone on the ranch gathered to see their friends off. It wasn't the best day in O.C.'s life, but it was a good one. He studied his son, who stood tall and proud beside him.

"Sure enjoyed myself last night, Pa. It was good to play

music again."

"It was indeed. I'm just sorry it was Horse and Horn's last night at the Ranch."

"You think we'll ever see 'em again?"

"Never can tell, Joe, life just comes." O.C. watched the threesome get their supplies together. It wouldn't be long before they had to say their goodbyes.

His mind drifted to the night before and he turned his attention again to Joe. "Speaking of life, yours seems to be taking a turn. You're gettin' awful sweet on Cindy. I can see it on your face when you look at her."

Joe met his father's gaze. "Yeah, Pa, I'm takin' by her bad. I think I'm gonna ask her to marry me. What do you think?"

"Hot damn! Maybe I'll have some grandkids running around here someday!" O.C. laughed when Joe's eyes widened and his face flushed. "It's nothin' to be embarrassed about, son. All married folks do it." He lifted his eyebrow. "You are going to wait 'til you take your vows, aren't you?" He watched Joe fidget a bit before he answered.

"Oh, yes, sir. Nothin' else would do. Miss Cindy is a proper lady."

"That she is." O.C. could see his friends were ready to leave and started toward them. Joe followed.

"It's gonna be strange without them around. I'll miss all three of them."

"I think we all will." O.C. approached Johnny One Horn while Joe and Charles said goodbye to Boy Horse and Wind. "Johnny, y'all be careful, you hear? Tunnie told me the Army's fighting the Indians in that part of the country. You keep these white man's clothes on. At least 'til you get there." It was stupid for him to try to tell this man how to take care of himself, but the two of them felt more like close family than friends.

"We will be careful. That is a promise. I feel like my little buddy Carl will watch over us, and Miss Martha."

A tear welled in O.C.'s eye at the mention of his lost loved ones. "They're watching over all of us, Johnny. I can feel it."

Boy Horse walked up to O.C., grabbed him and gave him a bear hug. "We will miss the Armstrong family. You are our brothers."

One Horn joined in the hug. "Yes, you are."

Tears streamed freely down O.C.'s face when Charles, Joe and Kicking Wind put their arms around the three of them the best they could. He felt love from all angles and enjoyed the moment. "We will always be brothers. Forever and a day."

O.C. backed away, and wiped his face with the back of his hand. "Okay, enough tears and goodbyes. Y'all better head out. You've got a long road ahead."

The three mounted. Johnny One Horn had told O.C. at the party that they left some wild flowers at the grave sites and he'd personally left something on Carl's marker. The memory of the big man and Carl's relationship would always be a good one for O.C.

All stood and watched the trio ride away. They reached the top of the hill and O.C.'s breath caught in his throat when they turned their mounts back toward the ranch, gave the chest sign, then waved their last goodbye. He saw Joe, who was trying to be strong, turn away first.

"I've got some work to do. I might as well get started." Joe had only taken a few strides when Cindy, without a word, took her place by his side.

As the riders disappeared from sight, O.C. felt Charles' presence beside him. He turned toward his middle son. "You okay?"

"I can't believe they're gone, Pa. They've been around all my life and now I may never see 'em again."

"Maybe someday they'll be back, son. Maybe someday." He could only hope that was true.

The Final Chapter

Summer 1865

"Damn it!" O.C. threw the spent match into the river.

"Shhhh." Jack Tunnie held his fishing pole still in front of him. "I think I'm getting a bite."

"Oh hell, Jack." He lit another match and this time hit his mark. "I swear this getting old is tough. If my damn hands didn't shake so bad I'd be able to get it lit the first time, and it wouldn't make me mad. Besides, those fish can't hear me trying to light my pipe."

Jack's voice was quiet. "Maybe not, but they can hear you cussing. You should know that if you make a lot of racket you won't catch anything."

O.C. glanced over at his old friend. "How long have we known each other now?"

"Well, I guess since '53 when I sprung you from that Arizona prison cell."

"I can't ever thank you enough for that, old friend." O.C. glanced over at his grandchildren. It was always nice when Charles visited and they could all be together. He loved each and every one of those children his own way. "That was many years ago. Hell, we've been on the ranch for over twelve years now." He nodded toward the children playing. "Look at those kids. By golly it's a pack ain't it? How about it, don't they look just like me?"

"Well, I can't say that they do, but I do know one thing."

He looked back to John. "What's that?"

Jack pulled in his line. "Those kids out fish us every time." He re-baited his hook with a worm, then threw his line back in the water. "Because they're quiet when they fish, old man."

O.C. laughed. "Yep, they sure as hell do. Maybe quiet is the reason. Who the hell knows?" He sat back in his rocking chair. They'd made their special place by the river quite comfortable so they could enjoy it, and it was where he loved to relax and rest his weary bones.

The war had been all around them for the last few years, but it hadn't interfered in their lives much. Their place was pretty secluded between the bluff, the woods and the river. However, now the fighting was over. That was just one more thing they could be thankful for.

Thoughts of the years past ran through his mind, as they did more and more these days. He rocked and watched the beauty of the river as the sun danced on its surface. "You know, Jack. Life has turned me some bad cards, but overall I've had a pretty good hand." He drew off of his pipe, then blew the smoke out. "I lost 4 years of my life in that hellhole, my wife died and I wasn't there for her, Carl died, but I feel blessed to have gotten to see him one last time before he joined his ma in heaven."

Tunnie sat back in his chair holding his pole. He listened as O.C. continued.

"Looking at life now, the years on this ranch have been some of the best. Even with the war going on."

"I have to agree."

He was so proud of Joe and Charles. "I mean, since Joe married Cindy, he's been so happy. They named their first born after Carl. Can you believe he's ten years old now?"

"No. It seems time passes faster the older we get. Hell, Joe and Cindy's second boy Earl is seven and the young'un James is five.

"I remember when my and Martha's boys were that age. They were working the crops on the farm. I'm glad Joe is instilling that same work habits in his sons. Hell, they can all ride a horse and herd cattle almost as good and their daddy!"

"You ain't kidding about that." Jack pulled back on his

pole. "Hey, I think I've got me a big one." He hauled in a trout and took it off his hook. "That'll make me and Amy a real nice meal for supper."

"Amy's a good woman. I'm glad you found her."

"We've all had life changes for the good I think. Hell, look at Charles. He moved back to Great Bend and now he's a big time lawyer and writing books. Making money hand over fist. And that pretty wife of his sure has made some pretty babies."

"Hey, I'm here to tell you that my good looks, and especially my Martha's, had a lot to do with those girls being so pretty."

Tunnie threw his line in and sat back again. "Martha maybe, but you?"

"Damn, you just won't cut me a break, will ya?"

"I don't want you to start thinking too highly of yourself, that's all."

"You're an ass." O.C. had grown to love Jack Tunnie. He was the best friend he'd ever had besides ole black Neil and Bud. Those memories seemed like another lifetime ago.

Jack laughed. "That makes two of us."

"Well, no matter, Martha, Minnie and Estelle are almost the same ages as Joe's boys." O.C. dumped the tobacco, then put the empty pipe in his pocket. "Funny that Joe had all boys and Charles had girls."

"Yeah, but like you said, they're all good looking. It took you a long time to get as ugly as you are."

O.C. welcomed the laughter. He picked up his fishing pole and bated the hook. Tunnie was good company, and having all of the Armstrong family on the ranch that evening was very special.

"Hey, O.C?"

"Yep?"

"You gonna tell your grandkids stories tonight like you usually do?"

"Jack, you know I've told them just about everything I can tell. I'm going to leave it up to Johnny One Horn to tell them the rest. Carl used to think Horn was the best story teller there ever was. I'm really glad he found it in his heart to come back to the ranch after the trip to the Black Hills. I wasn't surprised that Horse decided to stay with Kicking Wind. I think he felt like he was her father."

"Yeah, me, too, but I ain't playing cards with Horn anymore. He's the damn best card player I've ever seen!"

O.C. pulled his line in, then threw it out again. "Shhhh, I'm tryin' to fish."

"Oh, kiss my ass, Armstrong."

They sat quiet for some time. O.C. listened to his grandkids in the distance, pleased they would have a better life then his boys did. Tunnie's voice penetrated his thoughts.

"Have you looked at the ranch lately, O.C.? It's like a little town. We've got a small church, picnic grounds and over the years we've built twelve houses. Hell, you've even got a one room school house for your grandkids and the hands' kids. It's amazing!"

"It is quite amazing and I thank the Lord every day."

Tunnie continued. "Since Levi's gotten too old to help with the cooking, all of the hands' wives have chipped in to help. Joe says he's going to build at least four more cabins to house future hands and their families. Did you know that?"

Lost in thought, it took O.C. a moment to answer Jack's question. The growth of the ranch astounded him, but he always knew Joe had a special gift to make things work. He nodded his head and smiled. "Yes, I know, Joe's a good man. It's been quite a journey, my friend."

Again he thought about Mississippi. In a way, their farm by the swamp was like a small town, too. Three cabins, although two were up the road where the other families lived, but we had Sunday picnics, Neil Carter preaching the gospel, sharing meals and frequent visits by their Indian friends. Now, it was just a ghostly memory.

O.C. rubbed his forehead. "You know, Jack, sometimes I think my mind's leavin me and goin' back to the swamp. I think about it a lot lately."

"Don't keep letting it go there. From what I saw, it wasn't much to leave."

"Yep, but part of me is back there, buried on that little mound."

"You've got to live for the living, O.C. not those who have gone on."

"You're right, but you know the boys only got half that gold. I wonder if the swamp is still under water. Maybe we should go find out."

"That sounds like a mighty fine idea, O.C. I'll go saddle my horse."

Laughing, O.C. said, "Aw, I'm just talkin'. These days I'd never be able to make the trip." He stood and glanced back at his grandkids. "Y'all don't stay too long. It'll be gettin' dark soon."

With that his oldest grandson Carl came running. The boy sure looked like his namesake.

"Need some help, Gramps?"

"No, I'm having a pretty good day, but thank you for askin'." He rubbed the top of the boy's head. "You know, you sure look like your Uncle Carl did when he was your age. Same color hair and everything."

Carl took his grandfather's hand. "Yes, sir, that's what my pa tells me, too." Carl led O.C. to the area where all the graves were marked.

"I know about Uncle Carl and how he died, and Grandma, too. But what about the marker that only says 'The Lady' on it? Who is she, Gramps?"

O.C. smiled at the boy's question. "Well, son, we never really knew her. She was…at least she acted like she was a little crazy. Johnny One Horn called her Runs in Circles."

Frowning, Carl asked, "Why?"

"Because, she used to laugh real loud and run in circles all the time. We didn't see her a lot, never knew where she went when she'd disappear."

"How'd she die?"

O.C. was glad the boy wanted to learn the history of what had happened on the ranch. He would live to tell the tales. "Earl Stockton found her downstream. Drowned in the river I guess. I don't know how it happened, it just did."

"I think I get it. What about those other folks? The unknown ones? Maybe they were the lady's family."

"Maybe so." O.C. gazed over at Carl's grave. "They all died from the pox, just like your uncle did." He'd spare the sad details, he didn't want it to weigh heavy on the boy's heart, and the answer seemed to satisfy his curiosity.

Carl dropped O.C.'s hand and went over to stand closer to the graves. "Runs in Circles probably went crazy when her whole family died at one time. Hell, that would drive anybody out of their mind."

O.C. smiled and his heart soared. Like uncle like nephew. "Hey, now, you better watch your cussin', your ma will have your hide." He looked down at his grandson and fought the urge to laugh. The boy's face was crimson red.

"Yes, sir, sorry."

"Hey, O.C. You about ready to head to the house?" Tunnie gathered up his belongings.

"Sure 'nough. Looks like Joe's got the open cook fire goin'. Must be gonna have a shindig."

"Oh, boy!" Carl looked up at O.C. "You sure you don't need no help, Gramps?"

"I'm sure. You run along, gather up your brothers and cousins, too. It'll be dark pretty soon."

"Yes, sir!" Carl took off running.

O.C. joined Tunnie by the river. "I think I'll go talk to Horn and see if I can get him to tell some stories this evening."

"Sounds good. I bet Nate's got some of his moonshine all bottled up. Maybe we'll take us a few swigs."

"Now that really sounds good." O.C. patted his friend on the shoulder. "I'll be back directly."

O.C. approached the area where Joe and the hands had built a water tank. It stood about six foot off the ground and had a wooden fence around it. They had a water spout fixed up so they could stand under it to bathe, the fence allowed privacy. The water was cold, but it felt pretty good when a person got done.

Johnny found a cave near the tank, and took it as a dwelling. That's where O.C. figured he'd find the big man. Horn sat on a tree block sharpening his ever sharp Arkansas Toothpick. "How's the leg, Horn?"

O.C. hated to see his old friend limping so bad when he walked, but being mauled by a grizzly bear was usually fatal to a man. Not Johnny One Horn though. He was one man who lived to tell the story, though it was something he didn't like to do.

"Good today. I can walk."

"I see those women coming out here to pamper you. I think sometimes you pretend it's worse than it is so they'll give you the attention."

Johnny threw his head back and laughed. "You know me too well, O.C. Armstrong." The big Indian gestured toward the river. "I see you got no fish today. Grandchildren out fished you again. Maybe you should give up."

"Did you ever think I just let them out fish me?"

"If I were a betting man, I would say this is true."

"And you are a bettin' man for sure."

O.C. turned his attention to the aging wolf Johnny had taken in as a pup and brought back from North Dakota. The old dog stayed next to Johnny and never bothered anybody. However, he was well trained and with a simple command from Johnny, the wolf would tear someone's arm from their body. "What's old Chacha lickin' his foot for."

"He got a thorn. He hasn't been feeling well lately. Getting old like the rest of us."

"Guess I won't be tryin' to pet him then."

"Good idea. He might bite your worm off. What brings you here, O.C.?"

"We're having a big to do at the house tonight. This is the last night before Charles and his family head back to Great Bend. I was hopin' you might tell the grandkids and everyone about you and Horses journey to the Black Hills."

"It is hard to tell."

"You can skip the really bad things that happened, but tell what you feel comfortable with. Charles wants to put your story in a book he's writing about the family."

Johnny slipped his knife back into its sheath. "He has already written one story about me. I cannot read, but Nate read it to me. Charles is good at writing. He tells the truth in what he says."

"Does that mean you'll do it?"

"Yes, I will tell the story of our trip, but at any time the Great Spirits give me a sign to stop, it will be done."

"That's only fair. Thank you, old friend. I know this is something Charles really wants to do. Maybe someday a lot of people will read his books. They will be hard to believe, but I guess the truth always is."

****

The fire roared and the sun had gone down. Everyone's bellies were full and the hands sipped on Nate's moonshine and played some dice. O.C. listened to one of the Mexican girls play the fiddle. She was really good and he knew Joe would join with his guitar and Charles with his banjo, but not until after the story telling.

He watched as Charles and the children gathered around Johnny One Horn, their faces full of anticipation of what stories he was going to tell. Charles had a paper and pencil in his hand, ready to write by firelight.

The only two people that were missing had the names Martha and Carl carved into markers down in the small makeshift cemetery. Neither of their bodies were there, but that's where he paid his respects.

Listening to the excited chatter of the children before Horn started his tales, O.C. knew Martha would love to be there with her grandkids. He saw some lightning flashes in the far north at that moment, felt his wife's spirit hovered over the little ones like a guardian angel. He took the distant storm as a sign and in his mind he heard her voice.

"Go, talk to Carl."

O.C. nodded to himself, picked up a canvas wrapped jug from the table and began his walk to the river and Carl's gravestone. Once he was there, he took a long drink of the moonshine, knelt on the ground in front of his son's marker and poured some of the liquid on the ground.

"We never got to share a grown man's drink, son." He chuckled. "Knowin' you, you probably wouldn't like it anyway, and that's a good thing."

He put the jug down, placed his hand on the headstone and didn't try to stop the tear that trickled down his cheek. "I'll see you and your ma one day. Sooner now than later. I know y'all are just playin' on the road to heaven, just waitin' for me to join you. The Good Lord willin', we'll all be together again. Me, you, Ma, Joe, Charles, Horse, Horn, hell ole black Neil may already be there with you for all I know."

Standing, O.C. brushed the dirt from his knees then picked up the jug of shine. "I miss ya, boy." He started to walk back to the ranch but something made him pause. He turned back around and whistled the sound of a Whippoorwill.

He looked into the trees hoping for a response. An eerie light appeared through the tops of the foliage. The wisp? His heart pounded as it got brighter. It couldn't be!

Then the sweet sound of a Whippoorwill answered his call, and he realized that what he imagined was the wisp was actually the light of the full moon. O.C. grinned from ear to ear. "I love you, too, Carl."

About the Authors

JAMES ARMSTRONG

James (Jim) Armstrong, originally from South East Missouri, now makes his home in the Ozarks with wife Susan, their two Boston Terriers and countless other creatures of the wild. He loves to spend time with grandkids, and when he's not doing that, he spends time in his music studio or writing.

As a, now retired, oil industry consultant and professional musician, through the ups and downs of the oil business, Jim spent many years bouncing back and forth between the two careers. His passion is music, and Woodstock is his one of his best all-time memories, yet that is a different story.

As the 6th son of a cotton sharecropper, he spent the first ten years of his life on a small farm near Steele MO. Many spring storms rumbled across the boot heel of Missouri, and on those dark nights the family would spend time in their musty old dirt floored cellar. Jim remembers the smell from the kerosene lamp thickening the air. Aunts, uncles, and sometimes neighbors, would crowd in to weather the storms.

It was those nights that many stories were told. The tale of the Wisp intrigued Jim the most. He dreamed of one day writing it just as he'd heard it as a child, and so he did, but the manuscript was destroyed in a fire.

It took seven years to write it again, and with the help of Sharon Kizziah Homes it is a reality once more. Please enjoy 'The Will and the Wisp'.

SHARON KIZZIAH-HOLMES

I live in the beautiful Ozarks with my husband and two Cocker Spaniels, Dude and Lacy. I have seventeen grandkids and two great grands…that's right, I'm too young, I know… =) However, I love each and every one of them with all my heart, and wouldn't change a thing.

My interest in writing novels came in the early 1990's. A friend suggested we write a book together, so I took her up on it. I joined Ozarks Romance Authors and a whole new world opened up for me. I'm now a member of many other writing groups. I absolutely love writing, editing, publishing and teaching the basics of writing to others.

Hubby and I are retired road musicians. We have a boutique recording studio in our home (thanks to Jim) and record everything from karaoke singles and live bands, to audio books.

Working with James Armstrong on The Will and the Wisp has been a long journey, and I'm proud to say we've reached the time for publication. I've enjoyed every minute of it and cherish Jim and his wife Susan's friendship. I'm honored he chose me to help with this project.

Other publications by Sharon Kizziah-Holmes

Ride the Storm
Romantic Short Stories
Gamble for Life
Paranormal Short Stories
A Star That Twinkled
A Christmas Gift from God
A Dogs Life

ABOUT THE ARTIST

JAMES H. HUSSEY

Jim Hussey is a native of New Orleans who has become one of the country's artists of note. Born in 1936 Jim was educated in New Orleans, and upon completion of his academic training he began a career in the world of business. Later, in the summer of 1970, he decided to leave that career.

Equipped only with the paints and brushes his mother had left him, an interest in art from early childhood, and inspired by his surroundings, his family, his friends, and prominent artists, he decided to leave his successful career as a salesman and merchant to pursue his love for art on a full-time basis.

In order to refine his ideas, skills and techniques, in 1972 he attended the John McCrady School of Fine Arts. The decision to pursue art proved to be a wise one for his renditions of the Old South. Its many lazy bayous, and life along the Mississippi, shortly became wanted by many art collectors, galleries and museums throughout the world.

His paintings reflect personal feelings in the nostalgic and romantic moods, settings, and history of the South as seen through the eyes of numerous novelists and historians. Like most true artists, Jim is constantly driven toward self-improvement and growth through better interpretation, increased skill and authenticity in subject matter and composition.

"I believe when I display realism in a painting, it is as

important to reflect my feeling on the mood of that subject, or to tell a story much as a poet, using all of the color and feeling of one's mind. Otherwise, one might just as well take a photograph."

15906921R00202

Made in the USA
San Bernardino, CA
10 October 2014